Praise for

Tom Named By Horse

"You know you are reading a good book when you don't want it to end. Well, as the book thundered toward its conclusion, I didn't want it to end.... and when it did, I cried!

"As the action intensifies, the book becomes mesmerizing, meaningful and magical..... the reader is 'on the hook,' but Dutch takes care of the reader, too.... his willingness to be vulnerable and explore the complex emotional landscape of the characters is the hallmark of a great read. I can't wait to be back on the prairie with Tom, Soft Cloud, Buck and their ponies for the next two parts of the trilogy!"

— *Bobbie Jo Lieberman, Editor-in-Chief, trailBLAZER magazine, award-winning writer, and author of "Sassy Salad Secrets: Supercharge Your Diet & Recapture Your Health by Unlocking the Power of Living Foods"*

"A Story of Times Past – Hard-times with hatred, sorrow and grief. Then triumph, friendship, love. And Trust. War and New Beginnings. Obligations and following through. Follow Tom Named by Horse's journey – It will Captivate you. A GREAT Read."

—*Tina Mae Weber- Co-Host of "SADDLE UP AMERICA" Equestrian Legacy Radio, Trail Rider and Saddle Designer*

Tom Named By Horse

A boy's quest to be a man and understand love – a woman's desire to give love – a people's struggle to survive – a nation's fight to conquer a people and their land

DUTCH HENRY

TO MY WIFE, DAUGHTER
AND GRANDCHILDREN

ACKNOWLEDGMENTS

Often behind the story there are friends who have helped the author bring it all together. My dear friend Bob Hollinger helped with much of the research, sadly he went to heaven before publishing. Connie Bloss for proof reading the final manuscript and all my friends who read my manuscript along the way and encouraged me to publish. Bobbie Jo Lieberman, Editor of trailBLAZER magazine, who worked her magic in editing my story. My wife, Robin, for her encouragement, critiques and adding publishing to her list of things she can do.

A special thank you to Bobbie Jo Lieberman and Troy Locker Palmer, PHG Industries for a great cover. Troy can be reached by email at troy@phgindustries.com and visit her website www.phgindustries.com.

Thank you all.

AUTHOR'S NOTE

This is an historical novel set in the late 1860's in the American Midwest. While most of the characters and locations are fiction some are actual locations, occurrences and historical figures. In some instances just the historical figure's name is used and the stories and characters surrounding him are fiction. The historical figures are Chief Red Cloud, Bill Cody, Bill Hickok, General Sheridan, Chief Smoke, Chief Spotted Tail, Standing Elk, Chief Dull Knife, White Buffalo Calf Woman, Grandfather Mystery and Grandmother Earth.

Tom Named By Horse is a love story at its core and just as love can be powerful and at the same time confusing, so were the times just before what some refer to as the Great Plains Indian Wars. Parallels between Tom Named By Horse's awakening and brutal changes washing over the great plains weave together to tell the story of a time of struggle and confusion. While most of the characters are fictional, the struggles, love, hate, confusion and desperation are true. Tom Named By Horse's birth on the day of Chief Red Cloud's powerful vision of this terrifying change sweeping over Grandmother Earth bind the two together in powerful ways.

CHAPTER ONE

-Spring 1850-

It was a miracle that either survived the birth. She knew it was morning because a sliver of gray light peeked through the old blanket they had hung for a door. It had blown open with driving rain a day ago but she could not afford the strength to close it. Why, oh why, won't this awful rain and howling wind stop? Lying in the dark, cold dugout, she shivered so violently her newborn son trembled in her arms.

Oh darling, where are you? Please hurry back. These old blankets are wet and so very smelly. You promised you'd return soon with more blankets. Two days ago now I think, maybe three. I can't remember. I'm cold, darling. I'm wet and so cold. It's so dark in here. Our little baby can't get warm. He can't stop crying.

The new little baby found her cold breast and suckled … Soon her shivers stopped.

****

The rolling grasslands spread before him as far as his eye could reach, as broad as the universe itself. Each rise gave way to the valley beyond it. Every valley was the beginning of the next hill. Rain, falling hard from the

1

hands of Grandfather Mystery, soaked Grandmother Earth.

Chief Red Cloud sat on his favorite war pony all that dark day, and allowed the skies to beat him with raindrops pounding like rocks. He had told his uncle, Chief Smoke, of his terrifying vision. With sad eyes he looked into the rain. Today Red Cloud knew even Grandfather Mystery could not wash away the change about to sweep over their ancestral hunting grounds. His tears mixed with cold rain as he turned his faithful pony toward his village.

-Early fall 1865-

"Boy! Fetch me that knife, and do it quick or you'll feel my lash!"

The boy handed the knife to the grizzly-bear-shaped buffalo hunter and watched as the great beast was stripped of its dignity. He stood out of reach of the hider, knowing he should be skinning the buffalo, but he was still sore from last night's beating. It hurt to move. When the hider finished his work, he left a humbled, naked carcass, not at all resembling the magnificent animal it was moments ago. The boy always felt pity for the buffalo. But it was what they did.

The boy knew he was fifteen now. He didn't remember his life before the hider bought him. Not much anyway. Some townfolks claimed they had found him in a dugout, with his dead mama. They had never liked him much. He never liked them. At least with the hider he was never hungry. Never hungry, but too often kicked and beaten. "Get over here and pull on this hide, you stupid kid." Struggling together, they stretched the heavy wet hide and staked it for the sun to dry with the others dotting the landscape for a hundred yards around the wagon. Then the hider crawled on the seat, grabbed his long whip, and beat the horse and mule. The drunken fool struck them so hard they took off at a near gallop, throwing him down in the seat, evoking a string of cuss words and more lashing. The boy ran behind, as he had been taught by the hider's lash to do.

For days on end they wandered the plains searching for buffalo. The man rode the wagon, the boy followed a safe distance behind, like a whipped dog with nowhere to go except back to the master who brutalized him. At night the hider sat under the wagon sheet lean-to and drank whiskey until he fell asleep. Most nights when he woke he found a reason to beat the boy. For a long time now he had thought of running, and had run twice, only to be found by the hider. Those nights were the worst beatings.

Tonight was no different. He hadn't meant to kill him, but as he tried to shield his legs from the lash, his hands found the skinning knife. He only wanted to stop the beating. The fat drunken hider would never beat him again, or slobber his whiskey-fouled spit on the boy's face.

As if skinning a buffalo, he tore the clothes from the dead hider, propped the naked body against the wagon wheel, then sat cross-legged staring at what he had done. Some things were just too horrible. "But you're a horrible man," the boy muttered. Numb in mind and body, with the same skinning knife he'd plunged into the hider's chest, he cut loose a slab of the dead man's scalp. Just as when the hider had beaten him, it was as if he was watching himself from a distance. He could not feel the knife in his hands. He'd never cut a scalp before. He had seen some naked, scalped bodies of settlers, and he despised the practice.

By the meager light of the dying campfire, the stars, and sliver of moon, the boy took his time and gathered canteens, hard tack, and dried buffalo. He searched the wagon, and in a tin-covered box under the seat found the 52-caliber bullets and primers for the Sharps rifle, and the Henry's 44 rimfire shells. The 44s for the Navy Colt were in a soft leather pouch deep down in the box. In its own little can was the leather pouch that held the hider's coins. The boy had learned to count gold and silver coins from the old man, and found the pouch held nearly three hundred dollars.

It had been the boy's job to run the camp, so he knew how to prepare for his new journey. He gathered saddlebags and the wagon sheet, loaded the Henry and Colt, carefully wrapped the ammunition in canvas, and stuffed it in the saddlebags. With pieces of wagon sheet from the lean-to, he made two packs and strapped them on the mule. The first he filled with the jerked buffalo, hard tack, a bag of coffee beans, and a sack of flour. The knives, pots, and other supplies he crammed into the second pack.

Satisfied, he saddled the horse with the old McClellan, and slipped the Henry in the scabbard. He would carry the Sharps. The Navy revolver he strapped on over his ancient tattered shirt. Finally the boy stepped onto the tall gray horse and rode away, the mule in tow. There was no emotion, not loneliness or joy. The boy was free at last to go his own way. Whichever way that might be.

****

He sat poking life back into his tired campfire the next morning. With no one to answer to, and no lashings to avoid, the day seemed strange, empty. Even frightening.

The rising sun urged him to start his life anew. The horse and mule had not strayed far, and when he gave a loud whistle, the handsome gray came at a run. They had been friends a long time.

"Mornin' Tom Gray," he stroked the long mane, "Ready to find out what's out there?" The young man smiled when the horse nodded he was. Over the years Tom Gray had been his only friend. They understood each other. Both had feared and hated the old hider. They had leaned on each other to survive. The gray had even defended the mule from the old hider on several occasions.

He caught the mule, gathered his things, and was ready to head out, when a funny feeling washed over him. A warning, perhaps? He wasn't sure. But it was the same feeling he got before the old hider would beat him. "Let's keep our eyes open, Tom Gray." He told himself as much as the horse.

Before starting out he made a pouch from wagon sheet scraps, and fashioned a leather string around it so it could dangle from his neck. In it he placed a half dozen 52-caliber bullets and primers, then stuffed another in the rifle's breech. With the Sharps across his lap, and towing the mule behind Tom Gray, they started west. He could see treed hills far in the distance and set them as today's only goal, knowing there would be game and shelter there.

The years spent with the drunken buffalo hunter had been of some benefit. The boy had developed a keen sense of awareness and self-preservation. He was quick to sense danger and equally quick to notice opportunity. As he rode toward the far hills, the boy sensed he was riding toward danger. He argued with himself, trying to convince those worried thoughts that the only danger to him, Tom Gray and the mule was lying dead, leaning against a wagon wheel.

Longer shadows cast by Tom Gray meant darkness was on its way, so he hurried the horse, hoping to spend the night under the cover of the distant trees. Even at a fast trot it was well past dark by the time they rode into the first small grove and found a suitable campsite for the night. Old ashes and bones lying in a fire pit told him he was not the first to find the grove inviting. He hobbled the horse and mule, dined on jerked buffalo and a piece of hardtack, washed down with a swallow of hot water from the canteen, then went to sleep.

The mule's loud braying woke him in the morning. He paused a moment blinking into the rising sun, admiring the golden horizon, then with a start realized the mule and Tom Gray were gone. He followed the tracks of the hobbled horse and mule, and found them peacefully grazing on tall, dew-covered grass by a wide stream.

Bent low, inspecting the hobbles, he noticed trout in the shallows of the stream. "I'll have to work harder for my breakfast than you." He patted Tom Gray on the neck, jumped in the stream and began slapping the water fast and hard, to stun a fish or two. His crazy way of fishing created too much ruckus and spooked the horse and mule into a scramble as fast as their hobbles would allow. In less than a minute, he crawled from the stream wet and cold, holding a wriggling trout. His excitement began to temper when he realized he heard laughing.

A small group of Sioux braves stood just back from the stream bank laughing and hooting. The buffalo hunter and boy had sometimes been harassed by Sioux hunting parties, and whenever the old hider had the chance he would shoot them. "Always kill an Injun afore it kills you," the hider told him. "Any hider that don't kill Injuns is just plain stupid!"

The brave closest to him was wearing the hider's vest and hat, laughing the loudest, and pointing to the boy. The young man knew, they knew, he belonged to the buffalo hunter. He also knew they meant to kill him for the hunter's deeds. Then it hit him—he had foolishly left his camp unarmed. All his weapons lay carefully hidden under a blanket back in camp. His only weapons now were his wits and speed. Years of running behind the wagon had made him strong-legged and fast. He tossed the fish in the air and started to laugh and dance, flapping his arms and squawking like a wounded prairie chicken and kicking high. The braves, surprised at first, began to laugh, point, and jump about as if to mimic him.

That was the very reaction the boy had hoped for, and he took off in a flat run for camp. The braves gave chase, but he had so outmaneuvered them he beat them to camp, and stood straight and tall, holding the scalp of the dead buffalo hunter high. He offered the scalp to the three still-laughing braves. If they had found the buffalo hunter's wagon and searched it, they surely saw he had been scalped.

The first brave cautiously accepted the scalp, and the young man stepped back. The brave studied the scalp and showed it to the others. They passed it around, mumbling and laughing. The young man inched back and was just about to run when the three braves looked his way. The brave wearing the hider's hat made hand gestures the boy had seen before. He was asking him to follow.

Clenching fists by his side, the young man stood and stared at the braves, uncertain as what to do. They stood in silence for several seconds, but the boy was still unable to reason it out, and stood firm. Finally the first brave took the scalp, tucked it in his waistband, turned, and walked away. The others followed.

The young man stood rigid until they had moved a safe distance away. Still shaken, he set about finding the horse and mule again. He gathered his things and started out, holding the Sharps across his lap and chewing on hard buffalo jerky as he rode. That odd feeling from the day before still bothered him. Not having a plan, he allowed Tom Gray to slowly follow an Indian trail through the woods and drifted deep into thought. He pondered the fact the braves took his fish, but left behind Tom Gray and the mule. "Braves have no use for mules I reckon, Tom Gray, and maybe they thought you too tall."

Rifle fire from beyond the next rise tore him from his thoughts. He slid from Tom Gray clutching the Sharps and scampered to the top, dropped to the ground and crept through the grass. In a heartbeat he knew the story.

At the bottom of the hill a buffalo hunter sat on his wagon shooting at Indians. The boy recognized this hider. He would often stop at their camp. This man was even meaner than the other, and would help to do awful things to the boy. Things he could never forget.

The braves huddled in a low wash while the buffalo hunter enjoyed clear and safe shooting. They returned fire, but their arrows lacked the range to match the hunter's rifle.

The young man watched as their arrows hit the dirt, far short of the hider who sat cross-legged on the wagon seat, laughing and jeering, then carefully taking aim. Each of his rounds found their mark in the rim of the wash, sending dirt and dust flying high in the air.

The old hider had marveled at how rapidly the boy became a crack shot. Not only with the Sharps, but the Henry too, and even the Navy 44. Many times the old hider had gambled on the boy's shooting talents. Many times he had won the old man large sums of money. But the times the boy had lost the hider money, those are the times the boy remembered most. Most likely he would carry the scars of the hider's lash all his life.

Lying on his stomach, the young man raised the sight of his Sharps, just as he had been taught by the old buffalo hunter himself. He could see at least one of the braves lay dead. So could the hider and he jumped from the wagon and began dancing and hooting. After a brief celebration, the hider leaned against the wagon and raised his buffalo rifle, taking aim to send death toward the helpless braves one more time. The boy knew the hider would not stop until all the trapped braves were dead.

The boy touched the trigger on his own rifle, and watched through the high sight as the bullet plunged into the hider's back. Silence floated in. Nothing moved, no one cheered. Calmly, he gathered his things, mounted his horse and rode to the dead man.

He rode slowly around the wagon, studying the scene. Plenty of supplies lay in the wagon, tarps and sacks, too. Two mules stood patiently waiting their commands. A dead man lay sprawled by the wheel. The man he'd just killed. It felt like a world within a world.

He jumped from Tom Gray and promptly removed a large slab of the dead man's scalp. He would offer the hair to the braves. Then yanked the hunter's boots, and took his pants and shirt. This hider was more his size, and except for the 52-caliber hole in the front and back of the shirt, these were nearly new clothes.

As he rummaged through the contents of the wagon, the two remaining braves—one injured, one not—came to him waving their hands in friendship. This time he responded in kind, wondering though, what might have just happened here if he had accepted their offer earlier, and had been traveling with them?

At the boy's wordless urgings, they laid the injured brave on the wagon atop the canvasses. He and the other carried the dead brave to the wagon, and tied his Tom Gray and mule to the rear. Together they set out for the braves' village, sitting side by side on the wagon seat. Leaving only a dead, naked, scalped, buffalo hunter behind. Naked as any buffalo carcass.

As the two mules plodded along, the boy tried to understand the past two days. For years he had only known the mean buffalo hunter, a few of his kind, and a rare visit to some wild camp town. The only person that had ever wanted him was the old hunter. But what the hider wanted the boy for was unspeakable ... now the boy had killed the drunken, slobbering, old no-good. Not just him, but one of his friends too. The young man wondered why it had been so easy, and why the feeling he had was a good feeling. Almost satisfying. The boy knew there was one more of the three hiders that had so horribly treated him for years. Maybe he'd see him through his rifle sights too one day. He hoped so.

They guided the wagon west, never speaking, each lost in their own thoughts. The day faded as they trudged along. Occasionally the brave would offer an outstretched arm, pointing the way. The glow of campfires became visible on the horizon as darkness began to descend upon them.

The boy kept the mules stepping out at a good pace and soon they drove into the Sioux village. When the wagon stopped, they were quickly set upon by many interested Sioux—braves, children, and women. Two Sioux women helped the wounded brave from the wagon. A small group of women carried the dead brave away.

He sat quietly watching as those gathered around the wagon were told of the day's events in a language he knew only a very few words. He rested his hand on the revolver at his side, wondering how long he would need to sit there, wondering how long they would allow him to live, when a woman came to his side, and in perfect English asked, "Do you have a name?"

The young man spun toward her. His eyes must have betrayed his surprise.

"Yes, I speak English well, don't I?"

"Yea ... I mean ... Do you ... I mean ... why do you?"

"Why don't you tell me your name first?" Her voice was soft and kind. Kind as her blue eyes and soft as the feel of her hand on his knee. He wasn't used to anyone asking his name. Or even anyone caring. He had long ago tired of "Boy." What should he say? Until this very moment, the boy had never thought about a name. It had never been important. He sat looking at her, wondering why a white woman was in a Sioux camp. She looked like a Sioux, but he knew she was white.

"Well?" she urged.

"My name is ... Tom," he said, taking the name of his horse who had for so long been his only friend.

"Hello, Tom. My name is Rebecca, but the Sioux call me Still Water. I have been with them many years, but they still find me mysterious. Which I can often use to my advantage."

He studied her. She was a very pretty woman, and very white. She dressed like the other women in the village, but she stood out with her fair hair and blue eyes. Blue eyes like his own.

Now, many hands were going through the contents of the wagon.

"Would you like to come with me and meet my family? And oh, did you know you are a hero?" Tom climbed from the wagon and followed Still Water to her lodge. He had never been in a Sioux village before, much less one's tipi. "I have asked a young brave to care for your horse and mules," Still Water told him as they walked.

"What will he do with them?"

"Take them to the prairie where the Sioux ponies graze. The young boys watch over them there." She raised the flap entrance to her lodge and signaled he should enter.

He found it bigger inside than he imagined. Animal skins covered the floor, and a small fire made a peaceful warm light, creating dancing shadows on those seated around it. He stood inside the entrance and examined the faces of an old man, two grown braves, and the beautiful face of a young woman. All sat cross-legged on the opposite side of the fire. No word or gesture was exchanged. Tom stood rigid, as if ordered to, his arms hanging heavy at his side. The girl began to giggle, and the young braves laughed with her.

Unable to comprehend the laughter, Tom fled the lodge and picked his way between campfires through the village toward the grazing horses. He needed the comfort of his old friend. As he hurried along to the moonlit open grassland, he felt many eyes watching him, but no one spoke.

In the dark, with only the light of the stars and a thin slice of moon, he walked among the large herd searching for his friend. Having no luck, he let go a loud whistle. Tom Gray responded instantly with his familiar nicker, and they found each other along the outer edge of the herd.

"What mess did I get us into?" Tom sat in the damp grass, watched the ribby horses, and listened to their munching as they grazed. He'd always enjoyed just listening to his friend tear at the grass. Here was a peaceful place. A place he could stay forever.

Tom Gray raised his head and nickered, signaling someone's approach.

"The mother of the injured brave you retuned to us is in my lodge crying. Her son died in her arms." Still Water said in her soft, friendly voice.

Tom stood by his friend and faced her, not knowing what to do. The sadness in her eyes reached out to him, but no words came to him.

"The other brave you saved today, Buffalo Horn, is waiting at his father's lodge to meet with you. Come with me, I will take you to him."

Dogs followed at a safe distance as they weaved their way between campfires in the sleepy camp. Mothers holding their children slept on blankets near their fires. Most of the lodges had fires inside, lighting the village with shafts of light escaping through slits in the buffalo hide walls, and open door flaps. As they walked, they assembled followers, so that by the time they arrived at Buffalo Horn's campfire close to twenty curious Sioux arrived with them.

Buffalo Horn rose to greet Tom, and signaled a place for him to sit by the low fire. Those who had followed formed a half circle behind them around the fire. Tom returned the greeting, and took the seat offered. Still Water found her place next to Buffalo Horn, who was seated by his father, Chief Red Cloud.

A brave tossed a pile of branches on the fire, and for a few moments the group watched the flames jump, and a fine display of exploding sparks drift high overhead on the rising hot air. A bowl of meal and buffalo meat was passed around, and Tom took a healthy portion before passing it on. They watched the fire and ate for a long while, then when he was ready, Red Cloud turned to Still Water and spoke, using his hands to emphasize almost every word.

When the pause came, Still Water turned to Tom and translated. "Today you have proven yourself to be a brave Sioux warrior. You can take your place among the proud Sioux, and you will forever be welcome in our villages. You have saved the life of our great Chief's son, Buffalo Horn. Who will one day be chief of all Lakota Sioux.

"You have killed two of our enemy. But there is still one buffalo killer who also kills Sioux with guns that can shoot very far. Red Cloud believes you know this buffalo killer. For us you must kill him also. You may have from our ponies any two you choose to keep for your own. Take one day to eat and rest. Then take your ponies, and your gun that shoots today and kills tomorrow, and one brave of your choosing. And go and kill this man. You must leave him naked on the earth as you have the other two. You may keep all that was his, but Red Cloud will have his hair."

When Still Water finished she searched Tom's eyes. "You may ask any question," she told him as if she knew he was confused.

"I do know the hider he speaks of. He would often travel with us. He's a cruel man and should die. But why does he ask me to do this? Red Cloud has hundreds of braves in this village." Tom looked for an answer in Still Water's eyes.

Red Cloud understood white man's English, and gave Still Water his answer. She listened and then told Tom, "He has many braves who want to kill any white man. That is true. Some of his braves have already gone with the Sioux brave, Tall Dog, to kill whites. Perhaps there will come a day when a great war must be fought with the white man. But today, Tall Dog is wrong, and will only anger the white horse soldiers, who will kill many of our people. In this village, Red Cloud tells his people it may still be possible to share what Grandfather Mystery has given the Sioux. For now it will be better for Red Cloud if you kill this buffalo killer, who hunts Sioux women and old men ... He will hear your answer in the morning."

Buffalo Horn and Red Cloud stepped into the lodge, leaving Tom to gaze at the fire and contemplate. Finally he turned to Still Water and said simply, "I am tired."

Still Water led him to an empty lodge, "In here we have made a place for you. In the morning I will send my daughter to you with something to eat." She smiled. "You have a lot to think about. I'll leave you now so you can sleep and think." She raised the flap and walked away, leaving Tom very tired, and much confused. Stepping inside he closed the flap and made a soft bed with blankets and skins. He lay awake a long while, watching the fire light dance on the lodge wall, and thinking. He didn't even know what he was thinking about, he was too tired.

Noise from the village woke Tom from a deep sleep. Daylight snuck through slits in the lodge wall and dancing beams played on the floor. He threw back the blankets and hurried out where he was greeted by a very different sight than the night before. Everywhere people were busy, building fires, cooking meat, gathering wood. Children dashed after each other and chased their dogs. As far as he could see there were lodges and activity. More noise than he had ever heard hung in the air and trees. All this made his skin tingle. His breath short. He looked toward the horses. He'd rather go there.

Then he saw her. "Hello, I'm Soft Cloud. My mother told me to look after you. Are you ready to eat?"

Tom studied her, "I don't know." He remembered seeing her in the lodge the night before, but in the morning sunlight she was even more beautiful than her mother. Unlike her mother she had long black hair, and her skin was dark. Not as dark as the others, but a lovely light brown color. Her large, friendly eyes shone dark brown.

"I'll wait here while you get ready."

"Why do you talk English?"

"Would you rather I spoke Sioux?"

"No ... no that's not it. Why would a Sioux woman speak English at all ... I mean first your mother, now you. Were they your brothers last night? Do they speak English too?"

Soft Cloud giggled a little. "Yes, but not as well as I."

Still unsettled Tom went on, "How I mean ... Why. I just can't figure it."

"My mother wanted it. Actually I learned English before I learned Sioux. Although I speak both equally well. I can even read English."

"You can read?"

"Yes, of course, can't you?"

Tom dropped his eyes "No, I never got taught. I only ever saw one book." He looked back at those warm brown eyes, "Why would your mother want you to know English?"

"She understands it's important. Have you found an appetite yet?"

Already Tom was beginning to find it easy to speak with Soft Cloud. It calmed him. The peaceful surroundings of the Sioux village and her gentle company were having a strange effect on him. He felt as if he was growing wiser by the moment, and he seemed to understand things more clearly, in a way he had never experienced before. His thinking seemed easier, too. Never before did he need to organize thoughts, or plan things for a day. While this new clear headedness was frightening, it was also exciting.

"I think I can eat now," Tom's gaze fixed on her wonderful eyes.

Soft Cloud left for a moment and returned carrying a bowl of mush made of wild grass seed and stems of wild tea, and a fat bodied prairie dog. Using his fingers he began, timidly, to eat his meal while Soft Cloud sat patiently nearby, watching him.

"Will you do as Red Cloud asks?" Her soft voice, as lovely as her eyes.

"Yes."

"And how will you do this?"

"Just go shoot him," he wondered why she needed to know so much.

"How can you be sure he won't shoot you first?"

"Because that's not how I see it in my vision. This buffalo hunter will be sitting by his wagon, and I will lie down on the ground, and shoot him, and he will die. I see this clearly, so I am sure it will happen that way."

"And you can see this?"

Tom finished his meal and took a long drink from the water skin, then left her to find a sunny spot on a rise to watch the horses, and think. The hider must die, not only because Red Cloud asked, but for his own reasons, too. But he'd rather sit with the horses than kill another man. Why can't he just stay here where it is safe and peaceful? Why can't he just forget the hider? He'd heard an old man say, "If a man looks hard enough for trouble, he's bound to find it." He never understood what that meant, but today, he wondered if that was what he was fated to do. Look for trouble. He turned from the horses to look back over the village. The sounds of running, playing children floated out to him. For them? For their safety, must he look for trouble?

He decided to use Tom Gray as his saddle horse and the pair of mules to pull the wagon. Better to take the wagon to carry enough supplies in case they are gone a long time. Sitting in the grass, with the sun warming his back while taking in the sounds of the village, and gazing at the horses and the prairie beyond them, his mind continued to clear. There were five or six hundred horses grazing and engaging in small battles and short chases, each defending their own territory and supremacy. Tom quickly spotted the three mules and recognized his old friend, who was the most comfortable looking of them all, simply eating grass and having nothing to do with chases or battles. It made Tom proud, that even in a herd this size, his big gray horse stood out. He watched them for a long while, absolutely content. So content he fell asleep. Before he fell asleep, he told himself he would have a horse ranch one day. A horse ranch like the one he had seen near Ogallala when he visited there with the old hider.

****

Tom woke with a start at the braying of a mule. It was late morning so he hurried to Still Water's lodge. "I'm ready to tell Red Cloud my plans ... will you come?"

Nervously Tom waited for her response, expecting her to reject him. Instead she rose. They made their way through the Sioux village walking slowly between low campfires and lodges. They walked in silence past meat racks loaded with buffalo strips, rabbits and prairie dog. Women busily scraped hides, and young boys cut arrows. This village had more lodges than Tom could count, he guessed near two hundred. Today all the activity soothed him, unlike the worry it had given him the night before. Did he belong here? He glanced at Soft Cloud.

They waited by the fire at Red Cloud's camp until Buffalo Horn and Red Cloud stepped from the lodge, and signaled they should sit across the fire from Red Cloud. His dynamic black eyes stared straight into Tom's, demanding information.

Tom turned to Soft Cloud, "I will ride my horse. I have known him a long time, and I'll take the two mules and the hider's wagon. I will take as my brave Soft Cloud …."

Soft Cloud bolted to her feet. "I cannot be your brave! I am a Sioux woman not a brave!"

"I have heard that the Sioux tell the Crow, even their women can defeat them in battle …Tell him." Tom meant to offer a compliment but saw instantly he'd failed.

Soft Cloud moved to Red Cloud, they both saw Buffalo Horn smile. She stood over Red Cloud, her voice wavered. She flung her hands as she spoke. Red Cloud looked at Tom, not able to hide his amusement. Tom returned the look, but Soft Cloud caught him.

For a long moment Red Cloud said nothing, just looked at Tom over the low fire. Soft Cloud stood by Red Cloud. She glared at Tom, her brown eyes narrowed to dark slits on her tan face. Since Red Cloud did not respond, Tom continued, "Soft Cloud should choose from the ponies the one best for her. I ask for Sioux leggings and moccasins."

Soft Cloud stared at Tom, defiance and disbelief radiated from her.

"Tell him." Tom offered a faint smile and remembered from the night before that Red Cloud understood some English, but he wanted Soft Cloud to tell him in his own tongue.

Soft Cloud spoke again. With emotions high, and hands waving, she told Red Cloud the things Tom asked.

Red Cloud sat quietly, and Buffalo Horn's smile widened. Soft Cloud stood between them at the edge of the fire. When finally Red Cloud spoke, he looked directly at Tom, with a faint smile on his lips. As he spoke Soft Cloud became more agitated, then turned to Tom, "Red Cloud is worried because your horse is older than you, and he may not make the trip. But he is not worried that I must go with you!"

Tom didn't try to hide his smile, "Tell him my horse can smell old buffalo hunters, and Crow." She turned to Red Cloud and told him, and Red Cloud nodded. Then Buffalo Horn removed his moccasins, and leggings, and handing them to Tom, he spoke to Soft Cloud.

She turned to Tom, "They will bring you back safe and victorious."

CHAPTER TWO

"Yo, Buck Hawkins ... General wants to see you!" Sergeant Worly scratched his white beard, as he swung up on "Old Bedlam's" porch, the officers' quarters in Fort Laramie.

"Yea? Have a seat Sergeant. I'm still workin' on my morning coffee. Just got in two days ago from four weeks of scouting and tracking renegades and the only thing I want to ride is this lopsided old chair. Have a cup with me." Buck pushed his feet up against a porch post, and rocked back his chair.

"Can't Buck ... gotta get to the corrals and have look at the new saddle stock that came in while you were on your pleasure trip."

"What do you know about saddle stock? The last time you sat a horse we were still a British colony." Buck smiled wide at the Sergeant.

"I didn't mean I was gonna ride 'em, I gotta count 'em. General wants to know how many made it through the renegades his favorite scout told him weren't there."

"Well they weren't there when I was. Because if they were, I'd of seen 'em and run 'em off."

"Can't explain it, but maybe you'd better, to the General ... they sure gave the Lieutenant and his boys a run for their lives!"

"That's not good. Reckon I'd best get to him." Buck bounced down Old Bedlam's heavy plank steps. "Thanks for the warning, Sergeant."

Buck sensed the General's mood the second he saw him reclining on his porch. General Sturgis did not recline, and rarely could be found on the porch. "Morning Buck," the General didn't bother to stand.

"Morning, General, and a fine morning this is!" Buck tried to set the mood with his wide grin.

"Not if you have to answer to Washington for raided settlements, slaughtered livestock, burned fields and missing horses. Buck, what the hell's going on out there?"

"Well, we have Arapaho to our East. Sioux and Cheyenne to our South, and renegades and outlaws to our North and West. Go more than twenty miles in any direction, and you'd better have a fast horse." Buck settled on the rail facing the General.

Buck cut a good figure dressed in fringed deerskin pants, and leather moccasin boots. He always wore army issue blue blouses, a dark leather vest and his brand new Stetson "Boss of the Plains" hat. When he walked across the parade, any officers' wives that happened to be about would surely watch. His sparkling green eyes could pierce a man through when angered, and melt any woman he turned his soft gaze upon. It had been gossiped that Lieutenant Harris' wife had openly expressed desire for the man, causing a rift to exist between the two men. Although for Buck's part, it was simply a way to torment a man he considered a good friend.

"I need to know the location of Hooker's camp town. There's been a report they raided another settlement near Little Bear Creek, killed three men and stole the livestock. I've dispatched four men to guard the settlement, but we need to do away with the whole bunch. They cause more trouble than the Cheyenne, Arapaho, and Sioux combined. I want you to leave now and find where they hide like snakes in the grass. I want to know their numbers. Buck, I want this over."

"Numbers I can give you. They have close to fifty, mostly lazy outlaws and drifters, but they've begun to attract renegade Indians. A renegade

Sioux, known as Tall Dog, is sending word to all Arapaho, Cheyenne and Sioux villages to join him with Hooker."

"Well the Sioux and Cheyenne are fighting each other."

"Not when they can fight you," Buck pointed his finger at the General.

****

The old buffalo hunter guided his wagon horses carefully through the narrow pass that led up the last steep grade. His wagon carried the results of a successful hunt. Not just for hides, but also whiskey, and guns, that he could sell to the band of outlaws and renegade Indians. He stopped the wagon in the center of the camp.

The camp had grown into a small town since the old man had last visited. Shacks of board and canvas numbered over twenty, and now there were women in the camp. "Where's Hooker?" Bellowed the hider.

A crowd of mildly interested ruffians gathered around the wagon.

"What have you got for me this time, old timer?" Hooker strolled around the wagon pushing the curious aside and trying hard not to get mud on his fancy boots.

"Whiskey for everybody, hides for the Injuns, and ten of these new Henry repeaters. For anybody with gold coins." The boastful old hider flipped back the top hide to reveal a wooden crate.

Hooker ripped the cover from the crate and stared at the neatly packed rifles. Eagerness dripped from his eyes, he couldn't resist touching a shiny stock.

"Yeah," the hider spit tobacco juice on Hooker's boots, "I followed the sutler coming from Fort Laramie after he met with the Army buyer there. I knew he had these rifles along. I got 'im talking after a little whiskey. One of them fancy gents thinking he could get rich quick sellin' rifles to the Army. Fool was too new from the East. Come here representin' a big Army contract for these new repeaters. So I moved ahead about twenty miles, and when he came over the rise I, well you can just say I put him outta the repeater business and put me right in it. I took these here Henrys and six hundred dollars in gold coins he had on him … There's gonna be a big shipment moving from Fort Kearney to Fort Laramie, in a few weeks."

"That, you old cuss, is worth a drink!" Hooker slapped the hider on the back and led the way to the makeshift canvas saloon. They settled at a small table in the corner.

"I can tell you this," the hider held his voice low. "You need more men than you have now. The wagons with the rifles leave Fort Kearney with a cavalry escort of fifty troopers. They're expected in Fort Laramie by the end of October."

"Tall Dog will find us more. They're scattered all over the prairie just waitin' to kill soldiers. He can gather fifty in a week. Those renegade Sioux and Cheyenne will follow him anywhere. Almost every day another handful leaves Red Cloud, and wanders into the village Tall Dog started just north of here. What day do the wagons leave Fort Kearney?"

"To get to Fort Laramie on time, they need to get started in a week or two. That many men, horses and wagons, it'll take those soldier boys a good two weeks to make the trip."

"What other supplies are coming along?" Hooker's eyes held an evil glow.

"You'll be able to outfit all your men with brand new U.S. Troopers' clothes!" The hider wiped his mouth on his sleeve, grinned at Hooker and poured whiskey into the broken jar that served as his glass.

"Troopers' clothes? New Henry repeaters and new clothes!" Hooker scratched his cheek. "Ha, we'll have our own army. You get back to the fort, find out when they're leaving Fort Kearney, and get back here in a hurry."

CHAPTER THREE

Buck rode out of Fort Laramie just before noon, and headed straight for the high country. Planning to travel light and fast, he ponied along an extra horse. His saddle bags stuffed with jerked beef and a good supply of ammunition for his rifle, and his Navy Colt. The Colt that had saved him more than once in the war that just ended. He carried two canteens of water and started out pushing his horse hard.

He had seen Tall Dog at the foothills north of the fort two weeks back. Covering the open prairie fast, and making the foothills before sun up, he would stand the best chance of not being seen. That meant hours of hard riding, but with two horses he felt confident he could make it. Through the rest of that day, and into early evening, Buck maintained a fast lope, and just as the sun began to sink out of sight over his left shoulder, the landscape began to change from open prairie to brushy and rolling terrain. A clear sign he had covered half the distance, and could look for a place to water and rest the horses.

****

"Tomorrow we should head east, keep to the open prairie south of the foot hills." Tom brought the mules to a stop by a tiny stream in a lonely stand of trees. It was the end of the first day out of the Sioux village and Soft Cloud had suggested they stop to make camp for the night there when it first came into sight.

Tom hobbled the mules and horses, with a special request to Tom Gray not to wonder far, and Soft Cloud gathered twigs and dried grass and started a fire. She sat on the ground across the fire from Tom. "Now will you tell me why you chose me?" She handed him a strip of hard jerky.

Tom studied the tough black meat as if it held the answer. "I wanted someone I could talk to."

"My brothers both speak English almost as well as I do."

"I never talked to your brothers. I didn't know if I would like them."

"And you like me?" Soft Cloud cocked her head in a way Tom found cute.

"Well, I can talk to you."

"And do you like to talk to me?" Soft Cloud persisted.

"Yeah, sure, I mean you talk nice, when you talk. You didn't all day."

"I thought you were looking for the old buffalo hunter."

"You can see for most of a hundred miles out here. I think I'll spot him even if you talk a little."

"And if I did talk, what should I talk about?" She gave her head a devilish little tilt.

Tom was pretty sure she was teasing him now. But he had no idea what he should do. So he thought it best to answer her honestly. "I think I would just like you to tell me things."

"Tell you things? I don't understand. What sort of things?"

"Lots of stuff. I spent my whole life with one mean buffalo hunter, never got to meet many people. All I know about is guns, and knives, and skinning, and shooting. You know how to read, and do lots of things."

"Tomorrow we can talk, now we should sleep." Soft Cloud gave a kind smile.

Her smile told him she understood him. She understood he could ride, track and shoot as well as any brave. But he was lost inside. Her smile told him she would guide him.

Tom fetched a blanket from the wagon, covered her, and paused a second to absorb the warm, subtle beauty of her face, just as she closed her eyes. Grabbing another blanket, he flung it over his shoulders and walked to the horses and mules, slid down against the trunk of a cottonwood, and talked awhile to Tom Gray.

****

"Get Hooker in here." Tall Dog barked to anyone that could hear him, "and you come sit on my lap, and feed me." He snarled to a woman, as he dragged her to his side. She put up a feeble effort to resist, for which she received a hard slap across the face. Tall Dog was as big as his bravado, and always used his size to intimidate anyone he wanted to. His long black braids went so far down his back, they touched his horse. Never without his gun belts, rifle and knives, to look at him was to see evil. To disobey him was certain death.

She grabbed a piece of moldy bread, smeared it across his face, and tried to stuff it in his mouth.

Tall Dog punched her face, shoved her to the mud floor, grabbed his new Henry from the table, and raised it to shoot her.

"Don't kill her!" Hooker pushed the rifle aside with a laugh. "We need our women! Come on Tall Dog, let's talk."

Tall Dog fired a round into the dirt next to her head, splattering mud on her face, then laid the rifle on the table and turned to Hooker rage boiled from his eyes. "You better start teaching your women how to care for me!" Then waved her off.

"Come on, Tall Dog, take it easy now. We have to talk about business."

"You talk about your business!" Tall Dog grabbed the whiskey bottle.

"Listen to me. The Army's moving wagons loaded with new Henry repeaters and ammunition, and enough supplies for us for a year, from Fort Kearney to Fort Laramie in about two weeks. I want that shipment, but we need fifty more men to attack that train."

Tall Dog never liked Hooker. He was a little man trying to pretend he was a big man. His camp was useful though, and Tall Dog found it handy to hide here after attacking wagons and settlers, who came on the grasslands, and thought the Indian should leave. The horse soldiers from Fort Laramie have never been able to find Hooker's camp. "I can get the men you need." Tall Dog stuffed some moldy bread in his mouth.

"It'll take more than a week for them to cross the open prairie. We'll hit them midpoint, in the open."

"You fool! How will you get fifty riders close to soldiers in open land? Ha-Ha! You are a fool Hooker!"

"You're the fool, Tall Dog. We won't go to the soldiers, they'll come to us. We'll be camped along their route as a Sioux village. The Sioux from your village can help us. The U.S. army thinks Red Cloud's Sioux are no longer a threat in these parts. When they stop we will invite them to rest. When they rest they'll become careless, and we'll kill them and take the wagons. We won't kill all the white men though. Some we'll allow to escape to Fort Laramie, and these will report it was Red Cloud's Sioux who ambushed them, and the U.S. army will kill all the Sioux that follow Red Cloud."

Tall Dog studied Hooker's face, thinking what a puny white man he was. Always talking, always planning, but he never rode with Tall Dog's renegades. Just a puny white man hiding from the soldiers who branded him a coward. But Tall Dog would welcome the chance to cause the white man's army to kill Red Cloud's people. Red Cloud is a fool. He thinks he can talk to the white man. Tall Dog hated Red Cloud. Red Cloud drove him from his people, from his wife and children. "I'll go now, to gather brothers from the prairie." Tall Dog stood, grabbed his new Henry and admired it.

"When you bring the renegades, we'll drink!" Hooker held his glass high in a salute. Tall Dog smashed it from his hand with the barrel of his rifle as he marched to the door.

Outside, Tall Dog's eyes fell on the woman he had beaten, huddled on the ground by the canvas wall. "I will be back in three days, and you will see to me."

He swung easily up on his horse, and galloped out of camp.

She watched until Tall Dog was gone from sight, then went in search of the old hider. She had heard most of the loud conversation inside and knew he would be leaving the camp very soon. She did not have far to go, the hider was driving out of camp, and stopped in at the saloon. He disappeared into the saloon. She disappeared under the canvas on his wagon.

CHAPTER FOUR

Buck stopped by a stream to rest and water the horses and swallow a few strips of jerked beef. Darkness had settled in, but a bright half moon shone overhead. Switching horses, he rode on at a comfortable trot. Still aiming for the foothills and making good time, but it would be five or six more hours to the base of the high country. There he planned to rest until daylight, and in the morning he would start searching for signs. In the foothills among trees, brush, and hilly terrain he would have cover.

Riding into the foothills a few hours later, he realized he crossed somewhat of a trail, maybe even wagon tracks. Could this be the trail he was looking for? That would be too easy. Buck turned the horses, hopped off, and walked back to the spot. Sure enough, here was a trail, and the last traffic had been a heavy wagon. He paced, and tried to make sense of the trail. Deciding he would walk the trail toward the high country, and see what happened, he set out leading the two horses. He walked for another hour, and rested on a large rock. "Let's walk a little more, then we have to put our heads together and figure what to do next," he told the horses.

Overhead the half moon shone so brightly, Buck had no trouble understanding the trail sign. "It's not a very heavily used trail, but someone just went up to the high country alone, with one loaded wagon." He stopped again and stood with both hands over a horse's back, leaning heavily on the horse. He looked up to the sky, counted stars to one hundred. "There is nothing up there boys that would need a load of anything … Nothing but Hooker's camp by God!"

They continued walking the trail toward the high country, but now Buck was certain where it led. He'd had little doubt from the moment he first discovered the sign, his only real confusion was that Hooker's bunch operated so secretly, and for them to carelessly leave wagon tracks just bothered him.

With the moon fading, and the sun on the horizon behind him, he stood looking far up the trail and wishing he had brought along field glasses, when with his naked eye he spied a wagon headed toward him. He pulled his rifle from the scabbard and moved on toward the wagon. The wagon carried only a driver who slept sitting up, swaying as the horses picked their careful way down the trail.

"Ho there, wake up!" Buck shouted.

The old hider jumped awake and snatched up his buffalo rifle.

"Who the hell are you?" The sleepy hider leveled his rifle on Buck.

"I'm just a traveler who stumbled on a trail and decided to follow it, because I got real tired of being lost."

The hider held his old Sharps on Buck, and Buck saw the old timer had his finger on the trigger, hammer back. "Always ready, aren't you old fellow. Reckon that's why you lived this long." Buck thought.

"Dressed kinda funny, aren't ya?" The hider wanted to know. Then without waiting for an answer, "Travlin' light an' fast too, I reckon."

"Well I reckon I'm a weird kind of traveler." Buck offered with a silly grin and shrug.

"Well I reckon you're a damned Army scout. Yeah that's what I think, you're a damned Army scout, and I'm gonna blow you straight to hell!"

Buck sized the old fellow up, and slid his finger to the trigger of his Henry, but before he killed the old fellow he hoped to get some information, "Ha-Ha-Ha—That's a good one. Holy Cow! An Army scout! I wouldn't help this Army break a horse!"

"Yea, where'd you get them fancy duds?" The hider pointed up and down along Buck's frame, with his long-barreled Sharps.

"Bout a week ago, I won 'em off this fellow in a card game."

"Why the two horses?" The hider lowered the Sharps, a little.

"Won them too." Buck smiled his big smile. "Care for a game? I'll play you for your wagon."

"I guess not. Where do you think you're headin'?" The hider lowered his gun a little more.

"Like I said, I was planning to follow this trail and see where it takes me. I have no one to answer to, and nowhere I need to be. Say, where does this trail lead to anyway?"

"I'd advise you not to follow this trail."

"Why not? Seems easy to follow." Buck pointed up the trail with his Henry.

"You won't like who's on the other end."

Buck swung his arm toward his horses. "I can take care of myself. I won these clothes, and these horses didn't I?"

"You play cards like that with the fellows on the end of this trail, and you'll lose a lot more than a horse. Even if you win."

"A real rough bunch, are they?"

"The roughest. You ever hear of the Hooker bunch?"

"No. Not that I know," Buck lied. "Where are you headed?"

"I'm on my way to Fort Laramie, an' I'm in a hurry. It's over seventy miles."

"You know the way to the Fort? Holy Cow! That was where I was going when I got all turned around, Mister. Can I travel with you?"

The hider took his time, and studied Buck. Perhaps he'd tricked him into thinking he was some fool easterner that can't survive out here alone and he might offer help.

"Yeah alright, but you keep your distance!"

Buck moved around behind the wagon, mounted up, and began the long trek back to the fort. He felt very proud of himself, not only for avoiding getting himself shot but for the information so easily gained. Unfortunately, to preserve his story he would need to spend three days making a journey he had just completed in less than twelve hours, unless he could come up with some excuse to leave the hunter.

As Buck rode behind the old hider, he studied the back of the wagon. It carried a pile of crates, partially covered by a wagon sheet, shifting and bouncing with the rolling of the wagon. "Why would a delivery wagon, on its return trip, have so many crates on it?" Buck wondered. "Collect old crates, do ya?"

"Firewood." Came the one word answer.

CHAPTER FIVE

As the sun began to creep onto the horizon, Soft Cloud started a small fire. "I'll make coffee to help soften those hard buffalo strips."

Tom pondered the assignment he had accepted while tending to the horses and mules, and never heard Soft Cloud's offer to boil coffee. With fistfuls of long grass, he brushed the horses' and mules' backs while his mind labored to find an understanding of his new life.

Having spent his entire life under the heel of a mean and miserable killer of man and beast, he had never made a decision of his own. Or even realized he could. Until killing the buffalo hunter, his mind had remained closed. All he ever had to do was whatever he'd been told, carry water, skin a buffalo, shoot a buffalo, and scrape hides. And of course suffer the lashings and other horrible deeds.

Now he was out on the prairie that he knew so well, with a person who was so different. Tom could not understand her kindness and gentleness, although he could feel it.

Resting his arms on his horse, letting his eyes wonder over the openness before them, he needed the strength of this friend he could understand. This friend he could always count on to bring comfort and peace, whenever the old buffalo hunter had beaten him. This day though, his old friend offered no answers, only comfort. Tom turned and walked slowly to the small fire, his eyes still searching the vast prairie that surrounded them.

Pointing to the hills in the distance he said, "Yes today we'll go in the direction of the foothills."

"But the buffalo do not travel among the foothills," Soft Cloud said.

"The wounded and dying buffalo often drift to the foothills, and I think old and dying buffalo hunters do too. We'll find that hider there, and I will kill him."

Soft Cloud handed him a meal of coffee and dried buffalo and sat quietly as Tom ate, chewing each bite a very long time, as he studied the grasslands.

"Are you afraid of killing the hunter?"

"No ... Do you think I should be?"

"I don't know." Her eyes held him, offering only silence.

They hitched the mules and readied the wagon for travel. As they started out Tom asked, "What is Sioux coffee made with?"

"Hot water, coffee beans, and a few other ingredients." Her smile told him the few other things would remain a secret. The wagon bounced across the rough prairie ground, as the mules trotted obediently, with Tom Gray and Soft Cloud's Sioux pony following behind.

****

Still in a foul mood for not killing the woman who had so angered him the day before, Tall Dog traveled east on the prairie leading eight of his new recruits. "We will find Black Feather's camp today, and then we will kill those white men, and burn their wagons. And take their women! They can be useful in Hooker's saloon if they live!" He pointed to a tiny speck traveling west far in the distance under a cloud of prairie dust.

Tall Dog knew exactly the direction to lead his band of renegades. He had lodged with Black Feather only days ago. They galloped south until the horses had enough, but that proved to be sufficient. For when they loped over a high rise, Black Feather's camp lay before them. They kicked the exhausted horses into a gallop again, and the group thundered into camp. Tall Dog jumped from his blowing, sweaty horse, before it was still. "Where is my friend, Black Feather?"

Twenty renegades, from the Sioux, Cheyenne and Arapaho tribes, who were not yet convinced to live the new life the U.S. army was trying to enforce, lounged around a few campfires. There were no meat racks, no women, no dogs, and no lodges. This camp was an encampment of dangerous killers, and raiders. Just the kind of braves Tall Dog attracted, and needed. The kind that required no encouragement to kill white travelers and settlers. It took only minutes to convince Black Feather to roust his camp, and charge off with Tall Dog and his band, to kill whites.

A force of twenty-five galloped at top speed across the open prairie, each man carrying a lust for killing. Some armed with Henry repeating rifles, others with old muzzleloaders, and still others with bow and arrow. Whatever the weaponry, it would surely be deadly.

As the sun raised high overhead, Tall Dog and his band began to close the distance that lay between them and the two lonely covered wagons. When separated by still over five miles, those in the wagons spotted the threat, and pushed their mules for speed. Tasting the thrill of battle, the renegades began their assault yelling and hooting while waving their weapons high, and pounding their ponies' ribs with their heels.

The emigrants turned their wagons in an attempt to fortify their position atop a long rise. From here at least they could fire down on their attackers and stand a chance. Within seconds, fire from at least four rifles came roaring from the wagons. As well as screams from women and children. The rifle fire was not wasted. Horses and men riding with Tall Dog began to fall at the very first volley.

Tall Dog turned his band to regroup out of range of the wagon's rifles. His ranks already lessened by three horses and one man, Tall Dog's rage boiled. "We will go to the rear of the wagons, into the wind and set fire to the grass, and when they flee we will kill them! If they do not flee the fire will kill them. If they do not die, I want the women!" He thrust his rifle in the air and led the mob around the wagons drawing rifle fire all the way, but they rode safely out of range.

Behind the wagons five renegades tied bundles of grass together, and set them on fire using black powder and flint. Riders galloped through the tall dry grass dragging the blazing bundles, creating a wind driven path of fire a mile wide. Flames taller than a man sitting a horse raced toward the helpless emigrants and their wagons, faster than a horse could run.

The terrified settlers began to turn their wagons to flee, but Tall Dog had those with rifles shoot the mules and hungry flames swallowed the wagons. Cries of terror and pain mixed with screaming of wounded and dying mules sailed out above the roar of fire. Tall Dog gave the order to charge the whites, and kill all but the women. No rifle fire threatened the renegades racing toward the burning wagons.

Two women and a young girl survived the attack, and with ropes tied round their necks, were dragged to the spot where Tall Dog and Black Feather stood waiting. One woman had been badly burned and could not stop screaming.

"If you do not stop I will kill you now!" Tall Dog shouted in the face of the burned woman. Her hair had burned from her head and her face and arms burned a bloody black. She could not stop screaming in pain and terror. The other woman tried to hold her, but was pushed away by Tall Dog, "You are too ugly to sell." He turned and shot her.

The other woman and young girl huddled together, having had escaped the flames. The only damage they suffered was smoky ashes and falling into Tall Dog's hands. Tall Dog caressed the young girl's blond hair, her violent struggles made him laugh. "Hooker will pay fine money for these! Put them on a horse and take them to him now. Anybody that wants to go to Hooker's can go. Black Feather will go with me."

Tall Dog and Black Feather rode away, followed by only two renegades. The others, who were all too anxious for the taste of whiskey and women at Hooker's, rode north toward the high country.

****

Buck pulled up his horse to look over his shoulder into the sun, "Listen to that shooting!"

The old hider could not hear it. "What shooting?"

Buck stood tall in his stirrups, "My God man! It sounds like a skirmish!"

The old man turned his head in the direction Buck was looking, "Don't hear a thing." He returned his attention to his team and drove on.

"Look there, smoke! There's a fire over there, surely you can see the smoke."

The hider stopped his team again and turned his head to stare at the thick plume of black smoke swirling up into the brilliant blue sky.

"Yep, there's a fire yonder alright." He spat tobacco juice over the side of the wagon. "Don't mean nothin' to me. Like I said I'm in a hurry."

"Well I'm going to check on it."

"You go ahead if you need to. That fire's twenty miles away. Time you get there it'll be all over."

Buck spun his horse, grabbed the rope of his second horse, and rode away at an impressive speed, quickly leaving the wagon behind.

"Fool, now he'll be lost for sure. No matter to me. Sure can ride a horse though." The hider drove on. The only thought on his mind was to get to the fort to seek information, never aware of his hidden passenger.

The sun hung well past noon high before the old hunter stopped to rest his tired horses. "Whoa there! You two take a short breather. We been goin' five, six hours now, and I gotta pee." He stood to relieve himself over the side, when something in the rear of the wagon, under the pile of the canvas, caught his eye. "Hey! Who the hell's under there?" He gave the canvas a yank, revealing the beaten woman huddled in fear. "You're that woman from camp! What the hell are you doin' on my wagon?"

The terrified woman stood slowly, her legs cramped from the hours curled under the canvas. She stared at the filthy bearded man, not knowing what to expect. She stood motionless as she watched him sit down on the wagon seat, straddling it, so he could look at her, and cringed as he reached out to touch her face.

"Tall Dog sure fixed you up didn't he? Get down woman. I reckon we might as well have a bite now that I have a body to fix it. Fetch that grub box off the side an' get a little corn meal and jerky, an' start a fire. We'll have coffee too."

The old man tied his reins around the brake, and crawled off the wagon. He walked to the side, found a good place to sit and watched the woman take boards from the wagon and start a fire. "I might just have ta keep you." He said as she measured the coffee out of its tin can. She tried to wriggle free of his groping hands.

CHAPTER SIX

The fire had cut a swath more than a mile wide, leaving the prairie floor blank and lifeless. Tom pushed the mules for more speed through the lingering smoke. He had seen prairie fires before and hated the death they left behind. The soil black and smoking, the grass turned to gray ashes that blew away like ghosts in the wind.

Leaving the burned land behind them, they trotted on in a northeasterly direction at a steady pace, keeping the foothills in view. The terrain began to rise and fall as the foothills grew larger in front of them. Tom stopped the mules and studied the lay of the land. Between them and the foothills laid sharp hills and deep valleys, and the old hider could be out of sight behind the very next rise. He jumped from the wagon, ran to the top of the hill, and called to Soft Cloud. "I think he is out there, hidden in a valley." He turned and paced the ridge again. Soft Cloud ran to stand beside him.

"He's not far, in a low ravine, and I will find him now."

Soft Cloud moved closer to Tom. "And why do you think so?"

"I think he was along the foothills, and like us, the fire drove him east. He is somewhere, there." Tom said pointing again.

She noticed Tom had developed an air of confidence as he turned and walked to the wagon. She sat watching as he searched the wagon for the sack of hard buffalo, and took a generous bite. His white teeth glistened in the sun as he tore at the tough meat. He leaned against the wagon side chewing slowly and thoughtfully, and took a long drink of water from a water skin. She waited for him to say something. But he had nothing to say, and stood leaning on the wagon for what seemed too long. Finally, he took his water skin and, one by one, gave the mules and horses water, filling his hand and allowing them to slurp it out, pausing at Tom Gray to whisper in his ear.

Tom laid his arms over his horse, and stared across the prairie, and the sky, and the smoke from the fire. Finally he turned to Soft Cloud, "I'll run ahead with my rifle. You follow with the wagon. But never come over a rise until I signal. I'll crawl in the grass over each hill until I see if he is there. Just as we sometimes hunt buffalo. When I see him I will shoot him."

She watched his face change from the uncertain challenged look she had found so charming, to a stone cold threatening face that sent icy shivers through her.

They readied the wagon for travel, tied the horses to the back, and Tom boosted her to the seat. She watched in silence as he checked his revolver and rifle, then took the pouch from his neck that held bullets for the Sharps, and fingered through them. Satisfied, he hung the little sack 'round his neck again, then handed her the Henry. "There are fifteen shots in this rifle. If something happens. Well, you'll know what to do."

Without another word he turned and sprinted down the hill. She ached to call to him to be careful. But she knew the man running down the hill needed no advice from her. She hurried the mules, for Tom had already reached the bottom of the first ravine, and was starting up the next hill.

Just before he reached the crest, Tom fell to his stomach and crawled to the top. The old hider must not have been in sight for he stood and signaled Soft Cloud, then ran for the next rise. She followed with the wagon.

Tom ran down the hill and up the next, falling again to his stomach before reaching the crest, finishing the ascent crawling in waist-high prairie grass. Once again his search proved unrewarding. He stood and signaled to

Soft Cloud, but she had fallen so far behind that when he ran down the next slope she lost sight of him. She pushed the heavy mules into a trot and cleared the rise just in time to see Tom standing at the next hill, signaling her to hurry. This meant he still had no sign of the old hider. Again Tom disappeared, and she pushed the mules as fast as they could manage to the crest. They made their way though valley and over hill until the day began to fade, and so did Soft Cloud's belief that they would find the old hider where Tom believed he'd be.

****

As Tom crested yet another hill, crawling through the tall grass, he estimated they had maybe an hour of daylight left. On the way to the top he thought how strange to use a buffalo hunting style, taught to him by a buffalo hunter, to kill a buffalo hunter.

This time, he saw the wagon! He slid down, rolled on his back, and signaled Soft Cloud to stay in the bottom of the ravine. He crept back to the top and found the hider sitting with his back toward him, facing the wagon.

Tom dropped down, raised the sights on his rifle and crept to the crest. As he took aim at the middle of the hider's back he thought, this is really close, not more than fifty yards.

The buffalo rifle roared, the old hider flew forward. Tom loaded another bullet and primer, then stood and signaled for Soft Cloud to come. As he ran down the hill, he kept his rifle on the hider, for he had not fallen. Perhaps he was still alive.

He found why the hider hadn't fallen when he reached the wagon. In front of him sat a woman, clutching her chest, blood streaming through her fingers. At that range the bullet passed through the hider, and slammed into the woman's chest.

Tom shoved the dead man aside and tried to make the woman comfortable. Kneeling beside her, he lay her down on her back, and with trembling hands tried to smooth her clothes. What else could he do? Her blood was leaking out of the ugly wound. Tom had never tried to stop death, only cause it.

Holding her head in his lap Tom, stroked her hair. She opened her eyes and looked up at Tom, just as Soft Cloud dropped to her knees beside them. "I have a daughter."

Soft Cloud put her hand on Tom's shoulder, and they sat very still.

Tom's eyes wandered out over the rolling prairie they had just crossed, and he stared mindlessly at the smoke in the distance. In some strange way it pacified him. After a while he gently laid her head down. Then ran to Tom Gray.

Soft Cloud came to him. "You could not know." The uncertain face of a confused young man had replaced the cold hard determined face she had seen earlier in the day. She knew he needed her.

Tom went to the dead woman, and scooped her up, taking care to hold her head close to his chest. Soft Cloud saw his tears spot her dirty blue dress as he carried her to the wagon. He made her a bed among the canvas and covered her as if she were merely sleeping. With his sleeve he smeared his tears across his face before turning to Soft Cloud. "Can your people bury her?"

"We will send her spirit to the next life."

He turned and marched to the dead hider, stripped him naked, and cut a slab of scalp from his head. They left him lying in the brown grass as they drove the two wagons away, headed for the Sioux village. Tom sent Soft Cloud first with the mules, so he could watch over her as he followed; and he didn't want her to see he was still crying. As they traveled away from the place where he had killed the woman he continued to struggle with himself.

CHAPTER SEVEN

Buck pushed the horses for all they had as he neared the fire, and galloped onto the black smoky ground before slowing the horses. The old buffalo hunter was right about one thing. Except for smoking grass and objects smoldering in the distance, it was all over.

"Whoa! Hold up!" Buck leaped to the ground feeling his rage build. Three men and two boys lay smoldering, like so many burnt logs. Twenty feet to his right lay the smoking remains of wagons, and bodies of the dead mules, still in their harnesses.

Buck knew what had happened here. He mounted and trotted to the fire's edge where his search revealed spent rifle casings strewn about, and looking back toward the wagons he saw burnt arrow shafts in the scorched grass. Then he found the dead woman.

"Tall Dog you lousy son of a bitch!" Buck's body trembled with fury. "Those poor souls must have been able to give Tall Dog too much trouble so he set the prairie on fire to burn them to death."

To the north of the blackened earth, Buck found the tracks of fifteen or more riders headed to the foothills and high country. "Going to Hooker's camp no doubt," he thought.

He also found tracks of four horses going south, and trotted his horses out of the scorched path, following those tracks that led into the unburned prairie. Buck followed them a short distance, then dismounted. He was sure Tall Dog would be with this bunch.

"Boys, we have about two hours of daylight. Need to ask you to stay at it a while longer. This is a bad animal and we're obliged to kill it." Buck took a canteen, filled his Stetson with water, and gave each horse a drink. Having covered nearly a hundred miles in fourteen hours, they all needed a rest. He pulled his saddle and the small pack off, then lay in the grass, giving the horses a short break to graze.

As he lay there flat on his back watching his horses graze, he puzzled over the meanness of Tall Dog. The son of a bitch had been terrorizing this part of the territory ever since Buck's first days as a scout, but now the time had come to stop him. Buck wondered if he was good enough to do it. He knew Tall Dog hated whites. Hell everybody in the territory knew that. Trouble with Tall Dog was, he still believed he could keep the whites out.

When he could lay idle no more, he grabbed a fistful of long grass and rubbed down both horses. Then saddled up, swung into the saddle and they trotted over the prairie following the tracks left by Tall Dog, guessing he might have close to an hour of light enough to track by. He was not going to let it go to waste and would ride so long as he could see the trail, and start again in the morning before the sun cleared the horizon.

****

Early in the morning Soft Cloud and Tom set out for the Sioux village driving their teams side by side. "How is it that you came to be with the buffalo hunter?"

Tom pretended to be concentrating his team. "Come on now, put your hearts in it." He flapped the reins to get their attention, and deflect Soft Cloud's.

They traveled a while longer then she called to him, "Tom, I am interested in knowing more about you."

"Why?"

"I don't know ... I guess I'm curious, about how you came to be with a man you hated enough to kill."

"I did hate him. I hated him for a long time. He needed to be killed."

"How is it that you came to be with him then?"

He did not look up when he answered. "I remember living with some people in Ogallala. That's the first people I remember."

"Were they buffalo hunters?"

"No. I don't think so." He held his eyes on the horses.

"How then, did you come to be with the buffalo hunter?" Soft Cloud persisted.

"He said they sold me to him. He said they owned me because they found me as a baby, in a dugout, with my dead mama. So they could sell me to him because I was old enough to work."

"Do you think that's true?"

"Don't know. Don't care. He's dead now and I'm done with him."

Soft Cloud could ask no more questions. She turned her full attention to the mules and drove on. She knew there was more she needed to learn about Tom. She had the feeling there was more Tom needed to learn about himself. She hoped he was strong enough.

****

Buck had been following the trail half the morning when he noticed a separation in the tracks. "Yea, sure enough, one rider has split off. Which one is Tall Dog?" Squatting on one knee he pondered the divided trail.

"My guess, the lone rider is Tall Dog. Yep, I think we'll follow this trail." He stepped back into the saddle.

Moving slowly up a long rise, easily tracking the one horse and rider,

Buck announced, "When we crest that hill boys, we'll take a break and I'll have a look around." He could see clearly where the rider he tracked crested the hill, so he pushed his horses into a fast lope.

The sickening smack of bullet hitting flesh sounded just before his horse crumbled, throwing Buck to the ground. Never losing his grip on the lead of his second horse, he swung up and turned downhill with all the speed the horse could give. Riding low, he leaned into the horse's neck, gripping a fistful of mane in one hand, and whipping the rope against the horse's flanks with the other. "Come on fella, get us the hell outa here! Go-go-go!"

They galloped recklessly down the way they had come, Buck whipping and hollering for all he was worth, knowing the speed and surefootedness of his horse was his only chance. At the hill Buck turned east hoping to stay safely below the ridge and hidden from view.

Flying across the prairie like a winged horse, another volley of bullets came hurtling at them. Buck turned his horse further north demanding more speed from the already winded horse. Over his shoulder he saw three men riding hard at him. Although out of range, they shot wildly and gained ground as they careened down the hill.

"Come on fellow pour it on!" Buck screamed.

****

Tom stopped the wagon and stood, his hands cupped behind his ears "Someone's in trouble! Listen to all that shooting and yelling … We gotta help 'em!" Before Soft Cloud could react, Tom grabbed his buffalo rifle and jumped to the ground running. He saw the fleeing rider headed in his direction kicking and whipping his horse as if knowing his very life depended on it. Not sure if Tom was friend or foe, the rider turned his horse, and raced by him.

With skills honed on the prairie, Tom sized up the moment in a heartbeat. The riders bearing down on him were renegades and coming fast. The man they chased looked to Tom like an Army scout. He fell to the ground, found the lead horse in his sight and fired. His rifle roared and the horse tumbled. Tom snatched another cartridge from his pouch, reloaded, sighted the second horse and dropped it.

The third rider spun his horse, grabbed the outstretched hand of his fallen friend, jerked him up behind and galloped up the hill. Tom had reloaded by this time and sighted squarely on the renegade riding double. He touched the trigger a third time, blowing the man on the back from the horse.

The remaining rider was slowed and knocked sideways by his friend desperately trying to hold on, and turned when Tom fired a fourth time. Tom knew his bullet struck, but the renegade stayed mounted and raced up the hill. As Tom reloaded, the scout thundered past him with amazing speed and pistol drawn. He caught up quickly to the injured rider, closed to less than fifty feet and shot him from his horse.

The scout caught the renegade's horse, and stopped to finish the life of the first fallen renegade. Tom walked toward him when the scout fired a round into the head of a horse trying to stand even though mortally wounded by the buffalo gun. "Lousy business, killing horses." The scout muttered.

Tom approached the scout and with a questioning eye. "You alright?"

"Sure am! You know you're right handy to have around."

Tom surveyed the horses and men he'd just killed, started to turn to leave then whirled to face the scout. "Who are you? And what was all this?"

"I scout for General Sturgis. That fellow up yonder is the renegade Black Feather, these two I don't know. Guess they rode with him. I'm trailing Tall Dog for killing and burning a couple of pioneer folks. Guess I gotta kill him."

CHAPTER EIGHT

"Just who the devil are you, anyway, and how is it you shoot so well and how did you get here?" Buck stepped back to size up Tom.

Before Tom could begin any explanation Soft Cloud trotted over the hill behind them with her wagon and two horses in tow.

"Like I said," Buck repeated, admiring not only the useful wagon, but also its beautiful driver, "you're handy to have around!"

Pulling the mules and wagon to a stop, Soft Cloud looked wide-eyed at Tom, barely noticing Buck. "Tom, what just happened?" For a while no one spoke. They just stood and studied each other, the dead men and dead horses. "Just who are you?" Soft Cloud demanded of Buck.

"Buck Hawkins. And might I ask the same of you?"

"This is my friend Tom, and I'm Soft Cloud."

"It is really good to meet you Tom!" Buck offered Tom his hand, but held his gaze on Soft Cloud. "You're Sioux?"

"Half, my mother, Still Water, is white."

"Are you Sioux?" Buck grinned at Tom.

"No ... I don't think so, anyway."

"Got any water? I just about ran this fellow's heart out." Buck rubbed his lathered horse's neck.

"Sorry we're all out. We were hoping to find a stream to camp by tonight."

Buck looked up the hill toward the dead horses and men, took off his Stetson and wiped his sweaty forehead on his sleeve. "Why don't we gather those saddles and guns and get away from here?"

Tom jogged to the nearest dead horse, cut the girth, yanked the saddle free, and carried it to the wagon. He carefully placed it next to the dead woman, then headed down the hill to where the other wagon waited.

Buck tied his horse to the side of the wagon with the other two, and rode the dead renegade's up the hill and gathered the last saddle. He sat behind the wagon holding the saddle as if not sure he wanted to toss it on the canvas. "Is that a body?" He looked up to find Soft Cloud by his side.

"Yes. A young woman." Soft Cloud said, her brown eyes surveying every inch of Buck's face.

"Why are you hauling a dead woman? Where are you taking her?"

"To my village, so my people can help her to the next life."

Rattling wagon chains and a dust cloud stopped their conversation as Tom bounced over the ridge with the hider's wagon. He pulled the horses to a stop next to the mules.

"I know that rig. Belongs to an old hider. I'd sure recognize that buckskin anywhere." Buck stepped his horse toward Tom. "Where is the old grump?"

"Lying dead on the prairie about fifty miles north of here." Tom said.

"You find him that way?"

47

Tom looked Buck up and down a second. "No, but that's how I left him."

"You know how he died?"

"I had to kill him, now … I'm sorry I did."

Buck took a moment to examine the team of horses, especially the buckskin. Before he asked, he studied Tom, "You kill the woman too?"

They watched Tom's eyes fill with tears. "It was an accident! I didn't know she was there … I couldn't see her…"

Soft Cloud went to Tom and tried to take his hand. He jerked it away, slapped the reins hard on the horses and took off at a full gallop, the wagon bouncing and swaying as he raced away.

"I must go with him. He is here because Red Cloud sent him to kill that hider." Soft Cloud stepped toward her wagon.

"Keep your wagons headed south, in about three miles you'll be in trees, there's a good stream there for camp. I'm going to find my saddle and rig. I'll meet you there later and try to help fix this thing." Buck tipped his hat and galloped up the hill.

Soft Cloud started out easy, she knew the mules were tired, she also knew if there were trees and a stream nearby she would find Tom there. She went along letting the mules set the pace, and thinking about Tom and the day they'd just had. She was wondering if Tom had learned anything about himself today, and wondered too, who this Buck fellow was, and if they would ever see him again. Her heart lightened when finally she saw trees and the wagon in the distance.

"I'm ready for camp, and would like some meat other than buffalo jerky." She announced when she stopped the mules under the trees.

As if her wish were granted by the Great Spirit, four shots rang out to their east. "We'll be eating range hen tonight!" Buck's voice floated toward them, and in a minute he raced into camp, a saddle in one hand and a fistful of hens in the other. "They just flew into my bullets!" Buck held the birds high overhead, leaped to the ground holding onto his saddle, but losing the birds.

"I wondered if we'd see you again." Soft Cloud gave a soft giggle and gathered the birds with exaggerated effort and more snickers. "We're pleased to invite you for dinner." She gave him a wink and Tom a soft look.

"I feel pretty lousy for the way I treated you Tom. And right after you saved my life. I'd sure like a chance to start over. Reckon we can eat theses hens, drink a little coffee, and talk most of the night away?"

Tom shrugged and started for his wagon. On his way he dropped a few sticks by Soft Cloud for the cooking fire.

"I'll cook them, after you two clean them." She arranged the kindling and dried grass, then struck flint.

"Yes ma'am. We'll sure take care of that." Buck assured Soft Cloud, and turning to Tom he said, "Let's get to it, pard!"

Tom busied himself carefully moving saddles and equipment to the front of the wagon, neatly arranging the load, and tossed half the wood from the empty crates over the side for firewood. He did not feel much like talking.

Buck sat on a rock, plucked and dressed the birds himself. "I shot 'em. I dressed 'em. Reckon I'll sure enjoy eatin' 'em!" He flashed that smile again.

"But I shall cook them, Mr. Hawkins." Soft Cloud said.

"And so you shall." Buck agreed, and with much swagger in his step he delivered the naked hens to Soft Cloud by the fire. "Why Mr. Hawkins, these are four of the fattest prairie hens I have ever seen!" They both stood and watched Tom as he fussed about the wagon as if its orderliness was his prime concern.

"Curious lad isn't he though?"

"Very! He is able to kill man or beast with the skill and reflexes of a mountain lion, but hates himself afterwards, and if the need should arise a moment later I have little doubt that he would kill again just as swiftly and instinctively."

"He's young. How'd he learn to shoot like that? I doubt I could even outshoot him." Buck's look gave a hint he just might admire the young man.

"I know very little other than he spent his life so far on the prairie with a horrible buffalo hunter he killed to escape. He saved the life of Red Cloud's son and for the moment at least he is living in our village."

"That's a lot of hard life packed into his young years." Buck looked toward Tom sitting on the wagon side gazing down on the dead woman. "Think I'll go check on him."

"Need a hand?" Buck leaned on the wagon next to Tom.

"She had a daughter," Tom muttered. "She had a daughter and I killed her."

"You're taking her to her daughter?"

"No, I don't know who she is…I just killed her."

"Well, why are you haulin' her then?"

"We're taking her to Soft Cloud's village so we can send her spirit to the next life as a Sioux…because I shouldn't have killed her."

"What happened?"

"I was sent to kill a man. I found him and I shot him…but my bullet also killed this woman that I do not know."

"Well now Tom, you didn't mean to kill her. Sometimes things happen and it's not our choosin'. Sometimes things just happen." Buck put his hand on Tom's shoulder and tried to calm him.

Tom ducked away from Buck's touch, spun to face him and yelled. "Today I killed more men."

"And by golly! I for one am mighty glad you did! You grew up on the prairie, you know it's tough, and it's never forgiving. Tom, you didn't do anything wrong."

"I think it is alright to kill a man that needs killing…but you should not kill a woman that has a daughter that you don't know."

"How about I help you wrap her in this canvas?" Buck offered and without waiting for Tom to respond he hopped on the wagon and wrapped her neatly. He was stepping from the wagon when his eyes caught sight of something shiny. "Hey what's this?" He handed it to Tom.

"What is this?" Tom turned it over and over in his hand, studied it.

"It's what you call a locket. Folks often put pictures of loved ones in them to keep them close, when they're away." Buck explained.

"How do you look at the picture?" Tom handed the locket back to Buck.

"Like this." Buck pushed on the release and the locket sprang open, revealing a picture of a beautiful little girl about five years old nestled inside, under a protective piece of glass. Tom froze, held rigid by the eyes of the little girl on the other side of that tiny piece of glass.

"The hens are ready!" Soft Cloud's cheery beckoning failed to move Tom.

"I'm ready to test her cookin' and feelin' plenty hollowed out!" Buck snatched Tom's arm and dragged him to the fire.

Tom held the locket out to Soft Cloud. "This is her daughter."

"She is a lovely child." She said almost in a whisper, then looked from the locket to Buck.

Buck inched closer to the fire, eyeing the birds on the roasting sticks and rubbing his belly. "Let's eat, folks! Been a long day!"

Tom closed the locket slowly, and tenderly slid it into his side pouch.

The day began to fade into evening as the little group settled around the crackling fire to feast on the long-awaited meal of prairie hens. Buck held up a leg of a roasted bird and toasted the cook and the birds. "Here's to the cook! My compliments indeed! And to the birds, I thank thee for thine attendance, for without thee we would have no supper!"

"Well thank you, Mr. Hawkins and I offer thanks on behalf of the birds as well." Soft Cloud giggled.

"What do you think, Tom? Darned good cook, isn't she?" Buck tipped his Stetson to Soft Cloud.

"The food is good." Tom mumbled.

"Come on Tom, you can do better than that."

"I mean the birds taste good. Better than buffalo jerky."

"Tom, I will take that as a compliment." Soft Cloud offered a gentle smile.

After picking clean the bones, they began to settle in around the dancing fire on horse blankets and boards from the crates. Soft Cloud kept busy tending the fire. Buck busied himself picking his teeth with a match. And Tom searched for the North Star. "I like to find the North Star before I go to sleep."

Soft Cloud looked from Tom to Buck. "Buck, are you in the Army? I'm curious, what were you doing out here? Is there a reason you found yourself being chased across the prairie?"

"I'm a scout for the Army, out of Fort Laramie, under General Sturgis. I was sent here to find Hooker's base of operations. He's real trouble. His renegades, along with Tall Dog and others, have killed, burned, and terrorized many of the new emigrants moving into this territory. General Sturgis wants to eliminate Hooker and his operation. Yesterday I found a trail that leads to his base. I understand he has quite a few men there, as well as some women that are being held captive. Tall Dog and his renegades started that prairie fire yesterday. They killed two families and left their bodies burning in the fire.

"That's why we had that skirmish. I was following their trail and got my horse shot out from under me, and when I was running away that's when Tom saved me ... Tom, you sure can shoot. How did you learn to shoot like that?"

"I've been shooting guns a long time, I lived with an old bastard of a hider, and did a lot of shooting. I can hit a buffalo between the eyes from a hundred and fifty yards with my Sharps. I can kill a running jackrabbit from fifty yards with my Henry, and I can hit a tin can three times in the air before it hits the ground with my .44. I don't mean to be braggin' but I can do it. The old buffalo hunter used to make money betting on me ... when he lost money he'd lash me good."

"That's why you had to kill him?" Buck asked.

"Yeah, he's dead now ... dead and scalped."

"Well Tom, I don't believe you're bragging, I've seen you in action. You just may be the smoothest operator I've ever seen, except, maybe for Bill Hickok."

"You know Bill Hickok?!" Tom could not contain himself. It was the first brightness they'd seen in Tom all day.

"You bet I know Bill Hickok. I served with him under General Sheridan toward the end of the war, on the Kansas and Missouri border. Boy, those were some wild times. He's one shooting son of a gun, I'll tell you that. But I'll bet if I put you up against him you could hold your own. You guys could shoot bean cans all day long and, by golly, there wouldn't be anything left but tin scraps. Yeah, I mean to tell you, those were some wild times.

"Many days we'd be running for our lives and the only thing could save us would be Bill's shootin'. Why that galoot could shoot rebels out of their saddle at a flying gallop with his .44, without even hardly turning around. I mean there would be rebs falling all over the place and we would get out of every tight spot. Just because Hickok could shoot faster than most guys can spit."

"You know Bill Hickok. I can't hardly believe it. Sometimes, when we would visit camp towns, I'd have to sleep with the wagon outside the saloons, and I would hear people tell stories about Bill Hickok. I just imagined that one day I'd get to see him. But I reckon that'll never happen."

"Well now Tom, you just never know. Could be I'll run into him again and I'll make sure we look you up, but tomorrow morning, I'd best head back to Fort Laramie. General Sturgis will sure want the information that I have on Hooker and his camp."

"Maybe it's time we get to sleep." Soft Cloud suggested.

CHAPTER NINE

"Where the hell is Hooker?" Tall Dog wobbled in his chair, pounded on the plank table top and sucked down whiskey as fast as he could bend his elbow. "I just about had my damn head blown off by that crazy Army scout, Buck Hawkins. He was out there and he had help hiding in the grass. He shot the hell out of us. It was all I could do to get out of there with my own skin. I want Hooker. I want him in this saloon and I want him in this saloon now!"

"Whoa! Whoa! Whoa! Come on, can't you take a little shooting? I thought you were tougher than all that!" Hooker laughed, running into the saloon, spurs jangling. "Those extra men you sent up here are gonna work out just fine. How many more you think you can get?"

Tall Dog reared back his chair and propped his feet on the tabletop, looking as mean as ever. He stroked his new Henry. "Hey look at this, Hooker. I took this from that crazy Army scout after I shot his horse out from under him. But didn't you know that bastard had another horse and got away, but I got his many shots rifle!" To punctuate his wrath, Tall Dog fired rounds through the ceiling of the canvas top.

"Come on, Tall Dog! Damn! Now it's gonna leak there. Sometimes I don't know if you're worth all the trouble." Hooker sat next to Tall Dog, put his hand on top of the Henry and forced it down on the table. Tall Dog laughed off the little man's bravery and downed another slug of whiskey.

The two men looked around the saloon at the muddy, slimy floor, the women working the tables, the bar, the rough looking renegades and money piled on tables at poker games. "Tell me Hooker, are we ready to build a Sioux village and kill us some damned troopers?" Tall Dog leaned close to Hooker, whiskey slobber trailed down his cheeks. Hooker studied Tall Dog and could not help but see what a vicious killer this man was. A man who truly enjoyed killing, who would kill for no reason at all. He especially enjoyed killing if given a reason. But tonight he was just drunk, and of no use.

"In about three or four days that old buffalo killer should return with information on when the Cavalry's gonna leave Fort Kearney, then we can plan. But you're going to need to get us about twenty more men."

"That damned Army scout, Buck Hawkins, killed two—and he killed Black Feather! I might have to take some time and hunt that son of a bitch down. I want his scalp on my Henry." Tall Dog reared back, sighted his rifle on the back of the head of the man drinking at the next table. "What do you think of that?"

"Damn it Tall Dog, we don't have the time to waste. You're gonna have to go get more men and we need to get ready because we need to set up that village and get those wagons. We need those supplies for the winter."

Tall Dog bent far over in his chair, grabbed a woman by the back of her hair, and yanked her on his lap. She threw her arms around his neck, and started kissing him hard on his face. He looked up and hollered, "Get me a bottle o' whiskey over here. This is the kind of woman I like. I am going to get us drunk and then we're going to your tent. Drink up!"

"Tall Dog, we must get our plans in place. We don't have time for this. I only have about forty-five men here." Hooker pleaded with Tall Dog.

"You get your plans. I'm getting drunk. And if I see your puny, ugly face anymore tonight I'll blow it in the mud!" Tall Dog jumped to his feet carrying the woman, pushed Hooker into the mud, and headed for the rear open flap, knocking men from their chairs as he carried the laughing woman.

CHAPTER TEN

"Come on, you lazy bums, get out of them blankets." Buck ordered from his bedroll with a chuckle in his voice.

"We've been up quite a while, Mr. Sleepyhead yourself." Soft Cloud's voice came from behind the trees. "I was just fetching water to start breakfast. We thought you might sleep until noon, the sun's been up almost half an hour already." She settled on a broken log by the fire near Tom and helped fan the tiny sparks into small yellow flames.

Buck ambled to the fire pit, rubbing his eyes and reclined on a saddle. "I've most always had a problem with mornings ... You're not making that Sioux coffee are you?"

"Well, Mr. Army scout, would you quibble about *any* coffee made for you out on the prairie?" Soft Cloud teased. "As a matter of fact, I found plenty of white man's coffee on the wagon. But I didn't notice any trout in the pan by the fire. I thought perhaps you were fishing when I realized that I didn't see any men about, but then I looked back and saw the two sleepyheads still wrapped in their blankets."

"You know that's kind of interesting." Buck grinned at Tom and Soft Cloud sitting by the fire. "Just what are we going to eat for breakfast. I was sort of planning on trout myself. I'd wager there might be a few in that little stream down there."

Tom sent a grin all around and sprang to his feet. "Give me ten minutes." Then raced away without another word.

"Guess we're having trout for breakfast." Buck said with a wink, and a smile.

"I suppose we are at that ... Just exactly what are your plans, Mr. Hawkins?"

"Plannin' on breakfast with you folks, then headin' to Fort Laramie, if I can wrangle a horse from you. I'll take the renegade's horse, and I'd sure like an extra. I'll trade you mine, he needs a few days rest after the miles he's done. Your pony's pretty fresh, isn't he?" Loud splashing coming from the direction of the stream gave them both a chuckle. When the racket stopped, Soft Cloud tossed a few more boards on the fire.

"Maybe we should ask Tom if we can send the woman to the next life here." Buck suggested. "This is a nice peaceful place, and Tom would be better to leave everything that happened here behind." Buck grabbed a stick, and prodded the hot ashes, sending crackling sparks high.

"It would be best to have the ceremony here." Soft Cloud agreed. Buck looked up from the fire and into Soft Cloud's eyes and for just a moment they both enjoyed a glance.

Their peaceful gaze was interrupted by crashing and thrashing, hooting and hollering as Tom, stumbling and fumbling, made his way toward the fire trying to control an armload of wriggling trout.

"Holy Cow! We are going to have trout for breakfast! I can't believe this kid! He can shoot, he can run, and he can fish! Yessiree. You are quite the man, Tom, I'm sure gonna miss you when we part company."

Tom stumbled to the fire and dropped the armload of trout at Buck's feet. Soft Cloud and Buck moved fast to grab the trout and began cleaning them, Tom broke into a hardy laugh and asked with his hands on his hips, "How do you folks like them apples?" He sat, resting his back in a saddle by the fire, putting his feet on a rock. "I'm gonna warm my wet feet, and dry my soaked leggings while you two make breakfast. And I think I'll have a cup of coffee too. But just white man coffee with no Sioux stuff mixed in, okay?"

Buck and Soft Cloud shared a good laugh at the seriousness of Tom's declaration.

Tom reached for the metal pot of boiling coffee, held it to his nose and took a whiff. "Woo Hoo! Good coffee!"

Soft Cloud and Buck could not contain their laughs, even though Tom showered them with questioning eyes. "Have to hand it to you, Tom, you're one heck of a fisherman and you have earned your keep today!" Buck's eyes streamed tears, his voice cackled in laughter.

All three enjoyed a hearty breakfast of coffee and fresh trout, and Soft Cloud even found the time to bake biscuits in a Dutch oven they had found in the wagon. The sun was just beginning to get serious about its morning journey toward noon. Soft Cloud looked at the two men, both quite proud of themselves, and stuffed on trout and biscuits. "Tom, why don't we send the woman on to her next life here in this peaceful grove of trees? We've had a lovely time here, around this little campfire sheltered by these tall cottonwoods. I believe that here she could find peace as she makes her way to the Great Spirit." Soft Cloud's voice held the tenderness of a whisper.

Tom sat silent and wrestled with his thoughts. He had planned to take her to Red Cloud's village. Perhaps it would be best to let her go now. Long, quiet moments passed, then Tom said, "We will put her to rest here … so she can begin her journey to the Great Spirit, and the next life."

Tom and Buck searched the grove of cottonwoods, and gathered long poles to build a Sioux burial platform, and before the sun reached its highest point they had her resting on it. As is the Sioux custom, a hot drink and meal was placed atop the platform with the woman. It is understood by the Sioux that as the meal loses its heat, the body gives up its spirit so that it may start its journey to the next life. It is required that the dead be watched over until the meal is cooled.

"Well folks, it has surely been an experience. It might be best if you spend another night here and start out in the morning. There's no way you

can make it to your village before dark. But I need to get to the General."
Buck gathered his belongings, strapped on his .44, swung aboard the
renegade's horse, and rode to where Tom stood holding the rope on Soft
Cloud's pony. "Thank you, my good man. I'll be leaving you now but I
know we'll be seeing each other again. You are both fine folks, and I'm
honored to know you." Buck turned his horse and trotted away.

Soft Cloud stirred the campfire watching Tom watch Buck ride over the
ridge.

CHAPTER ELEVEN

Riding hard for hours, switching horses twice, by the middle of the moonlit night Buck could see Fort Laramie. Without slowing the horses he rode into the Fort and stopped at the corrals. It was about two in the morning and the only people awake were those stuck with night guard duty. Buck spied a sleepy Private leaning against the livery wall and hated to disturb his nap, but better him than the Sergeant.

"Hey there young fella!" Buck rousted the drowsy Private. "Figure you could get pried loose from your guard duty long enough to take care of my horses? They ran their hearts out for me all night, and this little fellow here is a genuine Sioux war pony. They're hot, tired, and thirsty and earned a good rubdown, plenty of water, some oats, and lots of hay."

Buck tossed the reins to the young private, "Thank you young man. I'm headin' for Old Bedlam now for a long, hot bath then jump in bed and sleep 'til noon. I'd thank you to get word to General Sturgis I'm back. Leave word that I'll see him as soon as I wake up and that I found the trail he sent me to look for."

The Private, wide awake now, stood examining the Sioux Pony, "Wow, Buck, how'd you get him?"

"I traded my Government horse for him." Buck said with a chuckle. "Don't tell the Sergeant."

Buck's long, hot bath included three stiff drinks and a fine cigar. He thanked the cook, with one of those fine cigars, for leaving his comfortable bed and not only fixing Buck a fine meal of cold roast beef and cold potatoes but also for making enough hot water for him to soak for half an hour.

Doggone, that's an awful lot of racket out on the parade for this early in the morning, Buck thought, as he stretched and sat up in bed. He fumbled on his nightstand for his watch and flipped it open. "Holy cow, 12:30! I'd better hightail it before the General sends the Sergeant to drag me down in chains." He dove into his deerskin leggings, army blouse, deerskin vest and Stetson, which now hung slightly droopy. He yanked on his moccasin boots, strapped on his Navy, gave his Stetson a slight tilt, and bounded down the steps two at a time, and out the front door.

"Good afternoon Mrs. Harris." Buck tipped his hat and flashed his grand smile. "I swear. I spend a few days out on the prairie and come back to find you've gotten twenty times more beautiful. I just cannot get over what a gorgeous woman you are! Does your husband fully appreciate you?"

"Why Mr. Hawkins! You fresh thing! You always say those things just to make me blush. And if Mr. Harris were to hear you! Why, you just know how angry he gets."

"Well, you simply are beautiful. And if it upsets the Lieutenant to hear me say those things well then I reckon he'll just have to be upset because one thing I cannot abide is unrecognized beauty. But I better get into see General Sturgis. I seem to have overslept a bit."

Buck hustled across the parade to the General's office, leaped up the porch steps, banged on the door and barged through. "Afternoon, General, and a good afternoon to you Lieutenant Harris. I just saw Mrs. Harris out on the parade. I must say Lieutenant, she looks finer every time I see her. I'll have to see if I can get a photograph of her... Hey! Could you provide me with a photograph of Mrs. Harris that I might take with me when I'm out scouting? Then the separation would not seem so painful."

"WHY YOU – TWO BIT SCOUT!" The Lieutenant grabbed Buck by

the vest and hurled him against the wall.

Buck crumbled to the floor laughing. "Why Lieutenant Harris, you're so touchy these days. I merely requested a picture of your fine and beautiful wife that I might not find the nights on the prairie so lonely. Why I could follow tracks just by the glow of her beauty reflected from a photograph carried in my vest pocket." Buck continued to torment.

Lieutenant Harris lunged across the room and kicked wildly at Buck lying on the floor in front of the General's desk.

"ALRIGHT! ALRIGHT YOU TWO!" General Sturgis bellowed as he leaped to separate the two rowdies. "I'll have you both in chains and maybe flogged! We have serious business to discuss; and Buck, I really don't appreciate your antagonism. You know that the Lieutenant here is thin-skinned in matters of his wife … But Lieutenant Harris, you know she really is gorgeous."

"General I can't believe I have to put up with it from you too. If this keeps up, I'll ship her back east to live with her mother until my enlistment's up."

"Come on Lieutenant." Buck almost choked on his laugh. "If you send her back east half of the cavalry west of the Mississippi will follow her and then how would the General fight the Indians and Hooker's bunch. And he damned sure wouldn't have a scout. I'd be back East!" The Lieutenant spun and punched Buck in the face, knocking him flat on his back. He laid laughing, but rubbing his cheek while Lieutenant Harris shook and massaged his bruised right hand.

"GENTLEMEN! THAT WILL BE QUITE ENOUGH!" General Sturgis stormed around the front of his desk, grabbed Buck's vest, and slammed him into a wooden chair. He spun and addressed the Lieutenant. "You sir will stand at attention." He turned to Buck. "You will sit and hold your mouth, or by God I WILL have you in irons!"

The General glared at both men, turned and stomped behind his desk. He towered tall, leaning with his fists on the desktop. "The young Private told me this morning you found the trail to Hooker's camp." He said looking at Buck. "I'm not sure I'll be able to deal with Hooker's town full of outcasts, renegades, and outlaws, at this moment."

The General held up a letter. "This came by dispatch from Fort Kearney yesterday. I'm to send thirty troopers to Fort Kearney, meet an additional twenty troopers there, and escort a wagonload of the newest Henrys and ammunition, and several wagons of supplies including new uniforms for every man in this fort. There will be five loaded wagons which we have the responsibility of escorting. I expect Lieutenant Harris to assemble his thirty men and to be ready to travel by noon tomorrow. Buck, I'm sending you with the Lieutenant. Any and all shenanigans stop right here and now! That my boys, is as FIRM an order as I can possibly give! Lieutenant, you're excused. Start assembling your men. Buck you go with me to the mess and fill me in on Hooker's outfit."

They walked side-by-side from the porch and across the parade looking very much like two old friends, even though General Sturgis was more than twice Buck's age. "Buck, why the hell must you torment Lieutenant Harris like that?"

"Well General." Buck started as he rubbed his chin with his right hand, and slapped his hat against his leg with his left. "It's just so damned easy, and I truly get a kick out of it. He sure is thin-skinned though, ain't he?"

"Damn it Buck. Can't you knock it off for one damned minute? I need to send that escort to Fort Kearney, and I need you to scout for it! I'll not tolerate one more word of this bullshit." The General gave Buck a playful shove, followed by a very real cautioning glare.

They crossed the dusty parade and climbed the rough plank steps to the porch of the mess and stood a moment while the General surveyed the activity inside the fort. Several troopers' wives were busy hanging laundry in the dusty early afternoon sun. A small group of friendly Sioux was leaving the commissary and two blacksmiths worked busily at the corrals readying horses for the journey ahead. "Sure is a peaceful day today." the General said. "At least when I can keep you two apart." Buck flashed a broad "I'll behave, General." But his chuckle belied his promise.

Inside the large and noisy mess hall, over plates heaping with roast beef, potatoes, and green beans, they discussed the inevitable reckoning to come with Hooker. "So you know the way to Hooker's camp town in the high country. As soon as we have this escort from Fort Kearney out of the way, I'm planning to send you with enough troops to clean that mess out of there."

"I never made it all the way to Hooker's outfit. I ran into an old hider coming down a rough mountain trail with a wagon. I rode with him for a while and he told me the trail leads to Hooker's."

"Are you sure that trail leads up to Hooker's outfit?"

"Sure as I can be, don't know any other reason for somebody to be hauling a wagon up and down that trail. He said it's about twelve miles up into the high country. Mighty tight trail though and most likely the entire twelve miles can be seen from his camp.

"But like I was saying, I was riding with this rough, old hider for a while when I saw a prairie fire and went to investigate. Tall Dog and some of his renegades had killed emigrants that were traveling with their covered wagons. Burned 'em to death. It was ugly." Buck paused to push his pile of potatoes around on his plate; he hated living it again. "I picked up Tall Dog's tracks there. It looked to me like twenty or twenty-five horses headed up to Hooker's. But I followed four others that went south because I was pretty sure Tall Dog was in that bunch. It wasn't too long until I caught up with them. Maybe they were waiting for me, I don't know. Somebody shot my horse right out from under me but I was able to get away on my second horse, and more renegades came up over the ridge pouring on the lead! If it wasn't for this young fellow, Tom, lying in the grass with his buffalo rifle ... I mean he shot the hell right out of 'em. I believe they'd have killed me."

"Who is this Tom fellow?" The General's eyes grew wide.

"He's an unbelievable young man who's traveling with a half Sioux woman because Red Cloud sent him to kill the hider I'd met up with. Turns out that old boy had been killing more than buffalo and Red Cloud had had enough. They were heading back from killing that hider when they heard the skirmish I was enjoyin' with the renegades. So he came running to my rescue with his Sharps. He's cool as a horse in the shade. Laid there in the grass and shot two horses out from under the renegades. And then shot two of the renegades dead."

"Sounds like a good man to have around when you need one."

"Well there's a bit more. He saved Buffalo Horn's life a couple days before that, and Red Cloud is so grateful that Tom is allowed to stay in the Sioux village. Quite a story don't you think?"

"I am not sure I know what to think of that young man at this point but tell me ... what about the breed Sioux woman? Do you know anything about her?"

"Not much. She sure is a fine looking woman, and she speaks English better than any schoolmarm I have ever encountered, and she's got the manners, carriage and attitude of a minister's wife!"

"A good looking, well mannered, breed Sioux woman out on the prairie hauling a sharp-shooting kid that kills hiders. She speaks English and he lives with her in Red Cloud's village. Buck, if you're not beatin' up on Lieutenant Harris, you're out on the prairie meetin' the most damned interesting folks. Where do you suspect your English-speaking Sioux woman and your sharp-shooting kid are now?"

"They're heading back to the Sioux village about eighty miles south of here in Indian Territory. I've seen their village, over two hundred lodges, about two hundred and fifty braves, some old men, women and children. They're not one of the trouble-makin' bunches. You know Red Cloud and Buffalo Horn are quiet right now. They've not been any trouble for a year, since that Caspar incident."

"Well Buck, I guess we'll have to see what the future holds. I'll spend some time thinking this all over. I don't know if we can allow a Sharps-toting crack-shot kid to pick off any hider he thinks should be dead. Even if he is a friend of Red Cloud's. That one, friend, I need to mull over in this old brain of mine."

General Sturgis stood, gave Buck a quick nod and headed for the door. Buck propped his feet on the mess table, reared back his chair, and snagged a cigar from his inside vest pocket. He struck a match on the plank floor, lit the cigar and began blowing perfect smoke rings. He sat peacefully smoking, enjoying both his cigar and a good hot cup of coffee. Secretly hoping he would be able to scare up a good poker game after sunset.

CHAPTER TWELVE

"Any one of you miserable piles of crap see Hooker this morning?" Tall Dog shouted, food and whiskey spilling from his overfull mouth. Earlier that morning he had stormed to the saloon, meaner than normal even for him, and pushed two cowboys from their chairs to take their table. Several quiet moments passed while Tall Dog stuffed cold biscuits and almost rotten meat into his gaping mouth and washed it down with generous gulps of watered down whiskey. "Somebody get up off their ass and go find that worthless Hooker!"

A few renegades sat around a table far from Tall Dog's chair absorbed in a game of poker, and whispering too loudly. Tall Dog turned in his chair. "Somebody got something they want to tell me?" The men in the game looked studiously at their cards, ceased all conversation, trying their best to hide behind the cards in their hands. Tall Dog rose ominously and approached the men in the game. "I'm heading out soon. You five are coming with me. We're going to the Sioux village and I'm bringing my sons back with me."

Hooker burst into the saloon, wearing his customary concho-studded black hat, leather chaps, and jingling spurs. "How long Tall Dog?"

"As long as it takes to bring my sons! When I return with my sons and more men, we will prepare to fool the cavalry troopers. We will enjoy killing the U.S. Army cavalry troopers who think our lands are no longer our home."

Tall Dog turned, and without another word marched from the saloon. The five men left their cards on the table and hustled after him.

CHAPTER THIRTEEN

"I think we're ready to travel," Soft Cloud announced to Tom from behind the wagon. They had worked together in near silence organizing the wagons and readying themselves for their return trip to Soft Cloud's village.

"I want a slow ride back, and I don't need any old hiders, renegades, or prairie fires. Or even any fancy Army scouts who need saving."

"You know, Tom, a little more than a half day's ride from here is a pretty little valley, with trees and a stream we call Little Bear Creek, and there's an old mud cabin. Why don't we spend the night at the cabin? And I'm quite sure you could see to it that we have trout for supper."

The idea of a quiet day driving a team across the sunny prairie, to a night at a place as wonderful as Soft Cloud described suited Tom. He started his team and tossed a smile to Soft Cloud.

They traveled peacefully for hours through knee-high prairie grass, patches of fall wildflowers, up and down hills, through streams, and passing the occasional massive tree and prairie dog town. In the distance once, they even saw a sprawling buffalo herd. Tom had always loved the prairie but felt as if today he was seeing it for the first time. He had lived his entire life on the plains, but today he saw it with a new eye. Today he felt happy - a new feeling for him. Today he understood why.

They traveled on, neither of them needing to speak for miles. Soft

Cloud finally broke their contented silence when she pulled her mules alongside Tom's horses. "Tom, have you thought of your future plans, what you might do? You know you're welcome to stay in our village. I'm quite sure my brothers, Buffalo Horn, and others in the village will make you welcome and help you to understand the ways of the Sioux. You have already proven yourself to be a trusted and worthy friend to our village, and anyone can see Red Cloud respects you."

Tom had nothing to say for a while longer, choosing to let Soft Cloud's words mill about in his mind. He concentrated on watching the horses lean into their harness while thinking about what she had said. As much as he was beginning to like Soft Cloud, and Red Cloud too, he was pretty much used to being alone. He figured he liked it that way. He figured it should be that way.

As they neared a low-lying area with a few trees and scrub brush, Tom pulled up. "Let's give them all a break in the shade. We should rest here." Tom guided his wagon to the most shaded spot within the little grove, then jumped down and sprinted to Soft Cloud's wagon and, before she knew what to think, offered his hand in a most inviting way to an amused Soft Cloud … Just the way he had seen in a dirty camp town, when he watched a cowboy help a lady from her carriage. "May I help you down young lady?" He mimicked the cowboy.

"Well yes, kind sir." Soft Cloud continued the game. "It's kind of you to help a gentle lady. And I will surely repay the kindness this evening as we dine on fresh trout and wild berries and if there is any flour and cornmeal left in this wagon, I will make biscuits."

Accepting Tom's assistance she stepped gracefully from the wagon, and thanked him with a quick kiss on his cheek.

Tom felt a strange heat rush to his face, so he mumbled something about the mule's harness, scurried away and thoroughly inspected the harnesses on both teams. He stood a second by the wagon gazing at Soft Cloud, then went to the rear of the wagon to check on Tom Gray and the cavalry horse Buck had left behind. "You know, this fella's beginning to look better already." He called to Soft Cloud, and gave the good looking chestnut a few gentle strokes on the rump. Then he fussed over Tom Gray. "I have been thinking of what I want to do." He told the big gray horse. "You and me are gonna have our own horse ranch one day. Just like the one we saw near Ogallala that summer."

He found Soft Cloud behind the cottonwoods in the brush picking berries. "I think I would like that … to live in your village … but I don't know what I would do in your village with women and children and things … sometimes …" After a pause Tom turned, looked away and continued. "I mean, I like being with you and, except for the killing when we were with Buck, I liked that. How can I live in your village? I was always out on the open prairie with nothing too close, and I like being on the prairie."

Tom shuffled in circles around the low growing thick brush, kicking the dirt with the toe of his moccasin, while Soft Cloud busied herself picking berries. "Look at this, we are lucky! We will have some fat berries with the trout that I'm sure you'll catch for tonight's supper." She held up two hands full of shiny black berries. Then added, "Tom, let's not think about that other … Why don't we just get back in the wagons and go on for a while longer, and see if we can find the old mud cabin, have supper, and get a good night's sleep. Then tomorrow we will go to my village."

CHAPTER FOURTEEN

Buck spent the rest of that afternoon, and most of the early evening, relaxing on Old Bedlam's porch, amusing himself with cigars and a gallon of coffee while peacefully rocking his wooden chair on its rear legs. There was a lot going on in the fort today that required his watchful eye from the comfort of his chair in the shade of the porch.

Lieutenant Harris hustled from one small group of men to another assemblage of troopers to the corrals and back to another cluster of men, and in and out of General Sturgis' office. It was at that very moment Buck decided life as a civilian scout was certainly better suited to him than life as a Lieutenant.

Satisfied he had made the correct decision about life, Buck drank all the coffee he could hold for one evening, and figured he might just as well start preparing for his scouting mission. "I guess I'd better find Sarge and pick myself a couple a good saddle horses." He danced down the long plank steps and headed to the corrals.

He watched Sarge a few seconds before he interrupted his efforts. "Hey Sarge, how are you doin'?"

Sergeant Worly dropped the horse's foot, slowly and carefully straightened his weary back. "Well Buck, I got more horses' hooves that need tendin' and my back keeps tryin' to tell me this is a younger man's job."

73

"Aw come on Sarge, you got plenty left, don't let that old man's back talk you out of a good job. But if you need a break, I was wondering if you'd had a chance to look over the new saddle stock that Lieutenant Harris brought in the other day? I'm afraid the two that I came in on last night are just a little used up, and I need to head out on a scouting mission for the General. I figure on leaving mighty early in the morning because I reckon somebody should swing by the Miller homestead."

"Besides," Sarge said with a chuckle, "it wouldn't hurt any to check in with sweet Hannah Miller."

"Well, you know you're right, it can't hurt. It's been over two months since I've been by there. No telling how many lyin', dark haired strangers stopped by and tried to confuse her about what good lookin' is." Buck pulled off his Stetson and slicked back his hair.

"We sure wouldn't want her to be confused, now would we Buck!" Sarge laughed and laid his rasp down on the anvil.

They strolled to the saddle stock housed in the corrals behind the blacksmith shop. Buck rested his arms over the top board of the corral fence and studied the thirty-plus horses in the large corral. It was approaching dusk and while he had enjoyed relaxing all day, Tom and Soft Cloud snuck back into his thoughts. He wondered how the two kids were making out this evening.

He studied the horses, and could see that pretty much all were excellent stock. Buck was looking for two young, strong horses with solid legs and wide chests. It seemed he was always running the hell out of his horses. But then he was no mounted trooper guarding slow moving wagons. His mind wandered between studying the horses, Tom and Soft Cloud, and of course, anticipating a pleasant visit with Hannah Miller.

"Sarge, crawl in here with me." Buck climbed over the fence. "Take this big strawberry roan." He looped a rope around the horse's neck. "And that long legged paint over there, and put them up in a stall in the livery. Give 'em plenty of a water, hay and oats all night. Looks like they got a lot of horse in 'em."

"I reckon I can get that done for you. Get your saddle down here and tell me what time you'll be heading out, and I'll have 'em ready."

"I'd like to be sittin' atop that paint at 6 a.m. sharp with that big strawberry roan haltered up ready to tow. Now Sergeant, identify me a quick, easy poker game and I'll thank you for all your help."

Sarge and Buck led the two horses from the corral and tucked them comfortably into stalls in the livery. Buck said his good nights and ambled into the lengthening shadows in the direction of the mess, and hopefully a little whiskey and a few hands of poker.

CHAPTER FIFTEEN

Tall Dog rode from Hooker's camp with five outlaws, well mounted and well armed, headed for the peaceful Sioux village eighty miles southeast of Fort Laramie.

They made good time down the backside of the high country into the foothills and were on the flatlands of the grassy prairie by midmorning, already covering one-third of their journey. No words passed between the men. The renegades knew all too well if they misspoke Tall Dog would happily put a round between their eyes.

A few hours of hard riding later, the sun hung high overhead and Tall Dog knew they had completed half of their journey. Just ahead lay a small grove of trees by a wide stream. "We will stop and water the horses at that stream, then ride to Red Cloud's village. I want to be in his village of cowards before the sun sinks. I will have my sons before the sun rises in the sky tomorrow. We will kill anyone who tries to stop me from taking my sons."

****

Buck started down Old Bedlam's porch steps at exactly six the next morning, a little groggy-eyed from the smoking, drinking, and poker playing of the night before, but he managed to find his way to the livery. "Howdy, Sergeant. Have you seen Lieutenant Harris this morning?" He tumbled into a pile of loose hay.

"Sure have, in fact he is around the back talkin' with a few of his troopers about the saddle stock. I have a few more horses to ready before he can head out at noon."

"Thanks, Sarge. How about saddlin' up that leggy paint for me? And be sure my saddlebags and gear are loaded up good and tight."

Buck hurried to the rear of the livery where he very politely greeted Lieutenant Harris. "Good morning Lieutenant. Looks like a bright morning for riding. I'm gonna leave right away. I aim to swing by the Miller farm. It's been just about two months since anyone from the fort checked on 'em. All this carrying on with Hooker's bunch, I feel it can't hurt to check and make sure all is well, as long as I'm headed in that direction anyway."

"You do that. I'll expect you at the junction on the Fort Kearney Road just north of the Bozeman Trail cut-off at dusk."

"If I'm not there by morning send two troopers to the Miller farm." Buck held out his hand and accepted the Lieutenant's hand.

"I'll make that six troopers, Buck." The lieutenant told him and he could not resist touching the black bruise on Buck's chin with his finger while he performed a fake examination. "Better let the surgeon look this over. Could be you're starting to bruise too easily."

"Could be you finally learned how to land a punch?" Buck swung up on the paint, grabbed the roan's rope, tossed a wide grin the Lieutenant's way, then loped off across the parade and through the double gates. "At this rate, we should make the Miller farm by one or two o'clock. I sure hope Mrs. Miller has some coffee and apple pie."

****

"I was sure we would have seen the old mud cabin by now. Maybe we should find a place to camp for the night." Soft Cloud stood in the wagon seat to look far ahead.

"Yeah I'm tired. Let's head for those trees to the north. We can get there in time for supper if we hurry the mules and horses a little."

Soft Cloud stayed standing, whipped the mules with her long reins and let go a cavalcade of shrieks and howls. Her mules lunged ahead of Tom's horses. He gave his horses their heads and yelled for them to lean into those collars, and his heavy wagon bounced across the prairie as fast as those horses could run. But Soft Cloud and the mules could not be caught. They raced on with wagons bouncing, banging, and clanging, Tom never able to close the gap. Her mules never seemed to tire, but his horses gradually became winded so he yelled to Soft Cloud that she had beaten him and she could save the mules.

"Great race, Tom. Perhaps if you practice driving, some day you'll be able to keep up with me." She laughed when their wagons traveled side by side again.

"Where would a Sioux girl learn to handle a team of mules like that?" Tom yelled back, gasping for breath.

"I have been driving them for a few days now haven't I?"

"You never drove a team before our trip?"

"Never even rode a wagon." She sent him a devilish smile. "But I had a very good teacher."

As they neared the trees, the outline of the abandoned mud cabin took shape. "There! There's the old cabin. I was beginning to think we were off course. My brothers and I found it early this spring. They were hunting and I had decided to go along. We spent two full days here. Whoever built the mud cabin also dug a deep well."

They urged their teams into a fast trot toward the cabin. "Hold up. Let's stop right here." Tom dropped the reins and hustled around to help Soft Cloud step down. "I'll take your hand, Miss." Playing the part again.

"Thank you, kind Sir." She joined the fun. They paused a moment by the wagons, studying the tired but promising mud cabin, the horses and mules stood dripping sweat and blowing hard.

"I should tend the horses and mules. I'll make a rope corral in the trees, then look for the stream and see if any trout would like to join us for dinner," Tom said with a grin and a wink.

"I'll search the cabin. If I remember correctly, there's a table and a few other things. I believe there was a large cooking pot hanging in the fireplace."

In no time Tom had the corral ropes strung and the horses and mules comfortably grazing in the shade of the tall trees. He walked them two at a time to the stream for water. Then took a moment to visit Tom Gray as he surveyed the old soddy and smiled at the cloud of dust streaming out the front door. "Never been around many women, but it sure seems women like clean. Maybe your name should be 'Dust Cloud'!" Tom yelled.

"Must be the Sioux part of me. I have not seen very many clean whites." Soft Cloud poked her head through the door. "The pot is still here, table and chairs too. I'll make our cooking fire inside. You go and see about those trout, take your rifle in case we need to eat prairie hen, or antelope, or buffalo, or whatever runs into your bullets!"

"I'll be back in no time with our supper." Tom snatched the Henry from the wagon seat and raced down hill. The stream ran wide, bordered by a sandy bank on the near side sloping gently until it lost itself on the creek bottom. Standing ankle deep in the calm, cool water he saw shiny stones glistening on the streambed, but no trout, so he waded up stream where the water ran fast and cold. Trout preferred swift water.

Resting his rifle against a tree he slipped off his moccasins, and removed his leggings. The last time he fished with them on they took all night by the fire to dry. He sat resting on the bank dangling his feet in the fast water enjoying its coolness, and the sound of it rushing over the rocks.

From the stream bank he gazed through the trees, out onto the open prairie and far in the distance he found a herd of wild horses. He watched as they grazed until they disappeared over the hill. Even from this distance he admired their strength and beauty, and it made him anxious to start his ranch.

Finally he leaped into the rushing stream and began wildly slapping the water in the fierce technique he had mastered as a young boy to stun the fish. In a matter of seconds he tossed a pair of trout up on the bank, scrambled from the stream, gathered the wriggling trout, and wrapped them in his leggings. Then he scooped up his rifle and moccasins and hurried back to the cabin.

Soft Cloud's high-pitched, frantic giggling froze him mid-stride, leaving him struggling to hold his grip on the writhing fish, and his nerve. "Tom you are something to behold! I just never know what to expect! But I must say it is not totally unpleasant to find a successful naked young hunter, or shall I say fisher bearing gifts."

She stood in the doorway trying to stop laughing, but not able to. "Tom, why don't you take the fish to the back of the wagon and dump them on the boards." It was all she could manage before laughter overwhelmed her again.

Tom dashing to the wagon and exposing his bare bottom made her fall to her knees, folded over in laughter. As quickly as he could manage he dropped the still lively trout on the rear wagon, sat down and pulled on his soggy, fishy leggings. Using his hands he did the best he could to wipe clean his leggings, then turned to Soft Cloud, who was still on her knees laughing in the doorway. "I am not happy that you saw me with no leggings on."

Soft Cloud, still giggling, went to Tom. "I'm sorry. I'm not sure if I was laughing because you were not wearing your leggings or if I was laughing at the way you tried so hard not to let the trout escape. Don't you find it funny though that the trout were in the leggings that you wished you were in?"

With some of the jocularity wearing off, they began cleaning and preparing the trout for the fire. "Oh, there was enough corn meal and flour in the wagon to make biscuits. I have them in the fire now. And you were gone long enough for me to not only start a fire and make biscuits, but to wash the berries, too."

The red glow of the setting sun guided their walk to the cabin, which somehow looked a little less sad with the fire burning in the corner fireplace.

CHAPTER SIXTEEN

Long shadows danced on the ground when Tall Dog and his renegades first saw the Sioux village. "That is the village of my sons. We will ride into their village and they will come to me. Or I will take them! If any cowards in that soft Sioux village try to stop me, we will kill them!"

The six men readied their rifles and galloped toward the peaceful village. A small group gathered at the woods' edge to greet them. In that group stood Red Cloud's son, Buffalo Horn. As the riders neared, Buffalo Horn ushered the small group into a half circle. None of them carried arms.

Tall Dog and his men rode into the circle of Sioux braves. "I will see my sons!"

"You are not welcome here." Buffalo Horn stood between his brother, Tall Dog, and the other braves.

"I WILL see my sons!"

A young brave standing close to Buffalo Horn addressed Tall Dog. "You were told you are not welcome here!"

"Neither are you!" Tall Dog fired two fast rounds from his 'many shots' rifle into the young brave's chest. "I do not wish to be welcome here! But I will have my sons!"

Tall Dog kicked his horse to a gallop and trampled the brave lying dead. His followers did the same, galloping through the village, riding through the fires, over tipis, over meat racks, and sending old men, women and children, and dogs running. Several unfortunate braves confronted them with bows and arrows and were quickly gunned down. Tall Dog stopped at Red Cloud's Lodge.

"I will have my sons!"

"You may have your sons, if they wish to go with you." Red Cloud motioned to a brave standing by his side to run through the chaotic village and bring Still Water's sons.

"My husband, why must you always carry such hate and offer such destruction?" Still Water begged of Tall Dog.

"IT IS HE!" Tall Dog pointed his rifle at Red Cloud. "HE is no longer Sioux! He is friend of the whites! He would lead all his people to their death, or worse to their LIVING DEATH at the hands of the whites!" Tall Dog screamed at Still Water, his entire body quivered like rattles of a snake's tail. Lasers of hate fired from his eyes.

"My sons will go to their death as true Sioux warriors! We shall kill the whites! And we shall kill any Sioux, Cheyenne, Arapaho, or Pawnee that help the white man kill our brother the buffalo, and steal our land! We shall not allow whites to steal our land until every proud Sioux warrior rests upon a burial platform!" Tall Dog held his rifle high, his long braids whipping as he shook his head. His face, arms and chest painted. He forced his horse to step in the fire. "We will crush the white man as easily as my horse crushes your fire!"

His sons stood by Still Water, their mother. "My sons, it is now time for you to decide. I can no longer demand that you stay with me, and lodge with me. I can no longer choose for you whether you live at peace with me and our great Chief Red Cloud, or follow the hate that drives your father."

To Still Water's right stood a tall muscular brave with long black, braided hair hanging well past his shoulders. "I am my father's son, Black Hair! And I shall stand by my father because his words are the true words of a proud Sioux warrior!" With ear piercing howls, he fired his rifle and swung onto his father's horse behind him.

"I too am my father's son." Declared the brave standing to the left of Still Water. "But I believe the words of my great Chief to be true. My great Chief Red Cloud speaks words of peace. He speaks words of living in harmony with the whites. My great Chief Red Cloud tells how we shall be allowed to keep lands for hunting, for our lodging. I choose to stand by my great Chief Red Cloud!"

"THEN YOU ARE A FOOL!" Tall Dog aimed his rifle at his son and shot him dead.

Still Water shrieked and collapsed to the ground cradling her dying son in her arms. "You are no longer Sioux! You are no longer my husband! You are no longer the father of my children!"

Red Cloud stood on the hot coals of the trampled fire and grabbed his son's leg. "You are no longer my son Tall Dog. You must never again come to our village, for I will kill you. You do not see the future. You see only today. You will cause the deaths of many Lakota with your actions. You will cause the death of your son that rides with you today. You have always been strong medicine, but you have become bad medicine. I would kill you now but I am afraid to release your bad medicine among our people. Leave now and wander over the lands tormented by your bad medicine. One day Tall Dog, my son, I will kill you."

Tall Dog was unable to speak to Red Cloud. He tried but his voice would not come. Afraid, he turned his horse and led his men racing through the village, causing much damage as they fled.

They turned their attention to the herd of Sioux ponies outside the village. With the skill of true horsemen they guided their ponies into the herd and cut out twenty or more and drove them out to the dark prairie. They ran their mounts and the stolen ponies hard and fast, putting a great distance between themselves and the Sioux village.

"We will stop now." Tall Dog ordered, when even he was ready to admit the lathered horses had no more to give. "We will rest all the ponies and we will rest ourselves. And I will spend the night sleeping by a fire with my son. My son, who will help us kill many whites and many cowards who should not call themselves Sioux."

CHAPTER SEVENTEEN

The next morning, before the sun broke over the horizon, Tom led the horses and mules to the stream. He sat on the bank near the spot where the evening before he watched the herd of horses in the distance. In the early morning shadows the prairie laid empty. Tom relaxed, enjoying the calm of the little grove of trees and wide stream. Tom Gray waded into the stream and lay down in the water. "Are you trying to tell me I should take a bath? I got pretty clean last night catching trout."

"I like your way with horses Tom, they can trust you." Soft Cloud's tender voice surprised him. Lost in his thoughts, he had not heard her sneak up on him. "And this place, here by the stream, the trees, it suits you doesn't it?"

"It 's a peaceful place, it feels right to be here. When we return to your village and I give Red Cloud the buffalo hunter's scalp I am returning here. I will spend the winter here in this cabin, among these trees, and by this stream. There is game to hunt, fish to eat, and it's only half a day's ride to your village ... I would like us to be friends."

"We will always be friends." She stood on tiptoes and gave Tom a hug, then playfully turned and dashed to the front of the mud cabin. He ran after her. Catching her by the well, he scooped her up and sat her on the little wall by the well. "I like being with you." He almost kissed her, but suddenly wondered if he knew how. Instead he helped her down and started to load the wagon.

They loaded everything they needed on one wagon and were about to harness the mules when Tom changed his mind. "I'd rather ride my horse. If you take Buck's cavalry horse we can ride together, instead of bouncing along in the wagon." He opened the rope corral with a request to the mules and horse being left behind to not wander too far.

The cool morning breeze seemed just right for a lazy trip across the prairie. They rode quietly, leisurely through tall grass and the occasional patch of fall blooming prairie flowers. A perfect ride for two people becoming good friends, who both were pondering, in their own way, where the future might take them.

Without warning Tom stopped Tom Gray, jumped down, ran with his rifle, then fell to the ground. All was quiet while he waited for the dogs to pop back up. Then he fired three fast rounds, hopped up and ran to the prairie dog village and gathered three fat prairie dogs.

Proud as a strutting buffalo bull he held the fat dogs high for Soft Cloud to see, then stuffed them in his sack, stepped up on Tom Gray and they trotted on.

The sun hung high by the time the woods' edge that sheltered the Sioux village came into view.

"We're almost back home now, Tom. This was quite an adventure! I'm so glad now that you asked me to go with you." She kicked her horse into a quick trot, pulling away from Tom.

Tom put heels to his big horse's ribs and caught her as she was about to race, but as they neared the village they both began to sense something. They could see that there was too much activity, but they were still too far to understand what it might mean.

"Tom, something dreadful has happened! Hurry!" Soft Cloud screamed and kicked her horse with all she had and flew toward the village.

They galloped past four new burial scaffolds, and stormed into the village, stopping only when the wreckage of smashed lodges blocked their way. Soft Cloud leaped to the ground and ran through the debris. Tom, bewildered, stood with the horses. Just a moment ago they had been so happy, but now he stood amid smashed lodges, crushed meat racks, and new burial platforms.

Tom let the horses stand where they were and ran into Red Cloud's lodge. He found Buffalo Horn sitting with a weeping woman by a crushed and smoldering lodge. With no words, Tom handed him the scalp of the buffalo hunter. They allowed their eyes to meet, and while Tom could not understand what had happened in the village, he knew Buffalo Horn considered him a friend.

Tom walked, shrouded in worry and sadness, back to the horses, yanked the saddles and led them to the field where Sioux ponies grazed. He went in search of Soft Cloud. It was Soft Cloud who found Tom. "I need you to come to my mother's lodge."

CHAPTER EIGHTEEN

Buck held his paint in a fast canter all morning, and in only a few hours the Miller farm lay on the horizon. Asking for a little more speed, Buck made the appearance he liked in front of the large frame and board two-story farmhouse, flashy and noticed.

"Hey, anybody around here today?" Buck swung down from the paint. "Hey, I say again. Anybody about?" He tied his horses to the picket fence, hustled up the wooden sidewalk and jumped on the porch. As he was about to pound on the front door, it swung open. "Why Buck Hawkins, what brings you to our side of the prairie?" Mrs. Miller flung her arms around Buck's shoulders.

"I'm bound for Fort Kearney to escort a load of supplies to Fort Laramie. And it has been too long since I have seen my favorite family. Where the heck is everyone?"

Mrs. Miller took Buck's hand and led him to the sprawling farmhouse kitchen, where Mr. Miller, Hannah Miller, and two farmhands sat around the long table, plates laden with potatoes, beans and fried chicken. "Well howdy! I reckon I'm just in time for some famous 'Miller' chow! I am invited aren't I?" Buck teased and hurried to the opposite side of the table, put his hands on Hannah's shoulders, gently tilted her back as he kissed her forehead. "Mr. Miller." Buck held out his hand and accepted Mr. Miller's in a firm handshake. "Chuck, Sam, great to see you all."

"Are you going to join us for some of my fried chicken or stand about chatting all day?" Mrs. Miller offered a chair and a smile.

"I reckon I'll just sit and dig in!" He tossed a silly grin Hannah's direction.

"Any news on the renegades? We've heard they wiped out two families northeast of here." Mr. Miller asked Buck, looking at his wife with a face that wore concern.

"They're sure a mighty bad outfit. Some fancy dude named Hooker runs a camp town up in the high country. Yeah, they're turning into a real pile of problems. I was scouting for their camp the other day and I'm pretty sure I found the trail that leads to it. It's bad though, they got the meanest renegade of all, Tall Dog, scouring the territory looking for renegades and outlaws to join up with him and Hooker. I have a funny feeling they're counting on raising a whole mess of trouble."

"Do you think we'll have any trouble from them here?" Hannah's eyes reflected her deep fears.

"I don't feel good about it. You sure want to watch your back. Chuck, Sam, Mr. Miller. I don't think I'd go out of the house without a rifle."

"Buck! You're scaring us now." Mrs. Miller looked to her husband for comfort.

"I sure don't want to scare you, but I don't think these are safe times. And the Army doesn't have enough troopers to protect every settlement."

"We'll be darned careful, Buck. Chuck, Sam, we'll want to keep all the livestock under close guard and keep our eyes wide open." Mr. Miller passed the plate of fried chicken to Buck with a tense ease that failed to hide his concern.

"Do you really think it's possible those renegades could come this way?" Hannah leaned on the table, staring at Buck, obviously hoping for the answer she wanted to hear, not the one she knew was the truth.

"We just don't know what they're up to. I want you all to be damned careful and I'm not joking about that. Two days ago, I had a run in with Tall Dog and a few of his renegades and without a fast horse and help from a new friend, Tall Dog would have killed me that day. I do know he is looking to kill me. I reckon he knows I'll be lookin' to kill him."

Buck rose from the table and politely acknowledged everyone present. "I sure hate to be party to such a short visit but I'm meeting Lieutenant Harris at the Bozeman Trail junction tonight. I'd like to water my horses, then I gotta get."

"You bet, Buck, I'll come give you a hand." Mr. Miller squeezed his wife's hand and followed Buck.

They stood by the water trough waiting for the horses to drink their fill. "Couple a days more and you'll have that new barn all wrapped up."

"Been working real hard at it, Buck. I'll tell you, I'm damned uncomfortable thinking about those renegades coming here killing my family and maybe worse. If they mean serious business, there's not a thing we could do."

"Got to do all you can. Just make sure you all stay sharp. As soon as this little escort detail is done, General Sturgis will send some troopers with me up to that camp town. We will do our level best to clean it up and drive 'em out. That's a promise you can count on."

"Wow, Buck! This is the most handsome paint I have ever seen! What's his name?" Hannah hugged the tall horse around the neck.

"You know, Hannah, this old boy doesn't have a name yet. He is a good looker, isn't he? And boy howdy he's fast. He can run like the devil!"

"With that beautiful long mane and tail and fast as the devil. Let's name him – Diablo!"

"Diablo! There ya go." Buck swung up on the tall paint's back. "I'm serious now, folks. You watch out." Buck cantered Diablo away leading the roan horse.

"That big roan's a great looking horse too Buck! You sure can pick 'em!" Mr. Miller called after Buck.

****

Tall Dog arrived back at Hooker's camp the next day shortly after noon with twenty-two Sioux ponies and exactly that number of renegades. Some of the men took the horses to the far end of camp where crude corrals held the camp horses. Tall Dog went to Hooker who was standing in the dusty street.

"Appears to me as if we have all we need to take that supply train." Hooker boasted as Tall Dog approached him.

"I brought one son! The other coward I left dead." Tall Dog rested his hands on the shoulders of his son and shoved him toward Hooker. "This is my proud son, Black Hair! He is no longer a coward Sioux! Now, he stands a proud Sioux who will fight, not talk."

Hooker stared at the young brave, as if afraid to speak. "Let's go to the saloon. I have news about the Army supply train."

Hooker led them to a table in the corner and sat down. Grasping a fistful of his son's hair, Tall Dog shouted. "This is my son! He has come to join us as we fight the white man. He will kill many white men. He will kill many Sioux cowards for he is my son!"

Black Hair started on a bottle of whiskey, Tall Dog slammed his boots on the table, reared back his chair and yelled at Hooker. "Tell me the news, about the U.S. Army."

"Someone here found the old hider dead, scalped, and naked by the trail in the foothills. He won't be providing any information so we must make our plans now. Take fifty men and build our village two miles north of the Bozeman Trail junction."

"My son will have whiskey and women tonight! Tomorrow we leave. Tonight you send two wagons with supplies and tipis to Bozeman Trail junction. Send them now, they must not stop. It is a far way to the trail

92

junction."

****

Still Water sat next to an old Sioux man inside her lodge; Tom and Soft Cloud sat facing them across the low fire. The old Sioux lightly tapped Still Water's knees with a small pouch. "The damage you see to our village was done last night by Tall Dog and some of his renegades." Still Water spoke softly and slowly.

"He killed four of our braves. One was my son. He killed my son because he refused to go with him." Still Water continued. "He killed the other braves because they tried to stop him."

Soft Cloud sat quietly watching her mother speak, and watching Tom's face grow hard.

"My other son, Black Hair, went with Tall Dog."

"Why did Tall Dog want to take your sons?" Tom felt confusion, anger taking hold of him.

Still Water looked to the eyes of her daughter. "They are also his sons." She turned her teary eyes on Tom.

Soft Cloud watched the shock wash over Tom. "I thought he was their father." Tom pointed to the old Sioux.

"No. This is Light Feather, Red Cloud's brother."

With confused eyes, Tom studied Soft Cloud. He took a small twig, held it in the fire and watched it ignite. He concentrated on the tiny yellow flame as it slowly consumed the twig. When the fire was just about to touch his fingers, he dropped the twig. His eyes moved from the fire to Soft Cloud's. "And your father?"

"Her father is Tall Dog." Still Water said.

Tom sat rigid, slowly stroking the fringes on his Sioux vest. Trancelike, he watched as the old Sioux continued to touch Still Water with the small sack. His mind filled with a thick fog as he sat next to Soft Cloud, completely unable to comprehend this new situation.

His reasoning was slow, thorough, and determined, but still he could not understand. Soft Cloud is so gentle. She is so kind. So warm. Tom reached toward the fire, took another small twig and poked it into the hot coals until its end burst into a flickering flame. He watched again as the fire approached his fingers and sat motionless as the dancing yellow wings crept up the twig and suffocated between his fingers.

Not knowing what to do, Tom rose slowly and moved toward the flap of the lodge. Tears burning his eyes. "I will be with my horse." With great care, as if it were the most important thing, he closed the flap behind him and ran through the village to the grazing horses.

At first he could not find Tom Gray. He ran among the sprawling herd and still did not see him. Tom stopped and whistled as loud as he ever had. Again and again he whistled. Finally he heard the familiar nicker of his friend and he ran recklessly to the big gray horse. He gathered fistfuls of mane, pulled himself up on his back and wrapped his arms around his horse's neck. He buried his face in his old friend's mane. For a long time he lay that way, tears streaming down the neck of the tall horse.

CHAPTER NINETEEN

Buck trotted into camp as twilight settled over the prairie, hopped down near the picket lines where he stopped to talk to the young trooper in charge of the horses. "Reckon you could tend my horses while I go find Lieutenant Harris?"

"Sure thing, I'll give them both a good rubdown too. They look like they covered some ground today."

"They surely did, they surely did. You got some oats and hay too?"

"Sure do. I'll take right smart care of 'em."

Lieutenant Harris greeted Buck with a wave in the center of camp.

"Things look fine at the Miller farm, Lieutenant."

"Yeah, especially Hannah Miller I'd suspect." Teased the Lieutenant.

"Looking better all the time. But they sure are worried about the renegades. You know if Tall Dog and his bunch light down on that farm … they won't leave a man or beast alive … or building standing."

"I'd guess you're right, but the Army simply does not have the resources to protect every settlement or family farm in these parts. What we need to do is eliminate this renegade problem, including Tall Dog and the whole

Hooker outfit."

"I'm getting some chuck, then a bed roll." Buck nodded, set out for the cook's fire.

Buck sat squatted by the fire shoveling down the bits of ham and beans, when a trooper approached him. "Do you figure we're in for a scuffle with these renegades? I hear they're a mighty rough bunch."

"Yeah, I reckon so. Just no telling where or when. It would sure be my guess that they'd hit this supply train on our way back to Fort Laramie. So young fella, I'd stay real sharp. They're tricky bastards, so don't let your guard down."

"How do you mean that, Buck?" The trooper's expression telegraphed his worry. Several other troopers, now interested in what Buck might have to say, gathered around the cook fire.

"A couple of times in the past, when they thought they might be outnumbered, they set traps. That way they figured they could catch the Army off guard."

"I guess it would be one hell of a trap that could catch Lieutenant Harris." The trooper looked wide eyed around at his buddies.

"Yeah, would be. The Lieutenant has been around a while and still has his hair. But remember now, this supply train has got to be awful tempting to them." Buck finished his bowl of beans and ham.

"I am heading to my blankets, night gents." He found his saddle at the picket line, untied his bed roll, and lay down by the rope, his head resting on his saddle and the rest of him buried in the blanket.

Long before sun up, Cookie made enough noise to wake every man in camp. He and his helper tended three cook fires and ten pots of coffee boiling by the time a sleepy eyed Buck found the mess wagon. "Doggone, Cookie, just because you got so darned old you can't sleep through the night don't mean you shouldn't think of these young fellows."

"Mornin', Buck, you old rascal. It's these young fellows I'm thinkin' of, not old withered up scouts. Lieutenant wants to be movin' along the road by sunup. If you need to, you can sleep in my wagon 'til it's time for the older folks to kick back their blankets."

"Might come a day I take you up on that, but I figure I got a few years left to try and keep up with the youth of the cavalry!" Buck snatched a tin plate loaded with biscuits, gravy, and a slice of ham then found a seat on the wagon tongue. He was enjoying his second cup of coffee when the Lieutenant stopped and sat on the tongue beside him.

"As soon as you're through with your breakfast, saddle up and start out. Scout a few miles ahead of us and check back every two hours." The Lieutenant said, and moved on to more important matters.

The trail lay dry and dusty, most of the troopers had their kerchiefs up over their noses. This did little to keep boulder sized grains of dust from their eyes. They traveled at a fast cavalry trot in a column of twos. It was late morning before Lieutenant Harris ordered the men to stop by a wide stream. "Dismount men! Water your horses. We'll rest for fifteen minutes."

Troopers rode their mounts into the stream and jumped to the water from their horses. Every man dipped his kerchief into the water and washed out his and his mount's eyes. Some men took their hats and scooped water from the stream dumping them on their heads and dousing some on their horses' heads. Before fifteen minutes had passed most of the troopers were thoroughly soaked.

"MOUNT UP!" Lieutenant Harris ordered. Within seconds thirty troopers rode down the dusty road.

****

Tall Dog rode from Hooker's camp town the next morning with some fifty renegades and outlaws. It made little difference who followed him as long as they wanted to kill soldiers, they were welcome. They pushed their horses recklessly down the steep slopes of the high country. Then out onto the gentler foothills and finally they galloped onto the prairie flatlands. They traveled fast in a southeasterly direction toward Bozeman Trail junction.

They were a small army made up of shiftless cowboys, bitter renegades, and lazy good for nothing drifters. But willing killers were they all. Tall Dog and his son Black Hair rode lead; flamboyant and proud to be side-by-side and anxious to ambush U.S. Army whites.

They traveled at a fast pace from morning sun to the early evening shadows. When the shadows began to lengthen, Tall Dog stopped for the night. The horses were stripped, saddles and equipment gathered in a convenient spot and with the exception of a few men who stayed mounted to drive the exhausted horses to a nearby stream, others began to make small campfires and eat whatever they had brought with them. A few men gathered on blankets to kill time playing cards. With the start of poker, came the start of arguments.

"You filthy bastard! You're a cheat! I'll take my money back now!" A man too young to have yet learned the ways of a rough and tumble bunch of misfits, outlaws and renegades leaped to his feet and yanked his sidearm.

The other fellow sprang up, jerked his, leveled it at the accuser, and fired fast. The accusing cowboy, dead instantly, fell backwards.

"What the hell is going on?" Tall Dog bellowed. "Any killing in this camp, I will do!" He pushed his way through the men at the scene of the shooting. One fast kick knocked the revolver from the cowboy's hand, and swinging his rifle almost before his foot landed, Tall Dog slammed it across the cowboy's face knocking him to the ground. "No more killing in this camp!" And just to punctuate his authority while the cowboy was still on all fours, he kicked him squarely in the head.

"You killed him!" One of the cowboy's buddies shouted.

Tall Dog spun neatly on his heels, pointed his Henry toward the cowboy. "Like I said, any killing done in this camp, I'm doing!"

Most of the men watched Tall Dog walk to the perimeter of the camp, but a small group gathered their things and snuck to their resting horses. "I'm getting the hell out of here. I never had a good feeling about that crazy Sioux bastard in the first place. Let's ride to Ogallala, maybe get in some good poker games." One of the cowboys suggested. Five cowboys swung up on their horses, and trotted out of camp, intending to be finished with Tall Dog.

Tall Dog watched as the cowboys made their escape. He signaled his son and they ran for the horses, rifles in hand. Snatching the first two horses they found they swung up and galloped from camp.

Tall Dog and Black Hair began to gain on the five cowboys. One of the cowboys realized they were being pursued and yelled to the others. Tall Dog and his son gave a hard chase and continued to lessen the distance between them. When Tall Dog began to fire, the cowboys returned fire, but Tall Dog and Black Hair continued to gain on them.

The cowboys turned their horses in a single move and charged Tall Dog, firing fast and reckless. As fast as they could push their horses, they galloped straight for him.

Tall Dog and his son were not to be turned back and they drove their mounts toward the cowboys. Suddenly without slowing his horse, Tall Dog dove to the ground holding his 'many shots' rifle.

The stunned cowboys tried to stop, but were too near. Tall Dog fired until all fifteen shells were gone and five cowboys lay dead nearly at his feet. He remounted and gathered the wandering horses then rode back to camp with his son. "You can all fight over their saddles." He said, and as he walked away added. "Anybody else want to ask me about leavin'?"

****

Lieutenant Harris, his troopers, and Buck rode into Fort Kearney mid afternoon three days later. Every horse was spent and every man hungry. But Fort Kearney was well stocked with both food for the men and fresh horses for the return trip. Lieutenant Harris, being himself, marched promptly to the General's quarters. Buck, being himself, hustled directly to the barbershop. Bursting through the door he announced, "I'd like a shave and a bath, kind sir."

"Good to see you, Buck! By golly it's been a while." The barber greeted him. "There's hot water in a barrel in the back. Get yourself a bath and I'll beat your clothes out for you. They'll be ready when you're finished, then we can see about that shave!"

"Sounds like a plan!" Buck stripped off his vest and shirt and threw them at the barber, who nearly cut a man's ear off trying to duck out of the way.

****

Lieutenant Harris found the General in his office studying a stack of papers. "Afternoon, Lieutenant." He looked up from his papers long enough to point to the chair next to his desk.

"Good to see you again, General."

"You and your men take the rest of the day and tomorrow to rest. You can leave Friday morning for Fort Laramie."

"I'm sure I can convince the men to take a day off. We pushed pretty hard coming east." The Lieutenant walked to the General's desk. "Mind if I have a look?"

"It's quite a shipment, and I wish I could give you more men. Somehow we're always stretched thin. You'll have one wagon carrying twenty cases of those new Henrys, five in a case, and ten thousand rounds of ammunition. You know these hundred new Henrys are the only ones west of the Mississippi," he added with a little jealousy showing.

"Another wagon is loaded with new uniforms. Everything from hats and boots to socks and kerchiefs. Two more wagons of supplies, foodstuffs, coffee, soap, towels, and miscellaneous odds and ends and there will be one wagon with supplies for you and the troops on the trip. Ten days' rations for fifty men." General Peters tapped the desktop with nervous fingers. "Four heavily loaded wagons, going on a ten-day trek across the prairie guarded by only fifty cavalry. I'm more than a little uncomfortable, Lieutenant … rest your men today and set out Friday. Make your best speed, circle the wagons at night, and keep your wits about you."

"Count on it!" Lieutenant Harris promised.

CHAPTER TWENTY

Tom spent the night and most of the next day on the prairie with the horses. His seat a fat stump, his back against a leaning tree, he stared out over the grasslands away from the Sioux village. Although he could hear the cleanup and reconstruction work being done in the village, he was not interested in helping, or watching. He chose to allow the grazing horses and the open prairie the time they needed to clear the fog from his confused mind. Only once did Tom have contact with anyone, when a small boy sent by Soft Cloud brought him food and water.

The only comfort Tom found was Tom Gray, and he was still sitting on the stump leaning against the tree dozing for long periods at a time when he heard Soft Cloud approach.

"Won't you come with me to my mother's lodge and have something to eat?" Softly she touched his arm.

Tom pulled his arm away from her touch. "I don't think I'm hungry."

"Are you going to sit here on this stump all day?"

"I can't think what to do next." He looked to her, then turned to send his gaze over the prairie beyond the horses. "I was happy to be with you. It's hard for me to understand that Tall Dog can be your father. I don't know my father. It was better when I didn't know your father."

"I am still Soft Cloud. I am still, and always will be, your friend. All the people in this Sioux village are your friends." She reached for his hand, her eyes coaxing him. "We should go to my mother's lodge."

An uneasy silence cloaked them as they walked through the shadowy village to Still Water's lodge. Not even the giggling of playing children interested him. Inside the smoky tipi, Tom sat opposite the small fire from the old Sioux man he now knew as Light Feather.

He waited for Soft Cloud to prepare his meal, while drinking slowly from a water skin as even more questions forced their way into his troubled thoughts. He wondered why this old man, brother to Red Cloud, lodged with Still Water. How could Tall Dog kill his own son? How could that man be the father of Soft Cloud? He must be an evil man. Like the fat buffalo hunter who used to lash Tom, he needed killing too.

Soft Cloud interrupted his thoughts, leaning low and offering a wooden bowl filled with wild grass seed, tea sprigs, prairie dog meat, and dried buffalo.

"I hope you've decided to become part of our Sioux village." Still Water said. "Red Cloud has spoken to me and he is proud that you have killed the old buffalo hunter. He also told me he would make you a Sioux brave as he has made me a Sioux woman."

Tom studied the fire and somehow he knew Still Water meant only kindness toward him. And yet, more information served only to cloud his mind deeper and make it difficult for him to choose what to do. He decided to say nothing, finished his meal, set the empty bowl on a skin by the fire, and lay down using his arms to make a pillow. Soft Cloud gathered a blanket and covered him. She sat beside him and rested her head on his lap.

CHAPTER TWENTY-ONE

Tall Dog and his son started well ahead of the rest. By sunset they rode far ahead of the main body of renegades. Hours later, guided by the light of the nearly full moon, Tall Dog found Hooker's wagons and galloped the last half mile to overtake them. He stopped by the first wagon and yelled to the driver, "You keep moving east. We will go ahead and find the place to build our trap. Black Hair will return to lead you to the place I choose."

They spun their horses and tore from the wagons. Soon only the dust clouds they raised were left for the driver to see. Aided by the bright moon, the two skilled warriors raced on over the flat prairie riding hard, until they found a wide stream. Tall Dog rode splashing through the stream and up the bank on the far side. Sitting his horse on the bank he saw that the prairie sloped down to the main wagon road. Ordering his son to wait by the stream, he galloped down the slope.

Tall Dog rode in circles, examining the line of sight to the stream. Satisfied that the U.S. Army supply train would be able to see the village, he raced back to his son.

"I will wait here. You bring the wagons and men. We will make our village on this side of the stream. Even stupid white soldiers will see this place from the trail below. When you return with the men and the wagons we will rest. Tomorrow we will build our trap."

CHAPTER TWENTY-TWO

Tom slept through the night. His troubled mind had slowly quieted and allowed him to sleep and even though she was awake for hours, Soft Cloud never left his side. Finally he stirred, bolted up, looked around the lodge and saw they were alone. "I have decided to go back to the mud cabin by the stream."

"I'll help you to get ready." Eagerness and tenderness in her voice could not mask her deep disappointment. Tom felt the need to explain, but he had no words. Even in his sleep he'd felt her protective, caring presence throughout the night. He also felt she had hoped he would stay here, with her, and he wanted to. He simply did not know how. He did know, she knew, they both loved the little mud house by the stream. And he knew he wanted her company, and she wanted his.

As they weaved between lodges and fire rings, walking in silence to the horses, Tom noticed the damage done by Tall Dog and his renegades had been repaired. Not a single reminder of the terrible day. Save for the new burial platforms.

When the time came to say goodbye to Soft Cloud, Tom felt another new feeling. He was anxious to get back to his cabin but was in no hurry to leave her. "Tomorrow you could ride to my cabin. I'll kill two prairie hens and you can cook them."

Her pretty brown eyes swept over him tenderly. "I will be happy to come tomorrow." Tom felt the new feeling of hot blood rush to his face again, so he turned and jumped on Tom Gray; just before he put heels to the big horse's ribs, he stopped and leaned down to her. "You could bring your mother." He waited to watch her wave and then hurried on with a lighter heart, and almost missed what she called after him. "My mother likes boiled tea." His plan was to get back to the cabin before dark so he could spend time looking things over, and make his place worthy of a visit by Soft Cloud's mother. Tom Gray kept up an easy lope on the trip home.

Having seen Buck slide to a showy stop, Tom pulled his big horse to a long dusty slide just outside the cabin door. Dust flew higher than the roof of the soddy and sent the poor mules, who had been grazing by the well, braying and running for their lives. They didn't stop running until they reached the lean-to barn, where they stood braying at whatever it was that just tried to kill them.

"Hey, it's alright fellas, I'm not gonna eat you … till I get snowed in anyway." The mules kept up their racket and Tom was forced to amend his threat a minute later. "Okay I didn't mean I would really eat you. I was only kidding, and I'll put up plenty of dried antelope!" He yelled just as loud as he could and the mules fell suddenly silent and started to relax and graze alongside the shaky barn. "How about that." He told Tom Gray with a happy laugh in his voice. He slid the saddle down, hung his headstall on a peg on the porch post, then went in the soddy to take stock of what to do first.

First on the agenda, a bed. By the light of a cheery fire he worked into the night building a sturdy frame of boards from the wagon, with tree limbs for legs. Next he gathered a bundle of tall prairie grass, wrapped it in a piece of canvas, and made a soft base for the bed on top of the flat boards. Finally he fetched a saddle blanket, spread it on top, and with a satisfied look at the cot, congratulated himself. "Now that is a darned good bed."

Robbing the wagon of more boards, he built a sturdy set of shelves on the wall near the door. On the middle shelf he neatly arranged the ammunition for the rifles and revolver. The top shelf was for the Sharps and Henry, and he pounded a peg in the wall to hang his gun belt.

Under the glistening moon, Tom stood on the porch planning the repairs necessary to fix its sagging roof. Then he looked through the shadows at the remains of the lean-to barn. "That'll be a bigger job.'

CHAPTER TWENTY-THREE

"Hey Sarge, good to see you made the trip! You wagon sittin' old bag of bones." Buck teased Sergeant Worly as he ambled his way.

"Yo' Buck! General Peters wants to see you in his quarters, right away."

"Does he mean right away or can I finish my cigar?"

"I reckon he means right now." Sarge delivered the bad news.

"I'm on my way!" Buck hopped from his chair and sprinted across the parade.

He ran up the wooden sidewalk to the General's pine log home sitting in a yard of its own surrounded by a split rail fence that had recently been painted white.

"I was hoping I could find you in a hurry. I need you to leave for Fort Laramie immediately with a dispatch for General Sturgis." General Peters' voice carried an anxious tone.

"Need to leave right away? Some of the boys were about to get a friendly game of cards going in the sutler's store," Buck protested.

"Right now. Sorry, Buck, but I have no one else to take a dispatch. At least no one that I'm confident can get there on time.

"Take your two horses, they've had a day's rest, and a third from our corral. Start out on our horse and when he tires, just let him go. Here's the dispatch. We can't afford the time for you to use the wagon route. Cut across the top of the prairie. You can save fifty miles but you'll still need to run those horses. General Sturgis needed this dispatch a day ago."

"What's wrong?" A rare look of seriousness spread over Buck's face.

"It's all detailed in the dispatch. We've heard stories of some mighty big trouble brewing with Hooker's outfit and renegades he recruited with the help of a renegade Sioux. We can't wait for the supply train returning to Fort Laramie to carry the letter. Our information tells us to expect big, big trouble over there with that bunch in about a week. Maybe less. You have got to do your best to get to Fort Laramie in less than two days."

"Cutting across the prairie as the crow flies with three horses, I believe I can make that trip. I had a feeling something was up. But I thought sure they'd go for the supply train."

"We were thinking that way, too. But what we heard from a cowboy we have resting in our guardhouse who runs with Hooker's bunch, it's all going to happen west of Fort Laramie in the settlements scattered there."

"That's bad. Most of those settlements aren't settlements at all. Just one family sitting out there alone on the prairie trying to make a go of it. They're spread so far apart Hooker could hit one at a time for a week before we got word." Buck snatched the dispatch from General Peters and ran for the corrals.

Five minutes later Lieutenant Harris watched Buck gallop from the Fort on a huge black stallion trailing his roan and Diablo, and he understood immediately on the return trip he would not have the services of that talented scout. Curious, he sought out the General and found him still relaxing on the porch as the sun was slipping from the sky. "General, I see Buck has gone, with a dispatch no doubt. I hate to admit it, but I'll need three men to replace him. So I suppose I'm formally asking for an additional three troopers."

"Lieutenant, we've got trouble brewing. That dispatch was to inform

General Sturgis that we have rumors of raids coming on settlements west of Fort Laramie. We have information that Hooker has enlisted the aid of a Sioux renegade who is helping to recruit more Indians."

"That would be Tall Dog. He's a bad one. We believe he's been responsible for not only raiding settlements, but he burns and mutilates the men. He rapes and kidnaps the women. They take them to Hooker's camp somewhere in the high country, which we understand now is a small town, and forces them to work in the saloons as prostitutes."

"I'll be happy to send ten extra men with you but the more I hear, the more I worry about the supply train. We have to suspect this Hooker knows about it. It's quite possible the whole idea of him raiding west of Fort Laramie is a ruse to divert our attention from an attack on the supply train. Imagine what they could do with a hundred new Henry's and ten thousand rounds of ammunition." The General finished with a tight-lipped, grim stare over his porch rail.

"The men will be well-rested and ready for travel, and those ten extra men will mean a lot. I'll stop by the commissary and see to it we have enough rations for those extra men. Now, if it's allright with you, I'm long overdue for a hot bath, shave and haircut and then a meal and cot. Maybe tomorrow I'll pretend to be Buck Hawkins and sit on the front porch of your mess with my feet on the railing and smoke a cigar or two."

"You have my permission." The General let go a quiet chuckle. "You and your men relax tomorrow and get a good night's rest tomorrow night and may God go with you when you leave Friday morning."

****

In the very early morning hours, the wagons and renegades arrived at Tall Dog's location. Some men lounged about on their saddle blankets while others tended to their horses. But most were busy erecting tipis, building fire rings, and generally trying to make it resemble a Sioux village.

"Put the wagons in the rear of camp," Tall Dog ordered. "When we see the supply train, five men hide in each wagon with rifles. Twenty Sioux braves go to this side of the village," he yelled, pointing with his rifle where the braves were to stand. "I want the U.S. Army to see Sioux braves. Sioux braves that look like cowards! That is what the stupid U.S. Army must see. We will work until we are ready and then we will wait."

"No one will drink whiskey today, tonight, tomorrow, or any time until we kill the U.S. Army whites and steal their wagons! If any man gets drunk or fights, I will kill him! Three men go hunt so we have meat to show the U.S. Army and so we have meat to eat."

CHAPTER TWENTY-FOUR

"I need to cut windows through these walls." Tom examined the dark cabin the next morning while starting a new fire. The only light streamed through the open doorway. He pondered the interior, and being pleased with his cot and shelf for his guns, he now set his sights on a window, table and chairs. A few hides could cover the dirt floor. The roof of logs and thick sod showed no signs of leaking. First plan for today, after coffee and hard buffalo jerky, would be chair and table building.

Satisfied the horses and mules were content in the grass on the stream bank, Tom grabbed the axe from the back of the wagon and headed for the grove of trees for branches and limbs to make his chairs. By mid morning he finished the table and soon after that he had three stout chairs. One he would set on the porch, the other two were for the table.

But first the porch would need work. Small logs that supported the sod roof had rotted and snapped, allowing the sod to fall in a pile on the porch floor. His count showed four logs in need of replacement, so back to the trees he marched. This time, he grabbed his rifle. "Just might see those prairie hens I plan to invite to supper."

The sun, high overhead, found Tom wading knee deep in prairie grass dragging four neatly trimmed logs, tied together with a bit of rope. Engrossed in thought he never noticed the four hens until they exploded from the grass almost between his feet sending him rolling backwards. He never got a shot, but he did find a seat on the logs. "There went supper!

Well birds, the invitation still stands. You're welcome to come to supper any time."

The rest of the afternoon he devoted to hard work on the porch roof, and in a few hours he had the logs and sod replaced and the porch back in top shape. He strutted out in the yard like a proud rooster to admire his work. "Starting to look like a homestead. Yes sir!"

"I reckon I better get some meat for supper or my guests will decide that I make a mighty poor neighbor." He took his rifle and headed back out at a trot, stopping only when, about half a mile from the cabin, he spied a small herd of antelope slowly milling in the tall grass.

Being careful to stay downwind, Tom slowly circled to the rear of the herd. He moved in slowly, cautiously, taking two or three steps at a time, keeping the wind in his face. When he closed within two hundred yards, he lay flat down in the grass but continued to advance on the herd, crawling ever so carefully. His years with the hider had taught him antelope are quite different from buffalo and will flee much sooner if they sense any threat.

In the distance Tom saw the herd of wild horses, and reasoned they were distracting the antelope herd and helping him close in on them. Finally he was within shooting range. He stretched full out, rose up on his elbows, aimed carefully, and fired two shots. The herd dashed away leaving two dead antelope lying in the grass.

"That'll do, meat for dinner, and I have the antelope hides for the chairs." He hustled to the antelope, gutted them and tied a rope to their front feet, wrapped the rope around his waist and started to drag them back to the cabin. They proved heavier than the logs, and not as easy to drag. "I have a better idea than this." He dropped the rope, ran to the cabin, grabbed Tom Gray's mane, hopped up, and galloped back to the antelope. Swooping low, he found the rope and started back dragging the antelope behind.

His heart pounded with joy when he saw Soft Cloud and Still Water ride into the clearing. He reached as high as he could and waved his free hand. They sent waves of greeting back, then Soft Cloud galloped to him.

"I thought I ordered prairie hens. Don't you know that skinning antelope takes a lot longer than plucking hens?" Soft Cloud teased.

"I had a chance at hens but ... I guess I needed bigger targets today."

As Still Water began skinning antelope, Tom led Soft Cloud on a tour to inspect the work he had done to the porch, and the chairs and table he built. "My plan is to make the porch big enough to have a table out here. But first I need to work on the lean-to so the horses can get out of the weather."

"So you plan on making this your home?"

"I sure do, and nothing will stop me!"

"But aren't you used to moving all around the prairie following the buffalo?"

"I'm done with that. I want a place like other people have. A place I can make better. I want to make a horse ranch, like the one I saw near Ogallala. There are plenty of wild horses right here on the prairie to catch and break to sell."

"I have admired the way you have with horses. I'm as sure as I can be you will do it ... I wish I could be a part of it."

She looked up at him, her brown eyes searching his face. He felt the life, the eagerness in her eyes touch him. He liked the way it felt. But in some way it scared him. "You can help me!" And then to keep the seriousness away, he added, "I might need a mule skinner!" He allowed his hand to rest on her hip. He had an impulse to pull her tight, but thought the better of it. She took his hand, held it.

"Well I reckon I'd better get a fire started if we're to have any supper tonight." Gently he slipped his hand from hers, but the feeling of her hand in his followed him to the fire pit in the yard.

Before long he had a fine cooking fire started and Still Water began to roast the antelope. With supper roasting, Still Water and Soft Cloud began to skin and slice the second antelope for drying, hanging the strips on the wagon side in the sun. He fetched a chair from the cabin and sat comfortably on his new porch to watch Still Water and Soft Cloud and ponder the feelings he had holding Soft Cloud's hand.

Darkness had settled in by the time they sat to eat roast antelope. "I was wondering, Tom, do we have any tea?" Soft Cloud teased.

Tom felt his face warm. Soft Cloud had told him her mother loved boiled tea. "I forgot to find tea ... but I do have a couple of buckets of water from the stream. It's good cold stream water. I'm planning to dig a trench from the stream to my corral when I build it for my horses."

"Why not just let them roam on the prairie like Sioux ponies?" Soft Cloud showed him a questioning look.

"I reckon mostly because I don't have two dozen Sioux children to tend the herd and keep them from running back into the wild." He found it surprisingly easy to joke, laugh and smile with her. He realized and felt the change coming over him. The change she was bringing to him.

They chatted a long while about horses and the plans Tom had, and all the hard work that faced him. The fire cast a warm, peaceful light and Tom found himself recovering from the shock of two days ago. The shock of learning Tall Dog was Soft Cloud's father. It crossed his mind briefly tonight and he came close to asking Still Water how she happened to marry him, but thought the better of it.

"Why don't you two stay here tonight," Tom offered, hoping to stretch the visit. Together he and Soft Cloud gathered firewood and started a fire in the fireplace. Soon the little cabin was cheery and bright with the warm glow of dancing fire. With saddle blankets and canvas from the wagon sheet they fashioned a bed at the hearth.

"I think I'll walk out and make sure we still have all the horses and mules down at the stream." Tom was able to see before he had gone very far that all the animals were there but went all the way anyway to say goodnight to Tom Gray. With his arm around the horse's neck and his hand tickling his muzzle, Tom knew his friend was glad that he did. He said a brief goodnight to all the horses and the mules and hiked back to the cabin.

CHAPTER TWENTY-FIVE

Buck rode hard, covering large amounts of ground up and down the peaks and valleys of the high plains traveling west. Eventually the Army issue cavalry horse began to fade so Buck slowed to an easy trot. Although the moon was less than half full, it was a cloudless night affording good visibility.

In the distance stood the dark shadows of a grove of trees. "Hang in there, buddy. A few more miles and you'll get some time off. And hopefully a good drink, if there's water with those trees." Buck told the big stallion and patted his neck.

He trotted the horses for about a mile to catch their wind then kicked back up into a lope and held that speed until he reached the trees, where he was relieved to find a fast-running stream. He stepped from the cavalry horse, slid the saddle from his back, and removed his bridle. "Well son, the boss says you're free to go." Using the saddle blanket he did his best to rub the stallion down. "Now go on, son. Go make little horses." He told the big black as he gave him a smack on the rump. But the horse only moved about twenty feet, and then he walked out into the stream and lay down. Buck had two other horses to tend, but was fascinated by the horse in the stream. He watched as the black rolled in the stream, got up and shook, and shook. "If you aren't the most! Well son, you're free to do as you choose. These other two got a lot of miles to pull yet."

Buck made sure both the roan and Diablo had plenty to drink and filled the canteens. He decided to saddle the roan, saving Diablo for the last leg knowing that territory was the most open. If he ran into trouble he could abandon the roan and use Diablo's incredible speed to save his life. Buck checked his cinch, grabbed Diablo's lead rope, flipped open the saddle bag, took a handful of beef jerky, and stuffed his mouth full. Then climbed on the roan and kicked him into an immediate gallop.

They flew across the prairie bounding up and down the rolling grassland, the roan's solid legs and huge hooves pounding the soil in a rhythm that helped to keep Buck awake. Buck liked the power of this horse. He could feel the strong horse push the ground away behind them. Each powerful stride had them almost flying off the ground.

For hours the roan's stride ate up the miles. Buck began to tire but the roan surged on with incredible energy. The roan gathered speed and momentum as they galloped down the slopes and drove with powerful lunges up the inclines, sending chunks of sod flying behind his massive rear hooves. The big roan began to outrun Diablo, causing the leadline to tug on Buck's arm.

Buck made a chancy decision. He dropped Diablo's lead hoping he would stay with the big roan and both would increase their speed. For a while it seemed as if the plan would work. Diablo pulled even with the big roan. Matching stride for stride, eight hooves pounding the prairie sod. Buck was reminded of his pony express days as they flew across the grasslands.

They continued to gallop hard and fast, with Buck leaning into the roan's neck, pushing him for his top speed. Dawn was beginning to break and he knew that they had traveled a big chunk of the distance he needed to cover.

Buck was just beginning to consider changing horses and finishing the last leg of the journey on Diablo, when he heard the hoof beats of an approaching horse. He looked back under his right arm and saw a black horse straining to overtake them, but could not see the rider. This told him it was most likely a renegade Indian, riding low on the horse's back.

The two horses were still side-by-side, stretching as far they could for the longest, most ground-consuming stride they could manage. Buck could see the rope on Diablo flying high above his back. He leaned and grabbed the loose rope and demanded more speed from both horses but he had no free hand to grab his gun. The only option was to outrun the renegade. He looked under his right arm again. Somehow the renegade was gaining on him! Buck had a lead of about a thousand yards, but that lead was shrinking. He spied a small ravine ahead and turned his horses in that direction and asked for any speed they might have left. The big roan was blowing so hard he sounded like the roar of a tornado but there was no chance to slack off now even though Buck thought he felt the big horse quiver every few strides. "Just a little more, big boy!" Buck yelled, hoping he wouldn't collapse before the ravine. Buck planned to make a flying dismount and hopefully pull his revolver and blow this renegade to hell.

The plan worked magnificently! Just as they cleared the rim of the ravine Buck jumped from his winded mount, tumbled to the ground and came up with his Navy .44 leveled squarely on the chest of the renegade's black horse.

In the instant before he fired, he recognized the black horse as the cavalry mount he had set free all those miles ago! With a huge sigh of relief and a hearty laugh, Buck holstered the .44. The big black marched right up and nuzzled the winded scout.

"Well, you big son of a gun. You really are something." Buck walked along on foot leading Diablo and the roan, the black stallion patiently trailing along. He estimated he had only about forty miles more so he decided to walk the horses for a while. His legs could use the walk and the horses sure needed a break.

The sun was beginning its daily climb when Buck decided that he and the horses had rested enough, so he saddled Diablo, stepped in the stirrup, and put him in a fast lope. He was confident if he had no problems they would make it to Fort Laramie by mid afternoon. For several more hours, Buck and the three horses continued steadily onward in almost a carefree canter. Then, feeling Diablo beginning to tire and seeing no danger, Buck figured he could slow the pace and allow the horses to preserve any energy they may have left for an escape, and reined Diablo back to a nice easy Cavalry trot.

Buck made his traditional appearance of storming into the fort with a sweat-soaked horse, jumped down, opened the saddle bag, snatched the dispatch and ran to the General's office. General Sturgis had seen Buck gallop through the gate and met Buck on the steps of the porch. "This dispatch is from General Peters at Fort Kearney. He told me to hustle it on over here. Looks like the Army is expecting trouble from that damned Hooker outfit."

General Sturgis tore open the dispatch. Buck watched a look of disgust mixed with rage wash over the General's face. "Thanks, Buck. Go tend your horses, then take the day to rest up because you're going out again. I'll need you to lead a patrol to warn the settlers. You know where most of them are, and with most of my troopers out with the supply train, I only have green recruits here. Most of them haven't been west of the fort and none have seen battle."

CHAPTER TWENTY-SIX

Lieutenant Harris departed Fort Kearney with five heavily loaded wagons and a patrol of sixty experienced troopers. Most had served under one flag or another in the War Between the States. Nearly every man in the column had seen action on the battlefields of the Blue and Gray, or the plains of the Nebraska Territory fighting Sioux and Cheyenne. They made a wonderful show as they streamed through the front gate in perfect formation. It was somehow festive in its appearance. General Peters stood on his office porch until the last man and horse rode out of sight.

Lieutenant Harris intended to cover twenty miles a day and some days as many as thirty. His plan was to reach Fort Laramie in ten days or less. He wanted the rifles in the hands of the troopers stationed in Fort Laramie as soon as possible and he knew the General needed these men.

Half a day out from Fort Kearney, he called for a halt to rest the horses. Most of the troopers simply stood by their horses. A few wandered back to the mess wagon where Cookie was handing out old cold coffee and biscuits that he had stolen from the mess at the fort before pulling out.

The Lieutenant rode the length of the train and acknowledged each trooper and teamster along the way. Satisfied the men and horses appeared rested, he ordered the wagons on. The trail here was a well-worn wagon road, flat and wide, and great for making best speed.

"Corporal Smith!"

The Corporal broke from ranks and galloped to the Lieutenant. "Yes, Lieutenant."

"I expect we will cover more than thirty miles today. Take three men and scout ahead for a suitable stop for the night where we can protect the wagons, and water and graze the horses. You are to stay at that location and make preparations for night camp."

The young Corporal galloped back along the column, "Casey! Rennick! Taylor! Fall out! You're with me!" The four men sped away from the column and galloped from sight in a swirling dust cloud while the supply train and its escort continued on at its plodding pace.

Periodically Lieutenant Harris moved to the side of the trail, sat his horse, and watched the procession file by to keep watch for failing horses or wagon wheels. He was not in the mood for surprises that would cost him time. As much as Buck was a pain in his ass, he could move a supply train. More than once during the war it was Buck's talent for sniffing out danger and pushing teamsters hard and fast with supplies the Lieutenant's men needed that saved them. No man alive could move horses and men like Buck. Boy, how he hated to admit that. Even to himself!

Satisfied all was well, he loped back to the half-mile long train and resumed his position in the lead alongside his friend, Sergeant Peterson. The Sergeant, like Buck, had served with the Lieutenant in the war.

"Have the men break formation. Position twenty men to the rear of the last wagon. I want ten men flanking each side of the wagons, ten in a column ahead of the wagons, and send four scouts to stay two miles ahead of us. Let's show Buck Hawkins we can move a supply train through hostiles, too!"

The Lieutenant raced ahead on the north side of the trail and stopped his horse to watch the Sergeant reposition the troops. The wagon train soon took on the appearance of a well-guarded convoy and sent the warning the Lieutenant intended to send. Seen from a distance he believed Hooker, Tall Dog, and whoever might be planning to hit the train would understand it would be a long day.

The supply train and its military escort moved on throughout the day with no incident, and as evening approached and daylight faded, Lieutenant Harris spied the campfire of his forward scouts. They had set up camp on the south side of the trail next to a large creek. He turned to Sergeant Peterson. "Bring them in Sergeant, I'll see you when you get there." And dashed away.

The Lieutenant made a quick loop around the camp area before dismounting. "You boys picked a fine location," he told Corporal Smith. "As the column approaches, position the wagons on the four key points of this level spot. Picket the wagon stock and ride herd on the mounts."

The train and its escort soon filed into the bivouac area. All arrangements were made as per the Lieutenant's orders, and before it was completely dark campfires dotted the night's darkness like candles in windows, and the cook with his conscripted helpers were dishing out a meal of biscuits, gravy, potatoes and beef.

"Cookie this is going to be the first patrol I was ever on and gained weight," one of the troopers yelled, saluting the camp cook.

"And I second that!" hooted another.

"Three cheers for Cookie and his crew—HIP-HIP-HOORAY! HIP-HIP-HOORAY! HIP-HIP-HOORAY!" A rousing cheer from sixty men roared through the happy camp.

Cookie hopped atop a wooden crate. "You all remember that at the end of the trail when I run out of supplies and I'm feeding you rattlesnake and lizard bellies."

"If you fix 'em with gravy, we'll eat 'em!" yelled a trooper, and the men roared and clapped all over again.

After everyone had enjoyed their meal and men were stationed on lookout and herd patrol, and details arranged for rotation, bed rolls were rolled out near fires between the wagons. The Lieutenant took a stroll through camp and wondered if Buck had reached Fort Laramie. Fort Laramie, the picture of his lovely wife leapt to mind. Seven or eight days and he could sleep in her arms again.

No man had a better wife. A woman of culture and means, raised in Washington, DC, she left family, status, and comforts behind to come to this wild, dusty uncivilized world to be with him and endure the life of a military wife. Two short months to go and his enlistment would be up. He promised her they were DC-bound and he would take the position her father had offered. She could once again enjoy the privileges that wealth and status had to offer. Not the hardships that an officer's wife suffers at a fort on the furthest edge of civilization.

Morning comes early on a military supply train escort, especially for the cook, and by 4:30 a.m. Cookie had coffee and bacon strips on the fire and biscuits in the Dutch ovens. Breakfast was ready to be served at 5:10. Cookie couldn't resist. He jumped on a box, took a black skillet and hatchet and banged over and over again on the skillet until every sleepy trooper was sliding out of their blankets and nearly standing at attention.

"Come on men! The Lieutenant wants these wagons rollin' by six!"

"That'll get the men started." Lieutenant Harris laughed.

As fast as the men filed through the chow line they prepared for the day ahead. Most of the men gathered their horses, saddled up, and mounted. Some harnessed the driving stock, but everyone was soon busy with the day's duties. At five minutes to six the convoy was making dust on the rutted wagon road.

CHAPTER TWENTY-SEVEN

Still Water was sure to raise enough clatter to help Tom and her daughter shake off their blankets early in the morning. The fire she'd started had the soddy bright and warm.

Tom sat on his cot soaking in the comfort of the fire-warmed cabin and the company of Still Water and Soft Cloud. "I just may trade Red Cloud a few horses for you two. I could learn to live like this." He stretched his arms high, trying to chase the sleepiness from his long body.

The women spun around fast enough to raise dust on the floor and in unison and with their hands on their hips shot daggers from their eyes. "A few horses?" Still Water shrieked in feigned anger.

Feeling brave, he pulled on his moccasins. "Well, I do have the mules, too, but I'm kinda partial to 'em!"

"We'll show you why we're worth a lot more than A FEW HORSES!" Soft Cloud shrieked, and they raced across the dirt floor and beat him with their moccasins until he begged for mercy. It's possible the only thing that saved him was that the antelope Still Water had warming on a stick over hot coals caught fire and filled the cabin with smoke so thick they had to run outside for air.

They lay on the damp grass laughing, and then Tom ran back inside and threw the smoking meat out the door, grabbed a blanket and waved it in the smoky room until the air cleared. When all was clear Soft Cloud and her mother came back inside. "I'll bet the biscuits are ready," Soft Cloud said.

After breakfast they helped Tom gather firewood, chatting all the while about what a fine place the little cabin is and how the land there was just right for his plans, if he was looking to stay in one place, as Soft Cloud had put it. With a heavy feeling of emptiness, Tom watched until they rode out of sight in the cottonwood grove. I guess this will be a lonely day, he thought, but I can find plenty to do.

After staking out the antelope skins to cure, he moved to the lean-to barn. He sat in the grass studying the framework when Tom Gray came up behind him and gave a playful nudge. "What's that you say? I should get up and get to work on your barn?"

The barn looked worse than it was. Only three or four of the short logs in the roof needed to be replaced, and that job could be completed today. He hitched the mules to a wagon and drove to the woodlot with his rifle across his lap. Tom Gray and the old mule tagged along, never allowing the wagon to get more than a few feet ahead of them. Tom stopped in the shade of the tall cottonwoods and sat to survey the lay of the land around the soddy and lean-to barn.

To the west of the barn was a convenient vertical wall that could serve well as a fence for half the corral. The land sloped just right so by digging a ditch on this side of the wall, he could run water to the horses in the corral.

With those plans solid in mind, he spent the rest of the day dropping trees and trimming logs. When darkness finally halted all work, he not only had the logs needed for the barn roof repair, but also twenty-one fence posts for the corral loaded on the wagon.

CHAPTER TWENTY-EIGHT

Buck bounded from Old Bedlam before the bugler finished Reveille. He sprinted to the mess hall and quickly talked the cook out of a fine breakfast of eggs, potatoes, coffee, toast, and a slab of ham. Loaded down with two plates piled high, he marched to the porch where he used one chair as a table and another to recline and enjoy his breakfast while he amused himself watching a group of new cadets being drilled mercilessly by an overeager Sergeant.

Breakfast finished, Buck propped his feet up on the rail, lit a cigar, and enjoyed it with the rest of his coffee in a drowsy, satisfied kind of mood. All the while feeling sorry for the Sergeant. If that's the best this army can do for new recruits well, times will be hard on Sergeants.

Buck pondered the goings on of a group of settlers he watched on the parade. Four Conestoga wagons with four families headed west and he chuckled at General Sturgis trying hard to convince them it was sure the wrong time of year to continue west. Secretly though, he was hoping if he sat on the porch long enough, Mrs. Harris might walk across the parade. But after two more cups of coffee and two thirds of a cigar he decided Mrs. Harris wasn't in the mood for sun today. He took his dirty dishes to the cook, wrangled another cup of hot coffee and headed for the livery to check on his horses.

"Hey, Sarge, where do you have my horses?" Buck checked the inside stalls.

"Got 'em around back in a corral by themselves. They were sure beat. You know, that black stallion of yours sure is a strong, rank one, isn't he though?"

"One of the toughest I ever saw. Rode those three from Fort Kearney over the high lands, in close to thirty hours, and that black stallion proved his worth. I aim to keep him."

"You sure are one hard-ridin' son of a gun, Buck. Well all three are good to go now. If they have any wind left."

"Ain't going anywhere today Sarge, I get the day off and so do they." Buck took his time grooming all three horses, being careful to check for injuries. Satisfied that they were no worse for wear, he gave them each an extra ration of oats and forked a pile of hay into their corral. Making sure their water trough was full to the top. "There you go boys, enjoy the day, but don't get stiff on me we're headed out tomorrow. But we won't need to push it so hard this time."

Feeling good, well fed, and with his horses personally cared for, Buck found he was bored and would rather the patrol headed out today. He decided he would go to Old Bedlam to see if he could scare up a game of cards.

They were hardly through the first three pots, with Buck winning all three, when a private came bounding up the steps. "Mr. Buck, the General would like to see you, he's waiting in his office and says it's important."

"Yeah … It's always important. Not as important as my poker winnings though." Buck complained, but the Private was already down the stairs. "Thanks for the games boys, and the cash."

Buck sprinted down the stairs and across the parade to the General's office, hurried up the wooden sidewalk to the porch, and bolted through the door to find the General staring at a map he obviously had sketched himself. "Thought I had the day off, General."

"You do. I want you to look at what I've been thinking over. I drew a map of the territory west of here, where most of the settlements are. You told me before you left for Fort Kearney that you thought you'd located the trail to Hooker's camp town."

"Yes sir, but I don't see how we could ride up there with enough troops to do any good. That trail's narrow and winds up through the high country. It's tight and could be easily guarded. The way the vertical walls follow it up, hell any kid with an old Spencer single shot could hold off an entire regiment."

"Have a look at this map." The General turned the map to Buck. "About sixty or eighty miles southwest of here is Red Cloud and Buffalo Horn's village. For the moment Red Cloud is at peace with us, and yes, I am aware that could change. The Union Pacific has a group of surveyors on the prairie not fifty miles from his village. That's bound to stir him up sooner or later.

"But, I believe we could go out with a patrol and head due west to the first settlement over by the Little Bear Creek, check on those folks, follow the trail along Little Bear Creek ending up just a few miles northwest of Red Cloud's village. That would probably hit all the settlements west of here. Then you could take the troopers and check with Red Cloud. Just to make sure we're going to stay at peace for awhile. Then swing back traveling northeast along the old Jackson Trail to check on our sawmill settlement. I'll be sending you out with fifteen men and give you full authority for the mission." General Sturgis studied Buck's face for approval.

"Looks like a solid plan to me and should only take four or five days, maybe a week, but what about cleaning out Hooker's camp town?"

"Don't have the men to deal with that until Lieutenant Harris returns, but by God, we will deal with them!"

"I presume to be part of that hand you'll be dealing, and I think it's a darned good idea to check on those settlers in the meantime," Buck said.

"Good. I'll assign Sergeant Fetterman to pick fifteen men, have them mounted, armed and supplied by morning. They'll be on the parade at 7:30."

"What about those settlers with the Conestogas? Have you convinced them to winter here at the fort?"

"No, they won't be bothered with reason. They have family somewhere west of here along Little Bear Creek. All Germans, from some place called Lancaster in Pennsylvania. Tough folks they are but stubborn as the mules pulling their wagons. They're setting out any day now."

****

The morning of the eighth day on the trail found the supply train slightly ahead of schedule with nearly three-fourths of their journey behind them.

"Sergeant Peterman," Lieutenant Harris wore a comfortable smile. "I believe before we make camp tonight we'll be beyond the Bozeman Trail junction."

"I agree. Should I send Corporal Smith ahead to locate a bivouac area?"

"Sergeant, that's precisely why I keep you in my company. You're always in step with my thinking."

Sergeant Peterman cantered back through the first fifteen men. "Corporal Smith, take three men and ride to Bozeman Trail junction and select a suitable bivouac for the night. Start fires so Cookie can get dinner burning as soon as we get there."

Corporal Smith and three men left the column in a dash, overtook Lieutenant Harris, and continued down the wagon trail, creating the image of being pushed along by the dust cloud they raised.

"Sergeant, make note those four will do herd patrol the first half of the night." The lieutenant smiled as he gave the order. He grabbed his hat and slapped his thigh, then rubbed dust from his eyes with his kerchief.

The wagons rumbled along the rest of the morning and early afternoon with only one rest stop. Lieutenant Harris was eager to reach Bozeman Trail, knowing that Fort Laramie and Mrs. Harris were then within a day's march.

"Lieutenant. Up ahead to the south of the trail, I see Corporal Smith's fires," Sergeant Peterson announced.

"Two more miles men!" The Lieutenant spun his horse and loped along the train.

An hour later wagons began to pull off on the south side of the road and the now routine positioning of wagons, stock, and equipment was completed in short order. Lieutenant Harris handed his horse to Sergeant Peterson, "I'm checking with Cookie. I sure need some of his stout coffee to scrape the dust off my tonsils."

Corporal Smith stopped him before he reached Cookie's wagon. "Lieutenant, it's difficult to see, but if you look to our north and east you'll see the glow of low campfires. I believe, Sir, there's an Indian village on the top of that slope."

The Lieutenant's eyes followed along Corporal Smith's outstretched right arm and recognized the muted glow of small campfires. "I agree. Have the wagons moved closer together and double the men on herd patrol. Keep the stock tight and the men sharp. And Corporal, good job!"

The Lieutenant turned his focus from coffee to protecting the wagons and the lives of his men. "Sergeant Peterson, start a chow line now with half the men. Position the rest of the men in defensive positions around our encampment in groups of four along the northern rim. Have them dig in twenty yards apart and supplied with fifty rounds each. Rotate them through the chow line. And Sergeant, I want total position in fifteen minutes exactly!"

"Yes sir, Lieutenant! You'll have it!"

"Cookie feed these men in a hell of a hurry, see those fires? It may be nothing but they damn sure won't catch us sleeping!" Without waiting for a response he ran toward the detail in charge of herd patrol for the mounts.

"Private, I want five men mounted, armed and at the ready on herd patrol all night. Keep the patrol rotated every hour. Stay awake! Stay fresh! Stay sharp!" He ordered and went back to the chow line.

Standing with men as they moved through the chow line, he addressed them. "Gentlemen, this is what the Army pays us for. We cannot be sure those fires are hostiles but we'll be ready. Eat your groceries and follow Sergeant Peterson's orders. Get your rest. Stay sharp!"

Concern washed over his face, but he was also satisfied with the reaction and response of his men. Within the fifteen allotted minutes small batteries of men were entrenched on the northern perimeter, armed and ready; the saddle stock guarded by six mounted armed troopers. In another fifteen minutes rotations were completed and all men fed.

"Cookie, I'll have that coffee now." Lieutenant Harris held out his tin cup.

"Looking for trouble?"

"Not looking for it, Cookie, but I'm sure gonna be ready for it." The Lieutenant found a seat on a wooden box to enjoy his coffee. "Tonight I would like that pain in my ass scout, Buck, and one of his damned cigars." He said mostly to himself. "Keep the coffee hot and have one of the men keep the duty guards supplied all night."

"You bet, Lieutenant."

****

Tall Dog stood on the perimeter of his makeshift Sioux village and watched the U.S. Army prepare. "They will send a few men in the morning. We will invite their leader to our camp. When he comes we will capture him. Then we will capture the supply wagons and kill the horse soldiers."

Tall Dog had in his village forty-five men. Mostly renegade Indians and a small handful of hardened ex-cowboys turned outlaws. In his mind, the weak and cowardly U.S. Army was no match for his band of courageous fighters. He went to his lodge to rest. Content his plan was secure, he sat by his fire anxiously awaiting sunrise. His son joined him by the fire in the lodge of a true warrior. Together they would deal the white soldier a terrific blow. Not like Red Cloud who believes in words. "Before sunrise, get the men from the wagons in the rear of the village, move them to the front, and hide them in the tall grass."

"We will attack the train?"

"We will not attack until we have captured their leader. The white soldier cannot fight without a leader. He will come to us in the morning. We will rest until then."

****

Watching the sun paint the morning red as it began its journey upward from the seat of the wagon, the Lieutenant had a clear view of the Sioux village. Something about the village bothered him. He knew it hadn't been there when they had traveled east but that alone didn't tell him much. The Sioux move around with the changing seasons. It could simply be a small village on its way to winter grounds. But he didn't see children playing with dogs, and he saw no women there. He sat on the wagon seat and studied the village as morning activities began to make it stir.

"Sergeant Peterson, what do you make of the village?"

"It feels odd to me. I've been lookin' it over myself. I don't believe it's a Sioux village, I believe it's a pack of trouble."

"My thoughts exactly. Tell me, what would you do next?"

"I'd feed the men. I'd go on like we never noticed 'em."

"I like that idea. Have Cookie feed the men. Rotate the men from their positions to the chow line. Let's not hurry and let's stay alert."

****

Like the Lieutenant, Tall Dog studied his adversary as the sun rose. It was well into the morning, and he could not understand why the U.S. Army had not sent anyone to his village. But he would wait. Tall Dog knew he had a good plan. Black Hair had done as his father ordered. There were now fifteen men hidden in the tall brown grass. Before long, though, Tall Dog began to grow impatient. Why would the U.S. Army not send its leader into his camp? That is the way of the U.S. Army.

As the morning wore on Tall Dog grew increasingly intolerant but he could do nothing other than wait. His renegades and cowboys in the camp all began to grow restless. His army was a rough collection of troubleseekers. Waiting for battle was not what they did well. They were accustomed to creating battles. It was not long before some of the renegades began leaving their assigned tipis.

Tall Dog was an experienced warrior a survivor of many battles against the Crow, Blackfoot and white settlers and their soldiers. He knew the importance of control over those who follow him. This morning he could see he was losing that control. But what he could not understand was why the U.S. Army would not fall for his trap.

What he saw the white soldiers do next told him they were not going to come to his trap at all. His strong heart began to pound loud as war drums and rage swelled in his chest, while he watched the Army soldiers began to hitch mules to wagons and break camp.

****

"Sergeant Peterson, assume the defensive posture and protect the wagons, we are moving out!" Lieutenant Harris ordered and the five wagons pulled onto the road and resumed their plodding pace toward Fort Laramie protected by troopers, twenty leading, ten in the rear, five on each side, and the ten flanking scouts. The Lieutenant rode to the north of the trail and positioned himself in plain view between the wagons and the Sioux lodges. Making a statement to whoever was up there they intended to go about their business of transporting the supply wagons.

"Bugler, sound Forward! Keep it up until we have passed the Sioux village. In fact, aim your bugle squarely at them!" The Lieutenant ordered.

****

Tall Dog recognized Lieutenant Harris. The Pretty Soldier. He had visited Red Cloud's village to talk peace two times. He is the reason Red Cloud is now soft. The Pretty Soldier is the reason Red Cloud drove him from his village and now talks of friendship with whites. Watching The Pretty Soldier lead the wagons away from his trap was too much for Tall Dog.

"Every one of you get your horses and rifles! We will attack the U.S. Army white man!" Tall Dog ran for his horse, rage streaming from his eyes. Men grabbed their rifles, scrambled for their horses, and merged into a group of controlled chaos. Following Tall Dog the army of renegades and outlaws charged down the hillside to attack the wagon train.

"You've got them flushed out now, Lieutenant." Sergeant Peterson pointed up the hill with his hat.

"At my signal have the wagons move out as fast as possible. You and twenty men stay with the wagons. The rest ride with me. We'll make a head on attack and a flanking attack. We'll put an end to this nonsense!"

The Lieutenant turned his horse to look head on at the charging Indians. The rider out in front he recognized instantly as Tall Dog with his long black braids trailing behind him in the wind. Today is your day Tall Dog, he thought.

When about one mile separated them, the Lieutenant gave the signal for his command to separate and fly into action.

"BUGLER! SOUND CHARGE! SOUND IT OFTEN AND LOUD!"

Forty men pivoted their horses as one. Lieutenant Harris out in the front, his Henry in the air, galloped toward the charging renegades. The horses moved in time to the bugler's energetic tune. They stormed up the hill charging the renegades. On the Lieutenant's signal the speeding horses split in two groups, one charging straight on, one flanking west. The air was so thick with dust it was impossible to see more than fifty feet. The Lieutenant gave the signal to fire.

Tall Dog was caught completely off guard. His cowboy recruits split off and ran for their lives. Half of his renegades fell, dead or wounded, in the first volley. Tall Dog was forced to look for an escape. He and his son turned the remaining group north, and galloped hard up the hill trying to outrun the cavalry unit.

BUGLER! SOUND CHARGE!" Lieutenant Harris hollered as he swung his group to the north in pursuit. Half of the flanking horsemen pivoted with him. Tall Dog and less than twenty renegades found themselves being overwhelmed by forty well trained, well mounted cavalry soldiers.

"POUR IT ON MEN! POUR THE LEAD TO 'EM!"

They raced up the slope, dust and bullets flying through blackpowder smoke-choked air. Tall Dog and his men never had a chance to get off a single shot. They were running for their lives. It was, as Lieutenant Harris would later describe it, an absolute rout.

In the hell bent flight for life, Black Hair's horse stumbled and fell. It was Tall Dog's own horse that ran over him, trampling his son to death. Tall Dog rode a strong horse and he alone was able to escape The Pretty Soldier's charge. Every one of his renegades was gunned down on the slope near the Bozeman Trail junction that day. Tall Dog galloped away leaving his son's body and his dead renegade allies behind, yelling a vow that The Pretty Soldier would pay for his son's death.

****

"Bugler, sound Recall!" Lieutenant Harris ordered as he brought his horse to a stop and watched Tall Dog disappear behind a rise in the distance. He knew he would rue the fact that Tall Dog was able to escape. "Private, kill those wounded horses."

"What about the wounded renegades?"

The Lieutenant surveyed the hillside before him, littered with dead and dying men, and horses, some unable to move, others trying to crawl away. "I ordered you to kill those horses!"

"The wounded renegades, sir?"

"They'll die!"

Lieutenant Harris sat his horse, and watched his men relieve four horses of their suffering, and gather rifles, revolvers, and gun belts from twenty-two dead or dying renegades. None so alive that they could put up much of a struggle. The Lieutenant's men were able to catch the remaining nine live horses and then spent another hour piling the lodges and other equipment abandoned on the field of battle onto the two wagons. They pushed the wagons together and set them ablaze burning everything, including the fallen horses and renegades.

After watching the leaping flames and stinking black smoke long enough to be satisfied everything would burn, the Lieutenant reined his horse about. "Let's move out men!" The Lieutenant, his forty men, and nine captured horses galloped hard in pursuit of the supply wagon.

"Private!" Lieutenant Harris yelled to the young man galloping along beside him. "Break free and catch that train and bring them back to a walk! Go, man!" As if shot from a cannon the young private sped away from the pack of forty.

It took Lieutenant Harris and his troopers nearly two hours to overtake the supply wagons. "Sergeant Peterson, at the next available location, stop to rest the mounts and ourselves. We'll finish this journey tomorrow."

****

Tall Dog galloped until he knew he was safe, then jumped to the ground and cursed the U.S. Army, the white man, the cowardly red man, Lieutenant Harris, and his gods. He looked out across the prairie and saw the thick column of black smoke; he knew his son was part of that smoke. Then he looked in the sky, searching for answers and saw nothing. Inside himself, he felt nothing except hatred and rage. He vowed he would kill many more whites. The first white man he would kill was Hooker. Hooker must die. This plan to kill U.S. Army soldiers and capture five wagons was not a good plan. This plan killed his son.

He swung upon his horse and headed for Hooker's camp. He was east of Fort Laramie, and knew to stay north out of sight as he headed west to the high country and Hooker's camp town. He traveled all that day and all the next night without a stop. With the rise of the morning sun, he could see the foothills and the high country. He would be at Hooker's camp in the afternoon of the next day. Tall Dog pushed himself and his horse, stopping only briefly at occasional streams. Rarely did he dismount to walk, to stretch his own legs, or to rest his exhausted horse. He was a man driven. Driven by absolute hate.

When he rode into camp, he stopped outside the saloon tent, jumped from his exhausted horse, and entered, grabbed a chair and hollered for a bottle of whiskey. The tent and board saloon was smoky and dark. A few nearly naked women worked their way around tables hoping to do business. Several tables had men gathered playing cards but stopped talking when Tall Dog entered. The dark haired man behind the bar went to the far end to avoid being seen by the big renegade. One of the women brought him a bottle of whiskey and tried to sit on his lap. He shoved her to the dirt. "What I want now is Hooker! You find him bring him to me now!" She stared at Tall Dog from the slimy floor before rising to her feet. In one long gulp he swallowed a third of the bottle. "Let the flap open, get some air in! It stinks like white men in here!" He yelled after her.

Hooker ambled into the saloon, spirits high, spurs jangling, expecting an accounting of success. He laid his hat on the table, grabbed a seat across from Tall Dog, and reached for the whiskey bottle. Tall Dog grabbed the bottle and yanked it from his reach. "Get your own bottle."

"That's no way to treat a friend." Hooker reached for the bottle.

Tall Dog whipped his rifle across the table, landing a fierce blow on the side of Hooker's head knocking him from his chair to land lying on his back on the greasy floor. "You son of a white whore are not my friend! You are a stinking white man. You killed my son!"

"You bastard you!" Hooker struggled to get up.

"Stay in the mud you pig!" Tall Dog kicked Hooker in the chest and shoved him down on the muddy floor, aiming the Henry at his middle. "Your stupid plan to capture the Army supply train killed twenty men and my son. And it killed you, too!" Tall Dog fired five rounds into Hooker. Then laid the rifle on the table, snatched Hooker's black hat and, after he admired the silver conchos, put it on his head, sat down, and resumed drinking his whiskey as calmly as if a friend had just invited him for a drink.

CHAPTER TWENTY-NINE

In the days since Soft Cloud visited, Tom had worked hard at improving both his back muscles and his ranch. Today had been like all the others: cut logs, load them on the wagon, haul them to the corral. Dig post holes, set posts, and fasten rails to the posts. He had worked steadily all day in the hot fall sun and was taking an overdue break, sitting in the stream's cool waters. One more day and the corral would be finished. Well, almost finished, but building two gates would be a lot easier than some of the other jobs he'd bit into.

The barn and the mud cabin were both completed and in good shape. The well was clean and usable, with a new cover and a wooden bucket attached to a thirty-foot rope. A small corral adjacent to the lean-to barn was in place and the large corral, big enough to hold at least twenty horses, would be finished in one more day.

His eyes wandered across the prairie and sure enough, far in the distance grazed the band of wild horses. Every day as he worked Tom saw them. It was as if they wanted him to see them. Today he would ride out and visit them. He jumped to his feet and ran sloshing to grab a bridle.

The big buckskin, who Tom named Big Fella, had been snoozing in the shade of the lean-to, and as Tom slipped the headstall in place he got a very clear signal that Big Fella thought it was too hot to go racing over the prairie.

"I hate to interrupt your nap Big Fella, but today I just gotta run those horses." Tom grabbed a fistful of mane and slid up. They left the corral at a full gallop as the mules watched from the shade.

As they splashed through Little Bear Creek, Tom knew if he even had a chance to get close to the wild horses, he would have to circle around them and come up from behind. He kept Big Fella in a flat-out run, making a long circle through the tall prairie grass. In no time he was miles from his homestead and venturing into unknown territory. Already the distance between him and the wild horses had been cut in half. He kept the arc wide, knowing if he made a straight line toward the wild ones they would bolt. So far, they gave no sign they considered him a threat. Tom and Big Fella kept pouring on the speed, the big horse showed no signs of fading and those huge, tough hooves turned up chunks of sod with each stride.

All of a sudden the wild horses spooked. Heads flew up, a few horses snorted, and they made a mad dash away from Tom and Big Fella. Tom let the buckskin feel his heels, the thrill of the chase exciting him and the horse all the more. "Keep it coming Big Fella, let's run 'em awhile and see if we can turn 'em."

As Tom swung ever wider with his arc, and they traveled farther north, he saw a thick cloud of swirling smoke. "Whoa, whoa, hold on fella!" Tom turned to face the mountainous column of black. "Let's check on that!" Tom urged Big Fella back into a gallop toward the smoke.

They raced toward the black smoke until finally they were near enough to see outlines of burning buildings. Still miles away from the fire, Tom pushed Big Fella to stay at it, even though he knew the big horse had begun to tire.

Closing fast, Tom saw people around the fire. "Come on Big Fella, don't fade now!"

Tom recognized the people as renegades. He knew what they looked like and he knew what they did. Even though he rode unarmed he continued in the direction of the burning homestead. The renegades saw his approach and ran for their horses, fleeing in the direction of the foothills.

Tom counted eleven as they rode away.

The buildings had burned nearly to the ground. He jumped from his sweaty, blowing horse and stared at the destruction caused by those evil men. The thought of the work and effort he put into his own homestead came to mind as he looked at the ruins of what must have been a fine house, barn, and storage shed.

Just outside the smoldering barn lay two dead cows, six dead pigs, and four mules with their throats cut. For a moment Tom stood frozen, staring at the slaughtered livestock. Renegades had no use for mules. Then he went to the burning pile of rubble that was once the house. In the rear facing the prairie, he found a dead man—scalped, stripped naked. Nearer to the house were bodies of a woman and three children and another man, all scalped.

Tom's knees buckled as he crumbled to the ground nearest one of the dead children, a little girl maybe eight or nine years old. She wore a pretty blue and white floral dress. He picked up the little girl and held her tight while he rocked her as though she were only sleeping. Blood from her naked head smeared over his shirt. With eyes almost blinded by tears, he stared at the dead woman, her face frozen in terror, her eyes and mouth open. In her final moments she must have been cradling the smallest child trying to protect it. She died with her arms still clasped around her tiny baby.

It took all the strength he could summon to stand. He ran for the burning tool shed and kicked his way in through the flames. He knew what he needed—shovels, their handles just beginning to burn, and a pick. He threw the tools from the burning shed to the yard.

The ground was too hard to dig six graves, so he put the mother and the baby together. Maybe she would have wanted it that way anyway. For the two older girls, he made the grave wide enough for them to lie beside each other. He cut the bell from the dead cow's neck and laid it with the girls, so they could have a toy. The two men would need their own graves.

He finished the final grave by moonlight and glowing embers from the smoldering buildings. From the bottom of the last grave where he worked carefully placing the body of the last man, he heard approaching hoof beats. Armed with only a shovel he squatted on the dead man ready to face with a vengeance any trouble riding in.

"Looks like we're too late to help these poor folks but I never knew renegades to bury their dead before." Tom recognized his friend Buck Hawkins.

With tremendous relief, Tom scrambled from the grave totally unprepared for their greeting of over a dozen guns drawn and leveled on him. "You'd better speak up son, or you'll go right back in that grave." Buck ordered.

"Buck. It's me, Tom, it's Tom!"

"Holy Cow, Tom! What are you doing in this part of the prairie? Digging graves?"

"I was running wild horses, and I saw the smoke."

"This is some real mean business, Tom. I'm out with these troopers under the orders of General Sturgis to warn folks like these about Tall Dog. Looks like we were too late again. A few days ago we came across what was left of a small Cheyenne village. The renegades killed them all, fifteen men, women, and children. They killed their dogs and old people too, and stole the horses. If they don't go with Tall Dog, he and his renegades butcher them." Then he asked Tom, "Are you still traveling with Soft Cloud? Is she around here too?"

"She's back at Red Cloud's village."

"What are you doing? How'd you find this mess?" Buck waved his hand, pointing to the burning nightmare.

"I have a place some twenty miles southeast of here. An old soddy I fixed up. I'm starting a horse ranch." Tom looked around again at the smoking piles that a day ago were this family's house and barn. He couldn't make it make sense; that tiny little girl. "That's how I found these folks. Never knew they were out here. I was out running wild horses and saw the smoke ... I saw the renegades leaving. I was too far to see if it was Tall Dog. But it was Indians for sure."

While Buck and Tom talked, a trooper grabbed a shovel and filled the last grave.

"Where's your horse? You've done all you can for these folks, ride with us awhile. We're headed for Red Cloud's and it sounds like your place is on the way."

"This your horse, young fella?" yelled a trooper running up with a sweat-crusted horse in tow.

"Sorry about that, Big Fella, I forgot all about you." Tom gave him a good scratching on the withers. "I'm heading home, Buck. My place is only about eight miles northwest of Red Cloud's village. I'd consider it a favor if you and your patrol spent the night at my place. This mess could take me a bit to get over. Company would do me good."

"We'll do that Tom," Buck said. "Men, we'll ride to Tom's and spend the night. Our horses covered plenty of ground the last five days, they've earned a day's rest. Each of you gather any tools that survived the fire. These poor folks can't use them anymore and Tom sure can."

They rode mostly in silence from the burnt out settlement to Tom's place, but Buck managed to tell Tom about the incident at Bozeman Trail junction. "They took care of the whole rotten bunch, including Tall Dog's son, Black Hair. Would've been better all around if the Lieutenant and his boys had finished Tall Dog there too, but the slippery cuss got away"

"I have some news for you that'll rattle you to the soles of your moccasins" Tom struggled to say the words. "Tall Dog's son was Soft Cloud's brother."

Buck jerked his horse to a rough stop, yanked his Stetson from his head and stared blank-eyed at Tom. "Holy Cow Tom! Does that mean, Tall Dog is Soft Cloud's father?"

"He is, and he killed his other son for not leaving Red Cloud to go with him. Shot him dead in front of Still Water, his wife."

"Still Water, Tall dog's wife?" Buck's eyes grew even more blank. "He is a madman for sure. I hear he killed Hooker and took over the camp. Stories have it there are over one hundred renegades and outlaws up there in the high country again." Soft Cloud is Tall Dog's daughter, Buck thought. He wondered about his new young friend here. Hell of a kid but life sure keeps kicking him in the teeth. First he has to deal with the son of a bitch of an old hider, then kills that woman, now a girl comes along and treats him alright and turns out her father is Tall Dog. Right here and now, Buck decided, he would do all he could for Tom. Of course it's true he owed Tom anyway.

The small band arrived at Tom's homestead with several hours before the sun would slip below the horizon. Buck studied the lay of the land. "Troopers put two men on herd patrol, everybody else shake out their bed rolls and camp at the barn. Somebody get a fire going. You have coffee, Tom?" Buck's sparkling-eyed grin let it slip he guessed Tom did not.

"No, I'm real low on supplies. I've been livin' mostly off antelope meat, couple of trout, and a little bit of flour that was left in that old hider's wagon."

"Somebody make this man some coffee!" Buck ordered, and he looked around with a quick eye, "Even in the dark Tom, this place looks like it'll be something fine one day. Sure sets at a good spot don't it?"

"You know my story. I covered a lot of miles on this prairie and I like this spot. I have a darn good stand of timber, a good strong stream, and somebody dug me a well. And look at that sheer bank there, half of my corral is already built. I figure just this side of that wall I'll dig a ditch to run water to the corral, and maybe even build some more small corrals right over there." Tom pointed to the flats between the existing partially completed corral, and the widest part of the stream.

A pleasant young trooper came and handed each of them a cup of freshly boiled, very hot coffee. "Go ahead Tom, suck 'er down."

"I never had much coffee, Buck. I guess I just never got in the habit, but

I figure to change that." Tom held the tin cups to his lips. "Whew! This is hot stuff."

"Sure is. Just the way I like it. Coffee gotta be hot!" The two friends finished their coffee with no more conversation. Tom, not being a practiced host, handed his empty tin cup to Buck and just walked away to the soddy and his cot.

Most of the troopers were quick to fall asleep. The few on herd patrol rode around the small herd of horses, which in short order included both of Tom's and his three mules. Occasionally, a trooper would get up, and gathering sticks and branches from the pile Tom had made, they kept the fire burning all night.

In the morning they still had a good fire and a considerable pile of glowing hot ash. Buck crawled from his bedroll and ambled to the fire. "Gentlemen, that is as fine a cookfire as I have ever seen, and I've set around a lot of good campfires. Why don't a couple of you go scare up some prairie hens or antelope or buffalo or something. We got a day off and a hell of a fire, a good place to set, and we need to eat all day long 'till we burst our bellies." Three young troopers scrambled for their horses.

Buck leaned against the corral fence, surveying his friend's homestead in the morning light. With the same pride as though it were his, he admired every detail while listening to the casual conversation of the troopers relaxing around the fire. In a way it pleased him to hear that their main topic of conversation was finding Tall Dog. Words like filthy bastard, renegade son of a bitch, and murdering animal were the words Buck heard used to describe Tall Dog. He decided to let the men just talk and walked toward the soddy admiring the full front porch. "Tom, this is going to be all right. You know I always like a good porch. I feel right at home here. All I need is a chair, a toothpick and a cigar, and I'll move right in!"

"If you ever feel the need, Buck, I'll share everything I have." Tom spread his arms wide like an eagle.

"I might take you up on a few visits, but this is your place Tom. I figure when I get done with this Tall Dog stuff I'll come by and help you get your herd started. And that's a promise."

Thundering hooves announced the return of the three troopers storming back to the fire with two dead antelopes draped across one of the horses. "By the looks of those hides staked out over there, this isn't the first time you're going to roast antelope here," Buck said.

"Hunting is good here. Living is good here. I'm happy to be here, and I'll make a good horse ranch right here."

They sat on the porch and watched the troopers skin and prepare the antelope for the fire. In no time they were roasting above the flames on a quickly fashioned but stout spit.

The day wore on into early evening, and the men enjoyed their day of relaxation and the roasted antelope. "You know, Tom, you need a few dogs. Yes sir, a few good strong, mean dogs. Why don't you go along in the morning to see Red Cloud? I'll bet you could talk him out of three or four good dogs."

"What do I need three or four good dogs for?"

"You don't want to end up like those settlers you buried, do you? Good dogs will give you plenty of warning, and I've seen your shooting skills. I'll wager to say, if you had two minutes' warning, Tall Dog and I don't care how many renegades wouldn't be able to shoot you out of that soddy. I'm not kidding, Tom. I'd like to see you get three or four good big dogs."

Tom could see that his friend meant what he said and he decided he would follow that advice and go with him to Red Cloud's village in the morning.

****

Buck, Tom, and twenty troopers approached Red Cloud's village midmorning the following day. They rode past the herd of Sioux ponies as they neared the outer edge of the village and Tom looked them over with a different eye than he had a few weeks ago. The riders dismounted outside the village, where they were greeted by Buffalo Horn, Soft Cloud, and Still

Water and a large group of Sioux braves and children. Buck swooped down, snatched up a young Sioux boy, hoisted him to his shoulders and carried him along. The troopers waited with the horses. Buffalo Horn and Soft Cloud led the way to Red Cloud's lodge, Tom walked behind with Buck.

They found Red Cloud waiting by his lodge, and with a nod and wave he invited them inside. Acting according to custom, Buck and Tom stood until Buffalo Horn and Red Cloud sat. When Red Cloud motioned, they settled deep into comfortable seats among the skins surrounding a small, smoky fire with Soft Cloud next to Tom, across from Buffalo Horn. A worn wooden bowl half full of cooked meal was passed around the group. Everyone dipped their fingers in as the bowl came to them, taking small portions and chewing slowly, as if the most important thing of the day was to watch the fire while savoring ground meal. For a long while, no one spoke. Occasionally Soft Cloud and Tom's eyes met. Soft Cloud placed her hand gently on Tom's knee.

Finally Buck broke the silence. "General Sturgis of the U.S. Army asked me to tell you we are grateful for your peace toward the white man."

Red Cloud watched every word leave Buck's lips as Soft Cloud interpreted. Red Cloud studied Buck. Tom watched his eyes move up and down as they surveyed the muscular scout, and finally Red Cloud addressed Soft Cloud. It was a long speech, and there were several times when Soft Cloud's face grew sad. When Red Cloud finished speaking, Soft Cloud looked directly into Tom's eyes, not Buck's. It took her some moments to begin.

"I, Red Cloud, and my Sioux are at peace with the whites for this time. But I do not understand why the white man is building a road of iron through the land, on which the Sioux hunt buffalo. This is not the way of a people who want peace.

"We who live in this village welcome the peace in which your white fathers allow us to live and hunt on this land. But all Sioux do not follow my advice. There are many who hate the white man. There are also those who hate Sioux who are friendly with the white man. These I cannot control. These Sioux follow an angry warrior named Tall Dog ... my son."

Tom, unable to control himself, jumped to his feet. Buck grabbed the back of his shirt and yanked him down to his seat atop the skins. Soft Cloud rested both hands on Tom's knees leaned forward and, with tear-filled eyes, told Tom to be strong.

Red Cloud waited for calm and then he spoke again. Again he spoke for a long time. Soft Cloud addressed Tom as she spoke Red Cloud's words.

"Tall Dog has become an enemy of the peaceful Sioux. I lead my people in peace, but understand, I am not Spotted Tail. Chief Spotted Tail is a coward. He lives in the shadows of your Fort called Laramie, and those who follow him take food and trinkets from the white soldiers. He allows his people to forget the ways of the Sioux. That is wrong and the way of a coward. I am not a coward. I am Red Cloud. Perhaps the time for war will come. But for now, we will try peace.

"Tall Dog will not try peace. My son has very strong medicine. Strong medicine that has become bad medicine. He has killed many Sioux. He has also killed many white men. Red Cloud has many Sioux who wish to live in peace with the white man. They, as I, wish only that the white man leave us alone to live in peace and hunt our lands. Tall Dog has Sioux, Cheyenne and Arapaho that do not wish for the white man to live here. He does not understand. There are too many white men to kill. He will only cause many peaceful Sioux to die at the hands of the white man. If we do not stop Tall Dog there will be great war between the whites and the Sioux, Cheyenne, and Arapaho. Many will die. And in the end the Sioux will lose."

Buck addressed Soft Cloud. "I come to your village with U.S. Army troopers. We have been searching for Tall Dog. We have found many whites and peaceful Cheyenne dead at the hands of Tall Dog. We will continue to search for Tall Dog and one day we will find him. Then we will have peace." She turned and spoke Buck's words to Red Cloud.

Red Cloud nodded and began to speak, this time as he spoke, he saw no one but Tom.

When Red Cloud finished speaking, Soft Cloud translated through her tears. "Tom, you have become a great friend of Red Cloud and his Sioux village. Sometimes a Sioux brave is given a thing to do that must be done by that brave. Even if the brave wishes not to do this thing. This is the way of the Sioux. You have already done things for Red Cloud and his people. Red Cloud must ask you to do yet another thing for the Sioux. You must go and find Tall Dog. You must go and stop Tall Dog's bad medicine. You must go and you must kill Tall Dog. The Sioux of Red Cloud cannot trust that the white soldiers will find him. When you find Tall Dog you will kill him and you must cut out his eyes so he cannot see how to take his bad medicine to the next life with him. Only in this way can his son find peace in the world beyond. You must raise him high on his burial platform and cover him with this robe from our brother the buffalo. You see it is a sacred white buffalo robe. This will insure his son will not suffer in the next life."

Tom felt a suffocating weight descend upon him as the words came from Soft Cloud's lips. Soft Cloud was struggling with her emotions and it took all her strength to say the things Red Cloud made her say. He knew she too was finding herself in a new world. Just a short time ago she was living happily with her mother and brothers in a peaceful Sioux village. Now her brother is dead. Killed by her father. Another brother is gone from their village, and her grandfather asks Tom to kill her father. Even though Soft Cloud understood her father must die, when she was made to say it, Tom saw the pain in her eyes.

He liked Soft Cloud more than he had ever liked anyone before, felt a connection he'd never felt before, or fully understood. She'd told him she was planning many visits to his mud cabin. She was anxious to help him gather the wild horses and to cook more prairie hen and antelope for them to eat together. Now Tom must leave to find her father and perhaps he would never return to his soddy for they both knew her father was a very powerful warrior and his medicine was very strong.

Tom was first to rise. With a tight fist he hit his chest. A sign to Buffalo Horn and Red Cloud he understood. He stepped to Red Cloud and accepted the white buffalo robe and left the lodge. As he walked slowly in toward the troopers, Buck grabbed his shoulder and spun him around.

"I know you're a terrific shot and maybe a great tracker, but you're no match for Tall Dog. If you go out after him as Red Cloud asks, I'm afraid you're a dead man. Why don't you just work on your horse ranch and let the Army take care of this? I promise you I'll catch up with the bastard and bring you his eyeballs. Listen to me on this one, Tom. You're too young and too green to do this."

Tom's mind was clear, but fogged at the same time. He liked Buck and trusted him, and yet he felt, somehow, an obligation to Red Cloud. Maybe not an obligation, he could not be sure, but because he was asked by the leader of the Sioux to do this … kill this man. He felt he must. Maybe Red Cloud knew only Tom could place the white robe on Tall Dog.

No more words passed between them as they walked through the village to the waiting troopers, where Buck swung up on Diablo and Tom stepped into Tom Gray's saddle. Without any parting words they rode away, each of them following their own path.

CHAPTER THIRTY

Buck and the troopers made good time as they traveled to the settlements at the fort sawmill. Even from a distance Buck could tell all was well at this settlement. The sawmill was established by Fort Laramie about three years earlier to provide lumber and firewood for the Fort. Situated on the banks of Squaw Run River, which enjoyed a steady flow of water, the mill never lacked for power. They rode past the big wooden structure of the sawmill, through the gate at the end of a dusty street that was flanked on both sides by a barricade made of slab wood and tree stumps. During the past three years twenty families had moved in, built houses and worked at the mill. The sawmill settlement was now beginning to take on the appearance of a small town. Buck noticed a small chapel under construction in the center of the settlement. To Buck the settlement looked downright inviting.

The troopers halted just beyond the chapel in front of a building that served as the settlement's main gathering place. A long one-story wooden building, unpainted with a sign leaning against the wall under the porch roof that read, "GOOD EATS."

"This looks as good as any a spot to stop for awhile, fellows." Buck suggested. "A couple of you boys go find the livery and get these horses tended to, and if they have any beer in here, I'll buy the man a beer that gives Diablo a rubdown. If not, I'm sure they got milk." He pointed to the three Jersey cows in the yard by the porch.

A few troopers went in search of the livery, walking the horses down what appeared to be the main street toward a building on the far end which surely should be the livery if it wasn't. Buck and the rest of the men entered GOOD EATS.

A long bar flanked the rear of the building separating two ladies, busily preparing meals on a huge black cook stove, from the rest of the wide open, plank floored room. The troopers filled the room but as orderly as possible found seats at the tables and waited in anticipation to see what Buck would do next. The ladies at the stove stopped cooking and looked across the bar obviously surprised by the invasion of the U.S. Cavalry. "Ladies can you tell us what choices we might make? But don't make them too many because we're used to Army chow." Buck's voice carried his familiar chuckle.

"You fellas just barge in and take over a place, don't you?" The large woman from behind the bar pointed to Buck with a very threatening spatula.

"Sorry ma'am, we didn't mean to take it over, we just meant to conquer it and eat the spoils." Buck flashed his famous ear to ear smile.

"Well today, the spoils are beef stew and biscuits."

"How about that, men? Can we do with a little beef stew and biscuits? What about beer?"

"Got no beer. Milk, water, and coffee."

"That will do mighty fine. How about serving us up and sending the bill to General Sturgis."

As the ladies began to serve, Buck asked if he could see whoever was in charge of the sawmill settlement, and a young boy was dispatched scurrying out the front door. Buck attacked his Stetson sized bowl of stew and tried to drown several biscuits in the broth. "That's a mighty fine stew ma'am and these biscuits, why I would not be able to describe how wonderful and fluffy they are if someone held a gun to my head. I can guarantee you one thing, right now, when all them Indians are tamed and I give up scouting I just might find myself working at your sawmill!"

"Is that because you like my biscuits, or do you have your eye on something else here at the mill?" The youngest prettiest cook flirted back with Buck.

"Well, these boys will tell you. I've always been partial to fluffy biscuits."

"Why you ..." and she threw a soggy, soapy dishrag square into Bucks face giving the troopers reason to hoot and holler while Buck wiped soap suds from his goatee. Just then Mr. Buchanan walked through the heavy wooden door. "Buck, I see you still have a way with the ladies." He sent a wink to the young lady. "I hope all you gents are leaving here with full stomachs. Of course, had we known we were going to be paid a visit by half of the cavalry west of the Mississippi, we would have butchered a steer." He pulled up a chair and sat at the table with Buck.

"Now, what can I do for you, Buck?" Mr. Buchanan, a wise old gent with soft wavy gray hair and a strong build was well suited to sawmill work. He was wise enough to turn a small opportunity given him by General Sturgis into a booming business supplying cut lumber to settlers for many miles in all directions.

"Have you heard of the renegade Tall Dog?"

"I have." Mr. Buchanan replied. "I hear he's real trouble. Do you think we're in danger of his renegades? We've heard there have been a number of attacks and killings and burnings and such."

"We don't know for sure. We do know he's stirring up all kinds of trouble. Just two days ago, he killed an entire family and burned down their buildings about a hundred miles northwest of here. We believe he has at least a hundred renegades. Sioux, Cheyenne, Arapaho, and some outlaws, drifters, whoever he can get."

"I appreciate the warning, Buck, but what can I do with it. We have eighteen families living here now. We're building a church. We've built a small school. We have even selected one of the mothers as schoolteacher. There are close to forty children here! We usually have four or five men working in the mill. Most days eight or ten men are out with the mules cutting and dragging logs. Yes it's true we all have firearms but what chance would a handful of men have against a bunch like that?"

"Not much, I reckon." Buck admitted. "I suppose when I make my report to the General I could suggest he send a detachment of troopers here until this trouble is over."

"Why can't you leave these men here now? It could be a week or more before the General sends help."

"I don't believe I have the authority."

"Buck. Isn't this Fort Laramie's sawmill? And aren't these Fort Laramie's troopers? Why not just simply leave Fort Laramie's troopers at Fort Laramie's sawmill?"

"You're a tough one. And you put me in a tough spot."

"I can't see what General Sturgis could do to you. You're not official military, you're a scout."

"I've seen Army scouts in Army guard houses. And I sure don't want to get any of these boys in trouble."

"Buck, I think I can speak for all of us." A young Corporal pushed back his chair and stood at his table. "We'll gladly risk the wrath of General Sturgis to defend these folks. And eat their chow!"

"Well, Buck?" Mr. Buchanan wore the grin of a victor.

"Do you suppose you boys are up to it?" Buck looked around the room.

In a simultaneous cheer led by the young Corporal the men let go a rousing. "Hell Yeah!"

"I suppose an Army scout can be outranked by a Cavalry Corporal. I reckon you have your troopers, Mr. Buchanan. Corporal, rotate your men, make sure they're well rested and well fed. Mr. Buchanan put some of your men and women to stacking that barricade higher. That may become very important to saving your lives. Corporal, I'd suggest a daily patrol of two men about ten miles out."

Buck rose, shook Mr. Buchanan's hand and walked across the room to the Corporal. "You're in charge son, and the lives of these people depend on you. I will make best speed back to the Fort and have General Sturgis detail ten more troopers. I'll be back in the Fort tonight and suggest they leave right away." He shook the Corporal's hand, winked at the waitress and cook then headed out the door on his way to the livery and Diablo.

Moments later Buck and Diablo galloped past GOOD EATS, waving his Stetson to the troopers standing on the porch hooting and urging him on. From the sawmill settlement back to Fort Laramie was only about thirty miles. Buck reasoned he'd be receiving a military ass chewing by sunset.

His mind though, did wander to the Miller Farm. It is one thing to convince the General to supply troopers to protect a small town and the Fort sawmill. It is quite another to dispatch troopers to protect a single farm family. The best protection he could give the Miller's, and all the other settlers in the area, was to deal with Tall Dog.

Buck's mind and thoughts seemed to be driven along by Diablo's pounding hooves. One thing Buck truly enjoyed was running a great horse mile after mile across the prairie and Diablo was a great horse. He found himself almost wishing he had a renegade to chase. But then his thoughts drifted back to the meeting that morning in Red Cloud's lodge.

He was glad he had several hours alone on horseback to ponder over Soft Cloud, Tall Dog, Tom, and himself. Buck liked that kid Tom a lot. Something about his toughness reminded Buck of himself fifteen years ago. Tough and eager, but with a lot to learn. Well, Tom would have Buck to help him learn. He knew that Tall Dog was going to die. He believed he would need to be the one to kill him. Buck could see that Soft Cloud was a good friend of Tom's and he was not sure how she felt about her father. Buck believed that Tall Dog must surely be killed but Buck was not Sioux nor was Tall Dog his father. He pondered about Tom's horse ranch and how Tom had selected a most perfect location for a ranch. As he sped along with Diablo, he could see pleasant imaginary pictures of Tom's horse ranch. Horses by the dozens, several corrals, a nice new wood board house. Yeah, that could turn into something great. If the kid doesn't go get himself killed by Tall Dog.

****

Tom rode only a few hundred yards from the Sioux village when he turned and went back. At the edge of the village he hopped down and walked in, leading Tom Gray. He was looking for Soft Cloud, and his search was a short one. She had been watching him leave and saw him turn back.

"Tom, my friend, have you more to say?" Soft Cloud held his eyes.

"I would like some dogs."

"Oh ... I thought you might want to see me, for something else."

"No. Buck told me I should have some dogs to help protect my horse ranch. Could I have some dogs?" He tried to understand the twinkle in her eye and the confusion painted on her face. "Your village has many dogs. Are your dogs no good to protect a horse ranch?"

"I'll ask Buffalo Horn to personally select four from our dogs to protect your horse ranch. Buffalo Horn and I can bring them to you tomorrow. Do you feel like talking? Would you like to spend the night here? We could all travel together in the morning. You should eat more."

"I want to go to my ranch. Did you know that Buck called it a horse ranch? I like to say 'my ranch'."

"Well then, Buffalo Horn and I will see you at your ranch tomorrow with four dogs to protect you and your *ranch*. I'll ask Buffalo Horn to select large, strong dogs."

Tom stepped back up on his old friend and paused to wave goodbye. As he rode away at a quick trot, he thought he could hear Soft Cloud giggling at him. Although he wanted to know for sure, he could not look back and he pushed Tom Gray into a lope, that irritating hot feeling filled his cheeks again.

Even though his mind lay heavy with the thought of having to leave again, he enjoyed the ride back to his home. He slowed to a walk to take pleasure in the scenery of the open prairie and the sun on his back while he did his best to think. He liked having Buck as a friend and he liked Soft Cloud, a lot. He understood he must kill Tall Dog. He pondered, would she still be his friend after he killed her father?

What Tom wanted mostly to do was build his horse ranch. His whole life, until a few weeks ago, he had traveled the prairie. His home an old wagon, an old drunken buffalo hunter, and his trusted friend this good horse. He reached, patted his friend on the neck. Now he had a place. A place like he had seen as he traveled with the old hider. He wanted to make this place seem like other places that looked so happy. But first he must kill Tall Dog. "Yes, old friend, I'll finish the corral, and I will dig a ditch for the water, then I'll go kill Tall Dog."

A small herd of mule deer jumped from the brush a short distance ahead of them. Acting quickly, Tom snatched his Henry from the scabbard and neatly dropped two. "Whoa old boy, hides for the floor, one deer for the dogs, and one for me. But you get to carry us all home." Tom dressed the deer, tied a rope to the front legs of both deer hopped back up on the horse and started home at a brisk walk.

"See that up ahead—that's our horse ranch!" he told Tom Gray when the soddy came into view. For a few long moments he sat quiet and surveyed the lay of his place. The little mud cabin sure looked happy now and the new cover on the well made the yard look like a place to rest and think of the future. He had a hard time asking the horse to move on toward the cabin. He enjoyed sitting his horse and studying the place too much. But finally he put heels to the tall horse and walked home.

By early dusk Tom had the mule deer skinned and hides staked out to dry. Over a fire in the yard he had one deer on a spit roasting. The other deer he was cutting and jerking into strips to hang on his newly constructed meat rack. He was feeling quite proud of himself as the evening sun lit the western horizon with a deep red glow that seemed to stretch to the ends of the earth.

He brought a chair out to the porch, and by the light of the fire cleaned and readied his buffalo rifle. Later he cleaned the Henry and the Colt. The red glow on the horizon faded as the moon began to make its appearance. Tonight the moon was only a sliver, but many stars lit the swimming black sky in a way that comforted him.

He dragged his chair to the yard so he could gaze at the moon and the stars. He found them different tonight. Out on the prairie with the buffalo hunter he would often lie on his back and look at the stars and each night compare their positions. He marked how they would move across the sky and how the moon would grow and shrink. He'd made up names for clusters of stars. There was his old friend the broken wagon right above him tonight. Soon he spotted the galloping horse being chased by the running man. But they were different tonight. Tonight they were happy stars, and he watched them from his yard … on his horse ranch.

CHAPTER THIRTY-ONE

Buck stormed into Fort Laramie just after midnight and proceeded directly to General Sturgis' house, tied Diablo to the fence, ran to the porch, and pounded on the door. It took a few moments, but finally from inside he heard, "Who's at the door?"

"Buck here, Sir. Sorry to wake you."

Dressed in his nightshirt, the General opened the wide door and signaled Buck to enter. "Trouble, I suspect."

"All around, General. Most of the settlers are okay, for the moment. But Tall Dog is really stirring things up. We found a village of Cheyenne, fifteen all dead and scalped. And family of six brutally killed, scalped and burned out. From the tracks, there must have been sixteen or twenty renegades."

"Tall Dog?"

"Never laid eyes on him. My guess his main base is still Hooker's camp up in the high country. But it would be impossible to take a large enough force up that bottleneck trail. They'd be picked off one man at a time. The only hope is to catch him out on the prairie."

"We have the troops now. Tomorrow by God, I'll send Lieutenant Harris with fifty men west to scour the plains for this bastard!"

"That'll work to protect the settlers and the settlements. But you won't get close to Tall Dog with fifty men, unless you stumble on him by mistake. What I suggest is to send me out with one trooper, a sharpshooter, a sniper maybe, we take our time and sneak through the prairie. That way we can get close enough and kill the son of a bitch. How about that Private Cole?"

"He's a proven shot, that's for sure. Consider him yours." The General continued to study Buck's face. "What else is eating at you?"

"Well General, ah, left your troopers at the sawmill settlement."

The General's face washed pale, then red. It took a moment for him to compose himself. "I suppose you're going to tell me you made a field decision they needed protection."

"That's exactly what happened! You see, there are twenty families there now. They have a school, a church. A lot has happened in the last eighteen months down there. Most of the men are out logging and dragging logs to the mill all day, the women are left unprotected. Sure, there are always five or six men around, but if Tall Dog rides in there with fifteen, eighteen, or twenty-five renegades, he'll slaughter 'em. I promised Mr. Buchanan I'd request you send ten more troopers and post a guard until this business with Tall Dog is over."

The General stood, unable to hide his shocked expression, or his surprise at Buck's report. "Sounds like you've given me very little choice. I'll see to it that ten troopers and a wagon with ammunition and supplies leave first thing in the morning. Anything else? Or should I be afraid to ask?"

"Got a good cigar?"

"Would you like my commission, too?" He tossed Buck a cigar.

"Nope, just the cigar." Buck turned to leave, then turned back. "You could toss me a couple matches." He didn't wait for the matches; he ran through the front door, sprinted to Diablo and headed for the livery.

Still pondering Tom and Tall Dog, Buck took a long time rubbing down Diablo. His hands made slow, small, deliberate circles on the horse's back, his mind made random circles of thought. A lot had happened in a short span of time, and Buck had quickly become very fond of Tom. He couldn't help but worry about him. Sure he could shoot better than almost anyone Buck had ever seen, but he was still a kid, not around long enough to understand the sneaky side of an evil man. And Tall Dog was evil *and* sneaky. He knew the kid wouldn't listen. The way Buck saw it; it was up to him to get the bastard before Tom got himself in over his head.

He put Diablo in the corral with his roan and black stallion, stood awhile and studied his horses. He had ridden a lot of horses in his life. He even owed his life to some. But these three, they were special. Or was he just getting soft? At any rate, he couldn't stop watching the strawberry roan move about the corral. He had a way of carrying himself that was smoother than anything Buck had ever seen. Like water flowing down a wide, smooth river. "That's it!" Buck yelled to the roan. "I christen you River!"

With a lighter heart and a bounce in his step, Buck strolled to Old Bedlam's porch, grabbed a chair, and assumed his favorite position with his feet on the rail. Rocking back on the chair's rear legs, he lit the General's cigar, blew smoke rings and watched them drift lightly on the soft evening breeze.

****

Several weeks had passed since Buck had had a chance to talk to Lieutenant Harris, and he was happy to find him still in the mess having breakfast the next morning. "Mornin' Lieutenant. How's your beautiful wife?" Buck needled as he sat at the Lieutenant's table.

"My wife is just fine, Buck. And keep in mind she is My Wife!"

"Yeah, that she is. But I can't help but think somebody should rescue her. Maybe that's what the Good Lord put me on this earth for."

"Buck, I don't care how valuable a scout you are, one day. Yeah, one day."

"I hear you left Tall Dog slip through your fingers a couple weeks back but I also heard you gave him pure hell. Story has it you killed every damned one of his renegades that day."

"I sure do wish we could have finished him that day. He's as bad as I have ever seen and he's recruiting more renegades all the time. The General has me taking fifty troopers out today to scour the prairie for him. I'll follow your route, start northwest of here, and pick up Little Bear Creek. I'm considering taking two supply outfits, set up a base camp somewhere along the Walls of Buffalo Ridge and send scouting teams out regularly in all directions until we get this bastard."

"Sounds right. Just don't let that bastard catch you sleeping."

"Don't think I'll get much sleep until we catch him," the Lieutenant mumbled as he left the mess.

Buck moved to the porch where he enjoyed a late morning cup of coffee while he watched the procession of fifty troopers, four supply wagons, a brand new chuck wagon, an ambulance, a pack train, and four Conestogas parade from the Fort. In the lead rode Lieutenant Harris, and to his left his trusted friend, Sergeant Peterson.

It was a wonderful display of United States Cavalry with both Old Glory and Cavalry flags flying high. The horses were well rested and high stepping, the men all dressed in clean new uniforms with swords shining in the bright sunlight and new Henrys tucked in scabbards. The supply wagons had new canvas tops, and newly painted sides and wheels. It was a magnificent procession. A train of fifteen pack mules heavily laden with even more supplies brought up the rear. It took nearly half an hour for the convoy to file through the parade and exit the Fort. Following close behind were the people from Pennsylvania in their Conestoga wagons, bringing along two cows and a bull each.

Buck relaxed sipping his coffee watching until the last wagon drove out of sight, then went back to Old Bedlam where he spent the next hour meticulously cleaning his Henry, Sharps, and Navy Colt. Eventually satisfied with the condition of his weaponry, he arranged and packed his bedroll and saddlebags, making sure he had ample ammunition. He paused at the barracks mirror, making certain his vest, hat, and hair were positioned in a manner acceptable to him. Finally, content with his outward appearance, he strapped on the Colt, gathered his bedroll, saddlebags, and rifles and started for the livery.

"Mornin' Sarge, I need a horse, I'll take the roan out on this expedition." He greeted his old friend.

"Mornin', Buck, nice to see everyone so well groomed this mornin'. You'll find him in the third corral with your other two. All three of those horses are lookin' in fine shape."

"The General didn't get you a new uniform?"

"Oh, I got my new skivvies alright. I'm just not ready to dirty 'em yet. I like to sleep in 'em awhile before I get 'em all torn and grimy you know."

Buck's hands saddled River, but his thoughts drifted to the Miller Farm. "Hey Sarge, I'm going to take a quick run out to the Miller Farm. I'll be back in the morning. Could you get word to Private Cole that I'll be taking him to hunt down that lousy renegade Tall Dog? Tell him to have his new Sharps and Henry cleaned and ready."

"Sure thing, Buck. See you in the mornin'."

Buck made his customary flamboyant exit from the Fort breaking stride only for a second to wave his hat to the beautiful Mrs. Harris standing on her porch. He kept the roan traveling at a brisk lope all morning, his eyes searching the prairie in all directions, on his ever-vigilant search for trouble.

By early afternoon the Miller Farm came into view. From a distance, everything appeared as it should. He could even see the picket fence in front of the house and someone working a plow horse in the large garden on the south side of the buildings.

Buck jumped down at the garden fence. "Howdy, Sam, I see the potato plow is working as it should. I guess we could have fried potatoes for lunch if I was to invite myself."

"Well, if it ain't Buck Hawkins!" Sam stopped the horse and wiped his brow with a dusty, dirty paw leaving a muddy smear across his forehead. "If you came for fried potatoes you came to the right place. We been digging potatoes for three days now and we got enough to fill two wagons. If you came to bring more troubling news about Tall Dog, you can mount up and ride off." Sam offered a hand over the fence in a greeting toward Buck. "Why don't we wander on up to the house and see if the women have any lunch fixed."

"Buck, it's sure good to see you!" Mrs. Miller called from the porch. "Hurry up here and let me have a hug! Come on step lively, dinner's on the table. I was just about to call Sam."

"I just rode forty miles to look at your smiling face, and the whole time I was running that big horse I was thinking two things. I wonder what that beautiful Mrs. Miller ever saw in that rangy old husband of hers, and I bet by the time I get there that table will be heaping with fried potatoes, cooked ham and greens. About eight miles back I could smell the ham cooking."

"Buck, you go on in. I'm gonna throw my horse and yours in the corral so they can water while we eat." Sam took River's reins.

Buck devoured the marvelous odors of their fine cooking through the screen door. "Hannah, I sure hope you're paying close attention to how your mother does this stuff because if you and I ever get married I expect to put on a hundred pounds in two years."

"Well Mr. Hawkins, I can guarantee you two things. One, if we ever got married, you'd have a lot of changing to do, and two, if you ever gained a hundred pounds I'd be looking for a new skinny ex-Army scout."

"Hannah Miller! I thought you were attracted to me because of my wit and charm, not because I looked good in deerskin leggings." Buck protested as he sat and firmly grasped the potato platter.

"Any more news of Tall Dog?" Mr. Miller shot a worried look Buck's way. "Things are nice and quiet around here right now."

"He's been stirring things up west of Fort Laramie and we understand he's building a small army of renegades. Lieutenant Harris set out today with fifty troopers to patrol that area. Tomorrow I'll head out with a sharp shooter. We'll see what we can do."

"It all sounds so exciting to me. I would love to be able to ride that grand horse Diablo across the prairie in search of an evil villain." Hannah whispered, starry eyed.

"Hannah! How foolish you talk!" Mrs. Miller scolded.

"Just think of it mother. All day riding the beautiful prairie on your trusted steed just like knights of old searching for a dragon to slay." Hannah sighed; her head cocked upward, her eyes big as saucers.

"He's a dragon, alright." Buck agreed. "And there's nothing more fun than riding the prairie when it's 115°, or driving rain and sleeping in a wet bedroll. Or falling asleep on your horse and dodging bullets. You bet, Hannah, it is a fairy tale for sure."

"Oh Buck. I'll bet it's not like that at all. Mother, I want to be an Army scout and I want to slay dragons." Hannah held her knife high over her head.

"I guess you'd better get started quickly before Buck slays all the dragons." Mr. Miller slashed the air with his butter knife.

"Stop this, all of you. None of this is funny. This man is dangerous and it's not some silly fairy tale!" Mrs. Miller cast a worried look at Buck.

"You bet it's not funny, and it surely is dangerous. Hannah, I reckon a few good knights would be a handy thing to have around." Buck stuffed half a potato in his mouth.

When the ladies began to clear the table, and Mr. Miller and the men left to finish the work they started before dinner, Buck asked, "You might think this terribly rude of me but I wonder if I could just relax awhile in the parlor and finish my coffee?"

Mrs. Miller set a tray with a small coffee pot, two coffee cups, and some fresh hot cookies on the table in the parlor. Buck reclined in the tall wooden rocking chair gazing out the front window while Chuck and Sam resumed the business of a small frontier farm. From the window Buck watched Sam plow up more potatoes and Mr. Miller drive to the barn with a heaping load of loose hay. He didn't understand the words Mrs. Miller and Hannah spoke in the kitchen, but the sound of their voices soothed him.

****

"Let's break for camp here, and tomorrow morning we'll push onto Little Bear Creek." Lieutenant Harris liked the lay of the land and they had put in a long day already. They'd come upon a fine location for bivouac, bordered on the south by a small stream, so he halted the caravan on a rise, giving the night guards a good field of vision in the event of an attack. Early evening gray light was beginning to settle in.

In short order, campfires burned, sending happy dancing light high into the dark sky, the cook whistled and joked about starving horsemen being underfoot, bedrolls and blankets laid out amidst camp hosted tired troopers relaxing, chatting and playing cards. Horses rested in a rope corral, and the first shift of night patrol was on duty.

After chow Lieutenant Harris sought out Sergeant Peterson, offered him a cigar, and suggested they take a stroll. Their walk took them around the perimeter of the rope corral. "Tomorrow send Corporal Smith and six men out ahead of us to Little Bear Creek. When they find a good location for our permanent camp, tell him to send two men back while the other four begin to make camp preparations. I'll want at least one side of the camp bordered by a vertical wall, a good supply of water, and trees nearby to construct some barricade fortifications."

They stopped where they had a view of the night camp, stood enjoying their cigars and watching the men. Some on their blankets continuing card games, some still working on their evening chow. A few were with the horses tending to nicks and scrapes and addressing the wear and tear normal to a cavalry mount. For a long time they sat together smoking, and each separately planning the details of the coming day. Lieutenant Harris concerned himself with the mission in its entirety. Finding the killers, protecting the settlements, keeping him and his men alive.

Sergeant Peterson was thinking more narrowly. Who he would send with Corporal Smith in the morning, how he could keep the horses in top shape and still cover thirty to fifty miles a day, while keeping the cook in good spirits to keep the men well fed, and other countless, unnoticed but necessary charges of a Lieutenant's Sergeant.

Before long, most of the men had retired to their bedrolls except those assigned to night patrol. The Lieutenant excused himself to pay a visit to the families traveling with them. They too had their mules and cattle in a rope corral with one man on watch. "How are you folks doing?" He greeted the watchman.

"Doing pretty well, thank you." The big man spoke with a thick German accent.

"Meeting up with family, are you?"

"They are not family but we all come from the same county in Pennsylvania and we will homestead here, all together. Our friends have been settled for a year on the Little Bear Creek. We will join them and start a farming community. We plan to grow potatoes, corn, and wheat. We also have these cows for milk. We are aware of the railroad coming through this valley. One day this will be a prosperous valley, and we can make a good life for our families."

"Aren't you afraid you'll lose your scalp before you make this a prosperous valley? We have a lot of trouble with the Indians, renegades and outlaws out here. Settlements get burned out and families get murdered."

"Your General Sturgis warned us of the dangers. But we have plans and dreams. We also have God. You see, Lieutenant, if God sends you on a journey you must go. It matters not the dangers. Tomorrow we will go our own way and leave you to your mission. We must travel more to the south to find our friends. We thank you for the help you have given and wish you luck and success and may God watch over you."

Having no response, Lieutenant Harris grasped the big man's hand in a firm handshake, and bid him "Good-Night."

****

Cookie's singing and happy crackling and popping of his cookfires stirred everyone to consciousness early the next morning. Almost every corner of the camp relished the smell of boiling coffee and fires baking biscuits in the Dutch ovens. "Morning, Cookie." Lieutenant Harris poured himself a cup. "Without you, I fear no patrol could be successful."

"Lieutenant, I agree with you." Cookie saluted and he tipped his coffee cup to the Lieutenant. They watched the four wagons of the German families head away on their own, into the prairie.

"I sure hope God goes with them" was all the Lieutenant could say.

When the men were fed and in their saddles with mules hitched to the wagons, the camp moved out, heading northwest. "Keep your wits with you today, Corporal Smith. See you tonight." Lieutenant Harris shook hands with the departing Corporal and his six troopers. Traveling in a small cluster, not in formation, they galloped from sight while the Lieutenant and his troopers, supply wagons, and pack mules moved at a cavalry walk. In a matter of moments Corporal Smith and his troopers were miles ahead. The terrain moving northwest became more rolling with greater peaks and valleys and more clusters of brush and trees.

"Corporal, plenty of places for them renegades to hide hereabouts, wouldn't you say?" A worried young Private riding alongside Corporal Smith tried to not know the truth of their situation.

"That's for sure, Private. Keep your eyes open, men! Keep your horses moving and stay together." Corporal Smith shouted.

They pushed their horses at a quick trot for a few more hours and when the horses began to tire Corporal Smith called out, "Hold up men, we need to walk the horses. I believe we're more than halfway to Little Bear Creek."

The troopers dismounted and began to travel on foot to rest their winded horses. "Corporal Smith, reckon it's safe to be on foot this far out?"

168

The nervous Private's eyes darted here and there.

"Well, it's not as safe as being in the Fort but we don't get paid to sit in the Fort, and these horses need a rest to catch their wind. We'll walk them to the top of the next rise and mount up." Corporal Smith pointed to the hill still a mile away.

Those were the last words Corporal Smith would ever speak. Every man there heard the swish of the flying arrow and the slap as it plunged into their Corporal's chest … and the sudden gasp from the Corporal as he toppled backwards. In less than an instant the troopers found themselves surrounded in the bottom of the ravine by some twenty renegades, descending upon them shooting arrows and rifles, screeching, howling and screaming loud war-whoops. The Indians galloped their ponies straight for them, closing their circle tight as a hangman's noose.

Caught by total surprise the ambushed patrol could only watch as the renegades stormed them. Their horses screamed in pain and terror and reared high dragging troopers until they all managed to yank their reins from their riders' hands. Three horses fell, fatally wounded, the other four bolted, running away with four rifles and much needed ammunition. Regaining their wits, the men huddled down behind the dead and dying horses firing their rifles or revolvers at the renegades as fast as they could lever shells.

Private Cooper, the youngest of the men, had joined the cavalry only ninety days before. On his 17th birthday. He had his new Henry and it was fully loaded. He wore his Navy Colt and had strapped on two ammunition pouches that very morning. His readiness was a result of his fear of the unknown rather than experience.

The renegades stopped firing long enough to capture the escaping horses. They retreated just out of range but well within sight dancing and taunting the troopers.

"They'll be coming at us again in a few seconds. With our mounts and rifles! Make every shot count, boys. It's only about two to one and they have to come to us," one of the more experienced troopers advised. In seconds the next charge came—a full frontal attack. Arrows and bullets flying thick and heavy but with none finding their mark. Private Cooper fired three rounds and saw three renegades fall from their ponies through the sights of his Henry. "Good shooting Coop!" he heard someone yell.

A bullet slammed into the dirt by his left thigh throwing gravel into the meat of his leg but he barely noticed and continued to work his Henry. Powder smoke filled the ravine, dropping a cloak of near darkness over the terrified men. Renegades continued to circle, hooting, hollering and shooting. Private Cooper leveled his sights on a renegade racing head long at them holding his lance high.

Cooper squeezed the trigger only to hear the heart-stopping click of a firing pin hitting an empty chamber. Without a second's hesitation he yanked his Navy Colt, sprang to his feet and fired two rounds into the charging renegade, sending him tumbling from his horse and thudding to the ground at his feet. But the horse kept charging! With a tremendous leap he cleared the dead horses and desperate troopers. Cooper fell to the ground, rolled on his back, and reloaded his rifle. Within seconds his Henry barked again. "What's going on out there?" Cooper yelled. "Are we hitting anything?" Renegades continued the attack firing and hollering; the gritty smoke grew thicker and darker. It filled the soldiers' lungs, they tasted it in their mouths. It burned their watery eyes.

"Coop, what you got left?" A Private yelled, his voice cracking with panic.

"Don't know." Cooper answered.

"I'm out." The Private shouted. Private Cooper saw the men on either side of him dead, one still clutching his rifle. He tore it from the dead man's hands and threw it to the trooper who was out of ammunition, but before he could make use of his newfound weapon a bullet split his forehead. At the same instant, an arrow found its mark in Cooper's left hand. Without thinking he reached up and snapped the arrow off.

The three remaining troopers pushed the bodies of their dead comrades on top of the dead horses providing them a greater barricade.

****

Lieutenant Harris jerked hard on the reins, his horse reared high on its hind legs. Waving his arm overhead he shouted. "Sergeant Peterson, that's gunfire ahead! Our boys have found trouble! Take men and go to their aid!"

Before the words cleared the Lieutenants lips, Sergeant Peterson and twenty men galloped away at a speed that surprised even the Lieutenant.

"The rest of you surround these wagons and pack train! Teamsters push ahead best speed!" The Lieutenant's voice boomed above the clatter of hurried men, wagons, mules and horses. The column and wagons surged ahead as fast as horses and mules could move and still Sergeant Peterson and his men rode quickly out of sight.

Rapid gunfire rained, growing louder with every stride of the Sergeant's horse, giving him hope the boys were holding on. They kicked their mounts without mercy demanding every ounce of speed from the tough horses.

They rode at a full run, rifles drawn, ready to engage and raced over the summit, slamming head long into chocking smoke lying heavy as dense fog. Racing pell-mell into the ravine they saw the trapped men and assessed their hopeless position.

"BUGLER SOUND CHARGE! AND KEEP IT UP 'TIL THIS IS OVER!" Sergeant Peterson shouted.

The Bugler's crisp notes rang high, loud and clear above the rapid fire of Henrys and Colts. Twenty-one men galloped down the ravine at top speed into the chaos, and the renegades at the first sign of the charging cavalry turned and began to flee.

"Pursue, gentlemen, pursue!"

The charging soldiers reached the bottom of the ravine and lunged up the incline, closing rapidly on the remaining renegades. The pursuit was brief, and Sergeant Peterson turned his troops and raced back to assist the men at the bottom of the ravine.

They found a horrible mess. Four troopers lay dead and all three survivors were wounded, surrounded by bodies of dead renegades, dead horses and their fallen comrades. The air was dark with burned powder and filled with the groaning of wounded men and horses.

"Someone kill the wounded horses," ordered Sergeant Peterson. "Whoever still has a fresh mount, get to the Lieutenant, tell him it's all over here and he can spare his animals."

CHAPTER THIRTY-TWO

Tom woke eager for morning at the first inkling of sunlight. Not yet light enough to see far, he strained out the window for a glimpse of Soft Cloud, but no rider's silhouette showed on the horizon.

Kneeling by the fireplace, warming deer meat and himself, Tom was unable to keep his thoughts from wandering to pictures in his mind of a corral full of wild horses. He could see mustangs shining in the sunlight. Mustangs of all colors … chestnuts, bays, roans, paints. Maybe even a buckskin and a few grays. But mostly he pictured a corral full of horses ready to be worked and sold. Maybe one day people would come to his ranch. Tom's ranch. He liked that thought.

Finished with breakfast and his daydream, Tom left the soddy for another day's work on the corral. Ambling merrily to the corral area he spied Big Fella and Tom Gray grazing by the stream never far from the buildings. They were good horses. The mules lay stretched out in the sun. That's the funny thing about mules, he thought—they never wasted energy.

He worked without a break until fifty holes waited for posts. The sun hung high overhead and the sky shimmered a sparkling, never-ending blue. Cool fall morning air had long since given way to a hot day, and the hard work of setting posts went on, and on. Steadily dropping a post in the hole, tamping the dirt, moving to the next one, dropping another post in another hole and tamping the dirt. One after the other. Tom turned his head and counted. He'd set twenty posts firm, straight, and solid. Deciding he had earned a break, he went to the stream, splashed water on his face, then lay down and sucked up water until his thirst was done. Big Fella and Tom Gray came by to make sure the water he drank was the same as theirs. "You two are sure enough something." He gave them each a firm smack on the neck.

Something over the withers of Big Fella caught his eye. At first it startled him, then he saw Soft Cloud, Buffalo Horn, and four big dogs. He raced to the soddy with all the excitement of a young child and they reached the porch together.

Soft Cloud couldn't hide her enthusiasm as she surveyed the improvements to the place. "Tom you must have worked night and day!"

"Not much else to do. Been anxious to see you though." Tom was not able to hide his excitement either. He nearly gave her a hug but Buffalo Horn slid from his horse and with a demonstrative show of pride handed him a braided leather lead rope attached to the dogs. While he said no words, his smile made it plain he was happy to present Tom with the gift.

"Thank you!" Tom blurted as he accepted the leather rope.

"Buffalo Horn claims they are the four smartest dogs in our village and he is certain they will serve you well and keep you safe," Soft Cloud beamed.

Tom dropped to his knees hugging and patting them as they jumped play attacked him. He leaped up and ran to the meat rack where large strips of jerked mule deer hung drying. Curiously, the dogs knew to follow him, although they did so in a ruckus and rowdy manner, leaping over each other snarling and snapping. They just about devoured him as well as the deer meat, jumping on him and knocking him to the ground. He lay laughing and wrestling with the big dogs, feeling like a little boy without a care in the world. Soft Cloud joined in the silliness, giggling, laughing and tackling dogs and man alike. Buffalo Horn, being the son of a Sioux Chief, could not afford the luxury of being amused by such childish behavior. He stood, arms folded, looking very much like a cigar store wooden Indian, which only made Soft Cloud and Tom more giddy.

This, of course, fed more excitement to the dogs, who barked louder, wrestled rougher, and further embarrassed Buffalo Horn. As the dogs began to wear Tom and Soft Cloud down, and the craziness began to wane, finally Tom picked himself up and led Soft Cloud to the porch, the dogs following close behind. He removed the leather ropes binding the four dogs, gathered a pile of deer bones and threw them in the yard. The dogs understood and lay there ferociously gnawing on the bones, each defending their own with flashing bright teeth and growls.

"Well Tom, I believe your dogs have accepted you already." Soft Cloud offered her inviting smile.

"Seems they did, but what about Buffalo Horn?" Tom remained close to another outbreak of laughter.

As if to answer that question himself, Buffalo Horn walked to Tom, firmly grasped his hand and arm and shook it. Tom felt the power in the grip, and recognized the respect in Buffalo Horn's eyes. Tom motioned they step inside, eager to show off more of his handiwork. He had worked hard installing cedar window frames and shudders that closed snuggly on each. And while there were no glass panes, with the shutters open the windows allowed plenty of light in for the interior. They stood a moment feeling the cheeriness of the room. Tom sensed the feeling of friendship among them.

"Buffalo Horn would like to know your plans for Tall Dog." Soft Cloud changed the mood in an instant.

"I have a plan." Tom felt reluctant to discuss the matter with Soft Cloud, certain that she must be uncomfortable because Tall Dog is her father and Buffalo Horn's brother. "I will finish my large corral, then ..." Tom found himself unable to finish and turned away to hide his saddened eyes.

"Tom, what is your second name?" Soft Cloud broke the tension that hung heavy in the air.

"What? ... Why would you ask me that?"

"My mother says white people always have a second name. She told me her white name is Rebecca Wilson, and I have been wondering about yours."

"I don't know my name. I was always just, boy. Even when I was small and lived with the family in Ogallala I was boy. I hated that. I didn't want to be called boy anymore. The day in your village when your mother asked my name, I said Tom. That's the name of my horse. He was always my good friend. So I said Tom."

"I like the name Tom." With her soft and tender smile, she took his hands and looked into his eyes. "I like the man Tom too. I even like your horse named Tom."

Awkwardness swept over Tom, stopping his breath, so he went out to the dogs. It took a moment for Soft Cloud and Buffalo Horn to follow. "Buffalo Horn said when you are ready he will bring Sioux braves to help you gather your first horses."

The offer left Tom without words, for a while he simply stared at Soft Cloud. When he recovered he surprised himself with the happiness in his voice. "You know what? I'll count on that! I intend to gather twenty or thirty horses and turn them into saddle stock. Maybe I'll sell horses to the Sioux." Tom's heart lightened and he shot a grin to Buffalo Horn.

Soft Cloud told Buffalo Horn, and at long last he had reason to let go a hearty laugh. He spoke to Soft Cloud and even mixed in a little English.

"He said if you can teach your ponies to carry him to a place where there are no whites he will buy them all from you. He also said we must leave now, and he hopes his dogs protect you, and keep you safe."

Tom pretended to busy himself with the dogs as Soft Cloud and Buffalo Horn rode away. A longer visit would have suited him better but he was happy to have these fine dogs, and his soddy, barn, and corral were beginning to feel like home. To him it already felt like a horse ranch. After all didn't he have a herd of horses running on land he claimed as his own?

The dogs occupied themselves all day exploring their new territory, but they never strayed from Tom's sight. Big Fella and Tom Gray both accepted the dog's playful antics as they darted around them. But the dogs learned right away that mules don't play. And they have fast teeth and hooves! Finishing by moonlight, Tom planted the last post for the big corral, gathered his tools, called the dogs, and headed for the soddy.

****

By noon, Buck and Private Cole trotted from Fort Laramie, headed for the foothills. Buck rode his black stallion and ponied Diablo, who was a convenient pack horse as well as an extra mount. Both men traveled armed with Colts, Henry rifles, and the latest model Sharps long rifle, nicknamed "Big Fifty" by men of the plains. A fifty-two caliber percussion rifle, accurate to a thousand yards, but in the hands of marksmen like these two, hits of over twice that distance were not uncommon. "Private, we'll ride on for four or five hours, give the horses a break, and then continue 'til we get to those foothills. Be best to make camp in some sort of sheltered area."

"Do you think we'll get to see this fella Tall Dog? I hear he's hard to find, and maybe even harder to kill."

"That's our plan, Private. But the only time I was in range of the son of a bitch he shot my horse out from under me and if it hadn't been for that kid, Tom, I believe he would have killed me that day. If we watch each other's back, take our time and snoop around, we'll catch up with him. Tall Dog is itching for a fight. He'll be on the prairie fixin' to terrorize settlers. We'll get him alright. Yes sir, we'll get him."

****

Tall Dog lounged in the saloon drinking whiskey all day. When he got the news that twenty more of his renegades had been killed by the Lieutenant, he shot the man who told him. The saloon was only half full, and no one sat at a table near Tall Dog. Finally, a grizzly of a man left the card game he was playing and sat across from Tall Dog. "What the hell do you want, Sidewinder?"

"Got news you might want to hear. I know where them troopers is campin'. They sent about fifty troopers to catch you. The Army intends to hang you. But I can get you to their camp."

Tall Dog grabbed another shot glass, filled it and slid it across the table top, spilling most of it, to Sidewinder. "I'm listenin'." The big Sioux warrior had always liked Sidewinder, and Sidewinder always liked Tall Dog. They were two of a kind. One an Indian outcast, the other a half-breed killer of anything Tall Dog thought should die.

"They're campin' about forty miles south of here on Little Bear Creek. It's easy to find. They ain't trying to hide or nothin'. Fact is they're building a small fort."

Tall Dog gulped down a slug of whiskey, pulled his revolver, laid it on the table, and studied it. It was as if it was the most important thing in the world to him at that moment. Then he shifted his bloodshot eyes to Sidewinder. "I want to go kill U.S. Army troopers. This time we fight my fight. This time we fight like proud Sioux and Cheyenne. This time, I will be unbeaten. They will send word to all the forts to bring all the U.S. Army troopers because they cannot kill this man they call Tall Dog." Tall Dog looked around the saloon at the men playing cards and drinking whiskey. There were maybe a dozen men there. He knew he had at least seventy-five braves in the camptown. "You go, Sidewinder. Spread the word we leave now. We make our way to the place on Little Bear Creek where the U.S. Army is camping. We will fight a great Sioux fight! Go now and tell them!" Tall Dog stood holding his whiskey bottle, slapped Sidewinder on the back, and swaggered out the tent door and into one of the small tents in the rear.

Sidewinder told the braves of the plan in the rear of the saloon, raising a great "Hurrah." These men were eager for a fight. They downed several drinks more, and boasted wildly about how they would kill the Army troopers and how they would have their scalps, rifles and horses. This time would be different. This time they would be successful and they would kill this Lieutenant and all his men. Then they would drive all the white settlers from the prairie ... or kill them all!

****

Tom worked the morning preparing a wagon for travel. After many long hours of pondering how to proceed after Tall Dog, he had decided the best way to travel the prairie unnoticed and unquestioned was to go as a hider. He carefully packed ammunition under the seat of the wagon, made a poncho from one of the dried antelope hides and strapped the .44 to his waist, hidden under his poncho.

His Henry he mounted on the wagon seat in a saddle scabbard and the Sharps buffalo rifle hung in a specially constructed rifle rack by his right knee. The rear of the wagon he loaded with full water skins, dried antelope meat, bones for the dogs, his skinning knives, a chair and the rest of his hides. The nights were growing colder now as fall approached, and the hides might come in handy. The white buffalo hide Tom packed snugly under the seat.

The paired mules stood ready in the harness and Big Fella he tied to the loaded wagon's tailboard. The tall buckskin had more speed and staying power than the older Tom Gray. If he had to outrun any of Tall Dog's renegades, he was sure not many war ponies had enough stuff to catch his buckskin. They left the ranch at a slow peaceful walk; Tom driving the wagon, Big Fella walking behind, and four eager dogs barking and bounding along like puppies.

He set out northwest in a direction that would not get him to the foothills too quickly, offering time on the open prairie. After poking along for half the morning, Tom stopped the mules. "Whoa up, hold on mules." Tom stood on the wagon seat and pointed. "Look over there." He told the dogs. "That's our herd." He sat down and admired the wild horses. It was a good band, about twelve or fifteen by Tom's count, they were moving and quite a distance away. "I got a job to do now, but we'll be talkin' later." He yelled their way. "Okay mules, walk up."

Plodding on till moonlight, Tom never stopped the wagon again until he fell asleep and the mules drug the wagon wheels over a deep gully nearly dumping him from the wagon. "You're right, this is as good a spot as any for camp." He decided, too sleepy to think much about driving the mules. More asleep than awake he tended the horses, mules and dogs, stretched out on a blanket to watch the stars fill the sky and fell asleep.

Jolted awake at daybreak by dogs barking and snarling, Tom thought how stupid he had been to fall asleep with the rifles on the wagon. His hand shot to his waist as he rolled from the blanket, and before he stopped, held his revolver in his hand.

By the wagon an old Indian squaw sat a ribby pony with a travois tied behind, stacked with hides, clay bottles, and things Tom couldn't see. An ancient brave stood beside her. His face dark and deeply wrinkled. A blanket draped over his shoulders leaving bony arms uncovered. Looking past them to the north, Tom saw three more ponies carrying old Indian women and dragging travois, several more old men walked slump-shouldered behind. They weren't Sioux or Cheyenne, most likely Crow. Tom knew the Sioux had driven the Crow west from these plains just two seasons ago. It was in the Crow battles that Red Cloud had won the favor of all Sioux.

Tom was not sure what these old Indians were doing wandering the prairie, but he could see they were hungry. With as much sign as he knew, he told them to sit while he went hunting and he would feed them. They seemed to understand, and the little band of hungry old weathered Indians gathered around his camp and sat by the fire pit.

With Big Fella saddled, he grabbed the Henry, stepped up and rode from camp. He hoped they wouldn't eat his mules before he got back. The dogs he left behind, not sure if four dogs would let him get close enough to anything he saw to get a shot.

Tom couldn't believe his luck, twenty minutes from camp he found a herd of mule deer wading in a wide stream in the shade of a patch of willows. Maybe their Great Spirit was watching and wanted to help Tom feed them. He flipped the reins to the ground and jumped from Big Fella, snatching his rifle on the way.

The mule deer saw him, one snorted and the herd started to back up nervously. He had to take his shot now or lose them. Standing straight and tall, he aimed at the closest and fired two fast shots, sighted in on the next, and shot two more times. The herd bolted from the water, but Tom had two deer for the hungry souls in his camp.

He was happy to see his dogs and mules had survived his absence, and the old Indians had even started a fire. They greeted him with happy looks and a lot of chatter-filled signs. Tom did his best to understand and left them with the deer. As he drove away every Crow in the camp stood and waved. The old women shouted the shrill cry of a loud good-bye.

****

Under the cover of darkness Tall Dog, Sidewinder, and sixty-five renegades and outlaws left the camptown and started the steep descent from the high country toward Little Bear Creek. They rode single file down narrow rocky trails, slowly and cautiously, allowing their horses to pick their way. Every man was well armed and each carried a good supply of ammunition, whether that ammunition was arrows, bullets, or powder and ball. Tall Dog, this time, was going to fight his fight his way. This was not going to be a battle planned by Hooker. Tall Dog needed to avenge the deaths of his men and most certainly the death of his son who died at the hands of the Lieutenant. Since the battle at Bozeman Trail junction Tall Dog thought of nothing else except killing U.S. Army troopers and killing the Lieutenant. The Pretty Soldier. He would hang his hair proudly from his Henry.

They rode down the sharp decline for several hours. Gradually the terrain began to change as they left the high country and entered the rolling foothills, still traveling by the dark of night, silently making their way along the banks of Little Bear Creek. Although still miles from the cavalry camp, the renegades saw the campfires glowing in the dark night.

The first glimpses of daylight found Tall Dog and his renegades camped on the other side of Little Bear Creek safely out of sight, hidden by dense growth and sloping terrain. "No man speaks today. We will make no sound. Tonight as the U.S. Army sleeps we will cross the Little Bear and we will kill them."

****

The first troopers crawling from their bedrolls found Cookie tending a roaring fire preparing hot biscuits, bacon, and coffee. "It sure is a pleasure having you along, Cookie." Lieutenant Harris poured himself a steaming cup.

"Just doing my job, Lieutenant." Cookie piled the Lieutenant's plate high with bacon and biscuits.

The Lieutenant inspected the camp, making mental notes of the inadequacies of their position. The vertical wall to their north extending all the way to Little Bear Creek gave them a position of superiority on their north flank. Little Bear Creek concerned him. The creek ran wide, shallow and slow for most of their western position. Checking the barricade the men had erected all along the east side of the camp proved it to be solid. He doubted renegades would scale down the sheer wall or climb over the barricade. Scrub brush and timber and thicket were the only protection offered at the southern end of camp. Somewhat satisfied with their position, he approached Sergeant Peterson. "Take twenty men and head south. Check the first two settlements along Little Bear Creek. Spend the night there and in the morning continue south. I'll stay here improving the fortifications to our south. Tomorrow I'll take ten men and visit the settlements to our north. We'll meet back here in two days. Should you find it necessary to leave troops behind at either of the settlements, you have my authority."

Immediately following breakfast, Sergeant Peterson and twenty men left camp traveling south, leaving the Lieutenant and thirty troopers at the base camp, and Tall Dog less than half a mile away with over sixty renegades anxious for a fight.

****

Tom and his dogs traveled across the prairie at a slow walk covering only a few miles an hour but making steady progress toward the foothills. By late morning he'd entered the outer edges of timber growth. He stopped to investigate what appeared to be someone walking their horse. Snatching his rifle from its rack and checking to be sure it was loaded, Tom laid the Sharps across his lap, cocked with his finger by the trigger. As if ordered to, the dogs all laid down, two on either side of the wagon. As the figures drew nearer, Tom could see there were two walkers and three horses, and one of those walkers was Buck.

"Yo Buck! It's Tom." He uncocked his rifle.

"Tom, you son of a gun, that's a good looking outfit you got there. What are you up to? Looks to me like you might be out hunting buffalo."

"Hunting alright but not buffalo." Tom jumped from the wagon, happy to see his friend.

"How's that horse ranch coming? You ought to have made some mighty good progress by now." The dogs gathered around Buck growling and showing their teeth the moment Buck moved too close to Tom. "Mind telling these guys we're friends?"

"Aw, they're all right." Tom dropped to his knees ruffled and hugged the dogs.

"Well I guess you'll have safe traveling with these fellas keeping an eye on you. I don't reckon even Tall Dog would mess with your outfit." Buck gave Tom a hard look. "That's why the Private and I are out here. I aim to kill him."

"Well I guess we can travel together then 'cause I aim to kill him too."

Buck stepped back, cast a glance at the Private, then back at Tom. "Now Tom, we have already discussed this. Tall Dog kills ten men at a time by himself. Why he'll cut you to pieces and not even work up a sweat. Why don't you just get your wagon on back to the ranch and when I'm done with this business I'll stop by for a visit."

Tom felt anger swell in his chest at Buck's low opinion of him, raised his buffalo rifle, sighted out onto the prairie and fired a round. Buck and the Private stared in amazement as about two hundred fifty yards out a mule deer fell to its knees. "He's gonna have to get closer than that mule deer to do it. Why don't you send the Private out there to drag that deer in and for supper, tonight we'll have roast deer. The dogs are hungry anyway."

"Doggone Tom, that's just plain showin' off! It is damn good shooting though. Private go ahead and get that deer." Buck moved to the back of the wagon, tied his horses, and motioned for Tom to join him. "What was your plan? Where were you heading?"

"I figured to ride the prairie a bit, lookin' for sign. I know Tall Dog wanders around the area near Little Bear Creek and I figured to do a little hidin'. I was thinking that way, I might be able to get close to him 'cause he never made any fuss about lone hiders. Say that's a fine black stallion you got there. Yes sir, you sure can pick 'em. Try not to get him shot though, okay?" He teased, remembering the day he saved Buck's life.

The young Private dragged the mule deer to the side of the wagon. "Great shot Tom, right through the shoulder into the heart from over two hundred yards. Was that a '65 Sharps?"

"It's the newest Sharps rifle, come out this year. I liberated it from a dead hider."

"Tom, meet Private Cole and don't let him fool you. He's a hell of a shot too. That's why I invited him and his new Sharps along on this adventure." Buck said. "Let's throw this deer on the wagon and get on down the trail and find a cozy place to camp. It's a little early to settle in but I could do with a visit, some deer meat, and I have plenty of coffee beans and a government-issue coffee grinder!" Tom and Buck climbed in the wagon, Private Cole rode alongside.

Tom stopped the team a few hours later under a dozen tall cottonwoods and aspens where the trail widened and it was just a short walk to Little Bear Creek. Working together, in no time the horses and mules relaxed in a rope corral, a fire crackled, and the dogs dined on deer leg. Tom fetched his chair from the wagon, made a comfortable seat with one of the antelope skins and settled in at the end of the spit so he could rotate the mule deer over the fire. "Tom, I'm not sure I remember too many hiders bringing furniture along." Buck teased.

"I reckon I'm not your ordinary hider."

Buck studied the young man, shook his head and admitted, "No Tom, that you're not!"

CHAPTER THIRTY-THREE

Tall Dog occupied himself for the rest of the day watching the activities in the troopers' camp. He stood amused at the work done by the troopers fortifying the two barricades; they would work in his favor. The troopers were blocking themselves in. What he needed and wanted to do began to take shape in his mind as he studied the movements of the troopers.

At nightfall Tall Dog sent fifteen men to move south along Little Bear Creek for a distance, and then cross the creek with orders to conceal themselves in positions that would prevent the troopers from escaping to the south.

He sent fifteen of his braves most accurate with a rifle to the top of the vertical wall. They would begin their attack by each selecting a sleeping trooper in their bedroll, and firing together. This would reduce the troopers' strength by half with their first strike. Knowing the Lieutenant would have guards on top of the sheer bank, Tall Dog gave orders for his men to kill them first with their bows, and to make no sound.

Tall Dog considered the manmade barricade to the east an obstacle to the troopers' escape and was confident his men atop the sheer bank could neatly pick off any white soldier trying to escape over them. Twenty more renegades, including his friend Sidewinder, waited with him in his camp. When the time was right, before the moon was high, Tall Dog, Sidewinder, and the rest would wade silently across Little Bear Creek and conceal themselves just beneath the grassy creek bank.

Impatiently Tall Dog waited for signals from his men letting him know they were all in position. They were to strike one flint spark shielded so it would only be visible to him on the far side of Little Bear Creek. He busied himself by watching the troopers, smiling as they tied their horses to picket lines to the south of the camp directly in front of his well-hidden braves. Tall Dog's enemy, the Lieutenant, was sitting comfortably by the main campfire involved in conversation with several of his troopers.

A flicker, faint as a night bug, caught Tall Dog's eye from atop the vertical wall. He turned his attention to the position south of camp waiting for that signal. Almost immediately a quick, tiny spark flashed in the trees. He gathered his men and they slipped silently into Little Bear Creek. On their stomachs, with only their rifles and faces above water and without making even a ripple, they crossed in the cold water to hide under its grassy bank.

The Lieutenant and the four troopers sat by the large campfire, obviously involved in very important talk for they were completely unaware of the coming engagement. It had been detailed by Tall Dog that he would initiate the attack by firing first from the stream bank and hopefully his first round would kill the Lieutenant.

At Tall Dog's silent signal, two Sioux braves shot the two troopers who had been positioned at the top of the creek bank. With arrows through their hearts they fell to the ground barely letting go startled grunts.

Tall Dog raised his eyes and rifle barrel above the stream bank, Lieutenant Harris looked directly at him. He threw his coffee cup into the fire and shouted "WE ARE UNDER ATTACK!" Tall Dog's round slammed into his stomach knocking him back from the fire. Sidewinder and the others under the bank fired their rifles with deadly accuracy at the four troopers who had joined the Lieutenant by the fire. Ripped apart by rounds from fifteen rifles, they joined him in death.

Troopers leapt from their bedrolls, abandoned their small fires, raced for their rifles, and tried to take positions of defense. Hopelessness could not describe their situation. Tall Dog liked his place on the stream bank and never rose to his feet but fired round after round from his Henry at the confused and panicked troopers until it was empty. Waves of bullets slammed into the camp from atop the vertical wall. The firing was so fast and accurate, many of the troopers never woke and died in their bedrolls completely unaware of the mayhem. A few troopers made it to the barricade on the east wall, and just as Tall Dog had planned, it slowed their escape and they were cut down by fire of the renegades atop the sheer bank.

Several troopers made it as far as the cook's wagon and from beneath it they fired blindly into the dark. Their only targets the flashes from the Henrys firing at them. Their stand was short lived and soon their rifles lay silent. Cookie never made it from the chuck wagon as bullets from atop the vertical wall tore through the wagon canvas.

The entire attack lasted less than ten minutes and when the rifle fire ceased, the silence was broken only by the groans of men not quite dead. The raid had been so efficient the horses never broke free of their picket line. Tall Dog, Sidewinder, and the group from the creek bank were the first to come into the camp. "Every U.S. Army white dog must be scalped. You may keep the scalps. Load the weapons and ammunitions onto the wagons and gather the horses, mules, and supplies. Take the clothes from their bodies. We will leave the U.S. Army white dogs naked. We will take all they had."

Tall Dog, satisfied that vengeance had been his, went to examine the loaded wagons. "Hitch the teams to these wagons. Gather the horses and pack mules and take these things up to our camp." From the picket line he chose a tall strong horse, saddled with a McClellan saddle, and rode away alone.

****

Tom's small fire greeted Buck and Private Cole as they poked their heads from their bedrolls. "Holy cow, it sure is getting cool at night, isn't it boys?" Buck grinned, taking in a long deep breath of the fresh morning air.

"I reckon it won't be long now till these plains aren't fit to travel for a few months." Private Cole said.

Since Tom had the coffee available, he cooked some. In all that had happened to him in the last month or so, he had forgotten how much he enjoyed coffee. One thing for sure, the soddy would have a winter supply of coffee before the snows moved in and he had the money it would take. The money he found on all three hiders' wagons totaled nearly twelve hundred dollars in gold and silver coins.

"So what are your plans for today, Tom?" Buck snared a cup of steaming coffee.

"Well, either I'll throw in with you two or I'll strike out on my own. Either way, I promised Buffalo Horn I would kill Tall Dog. And that's what I'll do."

"You're a great shot, and maybe even a quick thinker, but you don't know what you're up against. Tall Dog is a warrior like nothing I've ever seen. He can slip about almost invisible. He's been known to kill ten, maybe fifteen, troopers single-handedly and slip away." Buck pleaded, as he accepted his first cup of coffee. "But if you are dead set on chasing after him I'd just as soon you threw in with us."

"I will, then." Tom said, not entirely able to hide his frustration with his friend.

They hitched the mules, loaded up and the small menagerie headed down the trail. Three men, four dogs, four horses, and two mules. Cole tied his horse to the wagon with Tom's buckskin and rode in the wagon.

"We're going to have to make a change of plans. This outfit is never gonna sneak up on anything," Buck said. "I'll take ol' Diablo and my black and head down the trail and wander about a bit. I'll be able to find you fellas anytime I want and be back for supper." He sped away.

Tom and Cole continued on their way across the prairie, their eyes searching for any sign of renegades and careful to stay within a couple of miles of Little Bear Creek. They were nearing an area of settlements and Tom figured if they stuck to the open prairie between the settlements, perhaps Tall Dog would see them and come to investigate, or maybe Tom would see Tall Dog first. Either way suited Tom. He was glad Private Cole seemed to enjoy not talking and was content to simply enjoy the slow ride.

****

A few hours after leaving the wagon, Buck saw a farm on the far side of Little Bear Creek. From a distance all looked fine, but his duty mandated he check with the settlers. The stream ran deep here and Buck held his legs on Diablo's neck to keep his leggings and moccasin boots out of the water. As Diablo and the black splashed up the far bank two young girls picking beans in the garden saw him.

"Mama! Mama! There is a man on a big black-and-white horse coming!" They dashed headlong for the house. Buck rode past a sod structure he guessed to be their barn and stopped in front of a nicely built log house, surrounded by a rough split log fence. He tied Diablo and the black to a wagon and was about to walk toward the house when he was greeted by a solid looking man wearing a full beard coming out of the sod barn, holding a double barreled shotgun on him. "Who are you and what do you want?"

"My name is Buck Hawkins. I'm a scout for the Army out of Fort Laramie and I'm just stopping by to make sure you folks are alright."

The bearded man walked a little closer to Buck and kept the shotgun leveled at Buck's midsection. "Why would the Army send a scout dressed like an Indian, ridin' an Indian paint horse, to check on a farmer way off out here? Why the two horses? You steal the black?" His eyes studied Buck.

"Well, that's sure enough the truth Mister, and up until a little while ago I had a fellow traveler with me. Private Cole, he's dressed like an Army private, and both these fine horses are cavalry mounts."

The gun stayed aimed at Buck's middle as the settler moved even closer. "I still don't trust you. My way of thinking is these are mighty fine animals to be government stock. Got any papers on you, says who you are?"

"No, no I haven't, you'll just have to take my word I'm an Army scout, I've been an Army scout for the past couple months now since the war. If you'll take a look on their flanks you'll find the government brand. But I agree; they are too good to be cavalry mounts so I don't intend to give them back." Buck watched for the bearded man to crack a smile, he didn't. "As I said, General Sturgis at Fort Laramie sent Private Cole and me out looking for that murderous renegade Tall Dog."

"You always travel with two horses?" The farmer kept one eye and the shotgun on Buck while inspecting the brands.

Buck actually enjoyed the inquisitive banter from the tough fellow, and tossed his famous bright smile to the girls standing on the porch with their mother. "Only when I need to cover a lot of country. So you folks are alright? You haven't had any trouble with the renegades?"

"Not so far. Heard stories though. I heard about that Tall Dog. I just pray we never get to meet him. We heard he burns folks." The settler began warming up to Buck and dropped his gun to his side.

"Let's not scare the girls." Called the mother from the farmhouse porch, "Why don't you come in for a piece of blackberry pie? The girls picked the berries just yesterday."

"I'll sure have a piece of blackberry pie. I believe it must be two weeks since I had a piece of blackberry pie. That was over at the Miller Farm, about forty miles east of Fort Laramie; or about a hundred miles from here."

"We met the Millers. We met them one time at Fort Laramie. We were there for winter supplies last year. Nice folks. German too," the mister said.

"I believe they had a daughter. We're the Schneck's. I am Sarah, my husband, Frank, and these are our girls, Beth and Mary. Won't you have a seat at the table Mr. Hawkins, the girls and I will cut the pie? It is just a wonderful thing to have a guest to share it with."

They've built quite a good-looking house, he thought as he glanced around the large kitchen. Must have taken one wagon just to haul the cookstove and the two panel stoves. The table and chairs had the look of being homemade by the farmer but he must have a horse-powered sawmill to cut the planks that way. "Mr. Schneck, I didn't see any stock. Where are your horses or cows?"

"They're roaming not too far from here. We have two cows, one bull, and eight good mules. We moved west with two full Conestogas, and I'm proud to say we lost not a single head of livestock on the four-month trip. Not even a chicken! And each of the cows had calves this spring so we've got milk and a couple of heifers. We spent most of this year building the house and barn. We got one of those sod plows at the Fort last year and I brought my saw along from Pennsylvania. This year I was able to get about twenty-five acres of corn planted. We've been busy these past three years. We are hoping to have enough corn to sell at the Fort to buy winter supplies."

"How do you keep the deer and buffalo out of your cornfield?" Buck didn't mind talking with a mouthful of delicious blackberry pie.

"Daddy shoots them," Mary giggled.

"Well, I reckon that's one way for sure. Now, seriously folks, I want you to take care to always stay together until we get this renegade mess cleared up. You settlers are in danger. If you should see someone coming that looks like trouble, run out of here. You won't be safe at the buildings. Maybe your cornfield would be a good hiding place."

"How likely is it that we would have trouble with renegades way out here?" Mrs. Schneck's face broadcasted her fear. "We haven't seen another person in over six months. But we do have friends from Pennsylvania coming to homestead with us, four families from Lancaster County. They should be here any time now."

"Well how about that! I met them a couple of days ago at the Fort. They left before I did so you can expect them any time now. They have some fine wagons. Those Conestogas sure look stout. They have some good stock, too. I have no doubt you folks will have the start of a fine community here by the sound of it. The Army will take care of those renegades. You folks get your crops ready to ship when the railroad starts running. With five families here, there should be plenty to ship out."

"Well, you've been so kind to travel all this way just to check on us. We thank you and we do hope to build a community here and have friends nearby. We liked this spot the moment we saw it and Mr. Schneck says the ground is very fertile here." Mrs. Schneck beamed toward her husband.

"Would you like to see our cornfield, Buck? It's standing nearly five feet tall and I expect an ear from every stalk," Mr. Schneck bragged.

"I need to get back on my horse and keep moving. Sure am pleased to have met you and maybe I'll see you at the Fort one day."

Buck walked flanked by Beth and Mary to Diablo who, with the black, had wandered just a few feet and stood grazing in the shade. "He is just simply beautiful!" Mary exclaimed as she stroked Diablo on the neck.

"Why thank you, Mary, and you and your sister are beautiful too." Buck stepped up, grabbed the black's rope, and cantered to the stream. The girls did their best to run along but soon Buck, Diablo and the black were leaving the stream on the other side and cantering out of sight as the girls waved good-bye.

CHAPTER THIRTY-FOUR

The mules pulled the heavy wagon from the sheltering woods early in the morning onto rolling prairie. Steep inclines and deep ravines made the going slow, but the sturdy steeds plodded along with hardly a care. Cole slept in the back on the soft skins. Tom pulled hard on the brake to help the mules hold back the wagon as they skidded toward the bottom of a deep ravine.

Tom hoped the brake would be enough to hold the wagon off the mules' heels but the wheels slid on the tall dry grass. The mules held true and filled their harnesses with their rumps, but the decline was too much and the wagon continued to gain speed as the wheels skidded faster and the wagon began to jackknife.

Fearing the wagon would turn over, he yelled with all his voice kicking the mules into a flat run, hoping they could out run the sliding wagon. He released the brake and tapped the mules as they careened down the hill, outrunning the wagon and gaining control. Tom continued yelling as the mules started up the next steep hill. A very bewildered Cole hung onto the rear of the seat trying desperately not to bounce from the wagon.

Leaning hard into their collars, they started the steep climb up the other side. All at once the dogs shot by them barking and snarling. Tom dropped the reins and grabbed his Henry; Cole bolted upright and snatched his Sharps. They were both ready with their rifles when the mules lurched over the crest.

Clearing the summit, they stared shocked at what lay before them. For miles in each direction the rolling prairie was painted dark brown with the rumps of buffalo. The largest herd Tom had ever seen went on as far as his sight could reach. So close were the buffalo they heard tearing of grass as the great beasts grazed. He and Private Cole watched in awe as the prairie turned from tired green to brown, one brown shaggy rump after another. "I never saw anything like this!" Private Cole shouted to Tom.

"I've never seen a herd this big, and I've been hunting buffalo my whole life!" Tom shouted back.

The buffalo seemed unimpressed by the presence of the wagon and continued their slow walking forage. Not even the barking dogs bothered them. The men sat watching, so absorbed in the fascinating sight of a herd of that size, they neither heard nor sensed the impending danger until it was upon them.

"What the hell is that?" Shouted Cole. The dogs began snarling and barking in the other direction.

A dull, thunderous roar of pounding hooves drifted over them from the south. A second herd, as massive as the first, stampeded toward them. It had managed to get within half a mile before cresting the rise and coming into view. The herd bearing down on them looked at least two miles wide and coming at them with the speed of a flash flood. Cole leaped to cut his horse and Big Fella free. "Get on your horse and ride!" Tom yelled above the roar. Cole swung on his horse and rode away with all the speed he could get, but the dogs stayed with Tom and the wagon.

Cole left Tom and the wagon far behind even though Tom whipped his mules with all he had. Tom's buckskin matched Cole and his horse stride for stride until together they disappeared down the next ravine. Tom realized he was miles from the end of the original herd to his left leaving him nowhere to go but straight ahead, try to run around their flank before the second herd closed the seam. His mules gave it all they had, digging deep with each stride, throwing chunks of sod high in the air. But to his right the herd of wildly stampeding buffalo bore down on him with terrifying speed.

If he stopped long enough to cut the mules loose from the harness they would all be trampled under the oncoming herd. Their only chance was to insist on more speed. The stampeding herd was less than a few hundred yards away, and over a mile wide. Tom stood on the wagon, mercilessly whipping his mules and screaming for all he was worth. "GO... GO... RUN NOW!"

The poor mules ran their hearts out. The terrain was just too hilly; they could not manage any real speed pulling the heavy wooden wagon. In an instant the gigantic herd swallowed the wagon, the mules, Tom and the dogs. Somehow the dogs, barking furiously, were able to stay with the wagon. The buffalo closed tight, squeezing the mules, forcing them and the wagon to travel in the same direction, running headlong toward the other herd, which was now just as panicked, and beginning to stampede away from the closing herd.

The mules ran crowded by buffalo on all sides, front and rear, their speed no longer their choice. The mules could neither speed up nor slowdown as they ran swept along as if caught up in a massive wave of rushing water. Tom heard a mule scream the high-pitched cry of a terrified mule. He did his best to guide them realizing their only hope was to move with the herd until they ran themselves out.

Great collisions of beast upon beast thudded all around him, and the roaring of gored buffalo as horns found their mark in those trapped animals unable to get out of the way.

The left mule slammed into a fallen buffalo, stumbled and went down, dragging down the other mule. Braying and kicking, the mules tried to regain footing, but the wagon turned over pinning them. Tom saw the wagon sail over his head. Scrambling as fast as his terrified legs and arms could move he scratched and crawled his way between the tangled mules to avoid the slashing of buffalo hooves. The roar of the great beasts rumbling over and around them seemed to go on for hours. The dogs stood firm snarling and barking at the stampeding herd causing most of them to pass by the upside-down wagon.

The herd thundered on, most of them turning to avoid the pile of buffalo, the dogs, mules, and wagon. Some stormed over them; one found its mark on Tom's thigh, tearing open a long gash. Disregarding the pain, he forced his way deeper between the animals.

Finally, it ended. Straggling buffalo still galloped by, but the herd had thinned to the point where Tom felt out of danger. He crawled to the top of his hiding place between the buffalo and mules and overturned wagon to examine the mess, and his injuries.

Without warning, he was sent reeling head over heels backward, by first one mule and then the second as they scrambled to their feet. Snorting, stomping and shaking their heads wildly, dazed and cut by sharp hooves of the buffalo, they appeared to have survived no worse off than Tom. Incredibly, the buffalo that had been gored and caused the whole accident sprang to his feet and galloped away with the departing herd, leaving Tom, an upside down wagon, four battered dogs, and a pair of dazed mules in their wake.

Tom's leg was bleeding badly. He also had a nasty wound in the back of his head and had lost a sizable chunk of his scalp. He limped to the mules, took hold of the harness that remained and tied them to the overturned wagon. Then he sat down to examine the wound on his thigh. He hadn't noticed his missing scalp.

"Hey buffalo hunter, could you spare a tired old Army scout a cup of coffee?"

"Buck, I think I need a little help." Tom managed to say before he passed out.

Buck sprang to the aid of his friend, cutting a long piece from his saddle blanket and tying a tourniquet around Tom's injured leg. He was washing the back of Tom's head where the scalp was missing when Tom regained consciousness, "WOW! Buck! That hurts terrible!" Tom pushed Buck away.

"We got to right this wagon and get you some help. Your leg's in a bad way."

Buck threw a hitch around his saddle and tied the other end of the rope to the side of the overturned wagon. "Come on, boy, walk, pull, and pull Diablo!" Finally the wagon cooperated and flipped onto all four wheels, shuddered and banged in a dust cloud to sit upright.

"This wagon don't look too bad, Tom, and you were lucky it landed on top of your things. Both the Sharps look fine. Here lay the Henrys, and look at this, here's your .44. Musta flew from your holster. Looks like the only thing broken is your chair... well, and your leg and head. I'm gonna fix you a place to lay on the wagon and high tail it for Lieutenant Harris' camp over by Little Bear Creek."

Tom crawled on the wagon and lay down while Buck made the repairs he could to the harness and doctored the mules' wounds with mud packs he made by dumping water from his canteen in the foot thick dust stirred up by the trampling of countless buffalo hooves.

Tom found the white buffalo hide still wedged under the wagon seat and used it for a pillow.

Buck put the harness on the black stallion and Diablo and tied the mules to the back of the wagon. They were on the move in search of Lieutenant Harris in less than an hour. The buffalo herd roamed still in sight turning every bit of the prairie to their north and east a woolly brown.

"Never, ever, Tom, have I seen anything like that! I was about five miles away when I saw that southern herd aiming for the other bunch of woolies. The only other time I ever saw two great herds of buffalo come together was back in '61 when I was riding Pony Express. I was fifteen miles out from my last relay station when off to my north I spied this mountain of a herd of buffalo. Traveling at the speed I was going, probably twenty-five miles an hour, I was soon on top of them and as me and my Pony Express mustang were flying by them suddenly there appeared another huge herd heading straight for 'em. This herd was so large and strung out so far they completely blocked my trail. I had nothing I could do but to stop my mustang for we would've galloped into the midst of them. It looked to be a herd about five miles long, which would double my distance to the relay station. I was trying to figure what to do when these two bulls cut out of the herd and went at it head-to-head. The first time they banged heads it felt like an earthquake. I mean, these were the biggest buffalo bulls I had ever seen 'til then, or now. They backed up and come at each other again with the same result, a thunderous bang. Two huge beasts each easily over a ton, running full steam at each other like locomotives. It seemed as if those herds were interested in the outcome of the battle as all forward motion stopped. There was a crease between both herds like the parting of the Red Sea, and I knew it was a dangerous chance to take but if I could make it through that crease, which looked to be only about a mile long, I could save precious time getting to the relay station. I sunk my spurs into my pony's flanks. He squealed and shot forward like a cannonball. Those burly buffalo actually stepped back and made the split even wider. I never knew the outcome of the battle for in about two minutes I was through the herd and leaving them in my dust … I do have to say though, Tom, I never was run over by an entire herd of buffalo and I don't know of anyone else in the whole wide world that was and lived to tell about it."

Buck turned to look at Tom and found him asleep on the skins. "I reckon that's a story I can tell again. How about it dogs?" The dogs had resumed their stations trotting alongside the wagon and seemed not to care how often Buck relived the story.

The figure of a man with two horses coming fast caught Buck's keen eye. As he reached for the Henry he recognized the rider as Private Cole. Seeing that Cole would overtake them soon he decided not to stop the wagon but continued on his way with the horses at a strong trot in order to get Tom some medical attention as soon as possible.

"I could see Diablo from five miles back. He was sure a welcome sight. What we need out here is a few more buffalo hunters." Cole hollered as he approached. "It was a remarkable thing to gallop between those two herds and Tom's big buckskin stayed with me the whole way! How is Tom anyway?"

"He's got a bad rip on his thigh and lost a chunk of scalp but he'll mend. I'm trying to get him to Lieutenant Harris to see if those Army boys can patch him up."

As Cole tied Big Fella to the wagon, Buck called out pointing north.

"Here come the Lieutenant's troopers!" Waving a piece of blanket high overhead, he signaled distress. The column of cavalry altered their course to intercept the wagon and came at a full speed run, raising a dust cloud over the prairie a half-mile wide.

Sergeant Peterson reached the wagon first. Laying low on his mount and whipping him wildly with the ends of his reins, he stormed ahead of his detail by a hundred yards. Sliding to a dusty stop by the wagon. "What's your situation?"

"Sergeant, glad to see you." Buck yelled above the clatter of the arrival of the rest of Peterson's troop, "we've got an injured man here, can your medic take a look at him?"

At a signal from the Sergeant, one of the men broke ranks and hurried to address Tom's wounds. "This'll take a little time, Sergeant. I'll need to sew this skin on his leg and he's got a good sized wound on his head that needs sulfur powder."

"Two men get to the wagon and hold that man down while the Private does his work." Sergeant Peterson ordered. A few seconds later Tom was in the grasp of Buck and two troopers, while the Private carefully bathed the wound, doused it with sulfur powder, and stitched his leg back together.

"He should be alright if infection doesn't set in. I got plenty of sulfur powder in the wound." The Private who performed the surgery told Buck.

"If everything else is alright, we have about five miles to go to base camp. You're all welcome to come along, I'm sure Lieutenant Harris would be glad to feed you and put you up for the night," invited Sergeant Peterson. Buck fell in line with the troopers and the group traveled the last five miles back to base camp in a quick cavalry trot.

Suddenly the Sergeant let go a loud yell for the detail to "Halt!" Ahead of them lay the remains of their base camp. Every man there sat heavy as boulders on their mounts, unable to utter a sound.

Buck flipped the long reins high in the air and brought them down smartly on the backs of Diablo and his black. The wagon lunged ahead almost leaving the mules and Big Fella behind. Peterson kicked his mount into a flat run and raced into camp. Making a flying leap from the horse's back he stood, his mouth gaping in awe, his arms spread wide as if to shelter the entire atrocity himself. At first he was able only to stare at the naked bodies strewn about, partially devoured by wolves.

The other troopers dismounted and walked through the camp in stunned silence. Nothing remained except the shredded corpses of their fellow troopers. Even Buck, the seasoned scout that he was, was overcome and leaned on a tree for support.

"How could this happen? Lieutenant Harris is one of the finest military officers in the west. How could this have happened?" Sergeant Peterson asked himself.

"Sergeant, you'd better come over here." One of the troopers had found Lieutenant Harris. "Oh my God!" Peterson uttered and he collapsed to his knees in tears in front of his dead Lieutenant.

Buck joined him at Lieutenant Harris' side. They stood together a long moment, each having their own private thoughts about their friend.

"Let's get these good men buried." Was all Sergeant Peterson could say when he raked the back of his dusty sleeve across his eyes.

Troopers worked that afternoon and into the evening to bury the dead, for the Sergeant wanted the graves deep enough to deny the wolves.

At sunset, Sergeant Peterson called the troopers to formation and with the flag bearer holding the Stars and Stripes straight and proud with all the dignity they could collect, they set out for the prairie. What they could not see was Tall Dog watching from atop the vertical wall.

The troopers, Tom, and Buck traveled together for about two and a half hours. Then Buck shouted to Sergeant Peterson. "I'll leave you here. I need to get Tom back to his ranch. I'll send Private Cole with you and I'll thank you to tell General Sturgis of my whereabouts. Assure the General I will report in as soon as possible. When my friend's out of danger."

Buck turned from the column and headed in a southerly direction. After a few more hours of travel on the hilly prairie, Buck decided to give the black and Diablo a break and stopped in the shade of tall cottonwoods and willows by the bank of the Little Bear Creek.

Before setting out again he checked the mules. One of them had fared pretty well and suffered only a number of bumps and minor scratches. The other though, had a nasty wound and Buck figured it would take some real doctoring to pull him through. He looked at Tom and found he was sleeping again but now had developed a fever.

"Step it up Diablo, let's make some time." He kept Diablo and his black stallion in a steady trot, and changed direction to go directly to the Sioux village where he knew he'd get help for Tom and the mule.

Four hours of fast trotting later Buck finally drove into the Sioux village with three very tired horses and two exhausted mules. Still Water was the first to greet him and knew immediately something was wrong. "I have Tom back here. He's been hurt." Buck jumped to the back of the wagon. Still Water ran to climb in. Placing her small white hand on Tom's forehead she looked at Buck. "Yes, he has a bad fever." Still Water motioned to the braves who had gathered about the wagon and they carefully picked Tom up and carried him to her lodge.

Buck busied himself tending the horses and led the injured mule into the small stream where he splashed cool water on the wounds and made new mudpacks. When he was satisfied he'd done all he could for the banged-up mule, he led him to join the other Sioux ponies on the prairie near the cottonwoods. "You take care of yourself now," he told the mule and gave him a gentle slap on the rump. Then he hurried to Still Water's lodge. Soft Cloud was kneeling by Tom gently sprinkling his forehead with cool water.

"Buck, what happened?"

"He got run over by a herd of buffalo. How's he doing?"

"He is hot with fever. My mother is making a poultice for that leg. Whoever did the sewing on that leg did a fine job, but I'm afraid there is already heat there. We will need to keep fresh mustard poultice on that leg until we can draw the heat and poison out."

Still Water stepped through the lodge flap with a wooden bowl containing a thick soupy mixture that smelled strongly of wild mustard. She squatted to her knees next to Tom and began to smear the substance liberally on his leg, which they had elevated on a roll of hide.

"He was run over by a herd of buffalo?" Soft Cloud studied Buck's face, concern and amusement painted on her own.

"It's amazing anyone lived. I was cutting across the plain and making good time when I was forced to make a wide berth around a buffalo herd of maybe eight or ten thousand. It was the largest herd I had seen for some time, maybe four or five miles long and over a mile wide. I was trying to get around 'em because I was hoping to catch up with Tom and Private Cole. Then I spot another herd just as big running flat-out in a wild stampede! I saw right away they were about to run smack into the grazing herd.

"Then I saw Tom's wagon in the path of the stampeding herd. Private Cole jumped on a horse and got the hell out of there but Tom stayed with the wagon and tried to outrun 'em. He was doing just fine and I believe he would have made it, but a buffalo fell down in front of 'em, knocking his mules down. I saw the wagon flip up in the air and then I couldn't see anything again until the whole mess passed. I high-tailed it over there and Tom looked up and told me he didn't feel too good."

Buck paced around the lodge a few seconds, pulled off his hat, and rubbed his forehead and his long blond hair with a sweaty hand. He sat on the far side of the tiny fire, crossed his legs and rested his hands on his knees. "Well, then I figured to hustle over to Lieutenant Harris and the base camp and get some medical attention for Tom. We met up with some of the Lieutenant's men who had been out on night patrol and we rode into base camp together.

"What we found was all hell-on-earth. Every man lay dead. They were all stripped naked, not a single item remained in the camp except for the dead men torn apart by the wolves. There were no wagons, no weapons, no clothes, nothin'... nothing was left except the mutilated bodies of the dead troopers. And then we found Lieutenant Harris' body.

"We buried those poor bastards and we buried them deep. There won't be any wolves disturbing their rest now." Buck rose and came back to Tom and put his hand on his head. "It was surely the work of Tall Dog." He let his shoulders sag.

"And then I brought Tom here." He added, staring into Still Water's eyes. He hated telling her about the massacre. But the words flew from his mouth as if they had taken on a life of their own. He wished he could take them back. He felt like a kid who just told a family secret.

"I'm very sorry for your trooper friends," Soft Cloud said softly. "Some way Tall Dog must be stopped. This will cause the U.S. Army to kill all Indians. This is very bad. Tall Dog has become insane with hatred for whites. Perhaps Red Cloud should move our village to the west, farther from the white soldiers. I believe we are now in danger because of the actions of my father," Soft Cloud concluded in a whimper as she smoothed the poultice onto Tom's leg.

"Red Cloud and his Sioux have almost always been friends to the U.S. Army. Sergeant Peterson and the rest of the troopers went back to Fort Laramie and he'll tell General Sturgis this was the work of Tall Dog and his renegades." Buck hoped he was correct. "I'll rest here for a day, then go back to the prairie and search for Tall Dog." Buck found a good spot on the other side of the fire, made himself comfortable and went to sleep.

****

Tall Dog found the atmosphere at the camp town very much to his liking. All the renegades were in high spirits, most were drunk, celebrating their victory over their enemy Lieutenant Harris. Tall Dog called out for Sidewinder to be brought to him and settled down in the saloon with a bottle of whiskey and two women on his lap.

Outside a light cold rain was falling and the canvas saloon roof leaked through its many bullet holes. It could do little to dampen the high spirits of the jubilant renegades. They had just eliminated a very capable cavalry officer and his patrol without losing a single man. Celebration was righteously theirs this day.

Sidewinder found Tall Dog still in the saloon being entertained by the two women. "They say you wanted me."

"The white men are building a road of iron through our land. They have a camp near the Squaw Run River. These men make maps and leave marks on our land; I have watched them. We should kill them. They have no U.S. Army soldiers but they do have many men with rifles, perhaps twenty men. We must kill them, and take their maps and destroy their marks that they have made upon our land."

"Tomorrow I'll gather the men, my friend, and you will lead us to another victory!" Sidewinder gulped his whiskey.

"Their camp is in open land. We cannot move secretly upon them. Even by night we cannot reach them in surprise so we will dress in the U.S. Army clothes from the battle at the Little Bear Creek. We can be upon them before they can know of trouble!"

Twenty-eight men were killed at the big creek called Little Bear, beneath the Walls of Buffalo Ridge. The next morning twenty-five renegade Sioux, Cheyenne, and Arapaho, led by Tall Dog, left the high country dressed in cavalry clothes, riding cavalry mounts, and armed with cavalry Henrys. To be even more convincing, bringing up the rear was a cavalry ambulance loaded with supplies and five more renegades, in case they were questioned on the open prairie.

CHAPTER THIRTY-FIVE

Tom's fever broke during the night, thanks to his youth and the constant care of Still Water and Soft Cloud, and he was able to pick himself up onto his elbows to an almost sitting position. In early morning light, he heard little activity outside the tipi. Soft Cloud slept, her head resting on Tom's good leg, while Still Water rested, her head on Buck's lap. Buck was awake and wanted to stir but didn't want to disturb Still Water. He nodded to Tom, and shook a finger at the two sleeping women.

That was enough to wake Still Water. "We had a long night with you Tom, but you look a little brighter. How do you feel?"

"Tired and banged up. How are my horse and dogs, and mules?"

"The dogs would be in here on your lap if we call them." Buck said. "They came through it a lot better then you. They haven't moved five feet from this lodge. I never saw dogs take to a man like those four. Big Fella weathered the storm without a scratch but I'll wager he's a might stiff from all those miles. Your wheel mule, well, I reckon he'll come along all right, but he's a fair bit banged up. A little like you. You're off mule got by with about thirty scratches. Best thing you could do next time you go riding through a buffalo herd is, Don't!"

They all got a good laugh at that and Tom was grateful to hear his dogs, horse and mules were in good shape. As Soft Cloud lay still leaning on Tom's good leg, she took a stick and poked the slumbering speck of a fire back to life.

"I'm going to check on your mule, maybe you should put some of that poultice on his wounds, Soft Cloud," Buck suggested as he and Still Water left the Lodge.

"Do you know what you are going to do now?" Soft Cloud asked Tom.

"I'm going home."

"That's a bad wound on your leg, and you should not be alone until we can be sure it will not bleed again."

"Maybe you could stay with me." Tom felt a growing fondness toward this gentle young half-Indian woman.

"I'll get you something to eat, you must get strength back. After that we can talk more. Maybe I should go with you." Tom had fallen asleep again and did not hear all she had to say.

****

Tom's mule had improved overnight but they applied a thick coating of poultice on all his wounds, just in case. "He's sure lookin' better than I expected. Now for Tom, I'll bet he'd make good use of a crutch with that hop-along leg of his. Yup, I reckon I'll fashion Tom a crutch, then start out for the fort and let you and your daughter get him mended." Buck searched the tree line and brush until he found the perfect branch and, with his Bowie knife, he began to fashion a sturdy crutch. Still Water sat quietly by his side, admiring his ability to wield the long blade.

They sat on a fallen log where they could watch the horses and enjoy the morning sun. Buck pointed with his knife to his black stallion, who stood out among the herd of Sioux mustangs. "I'm giving him to Tom to use as a sire to start his horse ranch. That stallion has as much heart and toughness as any horse I've ever known."

"He's a beautiful horse, and a fine gift. You're a good friend to Tom. Buffalo Horn has promised to help Tom with his first gathering. But now with his wounded leg, it should wait for spring. Soon snow will cover the prairie and the horses are best running free."

"You're sure right about that fact." Buck agreed, feeling the sudden change in the fall air. A stiff breeze had picked up and an unexpected dampness made him shudder. He felt as if he were already fighting a deep snow.

"Red Cloud has said when the new grass comes he will move the village. He has become very troubled about the railroad. At council braves spoke in favor of joining Tall Dog, which angers Red Cloud. He is also very worried, and knows he cannot stop the whites. His visions tell of great wars between the white man and his people. But Red Cloud also has visions of leaving peacefully with them. If the white man does not kill all the buffalo and does not build this railroad ... Red Cloud can perhaps hold the peace." Still Water's eyes held the sadness and worry heavy in her heart.

"Red Cloud must convince his people not to fight, Still Water. The Indian nations can't win. The United States has just ended a great war with itself. I was part of that war. I know of the powerful weapons the Army can turn against the Indian nations. It will be the end of his people if they fight." Buck looked Still Water in her worried blue eyes and tried to convince her.

"The Sioux are very proud people and can be peaceful, but they can also be fierce warriors. I know them, and I know Red Cloud. I will tell you a story. The buffalo are sacred to all Sioux. Each time a white man kills for just the hide, or tongue, or just to kill, that buffalo cannot go to the next life. That weakens the Great Spirit. It also weakens the Sioux for the buffalo are the brothers and the sisters of the Sioux.

"Too many times Red Cloud has seen the rotting bodies of dead buffalo which cannot go into the cloud that would welcome them into the next life. On the once-happy prairie now lay the bones of too many lost buffalo. He knows the railroad will bring more whites who will kill more buffalo.

"Tall Dog knows this as well but unlike his father, Tall Dog cannot remember a time when the white man was not here. He and other younger braves grew up listening to grand stories about the times when the proud Sioux ruled over all this land and more. About times when Grandfather Mystery made the entire universe and Grandmother Earth taught the Sioux to use her for their needs. They heard the story of when the Buffalo Calf Woman smiled on the Sioux and gave them their brother the buffalo, who give themselves so the Sioux may have food and hides for warmth and shelter. Now all things are threatened. Each time the braves who follow Red Cloud hear the stories of Tall Dog doing battle with the whites or killing white settlers, they urge Red Cloud to join him."

When Still Water finished speaking, Buck found he was overwhelmed. He knew the Sioux considered the buffalo their sacred brethren. But what he had not known was that Still Water might still admire Tall Dog. Watching her pretty face as she spoke of him told Buck that even though he had become a vicious killer and had killed both their sons, she could still love him. Making matters worse, Buck was beginning to have feelings for Still Water. Not the silly playful urges he would often have for women. No, what he felt for Still Water was much deeper.

"We're in quite a fix, aren't we?" Buck lamented as he handed Still Water the finished crutch for her inspection.

"This will be a great help to Tom as his leg mends," she said softly, not allowing her eyes to meet his.

In silence they walked to Still Water's lodge, each engrossed in their own thoughts about the future, the present and the past. Each worried about what they feared came next to the people of the prairie. They found Tom stretched out by the fire, Soft Cloud sitting by his side. Buck offered Tom the crutch. "This should make gettin' around a bit easier. Pad the top there with some leather strips and you'll be able to lean on it alright as you hop along."

"I was wondering how I could get around the next few days." Tom grinned and examined Buck's handiwork. "Let's give it a try."

"Perhaps you should wait a few days to try it." Soft Cloud placed her hand on his shoulder holding him down.

"Folks, I've got to ride." Buck's gaze hung on Still Water. "I have to get to the Fort. Tom, I wanted a better time, but I want you to have my black stallion. You should have a stallion like him to start your ranch. He's a powerful horse with a lot of heart. He'll give you some mighty handsome foals."

"And the first one is yours…" Overwhelmed at the generosity of the gift, Tom looked away.

"I'll be on hand for that roundup. When you're up to it."

Still Water watched Buck ride away on Diablo at a fast gallop, his big Stetson flying behind tugging on its neck strings.

****

The survey crew and their guards had been in full view for a little while before Tall Dog turned his horse and spoke to his men. "When we are close enough to fire, they will know we are not U.S. Army so we must attack quickly. When I am ready I will run my horse into them and you follow me."

As they neared the workmen, Tall Dog knew they were sighted. He continued to lead his renegades in a slow military trot. Soon the survey crew stopped working and began to walk out to greet what they thought were cavalry soldiers on patrol. Tall Dog gave the order for each man to have rifles ready.

It was a small group of unarmed men and fifteen armed guards, half of whom stayed at the work site. The lead guard realized the riders were not cavalry, raised his rifle and was sliced to bits by a volley of bullets before he fired. The others in the group turned to flee but were hopelessly surrounded by the renegades. The guards put up a valiant effort, dropping to one knee military style and even managed to get off a few rounds. But on the open prairie surrounded by a mounted fighting force as skilled as any the U.S. government ever produced, their efforts were short-lived.

At the work site, the remaining guards and surveyors took cover under the massive freight wagon and began to defend themselves. Tall Dog mounted a full and direct charge at the wagon. The band of renegades flew past the isolated wagon firing as fast as they galloped, then turned and charged again. Two more times Tall Dog led heavy assaults on the splintering wagon, never losing a single man or horse. Then he stopped the attack safely out of range. "Now that they have something to worry about, let's give them time."

Tall Dog ordered his men to regroup in a night camp and start fires. He chose several of his best Sioux braves to crawl close to the trapped men with orders to fire occasional rounds into the wagon to keep the trapped men from sleeping. The men under the wagon watched as their attackers sat illuminated by their campfires, hopelessly outnumbered.

The intensity of the siege mounted second by second as bullets slammed into the wagon, and the dust surrounding it, with sickening thuds. Unable to bear his fear, one man broke free of his companions' grasp and ran from under the wagon toward the Indians yelling. "I can't take it no more. Kill me!" Tall Dog's men obliged, cutting him down before he took five steps.

Under the wagon five men huddled together, two of them wounded, one gravely. "We're all gonna die, aren't we?" the youngest sobbed, a lad of only 16, who was there, "to see the frontier" against his mother's pleading.

Late that spring he had seen the poster nailed to the hardware store wall. SEE THE FRONTIER—LEARN THE SCIENCE OF SURVEY, the poster screamed. Tired of farm chores, he was ready to go. The days after he carried the poster home and informed his mother and father that he was now a man and headed west were filled with bitter arguments. After all, he'd argued, this family had a long history of being in the thick of things as the nation grew, right back to his great-grandfather who fought in the Revolutionary War.

"Oh no, Ben! You mustn't go, it is far too dangerous," his mother had pleaded. Sometimes she wept uncontrollably. He knew she loved him dearly and he hated to hurt her but he hated farming more. "Look, mother," he pointed to the poster, "each team will be protected by the railroad's own guards, in any hostile territories." It did nothing to quell her fears. "Father, tell him he may not go!" His little sister, Anna begged. Ten years his junior, she worshiped her older brother. It was hardest of all to tear himself from her small arms as she wailed and screamed at the train depot in Philadelphia.

His father too, pleaded for him to stay on the farm. "All the spring plowing is about to start, son. I could sure use your help."

"I'm sorry father, but Michael and Harry are old enough to help now," he remembered telling his father. How he would like to be behind that old mule now.

Ripped from his memories by a new volley of rifle slugs slamming into the solid wagon he sucked in a shaky breath. "We ain't dead yet, kid! See if you can tear any boards loose from the bottom of this wagon so I can get some shells for my 50 here, I'm down to my last three primers." Bill shook the boy until he focused. "You got buffalo rounds up there, right Jack?"

"Yup, and 44s for the Henrys. Sure we got plenty of ammo, just out of reach."

As Ben crawled over the outstretched legs of Jack Garner, Jack grunted, "Careful there kid, that leg's broke."

"You hit too, Jack?" Bill hollered above the rifle fire.

"Yea Bill, my leg's shot to hell."

"I'm not hit yet," Todd Harvey said. "But I can't see worth a damn without my glasses. That pretty much leaves you and the kid, Bill—Sam's just about bled out."

"Hey white man, why don't you come out from under that wagon? We have no place to go and soon you will need water and bullets!" Tall Dog taunted from the safety of his campfire. "Soon I will add your scalps to those of your friends and if you are lucky I will wait 'til you are dead to take them."

Ben clawed at the underside of the heavy freight wagon. "It's no good, these boards are like iron. There's no chance, maybe I can crawl up and get inside the wagon from the back."

"No good, kid. You get six inches off the ground and they'll slice you to pieces," Bill cautioned. "Can anybody see my horse?"

The Indians had long ago killed all the stock. The mules and horses lay where they had been cut down. "I can see 'im, Bill," Jack said. "He's just about fifty yards to our rear. His ass end is to us and I can see your saddlebags."

"Kid get on your belly and crawl out there and cut those bags loose, there's enough bullets in them to hold off all day," Bill shouted.

"Stay put, kid. I'll go, hell I'm bleeding to death anyway," Jack yelled. "Here kid, take my Henry and try to give me cover."

Ben took the rifle and positioned himself so that he could fire into the silhouettes around the campfires. Bill handed one of his pearl handled revolvers to Todd Harvey. "You can see the fires, Todd. Aim high and make some noise."

"You bet Bill, sure am glad you happened by today."

"Next time you host a get together, Todd Harvey, please don't invite me!" Bill readied his rifle. "Anytime Jack!"

Bill's fired, his big 50 roared like a cannon and an Indian dancing by the fire flew over backwards. "Aim high boys, make that lead carry!" Bill shouted above the racket of gunfire. Jack slithered like a wounded snake on his stomach pulling with his hands, and pushing with his one good leg. Ben fired over Jack as he made his slow journey to the dead horse. Just enough light shone from the cloud-covered moon for Ben to be able to watch Jack as he wrestled the bags free of the horse. As Jack turned and began the return trip to the wagon, the moon broke free of the clouds. Bullets began to rain down all around him. "Keep firing boys, give him cover!" Bill hollered, but Ben saw a bullet rip into Jack's back, smashing him to the ground. Ben's Henry clicked the sickening sound of an empty chamber. He spun and snatched the one from Sam's dying hands, resuming his cover fire, aiming now for the renegades lying in the prairie grass only a few hundred feet from the wagon.

"Damn it!" hollered Todd Harvey.

"Get stung, did ya Todd?" Bill yelled.

"Same damn shoulder as last time me an' you were stuck! Damn it to hell! Give me your other pistol Bill, this'ns empty."

They all watched in the light of the moon as a battered Jack Garner struggled to stand on one leg and fling the saddlebags toward the wagon. Before the bags touched the ground a full volley of fire from the Indians close to the wagon cut him down. The bright moon also betrayed the hiding places of the nearby renegades. Three would raise no more, as each man under the wagon placed well-aimed rounds.

"Thought you couldn't see, old timer?" Bill taunted.

"Well hell, Bill, I can see a hundred feet."

"They'll hold off a while now," predicted Bill.

Ben lay in near shock as he looked out at poor Jack Garner. He had been so good to Ben these past few months. And Sam. He had been teaching him how to calculate the grades. So much death. Probably should have listened to mother.

"Hey iron road men, why don't you come out and die quickly. I want to go to the saloon and get a woman. You are taking too long to die."

Bill recognized that voice as the vicious killer Tall Dog. He took careful aim and let his 50 roar. Another renegade fell by the fire, bumping Tall Dog as he flew backwards from the force of the huge round. "Get that bag now kid!" Bill ordered. "Go get your woman, Tall Dog! I came to party all night!" And he fired another round, killing another Indian. "Stay at my party and you're likely to run out of drinking buddies!" He taunted. "Stay sharp, if he gets real pissed he's likely to charge us then they'll be backlit. Load those Henrys and pistols an' give me that sack of 50s an' primers." Bill knew his taunting would give the big Sioux enough clues to recognize him. Bill planned it that way, maybe if he knew his adversary, it would worry him into making a heated mistake.

"First you die, Bill Cody! You have killed too many Sioux and too many buffalo. You must die today, Bill Cody!"

"Did he have to pick a day you're with me to kill ya, Bill?" Todd Harvey fired at the renegades in the grass.

"I ain't dyin' today, boys," Bill assured them. "Well come on then you long-legged son of a bitch!" He hollered to Tall Dog and he let loose another fifty and another renegade howled.

****

Buck pushed Diablo for several hours riding fast while trying to sort through the cobwebs in his head. Who the hell is this Still Water? Why is such a fine looking and well-mannered white woman living with Red Cloud's Sioux? And Tall Dog her husband? How could that be? What's more, why is he so strangely attracted to her? Her beauty? She is a fine looking woman, mighty fine, but he has been with many a fine looker. What about Mrs. Harris? She always had her head turned his way. For a long time he had wondered what it would be like to be with Mrs. Harris. Now Lieutenant Harris is dead, by the hand of Tall Dog. How queer is that? Should he pursue Mrs. Harris? God but she is beautiful. If he should manage to kill Tall Dog, what then of Still Water?

The unmistakable report of a 'Big 50' tore Buck from his thoughts. Another roar, then rifle shots. No doubt about it that's a 50 and rifle shot, but in the middle of the night?

"Hold on Diablo! Let me get my bearings." Buck stood in the stirrups, ears pinned in the direction of the thundering 50. The firing continued with several Henrys mixed with an occasional 50. He dug his heels into Diablo so hard the startled horse snorted, reared and raced in the direction of the gunfire. Up one hill and down another, through the valley and up the next rise, Diablo flew like the wind, his long mane whipping Buck's face. At the top of the next rise Buck saw campfires. He jumped down, grabbed his own Sharps 50, a sack of bullets and primers and raced to the edge of the hill, whipping off his "Boss of the Plains" hat as he ran, so as not to be an easy target.

In less than a minute Buck analyzed the situation in the valley. At a glance he knew a survey crew was pinned by a bunch of renegades. What he couldn't figure was how they were holding off over twenty Indians. And no crew he ever knew carried buffalo rifles.

By the light of the cloud-covered moon and campfires he could easily find targets. All the shots would be over two hundred yards but backlit targets are easier to sight, and their Henrys and Spencers would be out of range.

Buck went right to work. His first shot dropped a man. He slid down out of sight and ran fifty yards and fired his Sharps again with like results. Again he ran along the edge, dropped at the crest and fired another round. Whoever was pinned under the wagon figured it out and after each shot Buck fired, the 50 under the wagon roared. He almost felt sorry for the renegades. They began to scatter, leaving most possessions behind while running for their ponies to scurry away. Buck and the 50 under the wagon continued firing until all the Indians were gone from sight. On the heels of the fleeing renegades, Buck galloped down the hill to the stranded wagon.

"I'll be doggone! Buck Hawkins! Welcome to our party. Sure am glad you brought your fiddle!" declared Bill Cody.

"And Good Evening to you! You do make a fine dance partner, Bill Cody."

"Are you the real Bill Cody? You mean I pissed my britches in front of Bill Cody?" Flabbergasted, Ben tried to hide his embarrassment.

"None other than!" assured Todd Harvey. "How about somebody lookin' at my arm, boys?"

Buck tore Todd Harvey's shirt open. "Not good, Todd. We'd better hustle you to the Fort. Looks like the only horse we got is Diablo, and I had the spurs in him all day. We'll have to strip down that ambulance to make it light enough for him to drag."

They propped Todd Harvey against a big wagon wheel with his arm wrapped tight against his chest while they stripped everything from the ambulance but the wheels. When they were ready Buck looked around. "Anybody else alive?"

"Naw, you got all of us. How come every time I get in a scrape with Cody, I get this shoulder shot?" Todd Harvey complained.

"Saved our bacon though didn't I?" Bill Cody boasted with a good natured grin.

The four men set out to Fort Laramie some thirty miles northeast. Three walking beside and one lying in a stripped out Army ambulance pulled by a very tired long legged paint, all four with weapons at the ready.

CHAPTER THIRTY-SIX

Two days later, Tom's leg was beginning to heal and he felt well enough to insist Soft Cloud take him outside in the morning sun. Propped on a pile of skins, he watched two young boys wrestle with his dogs. Around the village the women were working hard preparing for the coming winter. He watched as great piles of wood were stacked. Some women rubbed hides with bear fat to soften them for winter clothes. Others filled drying racks with strips of antelope and buffalo meat for winter meals when the great herds wander farther south for the winter. While Tom had slept, the braves of the village had a successful hunt. "Little wonder," Tom rubbed his wounded leg, "with two giant herds passing by on their way south. Red Cloud sure picked a great spot for their winter village."

The morning was frosty and a chill swept over him as he sat enjoying the activity in the village. Seeing neither Still Water nor Soft Cloud, he took the crutch Buck fashioned and made his way to the horses being watched over by the youngest braves of the village. The first duty assigned to young men in a village is often to guard the all-important Sioux ponies.

Tom found a good spot in the sun and wrapped the hide tight around himself against the early winter chill. He was admiring the big stallion Buck left him and picturing the fine foals he would sire, when Soft Cloud's presence broke into his thoughts. "How did that leg do?"

"Leg's comin' along, thanks to you and your mother. I was just admiring that black stallion, then I got to thinking about my place and winter coming.

Watching all the goin's on here made me think I'd better get back and get ready for the snows." He didn't bother to mention that he had also been fretting about chasing Tall Dog and the fact that by the time his leg healed the plains would be swallowed by winter, making them unfit for travel, even for someone as knowledgeable as himself. Tall Dog would have to wait for spring.

"So you want to go home? Can your leg stand the trip?" Soft Cloud could not hide the concern in her eyes.

"If we use the wagon I'll be alright."

"We, are you expecting company?"

"I just figured you would come along ... I mean I would like you to help me. See, like the women in your village." Tom pointed toward the village with a huge grin on his lips.

"I see. You need a slave girl." Soft Cloud shot back, her hands firmly on her hips in mock disgust.

"I want you to come with me, but you might be snowed in all winter. I don't know if I have the right to ask such a thing."

"You have all the right you need, and I'll be happy to help you through the winter at your cabin, though I'd rather we stay here, in our village. We would be safer."

He stood and gave a parting glance to the herd. "We should gather things to leave—I would like to leave in the morning."

They walked through the camp, Tom relying heavily on his crutch, discussing plans. "I'll have mother gather dried buffalo and hides for the floor and to cover the windows, you won't be hunting for some time."

He left her to the duties of supplies, and started out in search of Buffalo Horn. He was not hard to find, seated at the fire ring at Red Cloud's lodge. With the help of sign, which Tom was trying hard to master, Tom explained it would now almost certainly be spring before he would be able to resume his duties, and pursue Tall Dog. Buffalo Horn indicated he understood and offered Tom a seat at the fire next to him.

They chewed buffalo jerky and talked well into the evening, communicating with a combination of sign, broken English, and butchered Sioux. They discussed many things of great importance, from how Buffalo Horn and his braves would help Tom catch horses in the spring, to the uneasiness the building of the Bozeman Trail, its two Forts (the Phil Kearney and C. F. Smith), and railroad were causing Red Cloud.

The Bozeman Trail would lead many whites to his people's favorite hunting ground along the foothills of the Bighorn Mountains by the Powder River, Buffalo Horn explained to Tom.

Work had also been started on the Iron Road that will cut through the very lands the "White Talkers" just one year ago had promised to Red Cloud forever.

"My father does not believe in the ways of his son, Tall Dog." Buffalo Horn explained. "When white women and children are killed, peace with the white leaders cannot be made. Many times my father has counseled young warriors that the ways of Tall Dog are foolish and dangerous. But I fear they soon will tire of talk. It is now important that you stop Tall Dog before my father can no longer hold our people in peace."

Tom had traveled all the areas of the Sioux and Cheyenne hunting grounds with the hated old buffalo hunter and knew well of the troubles these proud people were being handed. He had seen the work on the Bozeman Trail and the new Army forts being built on the Big Horn River. Watching the survey crews making marks on the lower plains, Tom understood that the great buffalo land was changing.

It was changing as fast as he himself was changing. Each day brought Tom new ideas, new challenges, and new friends, just as each day brought new changes to the plains, with more buffalo hunters, more white settlers, more forts, more roads. Tom wrestled to understand the impact of these changes.

What he did know was that the friendship of the Sioux drew him nearer to them; he had felt that tug since the second day in their village. Since the day he'd met Soft Cloud. But how could he help them? He too was a white man who had carved out a large piece of their hunting grounds that he planned to call his own.

Buffalo Horn slipped silently away, leaving Tom wrestling with his thoughts and the meaning of their conversation. Stirring the ashes, sending sparks high, did little to clear the fog from his mind. Lost deep in thought, Soft Cloud caught him off guard. "The wagon is ready for travel in the morning. You should come back to my mother's lodge to get your leg cleaned, and to put fresh poultice on your wound."

CHAPTER THIRTY-SEVEN

The pathetic troop of worn travelers, exhausted horse, and stripped-down wagon were spotted by the Fort sentry. "Travelers approaching!" the sentry called out. The young officer on duty that morning was a very green and very young Lieutenant Canady. He grabbed his binoculars and examined the approaching wagon. "Looks as though they've had trouble, Private! Grab a horse and get out to meet them!"

"What's the situation?" The Private stopped 20 yards from the jumbled collection of exhausted men, broken wagon and spent horse.

"Hurry back and get the medic ready! We have a seriously injured man aboard!" Bill Cody shouted.

Sawing on the reins, the Private spun his horse about and started off at a gallop, only to stop in a few strides and gallop back to the wagon. "You—you—you're Bill Cody! Aren't you?" he stammered.

"I am, son, and this here's Buck Hawkins, now get! Hurry up that medic!"

The private needed no further encouragement and flew like the wind to the Fort where he announced, "That's Bill Cody out there with that wagon!"

General Sturgis stood on the parade to meet them as they entered the fort. At his side waited the Fort's chief surgeon with two assistants and they immediately lifted Todd Harvey from the wagon bed and hustled him to the hospital.

"I reckon I'll get my bath before you fellas!" Todd Harvey hooted as they carried him away.

"How about that Todd Harvey? Still has enough spit to torment us about being dirty when he had a soft ride for thirty miles and we walked and sweated all night." Buck flashed a grin to Bill Cody.

"Good to see you gents!" The General shook everyone's hand and made dust clouds over each of them when he slapped their backs. "You boys get cleaned up and have some chow, we'll discuss everything in two hours in my quarters."

As he turned to leave, Buck called out, "How's Mrs. Harris doing?"

"Not too well, I'm afraid."

Later Buck, Cody and General Sturgis gathered in the General's quarters. At first the room hung heavy, filled with tension and uneasiness. It had only been a week or so since the massacre at Little Bear Creek, and Buck had not had the chance to discuss the matter, with either Mrs. Harris or the General.

All through the morning's bath and at breakfast Cody and Buck spoke of old times on the Pony Express and nothing of the battle at the survey crew. Buck had kept his comments regarding the massacre at Little Bear Creek to simply the facts. It was where Lieutenant Harris died.

"Mrs. Harris will be going back east. I'm afraid she's having a very tough go of it." General Sturgis said.

"When will she be leaving?" A sudden and chilled weakness smothered Buck.

"She plans to leave for Fort Kearney in the morning, with the returning freight wagons. I'll be sending an escort."

Buck's mind raced. He and Mrs. Harris had been casual friends for a year now and despite the good-natured ribbing he gave Lieutenant Harris, he considered him a good friend as well. Buck and the Lieutenant had known each other for three years. Buck had served as his chief of scouts during the war between the states. Now he was dead and in less than a day she'll be going back east. It just felt wrong for it to end this abruptly. To have her gone before he really had a chance to talk to her about his mixed-up feelings. Why did she have to leave so suddenly?

Bill Cody yanked him from his thoughts when he began to explain the battle at the survey crew. "I'm in the employ of the Union Pacific Railroad to scout and hunt for the survey crews. I'd just ridden into their camp when all hell broke loose. Tall Dog and his renegades came ridin' up on the crew dressed like regular cavalry and when some of the boys went out to meet them they cut them down like ripe wheat before a mower.

"General, it didn't take more than two minutes for those fine men to die. When we saw what was goin' on we ran for the only cover we had, the railroad's heavy freight wagon, and dove under it. By the time we were under the wagon, all the stock had been gunned down and the renegades were making mounted attacks, shooting that wagon to hell. If Buck Hawkins hadn't shown up … Well, no one would have gotten out of there."

Buck did not feel much like talking. His thoughts continued to be about Mrs. Harris. Not thoughts of jealousy, desire, or bitterness. He just had not been prepared for her to leave his life so suddenly. Some days he thought the life he'd led kept him from any true contentment or happiness. For the past ten years he had been risking his life on the prairie in one way or another. From running horses to hell on the Pony Express, to spying for General Sheridan during the war, now scouting for the Army and dealing with renegades, and dealing with Tall Dog.

He had always enjoyed the conversations on the porch with Lieutenant and Mrs. Harris. How he would taunt Lieutenant Harris. He wished very much that the Lieutenant could be here today to endure some witty irritation. Buck had nothing to say in the General's quarters this morning. The General knew all there was to report on the incident at Little Bear

Creek so he got up, looked at Cody and the General, and said, "I'll see you later fellas." Even though the General made an effort to stop him, he left the room and headed to the quarters of Lieutenant Harris.

"Mrs. Harris, it's Buck Hawkins," he announced as he knocked on the front door.

"Hello Buck. I'm afraid I'll not be very good at conversation today but I can offer you a cup of coffee and I believe there are still a few cigars. I know how you and my husband loved to smoke on the porch in the evening. Perhaps this morning we could just sit together while you smoke."

CHAPTER THIRTY-EIGHT

Cold wind roared outside, but behind the thick walls of the soddy, Soft Cloud and Tom enjoyed a cozy morning by a lively, crackling fire. They had worked late into the evening stocking the back wall high with firewood. This blustery morning found Tom reclining on his bed as Soft Cloud applied new poultice to his leg.

"You've got to stay off that leg now, it started to bleed again." She advised with a stern look.

He happily took that advice to heart, his leg and head hurt enough to keep him from moving much, so he resigned himself to relax and soak up the heat of the fire. And Soft Cloud's tender care. Last evening he knew he was doing too much, but the cabin needed to be stocked. They both felt the sudden change in the air foretelling the storm and cold weather coming. In minutes he drifted back to sleep.

As he slept, Soft Cloud piled heavy buffalo hides on the floor making a bed next to him, then went outside to the horses and mules and put them in the corral at the barn. Now that they were a small herd, she feared they may wander too far. The dogs made themselves comfortable out of the wind on the porch. She threw them a bundle of bones and some buffalo fat. She felt certain the first snow of a long winter would arrive that night.

She hurried to the fire to chase the chill away. Checking on Tom she was pleased to see he had fallen sound asleep, so she nestled into a buffalo

225

hide. Her thoughts drifted back over the past weeks since Tom had entered her life. She knew he had the heart of a good man. She also knew his good heart was heavy with the burden of keeping his promise to her grandfather and uncle. At least if the snows came tonight, he would have the time for his leg to mend properly, and perhaps things would change. She wished for snow.

What would it be like for her to spend a long prairie winter alone with this young white man, Tom? Did she have enough knowledge of white man's ways to cause him to care for her as she was beginning to care for him? Her mother had not wanted her to leave with him, preferring rather they both stay in the village. But Soft Cloud had understood he would not be happy away from this cabin built of mud and grass now that he had found it and called it his own. These thoughts and others ran through her mind as she tightened the hides over the window and built up the fire so it might burn most of the night, then lay down beside Tom on her bed of hides.

The dogs woke them before dawn. They barked and whined an odd sort of barking, not one of warning, but more a pleading bark. Tom started to rise up, Soft Cloud stopped him and ran to the door. Opening it only a crack to investigate, driving snow pelted her face and blew into the room. Struggling against the wind to close the heavy door, she fell backwards when all four dogs bolted into the cabin, bounded across the tiny room and piled onto Tom, scattering snow wildly along the way. Her premonition had been accurate. "I guess they were cold! Reckon they'll spend the winter indoors." Tom reasoned while being mauled.

"I would prefer if they had left the snow outdoors!" In mock disgust Soft Cloud pointed to piles of snow melting into puddles on the hide covered floor.

She stoked the glowing embers into a roaring fire again in defense of the cold air trying to invade their snug quarters. Making breakfast proved challenging, with the four dogs testing her guard every moment. But eventually she had a fine meal of dried buffalo, water made by melting snow, and a little coffee prepared.

"Could be a long winter, Soft Cloud, if we're already down to dried buffalo. And it's only our first snowing."

"Early snowfall means early spring, most of the time at least." She peeled back Tom's pant leg to examine and treat his wound. "I'm not sure about the horses, the snow is deep already. Sioux horses run free all winter and where the wind blows the snow away they can find dead grass to eat."

"We may have to turn them out. I did manage to put some prairie grass in the barn but not enough for three horses and three mules. We'll take it day by day. Let's at least keep them in until this first snow blows itself out."

Howling wind and snow continued through the day and night and, by the next morning, it lay as deep as the porch roof. Both Soft Cloud and Tom realized they were in for a tough time of it. Soft Cloud had melted snow earlier for water but was determined to dig a path to the well. She was also concerned about firewood. Of buffalo and antelope jerky they had plenty, and they may even have enough flour if she used it sparingly. Firewood would be the biggest concern right now. Even though they had enough for several days, Tom's leg was in no shape to battle the deep snow in search of more

CHAPTER THIRTY-NINE

Unable to bear the thought of Mrs. Harris caught out there in this early blizzard, on the second day of the storm Buck trudged from Old Bedlam to the mess where he sat fidgeting and fussing about, irritating the grumpy old sutler.

Finally he could abide his inner torment no more and followed a shoveled path to the livery. "No more welcome place on earth in the dead of winter than a sweet-smelling barn." Of course, the peaceful atmosphere and horses munching contentedly on hay did nothing to stave his anxieties. Even though it was only hours until nightfall, he'd had all he could take.

"Sure would like to have that big black right now." Buck mumbled. "I guess River will need to get it done."

"What the hell are you doing, Buck?" Sarge barked when he saw Buck toss his saddle on River.

"I gotta check on Mrs. Harris... "

"Buck! There's thirty inches of snow out there—and it's two degrees!"

"Exactly my point. And she is out there in it!"

"Buck, she has a cavalry escort and all the teamsters. You ain't gonna do her any good freezin' to death or killing a good horse." Sarge stopped

Buck's hand from tightening the girth. "Use your head man."

Buck shoved his old friend so hard he flew back against the stall wall and collapsed to his knees. "Don't make me hurt you Sarge. I can feel it in my gut that I need to get out there. Now you can sit there on your ass or you can help me. Get Diablo in here. I'll ride River to bust open the path and pack Diablo. I have everything I need right there." He pointed to a pack lying next to him.

He wrapped a piece of a wool blanket around his legs and feet then covered them with tent canvas and covered the rump of each horse with a large woolen blanket folded in half, and with the Sergeant's help ran leather ties around their legs to prevent the wind from flipping them up. Another wool blanket was ruined to cover Buck's face and ears.

Fifteen minutes later, Buck was plowing through chest deep snow, leaving Fort Laramie behind him. Nothing would prevent him from getting to that wagon train.

The big roan plowed through the fluffy snow for hours. Darkness had settled in five hours ago but the moon hung high and the sky was clear, providing light to travel. Icicles hung from the horses' whiskers. Buck's feet were already numb with cold. He rode with his hands tucked under the saddle blanket trying to keep his frozen fingers alive. No need to hold Diablo's rope, he would never leave the trail blazed by River.

On and on they struggled. Ahead of him in the East the red sun began to appear on the horizon. With never a sign of the caravan. Buck was relentless. Each time River slowed from a fast walk he would dig his heels into the horse's ribs. Numb from his thigh to the tips of his toes he wondered if his toes would fall away when he pulled off his moccasin boots.

All through the day, he pushed the roan mercilessly to plow the snow, never stopping. Not to rest the horses, not to stretch his legs which he could no longer feel, not for anything; a single-minded man driven by an imagined danger.

As the sun slipped under the horizon behind him, he began to wonder if he had gotten off the Fort Kearney Trail and would miss them all together. His heels asked River for more speed. The horse responded with a side step and a quiver. "Whoa! Whoa! Hold up boy." Buck shouted above the fierce wind. "You all done in? We'll put Diablo in front for a while." His cheeks hurt so when he spoke he thought they would shatter like the icicles on his mustache. When his feet hit the ground he collapsed.

He couldn't remember a time when any ride had taken as large a toll on him. After spending a moment limbering up his legs and stomping his feet, he switched horses and was back to making trail through the snow, which touched Buck's knees when mounted. Diablo lacked the massive power of the roan but he had longer legs, and the progress seemed to be about the same. Into the night they continued their dauntless journey. Again the bright moon offered good visibility, although there was nothing to see, save the endless miles of wind-driven snow. No need to stop. No need other than sheer exhaustion. But that was not acceptable. Diablo pushed through the snow, sometimes climbing drifts as high as his head, clearing a path River could follow while he rested as best he could while still carrying a heavy pack and fighting the snow.

Buck rode on increasingly disillusioned, now convinced he had strayed from the wagon road. On and on he pushed Diablo, as the persistent thought of missing the wagon train altogether tortured his mind.

The sun began to rise in the east again, the second sunrise from the saddle with no break. Thirty-six hours of riding through chest-deep snow and a wind so stiff that most times he couldn't see the ears of the horse he was riding for the blowing snow. Onward Buck continued pushing his poor horses, demanding far more of them than is fair. Many times he had been forced to use up a horse but he never had two horses like these two. As long as Buck asked, they pushed on, as if they knew his fears.

Ice covered Diablo's face and whiskers in a thick shimmering mask. Buck turned in the saddle to check on River; his face too, carried a thick mask of ice with only steaming nostrils and wide eyes visible. He really didn't know how much longer they could go on. Fatigue, bone-chilling cold and numbness tore at his body, and he wondered when he would fall from the horse and freeze to death.

As the sun rose above the horizon before them, its brightness irritated Buck's exhausted eyes, he saw something in the snow ahead. He pushed Diablo to keep at it … What he found made him wish he had fallen and frozen to death. For some time he sat heavy on Diablo. All he could do was stare. Too exhausted to control his emotions he fell from Diablo's back into the snow weeping like a boy.

He lay sobbing, trying to build the courage to investigate the carnage strewn around him. They must have been hit just as the storm began, for the wagons sat wheel deep in snow. But thanks to the efforts of wolves most of the bodies lay exposed.

Buck had known he needed to be with that convoy. If only he had been here. Why the hell had he let General Sturgis talk him out of going with them?

When finally he could stand, he began to walk among the broken wagons and bodies. The wolves had the snow packed surrounding the wagons. The bodies were easy to find. Twelve mutilated and naked cavalry troopers. Eight equally disfigured teamsters, sixteen dead mules, and four dead horses. But no woman's body!

He found no signs of Mrs. Harris. Frantically Buck dug the snow away from all four wagons, thinking perhaps she had hidden and escaped what he knew would be a horrible end. There was no one under any wagon. Carefully he inspected all the bodies again. No woman lay among the dead.

The sun now high, Buck began to tear boards from one of the wagons and build a fire … He had to drive the cold from his bones.

As the fire struggled to take hold on the snow-soaked planks, he searched the wagons, found a few blankets and immediately put one on each horse knowing if they went down he would never make it out of there alive. There was no hay, but under a pile of broken grates was a torn sack of oats, which he dumped liberally on the trampled snow for the grateful horses. He grabbed some jerky from his saddlebag and his Henry from the scabbard, threw the broken crates on the blazing fire, and sat in its warmth wrapped in blankets.

Warmth forcing its way into his body lulled Buck into a fitful sleep. He gauged he'd slept for close to an hour by the fire, a mere pile of shimmering ash when he stirred. The horses too, had lain down in the snow and were sound asleep nearly covered by the blowing snow. Slowly rising to his feet keeping the blanket wrapped around him, he gathered more wood from the nearest wagon and brought the fire back to a full-blown blaze. Not ready to think about, or do anything, he huddled again by the fire, his back resting against the wagon wheel while his eyes surveyed his surroundings.

A bright noon sun tried its best to shine through swirling snow. Staring at the body parts poking through the snow here and there he drifted back to sleep. Buck may have sat there and slipped into the darkness of death had Diablo not jumped to his feet, shaking and stomping so vigorously that his blanket slipped off. The roan, too, leaped to his feet! With sleepy, frantic eyes Buck searched for the problem.

His and his horses' presence and the blazing fire had kept the wolves away from the wagons. But now the horses spied them, about a hundred yards out, barking, snarling, fighting, ripping, and tearing at some poor dead bastard's body. He had not searched that far out from the wagons. Oh what the hell, Buck thought, and raised the Henry. At another time, he would have been proud of his marksmanship as four wolves lay dead or dying in as many seconds. The others scattered in the snow yelping and snarling.

Calmly, almost hypnotically, he reloaded the rifle. For the moment, his thoughts were to sit by the fire and to shoot the wolves as they came to rip flesh from the dead bodies.

Then he had a horrible thought!

He took off at a run, the blanket flying, racing to the site of the newly uncovered body firing the Henry hysterically as he ran. Diving into the snow Buck dug frantically, exposing the tortured body. Then he collapsed on top of the frozen, dead flesh that had been ripped to bits by the wolves. He wept uncontrollably as he tried to gather her broken body into his arms.

Buck lay in the snow with Mrs. Harris, hoping through some miracle to breathe life back into this mangled, frozen thing he held in his arms. He held her close, trying to assure her no further harm would come. His mind drifted briefly back to that last morning on her porch. That morning, she asked him to just sit quietly and enjoy her company, and her husband's cigar.

His thoughts were still back at Fort Laramie on Mrs. Harris' porch, when a wolf snarled directly in his eyes, its hot breath washing over Buck's face. Insanity gripped him. He jumped atop the wolf and, with his long knife, stabbed it to death. Over and over and over and over, he stabbed the lifeless body of the poor starving wolf. Others quickly surrounded him, the pack numbered at least ten. His Henry lay empty by Mrs. Harris. He had his Navy .44 with six rounds strapped to his waist. Jumping to his feet he pulled it and automatically dropped five wolves. The others scattered again.

Perhaps he owed the wolves some debt of gratitude. As horrible as that is, but for them he would never have found her. He raced back to the wagon, snatched up the blanket and ran back to Mrs. Harris.

Carefully, delicately, he picked her up and laid her in the heavy woolen army blanket. Bits of her clothing remained and he was meticulous about the manner in which he tried to redress her. He gathered the blanket in his arms and staggered back to the wagon, his tears freezing as they fell on her blanket. He wrapped his bundle in another blanket and tied it securely.

Gently tying the bundle that was Mrs. Harris on Diablo's back, Buck told him, "I'm counting on you to take care of this fine lady, Diablo." He swung up on River and they headed southwest, blazing a new trail through the ever-deepening snow. Buck knew going in this direction they would find either the Miller farm or the sawmill settlement.

Buck no longer felt the cold. He just didn't give a damn. Nor had he any interest in reporting his discovery to the proper authorities at either Fort Kearney or Fort Laramie. They could go directly to hell and kiss his ass on the way there.

The big roan pushed through the snow, ever diligently making forward progress. For hours they traveled again, on and on, the snow swirling around them. The setting sun dragged the temperature down with it. Buck never noticed. The horses walked on, exhausted and in a trance. Buck was numb not just from the cold but from the horrible pain in his heart. He knew he didn't love Mrs. Harris in that way. But he loved her in some way. She had always been so sweet and fragile in the way she flirted harmlessly with Buck. He knew she enjoyed teasing Lieutenant Harris as much as he did. It was their special game. It gave them a connection—a playful, tender connection.

She was so beautiful! Oh how furious she could make her husband with her innocent flirting with Buck … He would never see her flirt again. It was impossible to believe that this porcelain doll of a woman was dead. Murdered on the frozen prairie, stripped naked and raped by horrible heathens. How terrified she must have been.

Why had he not been there to protect her? She must have called out for him! She was supposed to make it back east, back to civilization. Not left lying in the snow torn to bits by wolves. That's okay for men and soldiers and heathens. But beautiful, soft fragile women must not, should not, suffer that. There can be no damned God! For as long as he shall live, Buck will never again believe there is a God. For if there were, he surely would never have allowed Mrs. Harris to suffer what she did. Death. Death is okay, death is part of life. But only the evil deserve a tortured death.

All through the night Buck sat numb on River as they continued their way southwest. The wind and the snow were unrelenting. By the time the sun peaked above the horizon far away in the east, the snow was as deep as River's chest. Somehow the big horse kept pushing on. The tough horse was exhausted now and the forward progress was slowed to almost nothing. River would pause after almost every step. Sometimes Buck could feel the big horse shudder—the shudder a horse makes when it has given its all and is about to collapse. Buck didn't care. He had no intention of stopping for rest. They would continue on until they reached the Miller Farm or the sawmill settlement.

Eventually, through the swirling snow, Buck saw buildings. Too deadened to feel any excitement, he simply allowed the horses to walk on. Although the buildings appeared to be as close as a mile, it took another hour to reach them. He recognized the buildings as the Miller farm. He pushed River on toward the house until the horse was stopped by the picket fence Buck remembered being there. Buck dug his heels into the roan's ribs until he forced him to break the fence in, then rode up onto the front porch. He fell from the horse to the snow on the porch as Mr. Miller fought to force the door open against the drifted snow.

"My God man, you're near dead!" Mr. Miller tried to help Buck to his feet. Chuck, Sam, and Mrs. Miller pushed through the door as Hannah watched out the front window. "Chuck, Sam, fight your way to the barn with those horses and see to them!" Mr. Miller yelled then he and Mrs. Miller part walked, part drug Buck inside the house.

They helped Buck to the couch. Mr. Miller tore his soaked and frozen clothes from him, Mrs. Miller brought slightly warmed water and towels, and started rubbing his frozen limbs, urging them back to life.

"It'll be a miracle, Buck, if you don't lose some fingers and toes over this. What the hell were you doing out there?"

Buck never answered. He slept through the night until awakened by regular morning activity in the Miller kitchen. "Sorry to wake you Buck, but I've got hungry folks to feed." Mrs. Miller apologized.

"I hope I'm one of those people." Buck said. "But my legs, hands and feet pretty much feel like they're on fire."

"I reckon you'll be a day or two getting back to normal," Mr. Miller told him.

"Yeah, I feel pretty low. How are my horses, they damn near killed themselves gettin' me here."

"Not a nick on 'em." Chuck said with a big smile. "They're sure worn-out, though. I reckon they'll take longer to be back on their feet than you will. They both got frostbit ears, eyelids and noses. Other than that, they ought to be just fine."

"Poor devils, I've ridden an awful lot of horses in my lifetime, and rode some to death … But those two, I have no words."

"What ya' got in that big bundle Buck?" Sam asked innocently.

Buck struggled to sit up, looked slowly around the room. Everyone was there so at least he would only have to say it once. Before he could speak, his eyes caught fire again, burning with the wet of sadness. Hannah sprinted from the kitchen and dropped to her knees next to Buck. "It's ... Mrs. Harris." He dropped his face into his hands, and Hannah hugged him around his legs as tight as she could squeeze.

Mrs. Miller busied herself putting the finishing touches on the breakfast.

The men sat in the living room waiting for Buck to say something else. When he didn't, Mr. Miller offered. "You're welcome to stay the winter."

Mrs. Miller announced that breakfast was ready, and she would serve Buck on the couch if he liked.

"I'd like to join you all at the table."

Later that day Buck stood at the front window watching Sam, Chuck, and Mr. Miller shovel a path from the house to the barn and privy. The snow and the wind had stopped, revealing a beautiful day. As far as the eye could reach, the prairie glistened white, painting a peaceful, inviting view. He wondered if Mrs. Harris would have enjoyed this view.

Hannah and Mrs. Miller sat whispering, quietly peeling potatoes for the evening meal. He was surprised at how hungry he was. It seemed ever since he'd been awake he'd done nothing but eat. He poured a cup of coffee, took a chair at the table, stole a potato from the peeled pot, and munched it like an apple. "Now Buck it would be a far better potato if you let me boil it first." Mrs. Miller suggested with a pleasant look his way.

"And I'm looking forward to eating a passel of your boiled potatoes tonight." He fussed with the edge of the tablecloth as if straightening the hanging tassels, then picked up a spoon and tapped softly on the potato bowl, his mind everywhere but with him. "Better go check my horses."

He found Diablo and River in big warm stalls bedded knee deep in dry prairie grass and dining on mountains of the same prairie grass hay. "Looks like you boys are doing fine. Don't get too settled in though 'cause in a few days we'll be leavin'. You fellas did alright. Don't reckon I'll ever be able to pay you back. Looks like you'll both lose the tips of your ears. Guess you can figure that as your medals for performance above the call of duty."

He walked across the barn to his belongings stacked neatly against the wall. His saddle and saddlebags had been cleaned and soaped. His eyes fell on the blanket holding Mrs. Harris. He didn't need to cry anymore. All he needed now to was manage his rage.

Mr. Miller came up behind him. "Doing better, Buck?"

"A little." He lied.

"Your horses look fine this morning. You sure can pick 'em."

"Yeah that pair I aim to keep." He turned and shuffled to the horses. "They'll look a little funny with short ears though, won't they?" None of Buck's normal joviality danced across his face, only eyes that held the blank, hollow look of a hurting man.

"What's clawing at you, Buck?"

"Been wanting to ask ... about Mrs. Harris ... she should rest in a happy place. If you'd allow it."

"Saw that coming. We've already agreed, and I was going to make you the offer when I thought the time was right."

The next morning found Buck in the Miller family cemetery digging through four feet of snow to uncover the earth below. One good thing about the blizzard coming so early and fast was the ground didn't have a chance to freeze.

By noon, Buck had the grave dug, then gathered the Miller family and asked Mr. Miller to read over her grave. Buck couldn't listen. He'd asked it for Mrs. Harris' sake. But it was a nice sound all the same. Mr. Miller had that kind of voice. One that can make you feel everything is going to be just fine, even if you're all tore up inside.

Buck stood solemn, staring at the mound of brown dirt covering the finest woman he'd ever known. He never noticed everyone quietly slipping away. Knees weak, mind blank, he fell on the snow pile next to the fresh grave and smoked a cigar, with Mrs. Harris.

****

The entire Miller clan gathered on the porch to see him off two days later. "Come back and see us soon Buck!" Hannah Miller yelled after him.

River did his duty again that day, pushing through the snow the entire day. Buck was comfortable in the saddle, snacking regularly on Mrs. Miller's goodies. As the hours wore on and the sun shone brightly, his mood began to lighten and the goodies kept his belly full, helping him keep warm. All too soon the sun began to set. At this rate his destination was a very long ten hours or so away. It was time to switch horses and, while on the ground, he noticed the snow wasn't quite as deep the farther west he traveled.

Traveling by bright moonlight, this journey seemed almost pleasant. The horses were not struggling as hard, his belly was full, and his thoughts were more of anticipation than sorrow.

Up ahead he finally saw it ... That little sod house with yellow light streaming out through slits in the hide covered window bouncing on the white snow. The last mile took too long; he was ready to be done traveling. He stopped at the porch, gave the snowbound homestead a once over, and felt a grin of satisfaction crawl across his cold face.

"Yo! The house! You've got company!"

"Buck Hawkins, what are you doing out here in this?" Soft Cloud ran to give him a welcoming hug.

"If you'll have me, I'm here for the winter!"

CHAPTER FORTY

Five weeks had passed since Buck stumbled onto the porch of the soddy. Most evenings were spent around the fire listening to Buck spin yarns of past exploits. Tonight was shaping up to be a humdinger of a story time.

"Well, Hickok and me had been behind enemy lines for almost two weeks and it was hotter than hell. Neither one of us had any ammunition left and we were on foot, both our horses having run off two nights earlier, and boy howdy, was there ever a skirmish going on ahead of us. We looked at each other understanding we were in a jim-dandy fix. There we stood, less than a mile from a skirmish, no horses, no ammunition, and the whole damn mess movin' our way like a swarm of bees and rattlesnakes. It was Hickok's idea to climb the tree. I said, Damned if I will Bill, they'll shoot us like treed 'coons!"

"Hickok didn't wait for me to cooperate, he climbed that big tree so fast, I wasn't sure he wasn't a treed 'coon! He was so skinny that when he laid down on that big branch he was absolutely invisible. Well, I was standing there with my mouth open and them Rebs an' Yanks kept on coming and I had to do something. So I shimmied up the same tree. Only I went higher than Hickok. Wouldn't you know, they fought right under us for nearly two hours and that damned tree branch kept gettin' harder and harder. After a bit the fighting ceased but the Yanks camped out right there. Right under our tree!"

"Yeah, but that was a good thing." Tom offered. "'Cause you guys were spying for the Yanks."

"Actually it was a bad thing, because we had on Reb shirts, and we didn't have any papers to prove we were Yanks."

"What did you do?" Soft Cloud leaned closer to Buck.

"We spent one whole night and most of the next morning up those damned trees."

"Then what?" Soft Cloud inquired, her eyes still watching every word leave Buck's lips.

"We got to walking after they decamped, and in about two hours we ran into one of General Sheridan's aides who had watched the whole skirmish. He claims he saw us up in the trees and had been pointing us out to his troopers all morning, thinking it was some grand joke. Knowing all the time we couldn't give ourselves up and we were flat stuck. Hickok got even for us though. He mixed a little black powder in his pipe tobacco and the whole camp got a hell of a hoot when the poor fellow's pipe blew up in his face!"

As he would often do while lounging about the fire in the evenings, Tom played with the beautiful silver locket that had fallen onto the wagon bed all those weeks ago. He opened it and looked at the little girl's picture, never quite getting over how much she really did look like her mother. It pained him to think this little girl might be out there alone. Maybe with someone mean like he had been with for all those horrible years. He was absentmindedly tapping the locket on the arm of his chair when the little piece of glass fell out.

At first, it simply startled Tom. Then he noticed the way the picture had been cut to fit into the locket. It left some folded edges. Acting on an impulse, he yanked his knife from its sheath and with its sharp tip, pried the picture from the locket. Fumbling with the picture, he turned it over. There was writing on the back of the picture!

Tom forced the picture into Buck's startled hands. "What does that say,

Buck? What does that say?"

Buck held the picture close to the fire and studied the faded gray words.

"Sarah Jane Hartman." Buck read out loud. "That's her name, Tom! Sarah Jane Hartman. Let me see if there's more, yes, May 5, 1865, Six Years, Ogallala."

"That would be just a few months ago, wouldn't it Buck?" Tom gripped Buck's hands.

"Yes … Yes, it would. It's January now, and it's '66."

Tom tenderly replaced the photograph and the glass and closed the locket. Poor little girl, he thought as he hung the locket back on its peg. He returned to his seat by the fire saddened again, thinking of Ogallala, and that poor little girl, maybe having a rough go of it. He could still remember the town of Ogallala. He was very young then but he remembered a loud, dirty place.

"I'll go for Sarah Jane Hartman and if she is unhappy I'll bring her back to my ranch."

Buck and Soft Cloud were not surprised. But they were concerned. Tom is a very young man even though he possesses extraordinary talents when it comes to firearms and hunting. These are skills needed to survive on the open plain, not really all that suited for life in the city.

"Tom, this picture's almost a year old. She may be in Santa Fe by now," Buck cautioned.

"I don't think so. I think she is in Ogallala and I think she is sad and unhappy."

"Tom, you're blaming yourself for something that just happened on its own. You didn't kill her mother on purpose. And it's not your fault, even if she is unhappy," Buck tried to reason.

"Well, whatever you think, it will be a few months before you can head out across the plains anyway." Soft Cloud pointed out the obvious.

CHAPTER FORTY-ONE

By the first days of March, much of the snow had gone from the prairie, and green dotted the land again. On warm days Tom and Buck worked side by side, completing the large corral and several smaller ones. The place had begun to look like a genuine horse ranch.

One sunny morning while Tom was putting the finishing touches on a gate near the barn, he paused to watch Buck walk to the pasture and come back with Diablo. "Going somewhere?"

"Got some unfinished business."

"Tall Dog?"

"Yep."

"Not gonna let you go alone, Buck."

"How's that?"

"I've begun to think of us as friends and partners. Besides, I'm in this Tall Dog business as thick as you."

"Best get your gear then, I reckon."

After gathering their weapons and ammunition, Tom rolled the white buffalo hide tight and strapped it behind his saddle. Ready to ride, the solemn pair left Soft Cloud and the dogs in charge of the ranch. She could have tried to talk them out of going, but knowing there was no point, she had simply helped them gather the things they needed. She stood by the well, and watched as they slowly trotted away.

Suddenly she ran for the barn, threw a rope on Big Fella, and charged after them. She galloped across the prairie leaving the dogs far behind to stop next to Tom on the black stallion.

"Soft Cloud?" He was able to mutter before she leaned toward him, grabbed his hair and yanked his mouth to hers. She pushed him back in his saddle, almost knocking him from his horse where he sat staring at her with a most bewildered look. Buck did an admirable job of keeping his mouth shut, although he was bursting at the seams.

"You had better come home to me in one piece—TOM NAMED BY HORSE!"

She whirled Big Fella about and raced away before either Tom or Buck could manage a word.

Tom was totally and completely overcome while Buck was beside himself in delirium. "I reckon I know where I stand in this triangle … Tom Named by Horse!" Buck hooted and galloped away.

"Wait a minute, Buck," Tom hollered as he tried to catch up. "What did she mean by that?"

They rode together across the prairie in the early spring sunshine. Mile after mile, poor Tom suffered the endless ribbing of his good friend Buck Hawkins. "Maybe this winter we'll hear the pitter-patter of little Injun feet on that dirt floor. What do you think—Tom Named by Horse?"

"You ought to knock that off, Buck. You know it makes me feel funny when you talk like that."

Buck did relent but not so much because he worried about upsetting Tom. Mostly he just couldn't think of any more jabs. So, for a while they rode on in peace.

Without warning Tom leaped from his horse, Henry in hand. Buck, not knowing what was up did likewise and stood searching for trouble when Tom's rifle rang out with five rapid shots. Buck had dismounted so fast he failed to keep hold of Diablo's reins and both horses bolted from their side and galloped away.

"DAMMIT! There goes our ammo!" Buck yelled as he hit the dirt alongside Tom.

"You figure them prairie dogs will put up much of a fight?" Tom laughed and rolled in the wet grass kicking his heels high and slapping the ground.

"Prairie dogs? Damn you Tom! I thought we were about to get it!"

"We are. We're just about to get prairie dog for supper and you're just about to get up and go get those horses."

Buck walked in the direction of the horses, muttering to himself all the while about how that kid should soon learn to think before he just up and starts shooting away. Tom headed out to retrieve his prairie dogs. He stood a second and looked out over the dog village stretching before him for several miles, picked up the three dogs he'd shot, and walked a few hundred yards to the top of a rise where he squatted to skin and clean them.

Finding fuel proved a little more challenging, since not all the snow had melted and many of the chips were wet. With some effort, though, Tom was able to find what he figured would be enough to cook the dogs and took the chips back to his campsite, then prepared everything he could. But he had to wait until Buck returned with the horses and matches to start the fire.

Tom laid waiting in the tall grass, nearly asleep, when rifle fire jolted him awake. He leveraged a shell into the chamber and ran toward the shooting, knowing if Buck needed help that he had only ten rounds left. He had been beginning to suspect Buck had run into trouble and now this told it. If Buck hadn't found their horses with his saddlebags, Tom figured this could get rough. He ran to the top of the first rise and saw nothing.

Two more shots shattered the prairie silence. At least he was headed in the right direction. He thought about firing a shot to see if Buck would respond, but quickly chose against that. He would need every round in his rifle. Buck could not be far, but where? Where were the horses? He ran with all he had to the next rise and dropped.

Like a sneaking coyote, Tom crept to the very peak and looked out over the prairie, his eyes darting left and right. Still he saw nothing. There was a good bit of daylight, even though twilight was beginning to cast its long shadows. Where was Buck? Who was doing the shooting? Sitting there would not find Buck, so he ran again in the direction of the last, long-faded shots. From the years of following the old hider's wagon, Tom knew he could run all night if he had to. His eyes and ears ached from straining. Not a sign, not a sound. The dark shape of the next hill lay ahead. Buck had to be just on the other side of that rise.

Again, Tom crept over the top. Darkness began to swallow the prairie. Frustrated, he lay flat straining his eyes into the far reaches of the thick darkness. He realized he could run over the prairie all night and not find his friend. Then in the distance he saw the tiny lick of light of a small campfire. That made no sense, Buck would not start a fire. The answer was simple. It wasn't Buck's fire.

Tom crawled for what seemed the night, creeping and waiting, until close enough to see there were five or six men huddled around the fire. Fortunately, whoever had Buck had built their camp in a small stand of woods and that offered him cover as he approached. He picked his way through the brushy edge of the wood lot. In the total darkness he felt a little braver. Tom heard the loud voices of renegade Indians liquored up. He breathed a sigh thinking their drunkenness might make things a bit easier, but it could also make them more dangerous.

Like a cat stalking its prey Tom moved ever closer to the fire and the renegades. Finally close enough to get a good look, he counted seven, but Buck wasn't one of them. Tom froze, not sure of his next move. Had they shot Buck? Was he laying somewhere out on the prairie, dead already? He decided to creep to the other side of the fire to get a clear view of the far side of the camp.

It reminded Tom of the times the old buffalo hunter would make him sneak into renegade camps to steal their whiskey. Never once had he been caught. Of course, some of the trick was to make sure they drank a lot of it first. From the looks of this bunch, they had.

Successful in his efforts to reach the other side, he poked his nose up and over a fat log and counted eight men. One lay on his back, perhaps having drunk enough whiskey to fall asleep. Tom figured he had the drop on them. But that was cutting it close, eight of them, and ten rounds in his rifle. Pretty darned tight. Then he realized he could understand some of what they were saying. They were talking Sioux. Two renegades stumbled to the sleeping man and kicked him in the ribs. The man refused to move. Tom snuck to the other end of the log to move closer to the fire for a better look. The man they kicked was staked, spread eagled, to the ground. Tom's anger swelled in his chest when he realized the staked man was Buck. His fingers had a mind of their own as they moved to the trigger guard of his rifle.

Buck lay less than twenty feet away, but how could Tom get to him? The renegades continued drinking, laughing and celebrating that they had captured the great army scout, Buck Hawkins. They wanted to kill him but they knew if they didn't save that honor for Tall Dog, Tall Dog would kill them.

Tom decided to wait for the renegades to go to sleep then sneak in and cut Buck free. He waited for hours. It was a difficult wait because they kept kicking Buck as he lay there helpless. Eventually one of the renegades slipped into the shadows. Taking a big risk, Tom crept around the edge of the camp to where he had seen the man go into the woods. Fortune was with him, as the man's back was to him and he was involved in his business.

Tom sprinted the last ten feet and slid his sharp edged Bowie across the man's throat. He never even grunted. As he crumbled Tom saw he was wearing Buck's leggings. Without a sound he removed them. No ammunition in the deep pouches. Behind him horses on the picket line fidgeted and snorted offering him an idea. Cut the horses loose and divide the camp.

He froze when laughter and noise in the camp stopped. Sneaking back to the fire Tom saw Tall Dog had arrived. There just before him, stood the most evil man on the prairie. The waistlong braids of black hair always identified Tall Dog. What would happen to Buck now? Tom watched helplessly as Tall Dog leaned over Buck and made long, slow cuts on his chest.

"I will let him die slowly as he has helped the white man to slowly kill my people!" Tall Dog told his men. "Get me whiskey. We will drink all night as we enjoy the slow death of the great scout. This is a good night for you to die, Buck Hawkins!"

Tom counted twelve renegades in the camp. He had to come up with a better plan. Watching from his hiding place and listening to the renegades as they continued to drink and boast of the settlements they would raid now that the prairie had begun to get warm and the deep snows were gone, Tom tried hard to think of a new plan.

After waiting for longer than he could bear, Tom could not stand to see Buck hurt anymore. He had to act. Buck needed him to act now. With a stealth born of years of hunting, he crept to the picket rope and cut the picket rope ever so gently, not wanting to spook them. This way it would take the horses a moment or two to realize they were free and he could make it back to the campsite.

Tom crouched less than ten feet from Buck and Tall Dog before someone realized the horses were making too much noise.

"Somebody go see what's wrong with the damn horses!" Shouted Tall Dog.

Running, staggering and yelling in their drunken stupor they only succeeded in spooking the horses. The camp bristled with confusion. Tall Dog left Buck to check the horses ... Just far enough away for Tom to take a chance.

With his Henry in his left hand, and his big bladed Bowie in his right, he raced to Buck. Fast as a rattlesnake strike, he cut all four leather ropes that held him to the stakes.

"Get outta here, Buck!" Tom pushed his knife in Buck's hand. For a second Tom was shocked at how cold and weak Buck's hand felt. Then he folded Bucks trembling fingers around the bone handle and yanked Buck to his feet, and gave him a shove out of the way.

Tall Dog charged Tom. With only his knife in his hand Tall Dog gave a loud roar and lunged toward him. Tom shot him in the chest then dropped two more renegades where they stood.

The renegades that had gone to chase the horses began to run back to camp. Kneeling beside Tall Dog as he gasped his last breaths, Tom dropped more renegades. The rest fled into the darkness.

Tom wrestled Tall Dog's knife from his hand and cut off such a huge piece of his scalp his left ear came with it. But Tall Dog still breathed.

"Your daughter Soft Cloud lives in my lodge," he told the dying man. Tall Dog continued to struggle and curse Tom with his final breath.

Tom slipped into the woods, searching for Buck. He wished he would have had time to search the camp for ammunition. His Henry was empty.

"Tom ... Tom." Buck had only traveled a few feet and lay in a crumble, in rough shape.

"Can you walk?"

"Not real good. They did a pretty good job on me. Got a few busted ribs, I reckon, and this one slice on my chest is bleeding bad ... You best just leave me."

"The hell you say!" Tom blurted. "Hang on!" Tom left Buck lying and worked his way back to the fire and ripped Buck's army blouse and vest from a dead renegade. He darted to the other side of the camp, picked up Buck's leggings, and found his moccasin boots. The camp was still deserted, so Tom searched for weapons and ammunition. He took the revolvers and loaded gunbelts strapped to the waist of two dead renegades, and from Tall Dog his revolver, gunbelt and ammunition belt loaded with .44s for the Henrys.

Tom stood grinning by Buck's side, loaded down with clothes and ammunition.

"Holy Cow." Buck managed a chuckle. "Did you go to the sutler for supplies?"

"Found your clothes. Sorry the shirt and vest got some holes in 'em."

"Not as many holes as Tall Dog, I reckon."

Tom cut strips of cloth from a dead renegade's shirt and wrapped Buck's chest. He helped Buck dress and was packing to leave when two renegades returned leading Diablo and Tom's black stallion, both still saddled with saddlebags and buffalo rifles in place.

Tom and Buck flashed grins. They were so close to the renegades, Tom worried they would be heard. But he had to load his rifle. Each time a shell clicked in place, it sounded like a thunderclap to Tom, but apparently they were too busy examining their dead comrades to notice.

Tom tossed Buck a revolver. The two snuck to the camp's edge and without a second's hesitation, gunned down the renegades. The stallion and Diablo bolted at the gunfire again but they collided with one another, giving Tom just the time he needed to catch Diablo's reins and then the black's.

"Got one more job to do for Red Cloud, Buck," Tom said after stopping the horses.

"You don't mean you're gonna hang around here and build a platform for that bastard?"

"Gave my word to Red Cloud. Besides, you'll keep a watch for me." Tom didn't wait to hear any argument from Buck; he tossed him the Henry and started to break long poles to build a burial platform.

Buck sat as straight as his wounds allowed and kept a sharp eye for renegades. After a little while he called to Tom. "Hey Tom, they're all dead. There were only twelve counting Tall Dog himself, and I just counted that many scattered around here not making any more trouble."

Tom sat atop the platform covering Tall Dog with the sacred white buffalo hide, and didn't bother to answer Buck. He hopped down and helped Buck up on Diablo, and the two friends rode away headed for home. Buck struggled in pain but managed, and in an hour's time they were miles from the renegade's camp where Tall Dog lay on his platform covered in the white buffalo robe as Red Cloud had asked. They slowed to a walk and continued that pace for about another hour, when Tom stopped his horse.

"How are you doing, Buck?"

"Reckon I'll hang in there. Want to ride clean through to the ranch?"

"Figure you can make it all the way on your own?"

"Something on your mind?"

"Ogallala and Sarah Jane Hartman." Tom pulled the locket from his shirt pocket. "Point me in the right direction."

"Can't let you go it alone."

"I don't figure you can make the ride, you're heading back to the ranch. Let Soft Cloud fix you up … I got to do this Buck."

"Tom, you're just a kid damn it. That town will eat you alive. You won't stand a chance!"

"Pretty much what you said about Tall Dog, isn't it?"

"Gotta give you that, you're hell in a prairie fight. But this won't be anything like that. Ogallala is a rough town full of tough hombres and you're just a kid."

"Call me a kid again and I'll give those leggings back to the dead Indian."

"How about this? You ride with me for about another hour, while I take you to school … And learn you about city life."

"Start learnin' me, teacher Buck."

Peacefully they rode through the night as Buck talked about corrupt sheriffs, rowdy saloons, horse thieves, cattle thieves, pickpockets, gamblers, outlaws and drunkards, dark streets and alleys. "Cover your back. And most important Tom—don't trust anyone. They're going to see you like a kid, fresh off the farm but looking like an Indian, and they'll try to give you the business. The sheriff in Ogallala used to be a fella named Brad Johnson. Not quite on the up and up. But start with him. Tell him you're a friend of mine. Keep your revolver strapped and loaded and don't go nowhere without your Henry … Just keep going north, and you'll hit the Oregon Trail. Go east, and it runs right into Ogallala."

Buck leaned, reached and shook Tom's hand. "You have about a two-day ride ahead of you." He untied the scabbard holding his Sharps. "You'll need money. You'll get plenty for this. Don't take less than $300 and make your transaction private. Be sure no one sees you with the cash. They'll kill a man in that town for a buck fifty. Don't let anyone see your money. You get in a fight, you kill the man who started it! Don't mess around. You drop him. Take the sidearms and belts, too, they should be worth thirty dollars each."

It suited Tom that Buck wouldn't be with him on this journey. He wanted his first brush with town life to be on his own. He decided then and there to be the toughest green kid Ogallala ever saw. Sioux leggings and all.

CHAPTER FORTY-TWO

Just as Buck had predicted, on the afternoon of the second day the black carried him over the last hill between them and Ogallala. Tom sat a few seconds taking in the view of the crowded little town.

Dust swirled as high as the shabby wooded structures as they approached the west end of town. Guiding the black down the busy main street, he heard as many comments regarding the fine horse as he did about himself.

"You got a lot of nerve, young buck, ridin' into town in the broad daylight," hooted one man from the wooden sidewalk.

"How much you want for that stallion, a bottle of whiskey?" taunted another.

"Naw, he ain't old enough for whiskey!" jeered the first man.

Tom rested his hand on his Navy and kept moving. He found the sign on the only brick building on the street. Buck had told him the sheriff's office was brick, so he rode to the hitching rail. He gathered the revolvers and gunbelts, leaving Buck's Fifty in the scabbard.

It took Tom's eyes a second to adjust to the dim light inside. "Are you Sheriff Johnson?" He studied the big man behind the desk.

"Who wants to know?" The big man's mouth overflowed with tobacco juice.

Thinking of the name given him by Soft Cloud, and how proud it made him feel, he identified himself. "Tom Named by Horse."

"Well, Sheriff Johnson is dead. Dead almost four months already, I'm filling in for the time being. What business does an Indian pup have with the sheriff?"

The puddle of tobacco slobber on the desk told Tom he'd awakened the big fella. He fought the urge to laugh and stepped up to the desk and dropped the gun belts on it, making sure they landed with a solid thud. "I'm not an Indian, I just lived with them."

"Who'd you kill to get these?" The sheriff demanded, his big eyes, buried beneath overgrown eyebrows, sized Tom up.

"Some renegades that ran with Tall Dog. Killed them two days ago. Killed Tall Dog too." Tom informed the fat man in a flat voice.

The sheriff fell back in his chair, first with a look of surprise, then his look changed to disbelief and anger. "You expect me to believe some young, living with the Indians kid, killed Tall Dog?"

"I did, and I have his scalp in my saddlebag to prove it."

"Let me see the scalp ... Then maybe I'll believe you, kid."

Tom went to his horse and fished the scalp from his saddlebag, now a shriveled stinking clump of skin and hair. But anyone would recognize Tall Dog's long black braids with silver conchos twisted in the hair.

On top of the desk, Tom did his best to stretch out the shriveled scalp while the sheriff watched in amazement, examining the long braids decorated with conchos from Hooker's hat and a mangled ear. "Well I'll be damned. Well I'll be damned. Half the United States cavalry is out there trying to kill that bastard, and you got his scalp dryin' in your saddlebag. How can I help you ... Tom Named by Horse?" The fat man's opinion of

Tom had changed.

Tom poked his fingers into his shirt pocket, and pulled out the locket. "I'm looking for this girl."

The sheriff reached across the wide desk, took the locket and studied the little girl's face. "Nobody I ever saw. My name's Clyde by the way."

"I'll need money to be in town, looking for this girl. Would you buy those guns? Her name is Sarah Jane Hartman."

"Why are you looking for her?" The sheriff studied Tom with puzzled but sincere eyes.

Tom's back stiffened, his heart hurt. "I need to find her for her mother."

Tom read on his face that the sheriff had more questions, and was relieved he chose not to ask. "Not in the market for used pistols, kid. Take 'em down the street to the Watkins gunsmith shop. He'll buy them from you. You killed Tall Dog? Just a word of advice, when you get those guns sold, your first stop better be to get a bath and some regular clothes. You won't last half a day in that Indian rig."

"But Buffalo Horn, son of Red Cloud, gave me these. They were his."

"Don't tell anyone else if you want to keep your scalp. Do like I told you and hurry on."

"Could I leave my horse tied to your rail 'til I'm done? It's shady there."

"I'll keep an eye on him, now git."

Finding Watkins gunsmith shop proved easy with its big window under the porch stacked with guns. The door clanged a bell when Tom opened it. Behind a long, wooden counter strewn with leather and gun parts stood a short, weak looking man with dishonest eyes and a greasy leather apron. "How much for these two guns and gun belts?" Tom dropped them on the counter.

Displaying an attitude of disinterest the little man examined the guns, "I can give you one dollar each."

"But Sheriff Clyde just told me they're worth $30 a piece."

"You know Sheriff Clyde?" The shifty man looked out the window nervously, as he fondled the gun belts with his greasy, dirty hands.

"I do. He likes me."

"I'll give you $20 a piece, that's my top offer."

Tom began to gather the guns and belts. "I'll have to check with Sheriff Clyde before I can sell them for less than $30 a piece."

A beaten Watkins relented, teaching Tom a valuable lesson in namedropping.

Tom had never bathed in a tub before but figured he could get used to it, and his new clothes and hat made him look taller, older. With his new rig Tom headed for the sheriff's office, mostly because he could not figure out where else to go and he wanted Sheriff Clyde to know he had obeyed him.

He found Sheriff Clyde still reclining at his desk. "Well I'll be damned, ain't you somethin'? You almost look civilized." Sheriff Clyde grinned at Tom's new getup. "Let me have another look at that little picture. Been thinkin' about it ever since you left." Tom had also purchased a new leather vest and it was in the breast pocket close to his heart that he carried little Sarah Jane Hartman's picture. He pulled out the locket and handed it to Sheriff Clyde.

"No. No. I can't say that I ever saw her ... I see you didn't put your horse up at the livery yet."

"Not yet, got him tied just outside here, standing in the shade."

"Take him down to the end of town. The livery's that big barn. Hank Reynolds runs it. Tell 'im I sent you and he should take real good care of your horse."

Tom had never seen a livery before, he found it dark and dank, and did not want his horse in it. "Can you keep my horse in an outside corral?" He assumed the stoop-shouldered old man at the door was Hank Reynolds.

"Sure can, 25 cents a day, a nickel extra for hay and oats ... Hey what's a kid like you doing with a cavalry horse?" Hank noticed the brand.

"He was a gift from a friend of mine, Buck Hawkins. He's going to be my first stallion at my ranch southwest of here."

"You expect me to believe a famous army scout like Buck Hawkins would even know a green-eared kid like you, let alone give him a stallion like this. Kid, I see a lot of horses and there ain't one in five hundred built like this."

"We've been friends ever since the day I saved his life, the first time."

"If you say so, kid. What are ya doin' with those two buffalo rifles?" Hank's admiration of the Sharps showed in the old man's darting eyes.

"The one is mine, the other belongs to Buck. He gave it to me to sell if I run out of money."

"You just keep spinnin' 'em longer and taller, don't ya kid?"

"Have you ever seen this little girl?"

The locket looked tiny in Hank's old grizzled hands. He turned it over and studied the picture. "Not sure kid. Maybe." His voice trailed off.

"You think you saw her?" Excitement colored Tom's face.

Looking at Tom with a mean, piercing stare, Hank asked, "Why ya lookin' for her?"

Tom had begun to understand that people seemed to have a hard time believing his honest answers. "I was asked to find her, for her mother." He was also learning to lie when necessary.

"Why would a girl's own mother have to find her daughter?"

"They say someone from the town of Ogallala stole her about a year ago. Look on the back of the picture." Tom was beginning to get the hang of lying.

"What does it say? I can't read."

"It says Sarah Jane Hartman, six years, Ogallala, 1865." Tom recited, bluffing.

"Yeah, I may have seen this little girl here last summer. Haven't seen her for a while, though. Important to you, is it?"

"More than I let on."

"Why don't you let me tend your horse while you go to the hotel and get some vittles, then maybe old Hank can sniff around a bit for the girl, Sarah Jane Hartman, right?"

"That's it!" Tom beamed, shaking old Hank's hand with a hard grip.

"What do you want me to do with all them rifles?"

"I'll carry my Henry. Buck says can't be too careful here. Got a safe place for the big rifles?"

"I reckon under my mattress is safe enough."

With a new spring in his step, Tom headed to the hotel Hank had steered him toward. He did wonder though, if trusting the old man was wise. Remembering Buck had warned, "Don't trust anyone." But the old fellow seemed helpful. So did Sheriff Clyde.

This was Tom's first visit to a hotel and he was overcome by the closeness of it all. People sitting around little tables, talking too loud, smoking cigars, drinking whiskey, eating. To someone used to the wide open prairie, this felt wrong, confusing. Tom stood a moment, allowing his mind and body to adjust to the smoke and noise.

"May I help you young man?" A stranger greeted Tom.

"Help me with what?" Tom sized the odd-looking fellow up. He wondered why he had so much grease on his hair, and why he talked as if he could barely move his lips. And why did he walk so strange?

"What do you need? Would you like a seat at the bar or a table?"

"I was thinking of a meal. That's what you do here, right?"

"Among other things." The stranger led Tom to a table by the large front window, but Tom noticed the welcoming nature had left the stranger's attitude, replaced with one of self-importance.

Tom was busy studying the busy street through the big window when another stranger approached him. "What would you like?"

He simply had no idea how to respond. What do they eat in a hotel in Ogallala? He wagered if he asked for a fat prairie dog this fella wouldn't believe him either. He looked around the room and saw someone eating potatoes and steak.

"What's that fellow eating?" He pointed to a well-dressed gentleman enjoying his meal.

"Why he's having our fabulous steak dinner."

"Buffalo or antelope?"

"Of course, neither ... it's beef." This stranger too appeared impatient with Tom.

"From a cow?"

"Not a cow, you fool, a steer. Have you never had beef before?"

Tom knew if he told him no, he wouldn't believe him. So he just ordered. "I would like that and could I have some water? I'm very thirsty."

The new fellow left Tom's side and disappeared into the busy, crowded room. Tom looked over the room and decided he was becoming quite interested in the goings on. People talking so loudly, they had to talk ever louder to be heard by each other sitting at the same table. He was glad he was alone. He wondered if any of them could help him find Sarah Jane Hartman. As he pondered, the stranger returned to his table with a glass pitcher of water and a glass. At first he was quite surprised by the look of a glass pitcher. It looked as if the water was holding itself. But Tom was a quick learner and, one glass at a time, drank the entire pitcher. About the time he finished his water the stranger returned with a plate full of food. "Here you are sir, let me know if you need anything else."

"More water?" Tom settled down to enjoy his meal. Luckily he did remember from his very young childhood that townsfolk used these metal things to eat. He almost remembered how and, after a few moments of studying the room, mastered the art of carving a steak and putting it into his mouth with a fork instead of picking up the entire steak to tear a bite off.

It did not take him long to clean his plate and down another pitcher of water. The stranger came back and asked him how everything was and Tom assured him it had been a very fine meal and requested coffee.

Sitting in a padded chair by the large window was beginning to become quite comfortable as Tom studied the sights of the dusty, busy street. Most of the buildings were wooden, a few had canvas walls, and some had plank boardwalks in front of them and were covered with wide porch roofs. People scurried by the window, and wagons and carriages passed on the street. Seems to be a lot of people in a hurry in this town called Ogallala, he thought.

Commotion at the far end of the street drew Tom's eye to a large freight wagon pulled by six horses. Tom wondered why the fool driving the rig would gallop down a busy street. Then he saw a little girl standing alone in the street crying, terrified. He grabbed his Henry, dove through the big window sending shards of glass spraying onto the unsuspecting people on the sidewalk, bolted through the crowd, knocking many of them off their feet, snatched up the little girl, and ran to the far side of the street. The out-of-control rig flew by, scattering people and horses, as it thundered recklessly on its way.

"It's okay now, I can hold you 'til you stop crying." Tom knelt and hugged her tight.

"My baby my baby. My baby! ... How can I ever thank you? You saved my little girl's life!" A tear-streaked woman nearly knocked him from his feet, she hugged and smothered them with kisses.

"I reckon that'll be thanks enough ma'am." Tom tipped his hat.

"Well, I guess I might have to start believing your tall tales!" Sheriff Clyde pushed his way through the ever-increasing crowd surrounding Tom, the young woman, and still screaming child.

"Sheriff! Sheriff Clyde! That fool smashed our front window! I want him arrested! I want you to arrest him and make him pay for that window! We had that window shipped all the way from St. Louis! Now you arrest him this instant!"

"Now settle down, Mr. Boscov. Folks, why don't you give us some room here."

"Sheriff, he saved my little girl!" The still-sobbing mother blurted out.

Tom stood, totally bewildered by the level of excitement. It seemed to him the natural thing to do was get to the little girl, so he did. All these people had been closer to her than he, but none had made a move to save her. Now they all come crowding in, talking, pushing and shoving.

"Mr. Boscov, Tom, and Mrs. Bradley, you all come down to my office and we'll sort this out."

The door hadn't even closed behind them before Mr. Boscov started. "Sheriff that man smashed a very expensive window."

Tom thought, what an odd, puny little man, and he was beginning to get on Tom's nerves. If he said one more time that Tom broke his window ... Tom might break his jaw too.

"Mr. Boscov, my family will gladly pay for the window." Mrs. Bradley offered. "Did you not see what happened?"

"I did, but our hotel has doors! But he" pointing his finger in Tom's nose, "broke my window."

Without hesitation Tom punched him in the nose. "Now I'll wager I broke your nose, too."

Sheriff Clyde wrestled Tom away, turned on his heel and pointed to Mr. Boscov, "Now you, get back to your hotel."

"I want him arrested. I think he broke my nose!"

"If you don't get out of here, I'll break your jaw!" boomed the Sheriff.

Tom felt a smile creep across his face as Mr. Boscov left, holding his nose, shaking his head and muttering.

"I'll have to go see him later," Sheriff Clyde said. "Mrs. Bradley, this is Tom Named by Horse. Tom, this is Mrs. Bradley. Her husband owns the largest cattle ranch in the Nebraska territory."

"Tom Named by Horse. Are you an Indian?" Mrs. Bradley looked him up and down.

"No. It's hard to explain."

"It seems, Tom, I owe you a great deal. What can I ever do to repay you?"

Sheriff Clyde excused himself after telling Tom and Mrs. Bradley they had the use of the office as long as they needed. Tom was beginning to feel comfortable with Sheriff Clyde. He had a gruff way about him that Tom suspected hid a genuinely caring fellow. Tom wondered what it must be like to be Sheriff in such a place.

"Well, I came to Ogallala looking for someone."

"My husband and I know a lot of people in the area. Perhaps we could help."

Tom pulled the locket from his vest pocket, opened it, and showed the picture to Mrs. Bradley. By the way she studied it, he knew she recognized the little girl looking out from behind the cracked glass. Mrs. Bradley spent a long moment gazing at the picture. Finally she spoke. "I have seen this little girl. I've seen her in town begging at the back doors of the hotels and saloons with other desperate children."

Her response sucked the breath from him. Could he be so near to finding her? He found it almost impossible to keep from shouting. With effort he managed to control himself.

"When did you see her last?"

"I can't recall that I've seen her any time recently. Have you checked the livery? Many times, the children will sleep in the livery until Hank chases them. Why don't you come along with us, I'm going for my carriage, we'll try to get some information from Hank together. He must have seen her."

They found Hank cleaning stalls. "Hank, I know you've met my friend Tom, and I know he showed you a photograph of a young girl he's looking for. Have you seen her?"

"I knew right off I'd seen that little girl. She used to sleep here some nights with the other kids. But none of them been here for a couple weeks."

Tom studied the old man dressed in a worn shirt and floppy old hat. He looked harmless enough but Tom had a sense about things that few people possessed and he knew there was more to this grizzled liveryman. He searched the old man's eyes as Mrs. Bradley continued. "When was the last time you saw the children, exactly?"

Both Tom and Mrs. Bradley could see the question made Hank uncomfortable. He leaned on the fork, his dark eyes fixed on the floor. Hank told them he just didn't know exactly, couple weeks, maybe three back, they stopped sleeping in the stables.

Tom was about to grab the skinny man and shake an answer out of him when Mrs. Bradley spoke up, but looked at Tom with a question, and knowledge, in her eyes. "Why Hank, when did you get that beautiful carriage?"

"Ain't she a beauty? I bought her just two weeks ago. Gonna rent it out to fancy dudes!" Hank bragged.

"Never saw anything like it." Mrs. Bradley offered a polite smile. "Could you please get my horse and carriage? I need to be on my way." As Hank left to get Mrs. Bradley's horse she turned to Tom, "Why don't you gather your horse and things and ride out to the ranch with me, Tom."

"I kind of figured on staying in town and kicking over some rocks."

With a stern look leveled directly into Tom's eyes, but with the most pleasant voice, Mrs. Bradley insisted. "Come with me back to my ranch. I want you to meet my husband ... tonight, Tom."

"Hank, could you please bring Tom's horse and gear along? He'll be going back to the ranch with us."

When Mrs. Bradley's carriage was ready and Tom had the black stallion saddled, he asked Hank for the buffalo rifles. "Buffalo rifles? What do you mean?" Hank seemed to squirm in his skin.

"I asked if you could keep my rifles when I went about town earlier today." Tom reminded the obviously shaken old man. Tom knew this was going to get touchy.

"I don't remember no buffalo rifles, kid." Hank insisted, doing his best to straighten his slouching posture.

In one fluid movement Tom slid his Henry into the scabbard, whirled about facing Hank, with his revolver pulled and cocked less than an inch away from Hank's nose. "This help your memory any, old man? Just so you know, in the last five days I have killed close to a dozen men and one of them was the renegade Tall Dog. I probably rode one hundred fifty miles, patched up my best friend, left my house, my gal, and jumped through a big ol' window. Shooting you in the face ain't gonna bother me one bit. Think you can remember my rifles?"

"Yes sir, I'll fetch 'em right away." Hank hurried toward his room.

"So you are a gunman," Mrs. Bradley said from the seat of her carriage.

"No, I just can't abide liars, cheats, and mean people."

"Funny how they slipped my mind. Gettin' old, I reckon." Hank mumbled and handed Tom his rifles.

"Try something like that with me again and you won't get much older," Tom advised as he swung up on the big black. "Ready to go, Mrs. Bradley?"

Riding down the crowded, dusty street, Tom felt different leaving town than when he arrived, Buck was sure right though. "Don't trust anyone." He had a strong feeling he could trust Mrs. Bradley though.

When town was comfortably behind them Mrs. Bradley motioned for Tom to come alongside her carriage. "I didn't think it wise to talk in front of Hank, but I have a feeling we can help you find Sarah Jane Hartman. There have been rumors of wayward children being gathered up and sold to miners in the mountains as labor."

"And you think Hank is involved?"

"That's a mighty expensive carriage he just bought and I know I saw her, and I'm certain they slept in the livery."

"What's the way to the mines? I want to go there now."

"No, not yet Tom. First come meet my husband, he may be able to help. And you should spend the night with us and get a good night's sleep."

Disappointed, he gave in and rode with Mrs. Bradley. Along the way, she told Tom how she met her husband on the wagon train heading west from St. Louis a little more than ten years ago. "He was such a tall, handsome man, he caught my eye the moment our family joined the train. He was traveling alone, hired on as a guide. My family was moving west, headed for California. The very first time I saw him I told my sister that I would make him my husband.

"On the trail we suffered several attacks from Indians and bandits, and my John fought valiantly. Because of him, the wagon master, and a few of the men along on the wagon train, we never lost a single head of stock and not a single person was killed or injured on the whole trip. Well, I made sure that Mr. John Bradley noticed what a fine woman I was. And when we put up outside of Ogallala and he heard of this ranch for sale I told him he just had to buy it. It took very little persuading. He collected his pay and went to the territorial land office.

"The wagon train had moved on by the time he finished his business with the territory. It was several weeks later when he came galloping into our night camp. He rode his horse directly to my family's campfire. I'll never forget how he jumped from his horse and fell to one knee like a prince in a fairy tale, took my hand in his, kissed it, and asked me to marry him. Before I could answer, the entire camp cheered and of course I told him yes. He scooped me up, I waved goodbye to my family and friends and away we galloped into our new lives together.

"Those first years were tough. The ranch had a lot of land, but the house was a one-room sod cabin. There wasn't even a well. We had our share of Indian and cattle thief troubles. Keeping the cattle safe was a full time job. We struggled along over the years and gradually the ranch began to take shape. After a few years we managed to build a house. Now we have a bunkhouse, two barns, and thousands of cattle.

"Perhaps this evening my husband will tell you of our cattle drive. In the spring of 1858, he and I and our five hands took our horses and rode all the way to South Texas and gathered a herd of one thousand Mexican cattle. It was the most thrilling adventure of my life."

Tom could have listened to Mrs. Bradley's stories much longer but as the shadows grew long the ranch came into view. They pulled up in front of a fine wooden house painted bright white and surrounded by a white picket fence. Mr. Bradley bounded down the wide porch steps, his smile and eyes beaming. "This is a treat, I didn't expect you until tomorrow evening."

"There was an accident in town." Mrs. Bradley lifted Amanda into John's waiting arms. "Amanda nearly got trampled by a runaway team, but Tom saved her life!"

Tom felt John's eyes sizing him up. The big house and John looking him over made him uneasy. As uneasy as that first night in Soft Cloud's lodge. But John offered his hand in friendship and washed away all the doubt. "Sounds like we owe you a debt of gratitude, young man. Come inside, spend the night, and we'll get to know each other. If there's anything you need, ask."

The inside of a well-manicured home was something brand new for Tom. The fine rugs on the floor, curtains on the windows, stuffed furniture, and fancy kerosene lamps kept Tom intrigued for several moments.

"I've never been inside a house like this before. I've seen them from a distance. Sometimes on the prairie with the buffalo hunter, we would see ranch houses but we would never go in them. I have started my own horse ranch, about a hundred miles south of here, but I just have a sod cabin and corrals. One day I'll build a fine house just like this."

The table they dined at was long and solid. Tom grew quite embarrassed as Mrs. Bradley went on and on retelling the tale of his daring rescue of little Amanda. Tom could see why she had been taken with Mr. John Bradley ten years ago. He was a tall, broad shouldered, dark haired man with intense yet kind eyes. Tom felt the kindness of the man just being at the same table, but the power of the man came through as well. He decided, despite Buck's warning, this was a man he could and would trust.

"Tom Named by Horse, you are forever welcomed on the Bradley Ranch and any help you ever need you can count on us. In the morning, I'll ride with you to town and together we will talk to Hank."

They left the ranch before sunup traveling side by side at a fast trot. The big stallion never seemed to tire. Tom loved riding this horse and challenged John Bradley to a race. "Come on John. Let's see what your boy's got!" They flew down the road nose to nose then Tom's stallion began to pull away. By the time they reached the stream crossing the black was out in front by three lengths.

"Never saw anything like that, Tom! This is my fastest horse!"

They let their horses drink their fill in the stream, while Tom explained his plans for the black stallion and how Buck had given him to him.

"Seems like you're always saving someone's life. You're a good kid, Tom." John pulled his hat and wiped sweat from his brow. "Let's go find this little girl!"

No jeers or strange comments came their way this time as Tom rode with John down Ogallala's dusty main street. The big doors of the livery barn closed as they approached. "Come on, Hank, it's John Bradley. I want to talk to you."

"I know who you are, and I don't want to talk to you. If you hurt me I'll get the sheriff."

"Hank, come out here, we're gonna find you. We can ask you about those kids or we'll ask Sheriff Clyde." John swung open the door and led the way inside the dark barn. Tom pulled his sidearm as he stepped into the darkness.

Hank stepped from the shadows with a shotgun pointed squarely at Tom. "If he makes a move I'll blast him to hell and back!"

Tom didn't blink an eye nor did he holster his gun as he stepped toward Hank. He put his finger in the barrel of the shotgun, and pushed it into the air. John's eyes grew wide in amazement. Tom kept advancing on the withered old man, pulled the hammer back on his .44 and backed him against the wall. "Tell me about that little girl. Tell me about all those kids or I'll blow you to hell right now and you know I will." Tom shoved the barrel of his revolver into Hank's gut hard enough to crack a rib.

"Okay ... okay. Sometimes when kids get too pesky I haul 'em up to the mines in the mountains and sell 'em to the miners ... She's up there. That little girl, Sarah Jane, I sold her a couple of weeks ago."

With the force of a mule kick, Tom struck the man on the side of his head with his bare fist. He collapsed in a crumpled heap. Tom grabbed him by the shirt, lifted him high overhead, and banged him against the wall. Again and again Tom thumped him against the wall. Finally John grabbed Tom's arms and pulled him off, letting Hank fall to the floor motionless.

"Tom, you got your answer. You don't need to kill him."

Tom looked down on the whimpering man. "Yeah, maybe I do."

"Let's get to the mines. We can get there today ... What are you doing, Tom?"

Tom did not respond. He simply continued to strip his new store-bought clothes and dressed himself in the leggings, shirt, vest, and moccasins that Buffalo Horn had given him. He did wear his new hat; the rest of the store-bought clothes he tucked into his saddlebag. They galloped their horses out of town and onto the wagon road that led to the mines in the hills.

"Have a plan, Tom?"

"Yep, I'm going up there to save her. And I'll kill anybody that gets in my way."

"They are a rough bunch up there. You could get her killed. You could get yourself killed. Hell, you could get us all killed. What are you going to do, ride in there and show them your locket?"

"Maybe." Tom pulled the black to a stop and turned him to face John. With a kind of mountainous presence, Tom stared down at John, eyeball to eyeball. "I appreciate your friendship, but if you're afraid, don't ride with me."

Tom galloped away. For a few seconds, John sat frozen in place by Tom's icy words. He dug his heels into the flanks of his own horse and did his best to catch the racing stallion.

They rode in silence for hours at a steady cavalry trot. The wagon road was easy to follow, and they both knew they were nearing the gold mines. Finally, they crested the last hill and looked down into the valley that was home to many of the gold mines, none of which had legal claims since the United States government saw this as land owned by the Sioux Nations. The only law in the mine camps was administered by the fastest gun on the toughest son of a bitch.

Tom kicked the black and galloped pell-mell down the hill. John had no choice but to follow. Miners stopped their work and stood to watch the two galloping horses as they careened down the hill and came to a dusty, sliding stop by a big, leaning shack.

Tom moved the black uncomfortably close to the first miner he reached. The miner stood firm and was about to confront Tom when he was overcome by his presence. "Can I help you, friend?" was all the miner managed to utter.

"Where can I find the kids?"

"What kids?"

Tom raised his leg and kicked the man's face, then moved the stallion to stand over him. "Wrong answer. Try again. Where are the kids?"

A crowd gathered. Tom never noticed or if he did, he gave no sign. The miner lying under the stallion said he didn't know anything about kids. Tom danced the black over him. "Wrong answer." Tom made the stallion rear, his front feet thudded on the miner's chest. He whirled the stallion toward the crowd, pulled his .44, and aimed at the nearest man's face. "Where are the kids?" He demanded in a horribly icy voice.

"I don't know nothing about no kids!"

Tom shot him in the leg. "Where the hell are the kids?" His .44 leveled in the man's face.

John pulled his rifle and lay it comfortably across his lap and sat watching young Tom handle the ever-swelling crowd.

"You can't come in here and take on like this. We got a right to work our mines!" A member of the crowd threatened.

Tom forced the stallion into the crowd pushing some aside, stepping on others. Then he spun the big black in fast circles. A number of miners fell, stepped on. Some undoubtedly suffered broken bones. "You, the man with the big mouth." He pointed his revolver at the man. "You got two seconds to tell me where the kids are. Then I'm gonna blow you to hell."

"The kids are down in the deep mine. They dig for all of us!"

"Somebody better go get 'em!"

"Who the hell do you think you are?" demanded a well-dressed newcomer to the crowd.

"Somebody better get those kids!" John advised. "He's gettin' really pissed off."

"I want to know just what in the hell do you think you're doing! There are over two hundred of us here. We can cut you to shreds!" the well-dressed newcomer informed Tom.

"You won't." With a bitter coldness Tom shot the man. He pushed his stallion to the man that said the kids were in the mine. "Get me the kids."

The mud-caked fat man ran as fast as he could waddle to the obvious mine entrance and disappeared.

"Look over there, Tom!" John pointed to a horde of men storming up the valley carrying picks, shovels and rifles.

Tom holstered the .44, pulled his Sharps, and looked at John with a certain glint in his eye. "Think they'll make it up the hill?" The rifle jumped to Tom's shoulder as if it had a mind of its own and roared. The lead miner scrambling up the hill flew backwards and tumbled down the hill. The others dropped to the dirt. Tom reloaded and fired another round, spraying dirt and rocks in the faces of the huddled, terrified men at the bottom of the hill.

"Look at that, Tom, here come the kids!" John pointed to the fat, mud-caked miner leading a group of about ten children in their direction.

"I guess one of you fellas better get us a team and wagon!" Tom waved his rifle over the crowd.

Several men scrambled to their feet, some to escape, others to secure the wagon and team. The men at the bottom of the hill stayed where they were, content to watch the goings on.

The children were hustled to Tom. Tom instantly recognized Sarah Jane Hartman, skinny and filthy, but he knew it was her. He wanted so to go to her right away but he knew his business with the miners was not yet complete.

In a matter of minutes a mule team and a miner's wagon were delivered and all the remaining miners helped the children into the wagon. Tom ordered John to leave with the wagon while he stayed behind to make sure no one would follow.

Tom watched as the wagon cleared the crest and started down the other side out of sight. "My name is Tom Named by Horse! Today I killed only a few! If I must come for more children, ever again, no miner in this hole will be left alive!" He turned the stallion and raced up the hill. None of the stunned miners even tried to get off a shot.

They thundered up the hill, the black kicking up chunks of dirt and rocks with each powerful lunge, and flew over the crest, quickly overtaking the wagon. Tom jumped from the stallion to the wagon bed with the children, dropped on his knees and hugged little Sarah Jane Hartman. Then he hugged all the children, cursing Hank and the miners, as he looked at their frail little bodies with fingernails completely worn away and bloody tips of fingers from digging in the rocks. Tom laid down on the wagon bed and let the children crawl on him and hug him and thank him over and over again. And he cried until his eyes burned.

John decided to drive straight through the night to get the children back to his ranch as quickly as he could. Where he, Caroline, and Tom could feed and bathe them.

Most of the children were too excited to sleep on the ride. Tom studied Sarah Jane Hartman and wondered how he would tell her about her mother and pondered if he should. Perhaps he would never tell her. Perhaps like him, Sarah Jane Hartman would never know of her true parents. Perhaps it would be better that way.

At last the wagon stopped at the Bradley porch. Caroline ran down the steps around the wagon and hugged her husband. Then the shock of the wagonload of orphans hit her. But for their sake, she was brave.

"Children," she announced. "We are going to the house where you will have milk and fresh baked cake, and then you will all have baths if it takes the rest of the night and all day tomorrow!"

CHAPTER FORTY-THREE

It did take the rest of the night, but what a night it was; splashing water, giggling, and happy, hungry and finally sleepy children. Tom stayed on two more days at the Bradley ranch helping with the children but mostly just allowing the past several months to catch up with him. The Bradley ranch was a comfortable and loving place. Caroline would make a fine mother for all those poor children, and Tom was content in the knowledge that Sarah Jane Hartman would be safe and well cared for. The plans the Bradleys made to build the orphanage on their ranch were already underway before Tom left on the third morning.

Sheriff Clyde had arrested and jailed Hank Reynolds. Mr. Boscov not only forgave Tom for the broken window but made the first donation of one thousand dollars toward the construction of the orphanage. Clarence, the man who walked funny and worked for Mr. Boscov, quit his job and came to work at the orphanage.

Tom patted the black on the neck. "One more stop before heading home, Thunder." He told the great stallion, calling him by the name given him by Sarah Jane Hartman.

Turning Thunder to the east, Tom asked for a quick canter. It was a glorious, clear and sunny day on the prairie. Tom's heart was as light as it had ever been. They enjoyed a spirited, frolicking canter. Thunder could sense the happiness in Tom's heart as they flew across the prairie. Up one hill, down another, through streams and rivers they splashed, dancing through patches of spring wildflowers. Tom and his great horse felt as one, and when he could no longer hold him at a canter he slackened the reins and hollered, "Go on then!"

Like a bullet shot from his buffalo rifle, the great stallion exploded with a tremendous burst of speed. Tom grabbed fistfuls of Thunder's streaming mane as the wind whipped tears from his eyes. He allowed the powerful horse to race along. He knew the horse felt the same as he did. Happy and free, and just needing to fly like the wind.

Mile after mile they flew across the prairie, Thunder never tiring. As they approached a familiar grove of cottonwoods, Tom slowed Thunder to a trot, coming to a stop alongside the Sioux burial scaffold. As was Sioux custom he was taking her bones to rest on sacred lands, on his ranch. Delicately he placed the bones of Sarah Jane Hartman's mother and the remaining fabrics of her clothing in the blanket Caroline had given him for this very purpose. He tied the bundle securely with long leather straps and then tied the bundle to the rear of his saddle.

A little more solemn now, he turned south and asked Thunder for his ground-covering gallop. Now Tom wanted to get home.

Tom and Thunder camped that night out on the prairie. No trees, no stream, no fire, just he, Thunder, the stars, and the sandwich that Caroline had made. Lying on his back he found the North Star. It had been many nights since he had said hello to his friend the North Star, yet like a true friend, its light shone there waiting for Tom to notice.

Thunder's muzzle tickled his face and woke him in the morning. "Ready to go, are you?" He set about the task of saddling and gathering his things, and soon they traveled across the prairie again. Tom guessed by nightfall he would be at his ranch with his friends, Soft Cloud and Buck.

He settled down to enjoy the pleasures of a peaceful ride on a magnificent horse. Thunder's even stride soothed Tom completely and, for hours, he rode lost in daydreams of what the future might hold for him and Soft Cloud, before he saw the vast village of lodges on the prairie ahead of him.

"What's that all about, Thunder?" They loped in the direction of the village knowing his position to be about twenty miles north of his ranch and just thirty or so miles from Fort Laramie. As they neared the Indian village, he recognized it to be the village of Red Cloud and Buffalo Horn. In the weeks he had been gone they must have abandoned their winter village to relocate on the open prairie, but why here?

Tom was greeted at the camp's edge by his friend Buffalo Horn. Buffalo Horn had worked on his English and Tom had polished his Sioux. The two friends no longer needed an interpreter. Buffalo Horn informed Tom they had moved the village to be closer to Fort Laramie for his father was demanding to be heard by the leaders of the U.S. Army.

"Why does Red Cloud want to speak with the Army?"

"My father is angered that the white man is now building a road to take the white man into our hunting grounds at the Black Hills beneath the Big Horn Mountain where the Powder River Runs into the Big Horn. Red Cloud told the General that was our land, wrestled from the Crow nation. He is also angered at the men who make marks on the prairie for another road. A road he has been told will be made of iron. Many Sioux, Cheyenne, and Arapaho will be coming to join my father's village here near the Fort Laramie. Their chiefs will speak with us one day soon of making war. They speak of a great war when thousands of braves will stop the U.S. Army. My father cannot allow these two roads into our hunting lands. This land that was our ancestors' since before time, and we stand on today is all that is left of our proud nations. Perhaps it is time now for us to make war. Perhaps it is time for us to stop the white man who only wants to take the shiny metal that is in our land. Perhaps it is time to stop the white man who kills our sacred buffalo only for it to rot under the sun of the prairie." Buffalo Horn's eyes showed his sadness.

"But your father is a leader of peace. He has not wanted to make war with the U.S. Army."

"My father wants only peace but most white men are greedy, they force my father to listen to the war councils. It is not for him alone to decide this great and terrible thing. My father believes that perhaps there is time still to save our sacred buffalo. He believes it would be a terrible thing for the once mighty herd of buffalo to disappear from the great lands. But he has seen a vision that tells him the white man will one day kill all the buffalo.

"The bones of our sacred buffalo already are scattered and white over the plains. To the greedy white man, these things are not precious. To the greedy white man the buffalo means money. To the greedy white man, shiny metal means money. To the ancient Sioux the buffalo means all life. The Sioux have no use for the shiny metals that lay buried in the great mountains. We have no need to scar the face of those mountains that were here since before the Sioux and Cheyenne, Arapaho and Crow. Grandfather Mystery has given us all these things. The white man must not be allowed to spoil them. Already there is a great gathering of Chiefs on this place, on our grasslands near the Fort Laramie. Chief Spotted Tail, Standing Elk, and also Chief Dull Knife have come to talk with my father. Many other Chiefs and their villages will be here soon." Buffalo Horn's dark eyes burned red with sadness.

Tom felt as if Buffalo Horn had delivered him a tremendous physical blow. He had no response so he turned to his saddlebags, almost sad that he had killed Tall Dog.

"I have brought you the scalp of Tall Dog." Tom pulled it from the saddlebag and handed it to Buffalo Horn. "Tall Dog rests on a burial platform wrapped in the white buffalo hide as Red Cloud had wished."

"You have done all that was asked of you. You and the great Sioux nations shall always be friends. You and your ranch shall always be safe. You are welcome to stay and lodge with us this night."

"I need to get home, Buffalo Horn. I need my ranch and I need Soft Cloud." Tom leaned down to shake Buffalo Horn's hand. The two friends smiled, waved goodbye, and parted company knowing trouble was coming, but hoping their friendship would endure.

CHAPTER FORTY-FOUR

The Sioux village soon lay far behind him, but uncertain thoughts hung heavy. At long last the flat lands of his prairie ranch came into sight, then the corrals, and finally the sod cabin. He hooted at the sight and yelled for Thunder to run. They flew into the yard and slid to a dusty stop. Before Thunder could straighten up, Tom's feet hit the ground and he ran to the cabin to Buck stretched out on his bed.

As his eyes adjusted to the dim light of the soddy, he searched for Soft Cloud. "Buck, where's Soft Cloud?" he shouted.

"She and the dogs are down by the creek pickin' berries."

Tom turned and flew out the door running top speed to the creek. "Glad to see you too, Tom! Oh yea, I'm mendin' right up!" Buck called after him, smiling that grand smile.

The dogs saw Tom first and raced up the hill yipping, barking and bouncing. He dropped to his knees and let them smother him with their boundless energy as they wrestled wildly in the grass. Breaking free of the rowdy pack Tom leaped up, nearly knocking over a laughing, crying Soft Cloud.

She dove on him sending them tumbling into the deep grass. They held each other, crying and laughing, rolling downhill. "I was so worried. When Buck came home and said you had gone on alone, I just wanted to come find you." She straddled him, pinning him to the ground, and fixed her eyes on his. "I love you, Tom Named by Horse."

"Marry me!"

The End

If you enjoyed this book by Dutch Henry you will want to read

We'll Have The Summer

Available on http://www.amazon.com

Dutch is very social. Join him on Facebook and his blog
www.dutchhenry.blogspot.com

Please turn the page for a sneak peak at the next book in the
Tom Named by Horse Series.

From the Banks of Little Bear Creek

Dutch Henry

Coming Winter 2015

Three years after the death of Tall Dog, Tom Named By Horse and Soft Cloud have turned the little soddy, the lands granted them by Red Cloud, and the lean-to barn into a thriving horse ranch, fulfilling Tom's dream. The Plains Indians Wars, or Red Cloud's war, is mostly behind them, and the lands have had their transformation as Red Cloud's vision had warned years earlier. Trailing horses from the ranch to Denver city has become an annual event for Tom, Buck and the rest, and this is the story of that trail. In the spirit of a good old John Wayne movie, vengeance, cattle and horse thieves, a dirty sheriff and corrupt mayor, and a wedding make this year's drive a ride you'll want to tag along on. ~ Dutch Henry

CHAPTER ONE

June 4, 1869

"Won't we be living high this trip, with Soft Cloud coming along to cook?" Buck flashed Tom a silly grin and rubbed his stomach.

Tom stood in his stirrups and shouted through the dust. "Nothing's too good for the finest horse ranchers in the territory!" He spun his horse, raced along the herd to the chuck wagon and from the saddle blew Soft Cloud a kiss.

"I'm along to cook, Buck, but you will carry the water and gather wood for fires!" Soft Cloud tossed a wink to Tom.

"For your biscuits I'll chop down a forest of cottonwoods and carry a lake of water!"

This was the third June in a row that Tom and Buck trailed horses to Denver City. The trip was a long one, but the two friends had grown to look forward to the drive south each spring. Ranchers there paid high prices for Tom's horses, and last year Tom had fallen short of demand.

This year they convinced Soft Cloud to join them. The first drive Tom and Buck had made to the horse auction, she had been with child. The second year, she'd insisted their son was too young to make the journey. This year she simply gave in to the endless pestering and pleading from Buck Hawkins, her dear friend, and Tom Named by Horse, her husband. Now she would happily drive the team of mules and their chuck wagon south across the prairie headed for Denver City with their two-year-old son, Hawk, on the seat beside her.

She remembered the first time she'd called her husband Tom Named by Horse. That awful day a little more than three years ago when he and Buck had ridden away to kill her father, Tall Dog. She'd given Tom that name and kissed him for the first time, so afraid she would never see him again. She shook away the thought and focused her mind on the happiness of today. All of them together trailing a herd of fine horses.

Buck rode point most days on his favorite horse, Diablo, the tall spotted stallion that had the heart of a mountain lion, feared nothing, and to quote Buck, could run like the devil. Buck preferred to stay out of the dust. He liked to keep his Stetson hat, fancy deerskin leggings and vest as neat as possible. How he could grumble if his shoulder-length blonde hair and goatee ever became dust-caked! But Buck, a great point rider, always kept the herd moving at a good speed. He always found the safest, easiest routes with the most water, so Tom happily obliged him.

The three hands who hired on the beginning of their second year, all having fought the Plains Indians Wars on one side or the other, rode herd. The wiriest of the three, Lone Feather, had fought valiantly alongside Red Cloud in the "wagon box fight" that hot August day in 1867. Coop had served under the late Lieutenant Harris and was one of the three survivors of the bloody day on the trail of Tall Dog. Nineteen now, he had grown to be a handsome, tall, strong, dark-haired man. Coop was worth his weight in gold when protecting the herd from the many outlaws and cattle thieves who now drifted into the plains looking for easy profits. And of course Cole, who had been with Tom the day they were overrun by the stampeding herd of buffalo. Cole had been a Private then, and like Tom, had barely survived the day. Cole was the shortest of the group and even though, tough as nails and an incredible shot, he suffered Buck's merciless ribbing, who forever offered to find Cole a 14-hand horse. Cole planned to marry when they returned from Denver City. "It just puzzles me something fierce," Buck told Tom this very morning, "what that beautiful Hannah Miller could want with a short legged, square box of a man who has to stand on an anvil just to get himself a kiss."

Lone Feather was a quiet man. Though his allegiance to Buck and Tom stood fierce, he would never stray from his Ogalalla Sioux roots. Choosing his tipi and campfire over the sod bunkhouse, on moonlit nights he could be seen dancing by his campfire, chanting and waving his long lance high. While Tom had been able to convince him to carry one of the new Winchesters, Lone Feather never traveled without his bow and quiver. On journeys such as these, both he and his favorite Sioux pony were decorated in paint, as Lone Feather declared he never wanted to be mistaken for a farmer. When necessary, Lone Feather could be a tremendous scout.

Before setting out on their three-week journey to Denver City and back, the duties of the ranch were left in the capable hands of Still Water, Soft Cloud's mother, and her new husband Buffalo Horn. The years of the Plains Indians Wars had been the toughest on Still Water, who'd lost her sons and her husband. But the past few seasons spent with Tom and Soft Cloud on Tom's ranch had helped her to put some of the pain in its own place—in the past. She was delighted now to serve mostly as ranch cook, and everyone's mother.

Buffalo Horn had lost the bottom half of his right leg in the fierce battle on John Bozeman's Road where the Sioux and Cheyenne had successfully forced the Army to abandon Fort Phil Kearny and Fort C. F. Smith. Still able to ride as wonderfully as any Sioux brave, Buffalo Horn was most happy on the days that Tom announced they were going out "gatherin,'" for this meant a few carefree days on the prairie chasing wild horses.

Buffalo Horn's most prized possession was the tired old crutch Buck had fashioned for Tom the day after the buffalo stampede. Though the leather padding on top had long ago become frayed and worn, Buffalo

Horn fought as fierce as any brave in battle whenever anyone attempted to repair it.

They trailed sixty-five horses this trip, four of them sired by Thunder, the powerful black stallion Buck had given Tom while he lay in Still Water's tipi recovering from injuries he had suffered in the buffalo stampede. Tom rode Thunder this trip. He wanted buyers to meet the sire of those fine black two-year-old stallions.

Tom galloped to the top of a nearby ridge and watched the herd trot over the prairie. Far to his left, well ahead of the herd, he spied Buck and Diablo.

Riding point fit well with Buck's nature. Not quite able yet to let loose of his youth, Buck rode the edge of the knife in anything he did, and nothing was going to change him. During the Pony Express days, he'd ridden eleven months for the great Alexander Majors, dodging road agents and hostile Indians. During those rough and rowdy days, he and Bill Cody forged the beginning of their lifelong friendship. Later there came the months he'd spend on the Missouri border spying with Bill Hickok for General Sheridan during the War Between the States and then after the war serving as scout for General Sturgis out of Fort Laramie, helping to tame the plains. Those times and adventures had made Buck Hawkins the man he was. Ranch life treated him well, and Tom became the best friend he had ever known, but nothing could set his blood to boiling like being outnumbered and pinned down, fighting for his life and those around him.

There had been times over the past three years when Red Cloud, Roman Nose, and Crazy Horse had provided Buck with all the excitement he needed, pulling him from the ranch and back into service as a scout for the United States Cavalry.

It had never been the same again, though. Not since the loss of his friend Lt. Harris that miserable day in the fall of '66 when Tall Dog had butchered the Lieutenant and his men at the Walls of Buffalo Ridge.

Was it the loss of Lt. Harris? Or was it the brutal slaying of Mrs. Harris later that winter on the snow-covered prairie? Mrs. Harris. A finer, more delicate woman had never lived. She'd understood Buck and she loved to participate in Buck's childish teasing of her poor husband. How Buck would torment that poor man, and as often as not Mrs. Harris would play along, sometimes driving the two friends to blows. Buck could never be sure if Lt. Harris had really been jealous or "just funnin'."

For each of the past three years on the anniversary of her death, Buck traveled to the Miller Farm to visit Mrs. Harris' grave. The grave he had dug himself, through four feet of snow, to sit alone on the bench the Millers had surprised him with, and smoke a cigar. Smoke a cigar and remember that morning, just days after her husband's death, on her porch at Fort Laramie. The day she'd invited Buck to sit quietly with her, and enjoy one of her husband's cigars as the three of them had so often done. That morning had been the last time he would see her alive.

Still Water had tried for Buck's affection, and he had often been warmed by her soft touch and moist kisses. Kisses he had never shared with Mrs. Harris. Was it simply guilt that kept Mrs. Harris alive in his memory, causing him to be unable to allow Still Water into his heart? The burden of that guilt! He should have been with her. He should have gone with that wagon train the day it left Fort Laramie, the day before the snows came. Why hadn't the General permitted him to go with her? Damn General Sturgis for allowing her to leave the fort in the winter!

Ripped to the present by Diablo's sliding stop, Buck dragged the back of his gloved hand across his weeping eyes. "Son of a bitch!" Less than one hundred yards ahead sat at least twenty mounted renegades. He spun Diablo about, gave him his head, "Go boy!" Diablo knew what to do and launched his bolt of speed that Buck knew no horse alive could match. They raced to the top of the ridge, circling back to Tom and the herd, purposely staying high so the boys would have good shooting at his pursuers long before they reached the herd.

Diablo's long legs ate up the prairie beneath them, easily gaining distance. Buck snatched his revolver from its holster and, leaning forward on Diablo's neck, emptied it, firing under his arm at the howling and shooting renegades.

Buck hadn't realized how far from the herd he'd gone. Racing along the ridge top, he finally saw Tom and the others. He hoped they realized fast they had company stopping in. Buck holstered his .44 and yanked his Winchester from its scabbard. Flipping it one time he levered a shell into the chamber, twisted and fired a shot into the mob galloping behind him. Diablo knew his job and kept up that eye-burning speed along the ridge crest.

Coop and Cole stopped the herd. Lone Feather charged the hill toward the action and even from this distance Buck read the delight in Lone Feather's eyes. Tom dropped to the ground and instantly his new 'Big 50' roared. Again and again, the buffalo rifle launched 50 caliber slugs of lead into the startled group of charging renegades.

Buck turned Diablo downhill toward the herd and stopped only after passing the charging Lone Feather. The renegades had begun to turn and flee but Tom kept firing into the group and Lone Feather charged on, hurling lead and Sioux insults their way.

Refreshed by this surge of adrenaline, Buck trotted the rest of the way to Tom's side, sitting tall and wearing his wonderful smile.

"You gonna call that crazy Indian back?" Buck stepped from Diablo and slid his new Yellow Boy Winchester into its scabbard.

"He'll come back," Tom replied with a silly grin.

They watched as Lone Feather continued his charge up the hill, shooting and hooting at the fleeing renegades. Eventually he stopped his war pony and waved his rifle high, shouting Sioux insults and challenges, making sure the renegades understood they'd been proven cowards this day.

"That was interesting. Guess this trip could be a bit of a adventure." Buck stroked his goatee.

"Reckon you'd best not stray so far next time, Buck."

"I was thinking."

"Tell Diablo to walk slower next time you go to thinkin'."

Deciding they'd had enough excitement for one day, Tom told Coop and Cole to hold the herd and asked Soft Cloud to start supper. She flipped down the chuck wagon tailgate, propped it up on its two legs, making a tabletop to mix her biscuit dough, and prepare beans for the fire. Little Hawk was relegated to a red woolen blanket at her side. Tom settled on the blanket, scooped up his son and watched a busy Soft Cloud, concern showed on his face. "You'll have to keep the wagon close by the herd. Tomorrow we'll travel a little slower, keep the herd tighter."

"So you expect more trouble?"

"Sure do. That was too easy. They're not done with us yet."

"Yeah, that good-for-nothing bunch got a good look at what we're all about. They'll be back." Buck snatched little Hawk and perched him on his shoulders.

CHAPTER TWO

Sun barely kissed the horizon when they moved out the herd. Soft Cloud guided the chuck wagon very near the right front of the herd. Tom rode by her side, his eyes tirelessly scouring the surrounding country, his Winchester in hand, the new Sharps in the scabbard.

They kept the horses in a neat, tight bunch with Coop and Cole guiding on point. Lone Feather brought up the rear, Buck scouted ahead, selecting only routes that kept them as far away from dangerous ridgetops as possible. In this fashion they moved along all through the morning and into the early afternoon hours.

The sun hung hot when Buck rode back to the herd. "We have a stream crossing coming up." Buck wore unease on his face. "Water's not too high and the stream's only a couple of hundred feet wide. Seems like good footing. Be a good place to hit us when we slow down to cross."

Tom pulled his black hat, pushed his hand through his wet hair and squinted into the sun. Just then he wished Soft Cloud and Hawk were back at the ranch.

"The horses could stand a break and a drink. Open ground? Could we see them coming?"

"Yeah, pretty flat. But I don't know about stoppin' there. I was thinkin' more like runnin' right on through and gettin' away from that low land."

"Gotta water the stock, Buck, and the chuck wagon'll slow us down anyway. Take Cole and Coop and scout it out a bit on the other side of the crossing. If you see anything, get back in a hurry and we'll make a stand right here. I'm getting a feeling in my gut I don't like."

"Yea, that feelin' of yours always wants to get us in trouble." He waved to Cole and Coop and they set off at an easy lope toward the stream.

Tom trotted to the wagon and pulled up by Soft Cloud, "Put Hawk inside."

"What did Buck tell you?" Soft Cloud tried to busy herself with the reins, but her stiffness told of her worry.

"No trouble, yet. But we're coming up on a crossing. If it looks alright, we'll stop for the night and water the stock."

Tom loped to Lone Feather. "Scout that ridge and beyond in a wide sweep, then hustle back. If you see anything, any trouble, get back here, don't try to tackle the whole bunch on your own." Tom held Lone Feather's look, he knew Lone Feather was easily tempted into a party.

With all the men gone, Tom rode herd on the left while Soft Cloud drove the wagon on the right. Together they kept the herd moving toward the waiting stream. An hour later Lone Feather rejoined them, riding a very spent horse, and reported all things clear beyond the ridge to their west.

The flat land by the stream stood thick with young prairie grass, offering easy grazing, and the horses settled for the night with full bellies and thirsts quenched. Soft Cloud started her regular evening routine, with Hawk on the blanket, biscuits in the Dutch oven, and beans on the fire. Tonight, prairie dogs roasted on the fire too.

"Mighty fine shooting, Coop!" Buck delivered a man-sized slap to the middle of Coop's back.

"Doggone, Buck, them prairie dogs were just jumpin' in front of my bullets." Coop flashed a grin.

"Reckon that's why we ain't had no more trouble from them renegades." Cole joked.

"Why's that, Cole?" Buck joined in.

"Well I guess they seen Coop's fancy shooting. I mean, five dogs with twenty shots ain't bad!"

Funny though it was, Cole had to rebut, "Five dogs, five shots."

"Puts me in mind of the time Bill Cody and me got stuck in this town with no money." Buck started on a story. "Well, Bill gets this idea that to get a stake for a card game we'd hold a shooting match. Now this wasn't just any ordinary town. No sir. This was one of those camptowns that followed the railroaders along the Union Pacific. Full of gamblers, killers, tough, hard working men, with liquor, loose women, and no law.

"Bill was there working for the Union Pacific. He was a scout and a hunter and everybody pretty much knew Bill Cody. Nobody knew Buck Hawkins. Bill had gambled away his script the night before, and I was powerful low on funds myself. So we just decided we'd start a ruckus, him and me, and I'd challenge him to a shootout.

"Now the plan was pretty simple. We'd keep gettin' louder and louder 'til we drew a crowd, and then I'd challenge him. After we got the crowd all lathered up for a shootout, Bill would chicken out. Course that would just make me all the tougher and bolder, so then I was to suggest some trick shooting, you see, and then Bill could throw it.

"So I got the crowd all goin' and Bill, he played hard to get. He finally gives in and I start taking bets. Taking bets I could outshoot famous Bill Cody. We raised $500. We decided on six shots each. Four still targets and two moving cans some onlooker would pitch onto the street.

"The trick worked just grand. I bested Bill, six to four. Well, we took our money and headed to the nearest saloon. Bill got in a game, and I was throwing back a few shots at the bar. The night appeared to be going along just swell when all of a sudden I heard Bill in a loud argument.

"Bill had been drinkin' pretty heavy, and for a moment, I figure he must have forgotten about our trick shooting scheme because he calls to me by name. Then he declares he's known me for nearly ten years and I can vouch for what an honest man he is. Not everybody in that tent saloon was as drunk as Bill Cody and some of 'em remembered losing part of that $500.

"Bill sobered up mighty quick, and jumped over the table, scooped up most of the money and high tailed it out that front door. There I stood! With about twenty sets of coal black eyes bearing down on me."

"How'd you get out of that one?" Coop leaned way forward as if he might jump into Buck's lap.

"Well folks, right then and there I knew I was doomed. There I stood, my back to the tent wall, with more than a dozen drunk, cheated, railroad workers slowly inching my way, and I mean to tell you, railroad workers got some muscle on 'em. I knew I was done for. Dang that Bill Cody!

"All of a sudden I hear this ripping sound behind me! Doggone! Didn't that crazy Cody come around behind that tent saloon with our horses and cut that wall open. We flew out of that town, dodging bullets and the loudest string of cuss words you ever heard in all your life!"

"I knew there was a reason you always had to have a fast horse." Tom tossed a wink to Coop and Cole. Laughter filled the camp, even Soft Cloud found the story silly and to her liking. "Tom, please remind me not to bet on any of Buck's shooting." Her soft smile tried to convince Tom the silly story had dampened her worry.

"Buck and I'll take first watch. We'll wake you at two, at first light we head out," Tom instructed the men.

CHAPTER THREE

Sidewinder boiled over with violent rage when he learned through camp natter twenty of his renegades had been bested by a handful of ranchers. The big man stomped through the saloon, kicking spittoons, flipping tables, and throwing chairs, not caring if they held men or not. His big, hair-backed hands tossed unwary men over the bar, sending broken bottles and whiskey exploding into the air. His greasy, long black, hair sailed airborne as he whirled from side to side. Loud, beastly roars escaped his froth-caked mouth.

Those lucky, and wise enough to stay out of his reach, soon found exits and regrouped in the muddy camptown street started by Hooker five years ago. Most of the men had seen Sidewinder's rage before. In fact, many of them had been there the day he found out Tall Dog had been killed by Tom Named by Horse. Hateful, vicious rage had so consumed him that day he strangled the man who gave him the news and gunned down four others who had been with his friend Tall Dog the day he died.

That day, Sidewinder assumed the roles of Mayor, Sheriff, and God in the camptown which had remained safe for the renegades and outlaws all this time, thanks to the bottleneck trail leading to it. Of course, the Army being busy with the Indian wars helped too. With Tall Dog gone, the inhabitants had shifted their focus to a few stage coach jobs, cattle and horse stealing, prospecting, gambling and the like.

The camptown had grown to a population exceeding five hundred.

Today even a few legitimate businesses were giving it a go; stores, eating establishments, a few hotels, livery stables, and a blacksmith. But mostly it was a town populated by ruffians, gamblers, soiled doves, and pretty much the seedier side of humanity. Having to sidestep a dead body in the muddy street was not an uncommon occurrence.

The big man finally stopped breaking chairs and tables, arms and jaws. He tugged on the bottom of his buckskin shirt, straightened himself up, and sat at a table. "Somebody clean this place up and get me whiskey!"

A rather timid, dirty little man, with a much crumpled felt hat, patchy beard and very buck teeth quickly brought a bottle, and settled in next to Sidewinder. "You gonna send somebody after them horses, ain't you?"

Sidewinder snatched the bottle from the eager man's hand, wrestled the cork free with his teeth, and spit it in the man's face.

"You know, they said that were Buck Hawkins and Tom Named by Horse running that herd. You ain't gonna get an easier chance to kill those sons of bitches," urged the little man, wiping his grimy hands on his tattered plaid shirt.

Sidewinder looked up and down the little man's pathetic frame and had to employ restraint to keep from pounding him into the floor like a railroad spike with his huge, hairy fist. "You wanna go?"

"No ... No, not me ... I just serve whiskey."

Hardly a man in the camptown, or woman, for that matter, didn't know about the absolute hatred Sidewinder had for those two. First they'd killed his friend Tall Dog. Then six months later, they'd helped the Army defeat Red Cloud and his Sioux, along with Roman Nose and his Cheyenne, on that hot, hot August day. The day Sidewinder chose to fight alongside his Indian friends, not against them.

Nine hours, the Sioux and Cheyenne had charged that little fort made of wagon boxes. Over and over again they charged and each time more braves fell. Sidewinder himself had been wounded four times, and took nearly a year to heal. All the Sioux and Cheyenne nations knew army scout Buck

Hawkins and Tom Named by Horse had been there that day and had defeated the spirit of the great Chief Red Cloud. And still Red Cloud remained friends with Tom Named by Horse, who had taken Red Cloud's only granddaughter, Soft Cloud, for his wife.

Ever since he had healed, Sidewinder yearned to go to Tom's ranch on Little Bear Creek and kill him. Kill him for killing Tall Dog. And yet Red Cloud had given Tom Named by Horse his word that he and his ranch would be safe on Sioux land forever. But Sidewinder was not Sioux. He was Cheyenne. Buck Hawkins and Tom Named by Horse on the open prairie, burdened with a herd of horses, was more temptation than he would try to control. Plans must be made, and he would make them.

****

Tom rolled over on the heavy woolen blanket, picked up little Hawk and held him high. He felt great joy and happiness in that little boy's giggles, and Hawk always had a giggle handy. More like Buck than his own father in that way.

Soft Cloud, as usual, had been up for some time already and a happy breakfast fire crackled and popped. Biscuits roasted and chunks of antelope meat simmered, and plenty of coffee boiled on the coals. They had at last reached a point where they never went without coffee.

Tom sat on the blanket next to the fire holding his son and watched the camp come to life as the early morning sun dried dew from the spring grass.

"Nary a bit of trouble from horse thieves, renegades, or horses. Just a peaceful night, riding herd listening to Cole try to hum a tune," Coop teased and settled on the blanket with Tom and Hawk.

"Cole, singin'? It's a wonder them horses didn't break into a stampede!" Buck know Cole was blessed with a voice only a sweetheart could love.

"Oh, I don't know," Soft Cloud defended. "I've heard Cole sing, and I am sure that's one of the many things about him that Hannah Miller finds desirable."

"Holy Cow! If she can tolerate that singin', that explains how she could fall in love with a tree-stump-shaped fellow." Buck's grin grew wider.

"Buck Hawkins, what a terrible thing to say!" Soft Cloud shook her wooden spoon inces from Buck's nose.

Cole wandered into camp reading faces, chuckles and glances tossed his way. "If I was an antelope and I knew you were going to cook me, I believe I could die satisfied," he told Soft Cloud with a gentle nod.

"Thank you, Cole. You're the only gentleman this morning to compliment my cooking. The others are too busy inventing insults."

"Finish your vittles, boys, and let's get the herd moving, let's shed this lowland before we get visitors." Tom meant what he said, but he also thought it was time to interrupt the banter; Coop and Buck could go on all day.

In short order, they had fresh horses saddled, the chuck wagon packed, and began moving across the prairie away from the lowlands of the stream. The cool spring morning and the herd well fed and rested gave the horses extra energy, which required everyone to be top notch in their duties. Tom positioned Soft Cloud and the chuck wagon ahead of the herd to serve as a calming effect, and hopefully keep the horses focused on the wagon and not on their spring fever.

Tom had experienced a lot of life since the day he'd killed the hated buffalo hunter. He understood how the world worked now. At least the world he found himself in. Even before leaving the old hider dead, he'd known it was a brutal world, and killing was sometimes necessary. But now he knew that other things were so much more important. Like friendship. A kind of friendship that develops quickly and deepens gradually over time. The friendship he and Buck shared had become indestructible; the kind of friendship that means you can count on one another, without question, without explanation. A bond of trust, and loyalty.

He had also learned about love. In his early years, those years spent with the old hider, he had never known love, except for the love he'd felt for the old horse, Tom Gray. He understood now love can come in many shapes and sizes and temperaments. Perhaps friendship does too, but love is something different, and he understood that love is important to make a man complete. Not only complete in the way Soft Cloud completed him. But complete also in the manner in which a man believes, lives, fights, and dies. He thought of Tall Dog. His love of his Sioux ways, people and lands had caused him to become an evil, fierce killer. Tom understood that, and respected him for it.

Tom had already learned the importance of protecting what's your own. Again he thought of Tall Dog. Tom knew he would protect his wife and child, his friends and his horses and ranch, just as stubbornly as Tall Dog had ever fought for what he'd believed was his and proper. He had learned the importance of helping others and how by helping others, you helped yourself. He remembered the time, three years ago, when he'd rescued little Sarah Jane Hartman and the other children from the mines in the high country with the help of John Bradley. Tom thought of the orphanage the Bradleys started on their ranch. The orphanage he visited once a year.

Funny how a good woman can change a man. Soft Cloud, his wonderful wife…from the moment they met he knew they would be forever together.

Tom hurried his horse to the wagon and eased up to Soft Cloud. "You doing all right up here?"

"Going along as easy as the day, and Hawk is sound asleep in the wagon."

"I'm heading up to Buck to have a look over things. You'll be fine?"

"Should trouble come calling, I have your Winchester by my side and two fast, strong mules in the harness."

Tom waved and put his horse into a strong run, pulling up alongside Cole. "I'll be riding with Buck. Swing out by the wagon and stay close to Soft Cloud."

Not waiting for an answer, Tom sped away, holding a run until finally he caught Buck.

"Howdy pard, what calls you to the lead?" Buck looked surprised to see Tom in such a hurry.

"Just have one of my feelings. Seen anything at all?"

"I hate when you get your feelings. No, and I've been lookin' real careful."

"Something's up, Buck. Got a real strong feelin'."

"Like I said—I hate when you get your feelings."

"I'm sending Lone Feather to scout out the territory east of us. Hang back a little closer to the herd. I want you within sprinting distance of the wagon when we get the company I feel's coming to call."

"Only two more days to Denver, Tom." Buck pulled his hat to wipe sweat from his forehead.

Tom glanced at Buck's saddle. "Where's your Sharps?"

"Got my Winchester; the Sharps is back in the chuck wagon. Gets a little clumsy riding with two rifles under your leg."

"Let's get it, and plenty of shells. I got a hunch you'll need it."

Soft Cloud studied them with worried eyes when they pulled up next to the wagon. "What's wrong?"

"Nothing at the moment." Buck answered for Tom. "But he has one of his feelings."

Cole rode close enough to be within earshot. "We don't like it when Tom gets one of his feelings!"

"Cole, hustle back to Lone Feather, have him do a wide circle. You tell him I'm looking for trouble. You tell him I said something's up." Convinced that trouble was imminent, Tom slid his Sharps under his leg and rode close to the wagon. He had to chuckle though watching Lone Feather gallop his painted pony up the ridge, waving his Winchester and howling.

"What will we do if we are attacked? How will we protect ourselves and the horses?" Soft Cloud looked more worried than her voice would tell.

"Guess we'll fight."

ABOUT THE AUTHOR

Dutch Henry is a freelance writer and novelist who resides in central Virginia with Robbie, his wife of 39 years, horse, dogs, cats and chickens. As a freelance writer he writes about "People & Horses Helping Horses & People." Dutch has columns in trailBLAZER magazine and NATURAL HORSE magazine. These stories tell of the wonderful people and horses who give so much to help others. He has also had articles featured in numerous equine magazines. He is active on Facebook and his Coffee Clutch blog where he writes about horses, birds and nature, writing and, of course, his Coffee Clutch where he begins the day having coffee with his mare Kessy and critters. He enjoys spending time with his wife, trail riding, bird watching, nature walks and interviewing the wonderful people about whom he writes. He also does free "Therapy For Therapy Horses," clinics at equine assisted therapy centers and equine rescues

Made in the USA
Lexington, KY
21 May 2015